"IT WOULD NO~~T~~...
PR~~O~~...

His touch was ~~...~~
and elegant fin~~...~~ ...~~Cather~~-
ine burned.

She wished heartily to rise from the bed, to
quit the room. But she was naked beneath
the covers . . . and Jase St. Claire was very
well aware of it.

The thought made Catherine's blush turn to
deepest rose. She had to find a way to extri-
cate herself from this situation. Only at this
moment it was impossible, for the very hand
which had caressed her cheek seconds ago
now moved down to cup her chin.

"You cannot avoid me," Catherine heard him
whisper. His kiss was leisurely, seductive. It
demanded from Catherine a response that
she was unwilling to give . . . yet helpless to
withhold.

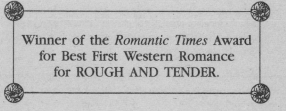

Winner of the *Romantic Times* Award
for Best First Western Romance
for ROUGH AND TENDER.

FORBIDDEN FLAME

SELINA MACPHERSON

AVON BOOKS ◆ NEW YORK

In loving memory of Amy Blondeaux Bonner . . .
and for her "Angel" Hugh . . .

And for my special long distance friend,
Debbie Minyard,
for lending a hand in friendship
to this beleaguered Yankee!

FORBIDDEN FLAME is an original publication of Avon Books. This work has never before appeared in book form. This work is a novel. Any similarity to actual persons or events is purely coincidental.

AVON BOOKS
A division of
The Hearst Corporation
1350 Avenue of the Americas
New York, New York 10019

Copyright © 1993 by Susan McClafferty
Inside cover author photograph by Studio VII Production
Published by arrangement with the author
Library of Congress Catalog Card Number: 92-97459
ISBN: 0-380-77250-7

First Avon Books Printing: July 1993

AVON TRADEMARK REG. U.S. PAT. OFF. AND IN OTHER COUNTRIES, MARCA REGISTRADA, HECHO EN U.S.A.

Printed in the U.S.A.

RA 10 9 8 7 6 5 4 3 2 1

Part 1

The Bounder

Chapter 1

Mississippi Territory
October 31, 1800

It was All Hallow's Eve, the sky moonless and the road black, a perfect night for devilment. Yet here in the stifling warmth of the roadside tavern, spirits were high and cares had been put aside for the duration of the evening.

Seated in the corner closest to the door, where the light of the tallow lamps failed to reach, Jase St. Claire took his ease, seeming to contemplate the swirling dregs of his whiskey.

The liquid was thin and watered, laced with tobacco to provide its amber color and gunpowder to impart its kick ... and a damned far cry from the fine Monongahela whiskey that even now aged in oaken casks at Rosemunde Plantation, and tasted poignantly of Jase's youth.

Since shortly after dusk he had been sitting in this chair, waiting, and his patience was quickly becoming frayed, stressed to the limits by the raucous scraping of a country fiddle and the fluting laughter of the bawds that Leo Hastings employed.

Hastings's House of Entertainment was one of many such establishments springing up along the lonely reaches of the wilderness road, the Chickasaw Trace, which stretched between Natchez and Nashville ... nearly five hundred miles teeming with all manner of treachery.

Mississippi Territory was still largely unsettled, a raw and lawless place with large areas of wilderness, numerous limestone caves, and dank secluded hollows perfectly suited to hide the outlaw bands.

It was common that small groups of travelers not wishing to dare the Trace after dark—returning flatboatmen forced to walk the long way home from New Orleans, adventurers, and itinerant men of the faith—all filtered through these roadside inns. They savored what scarce comfort was to be found, knowing with certainty that even the inns' slim security was preferable to what awaited them out in the stygian night.

But those seeking to spend the night for safety's sake were not the only ones to pass through Leo's door. It was rumored that Hastings was a familiar of the very criminal element which made the Trace so hazardous a route to travel—the roaming highwaymen who robbed and killed indiscriminately, and without the slightest flicker of conscience. Suspected to be among them was the Black Lion, a white renegade who had first emerged during the waning days of wars waged against the Indians for possession of the Ohio Country.

The conflict had been a long and bloody one,

beginning in 1755 with the French and Indian War, and culminating in 1794 at the Battle of Fallen Timbers on the Maumee River. For nearly four decades, the frontier had known only brief periods of peace. Waves of European immigrants, hungry for land, defied the edicts laid down by each new Indian treaty that said no settlement was to occur beyond the newest boundary line. The immigrants took the land by stealth, cutting away the forest to make their farms, wantonly slaughtering game with no regard for the needs of their red neighbors. Sometimes they took human prey with that same callous disregard.

Incident followed murderous incident. Retaliation and revenge became a way of life on both sides of the conflict. And when the complaints of the settlers became too strident, the Indians' retaliatory strikes carried out too close to established communities, the militia marched against the tribes.

Numerous campaigns were launched to eradicate the menace posed by the tribes. Many failed. Names like Braddock, Harmar, and Hand became as infamous as the tribal enemy against whom they fought, and by whom they were so miserably defeated.

Out of this conflagration a phoenix had risen, propelled to prominence on a tide of violence, a white man who had turned against his own and joined with the Shawnee to quickly become one of the most despised villains to ply his bloody trade in the history of the Northwest. Known for his lack of human compassion, the Black Lion had laid waste to farms along the frontier from Kentucky to Ohio and beyond. Years later, many of his victims still saw his distinctive vermilion-and-black war paint and faded blue headband in their nightmares.

In the summer of 1794 it all had ended. General Anthony Wayne and his troops met and defeated the combined might of the Shawnee, Delaware, Miami, and Potawatami at a place in the Ohio wilderness called Fallen Timbers. The subsequent Treaty of Greenville once again pushed back the boundaries; all captives were ordered to be returned; the might of the Indian Confederacy was sadly weakened. After that, the Black Lion disappeared. No one knew where he had gone or what had become of him—he had simply vanished from the face of the earth.

But now, six years later, rumor had it that he was back, committing murder along the Chickasaw Trace.

Jase St. Claire sighed, swirling the remaining whiskey in his glass. It was the search for the Black Lion . . . rather, for someone who had decided to borrow the renegade's identity . . . that had brought him to this place. Whether the impostor's motives sprang from a thirst for self-glorification or from a desire for revenge for some past slight, Jase didn't know. He only knew that the renegade's name was one he wished to see fade again into the dusty annals of history, where it should have remained.

Talk of the Black Lion nettled him. It had traveled from Nashville to Natchez, unwelcome news carried to his home, Rosemunde, by his factor, Alonzo Hart.

And so Jase had come to investigate, to see for himself this new threat to his own tenuous peace.

Hastings's inn was a good enough place to begin. It was rumored that Hastings gathered information, which he in turn sold to the bandits, concerning those travelers who carried their wealth with them and were therefore good marks.

That Hastings had a sharp eye for detail there was little doubt, for Jase had noted how the innkeeper's gaze had swept him from head to foot when he had first entered, missing nothing, as if taking inventory of Jase's worth. And yet Jase had no tangible proof of his suspicions, could not have gone to the authorities even if he had possessed such evidence, without gaining the very sort of notice which for four years now he had steadfastly avoided.

Jase stared into his near-empty glass, but instead he saw reflected in the pale amber liquid the fiery remnants of his past. A past which to this day could not bear close scrutiny ... a past which he had thought well dead and buried. ...

But that was before someone had cunningly chosen to resurrect the Black Lion, and thereby deny him the peaceful existence he had found at Rosemunde.

In the past four years he had worked hard to create a new life for himself from the ashes of ruin. Now that new life was being threatened by an impostor.

It was a situation he intended to rectify. He had worked too long and hard at attaining his present life to have it all torn down again. But tumble down it would, about his very ears, if he did not find this impostor, and soon.

Jase's lean jaw clenched as he thought of all that was at stake. A shadow fell across the table, drowning the amber lights in the remaining brew.

"Refill, mister?"

Jase raised his gaze to Leo Hastings's pudding face and nodded, which seemed to encourage the older man.

"Headed on up to Nashville, are you?" Leo questioned with an ingratiating flash of yellow teeth.

Jase considered the innkeeper a long moment before making a reply. "I'm bound for Natchez."

"Couldn't help but notice that black beast you rode in on. Fine-lookin' animal, he is. Spanish would be my guess. . . ."

"Your guess would be correct," Jase answered, not inclined to offer a morsel more of himself, nor his reasons for being there.

"Took him up to race him, did you?" Leo asked.

Jase's mouth, so grim a moment ago, curled ever so slightly at the corners in a strange semblance of a smile, which Leo took for affirmation.

Sadist was a source of pride for Jase, his first and wisest acquisition after his arrival in the Mississippi Territory. He'd purchased the black horse from Juan Carlos Delarosa, a breeder down by New Orleans. Delarosa had been loath to part with the stallion, but his gaming debts were overwhelming and he badly needed cash to see him through the sugar harvest. The black had cost Jase five hundred dollars, but he would have gladly given twice as much to own the magnificent animal if Delarosa had asked. He'd recouped the sum many times over since then, for there were few horses to match Sadist's lightning speed.

"Ha! I thought as much!" Hastings slapped his knee. "Pit that devil horse against those Nashville nags and by God I'll bet you're comin' home with a hefty jingle in your purse!"

"A man would be a fool to race a winning mount and not wager." The manner in which the other man's eyes kindled was not lost upon Jase. There was no need to say more.

Straightening, Leo sighed. "Wish I could 'ave seen it too, but a man has got to make a decent livin'." He glanced about the room. "Well! Good fortune to you, sir, and be sure to stop by again if you're out this way!"

The innkeeper's eyes shifted away to a great bear of a man who lounged on a bench by the hearthside—a nervous glance, Jase noted—then slithered back again as he bent to impart a final word in a near whisper. "Beware the Trace on lonely nights such as this! I tell you this as a friend," he insisted. "Many things come to my ears—evil happenings, sir! I hear there's one who plies his ill-starred trade along this very byway ... the Black Lion, he's called, an evil wretch with not a care of who he's robbing, whether it be gentry or penniless pauper. Steals for the very thrill of it, they say, and seldom will he leave a man with his life. A man such as yourself"—he indicated Jase's doeskin breeches and knee-length boots of finest Spanish leather—"traveling alone and late abroad, would make an easy target."

Jase's answering smile was cold. "Your concern

for a stranger's welfare is admirable." He paused slightly before continuing, a note of lazy interest entering his voice. "The Black Lion . . . the name is not unknown to me. . . ."

"Nor to any man with half an ear and a bit of memory!" Hastings propped his fists upon his hips. "One of Satan's most valued henchmen, come down here to plague good and honest men!"

"Have you seen this outlaw, by chance?" Jase asked, careful to keep his tone casual. "How can you know this new outlaw is the same Black Lion of so many years ago?"

"It's the same man all right," Hastings proclaimed. His vigorous nod set his jowls to jiggling. "A man don't need to see with his own eyes to know. I come from over Kaintuck way long about ninety-five. My own dear sister lost her husband to that lawless miscreant! She saw his heathen face, half-red, half-black, and demon eyes aglow with a fierce inhuman light!"

Jase shifted slightly in his chair. "You say this Black Lion wears the same paint as the Shawnee who attacked your sister's homestead?"

"Indeed, sir," Hastings replied. "One of my patrons talked to a man who glimpsed him and his little band. Wears that faded blue headband too. Covers up a gruesome scar, so I have heard. Oh!" Hastings flushed, noticing Jase's own similar scar. "Beggin' your pardon, sir. I meant no offense."

"None taken," Jase said. "I shudder to think that I have missed all this excitement while in Nashville. I thank you for your information, and for your concern."

"Wouldn't be Christian of me not to care what

happens to my fellowman," Leo said with a sniff, hitching up his baggy breeches. "Now, if you'd like to remain here the night, we could surely find the room."

Stay and find a cudgel in my sleep, Jase thought. Aloud, he said, "Thank you, no. As a man who loves a good gamble, I think I'll take my chances."

"Suit yourself, then, and best of luck again."

Jase watched as Leo touched his forelock and moved away to busy himself at the crude plank bar. If the older man harbored designs upon his purse, then he hid his disappointment well. Jase was given cause to wonder whether Leo Hastings was innocent of wrongdoing or simply an accomplished fraud.

Returning to a contemplation of the contents of his glass, he pondered the possibilities, but he didn't linger long. No revelations were likely to come to him if he remained, and there seemed but one way to draw out his enemy.

Rising from his chair, he reached into his pocket and produced a coin, which he laid upon the scarred table. Then he made his way to the door.

Free from the close confines of the roadside inn, he felt his blood quicken. He led his stallion through the yard of the hostelry and down a slight incline to a shadowed copse, where he settled down to wait.

Jase was hardly out of sight when a quartet of riders arrived at the stand belonging to Leo Hastings. The four had joined forces for the dangerous trek southwest along the Trace, but now the time had come for them to separate. George and Rhea

Richards, newlyweds from Nashville, were traveling to Bayou Pierre, where they would make their home with Rhea's brother, while their companions, a young Frenchman by the name of Breaux and his mulatto servant, Mose Aubrey, were Natchez bound.

Without success George had tried to convince his companions to remain the night at Hastings's inn, and now there was little left to say except farewell. "Sure wish you could change his mind," George said, directing his words to the mulatto. "I'd hate to hear that anything bad had befallen you all because of this young whelp's stubbornness."

The youth's slim shoulders stiffened slightly at the unkind reference, but Richards went on. "No reason to get your back up, boy. Better men than you and I have met their maker walkin' down this road, and that's a fact."

The youth said something in rapid French to the mulatto, who began a slow translation. "Monsieur Breaux thanks you for your concern, but we've been on this road nigh a month now, traveling from New Orleans on up to Buzzard's Roost and now to Natchez. He wishes you good fortune in your venture, but he's impatient to be gone."

"Yes, I can see that, and far be it from me to detain him," George replied. "Bid him Godspeed, and tell him that if we meet again, I pray it will be this side of the grave." With those final words, George turned his horse onto the small path that led to the stand. But Rhea hung back.

Her face revealed the depth of her concern as she searched the boy's shadowed visage beneath his velvet tricorn. "I don't know why you insist on going on tonight," she said softly, "but I bid you heed George's words. Terrible things can happen to our kind out here . . . unspeakable things!"

For an instant the youth's slim features, so set moments before, softened, and a spark of something entered the vibrant turquoise eyes. Perhaps it was gratitude, or the kinship one feels for one's own kind. Whatever it was, it quickly died, to be replaced by the singular light of determination. "I know of this place, and that your concern is not unwarranted, and I thank you for it. But I must go on. I must reach the governor."

Rhea shot a glance over her shoulder to assure she wouldn't be overheard, and whispered, "Do you really think he will listen to the entreaties of a woman?"

"I must believe he will," said Catherine Blaise Breaux steadfastly. "He was my father's friend. He's bound to listen. And when he hears my tale, he will surely act upon it! The bounty still exists for the Black Lion's capture. I looked into it myself. And I cannot believe that a man exists in Christendom who would not relish the sight of the Black Lion mounting the gallows stairs."

Rhea shook her head. "Men have tried to hunt him down before, and all have failed. He is elusive! A will-o'-the-wisp who surfaces when he wishes, then disappears again without a trace. Such a man as he will not be easily brought to justice."

"I have to try," Catherine said, looking suddenly small and forlorn in the burgundy coat and match-

ing breeches that had once belonged to her
brother.

The older woman swallowed hard and turned
her pleading glance upon the large mulatto.
"Watch over your mistress, Mose Aubrey, and try
to get her safe to Natchez."

"Yes'm, I'll do just that," Mose said.

"Rhea!" George's voice sounded from the distance. "Woman, where have you gotten to?"

Rhea turned and clucked to her mount, calling
back over her shoulder, "God's blessings on both
of you!"

Mose and Catherine cantered on, disappearing
quickly in the gloom, and headed, Rhea thought
as she listened for the fading tattoo of the horses'
hooves, for certain disaster.

It was a relief for Catherine to leave the Rich-
ardses behind. She had been fond of Rhea, who
had seen through her disguise from the first, but
the burden of her masquerade had borne heavily
on her in the company of the woman's husband.
She still found it amazing that she had managed
to travel all the way from Buzzard's Roost, near
the Tennessee River, in close proximity with
George Richards without him ever knowing she
was a woman.

Catherine had pondered at length the reasons
for his seeming acceptance of her bold lies, and
she had concluded that two things had aided her
in avoiding discovery: her reticence to speak English in George's presence, and her cropped hair.

Her exclusive use of French had discouraged
discourse of any length. Her naturally husky voice

had also helped to allay suspicion. But more than anything, the sacrifice she had made by cutting her pale tresses had been the decisive factor, for no man would believe that a woman would willingly part with that which was widely considered her crowning glory.

Catherine reached a hand to her nape and felt the feathery curls. Her fiancé, Alonzo, would be properly horrified when he discovered what she had done. But then, when this episode came to light, she could expect to feel his anger in any case. Perhaps he would even decide to call off their engagement once he discovered the depth of her deception. . . .

Responsibility for her deceit could be lain at the feet of one man. Catherine's brows drew downward. Were it not for the Black Lion, she would still be in New Orleans, preparing her trousseau and feeling the excitement natural to a woman about to be wed . . . and her brother, Andre, would be sharing in that happiness.

Catherine's thoughts turned to the day when her world had shattered, the day news had arrived of Andre's death. Five months had passed since then, and still the pain of her loss was excruciating. Andre had been more than just a brother to her; he had been a part of her heart, her soul! As twins, they had shared everything . . . but now he was gone, and Catherine was left alone to grieve.

If not for Alonzo, Catherine would have hastened to Levi Colbert's stand upon first receiving the news. Levi, a Chickasaw chief, owned the hostelry at Buzzard's Roost, and he had sent the news of Andre's death. An investigation must be conducted, answers found! Alonzo had insisted that her grief had crazed her, and that in time the pain would lessen. They had argued hotly, and for two weeks Catherine had refused all attempts at reconciliation. And then, quite abruptly, she had softened her stance.

Perhaps Alonzo was right, she had said; perhaps her grief had made her irrational. She needed time to heal, she needed rest and quiet, and what better place than Mobile, where her Aunt Thea lived? With Alonzo's blessing, she would prepare for the journey immediately.

Alonzo had seemed relieved, Catherine had noted as she informed him of her plans, then set about packing. But instead of venturing to Mobile, as she had said, she set out directly for Buzzard's Roost in the Chickasaw lands, where Andre lay buried. There she had learned the awful truth of how her brother had been set upon, then left to die upon the lonely wilderness path.

Andre's wounds had been grievous, but he had survived long enough to identify his attacker. The name repeated by Levi Colbert's wife was a familiar one to Catherine.

The Black Lion.

The sobriquet was synonymous with all that was wicked, a vile curse upon the lips of honorable men from the Mississippi Valley to the Eastern Seaboard. He was a murderer, thief, and rogue, and his frightful reputation had not dimmed with the passage of time.

Catherine recalled hearing the name as a young girl—and the terror it had brought. The Black

Lion's name was spat in the same breath as the name of Simon Girty, a white renegade who had fought alongside the tribes attacking isolated frontier settlements during and after the American Revolution.

Through the early years of the previous decade, tales had been common of the Black Lion's wild and hair-raising escapades, his very name enough to strike dread in the hearts of white settlers living on the fringes of the frontier. Then, after the Battle of Fallen Timbers in 1794, the deciding battle for possession of the Ohio Country, all talk of his deeds had abruptly ceased. Speculation as to his fate had soon become as wild as his reputation.

There were those who claimed he had returned whence he came, to guard the gates of Hell for his dark compatriot ... while others insisted that he had lost his life at Fallen Timbers, and swore the fatal blow had come from one of his own disavowed race.

For years the Black Lion's true fate had remained cloaked in mystery. When he had resurfaced six months ago, it was far from the Ohio Country where he had originally roamed ... as a different sort of outlaw.

During the Indian Wars he had fought against white encroachment into Indian treaty lands; now he waged a private war against the hapless travelers who dared the lonely byway connecting Nashville and Natchez. It was a new war with horrendous motives: greed and a love of wanton destruction.

Catherine had vowed to stop his reign of terror. To that end, she was riding to an audience with

Winthrop Sergent, the territorial governor. Something must be done to capture the Black Lion, and
Sargent had the power and authority to search out
the brigand and see him brought to justice.

"Miss Catherine?" Mose's voice came softly out
of the dark. "How they gonna catch this Mr. Lion
when he's been loose so long? Seems to me he
must be awful slippery, kinda like tryin' to catch a
catfish with your bare hands."

"Governor Sargent will know of a way, I'm sure
of it," Catherine said with hollow confidence.

In an attempt to keep at bay the doubts that had
plagued her over the four hundred miles they had
traveled from New Orleans to the Tennessee River
and almost all the way down the Trace to Natchez,
Catherine imagined that she could hear the ring of
bootheels upon the gallows stairs. She found the
sound strangely satisfying, and clung to it.

"Yes'm, I hope you're right." Mose glanced once
over his broad shoulder at the fading lights of
Hastings's stand, then kneed his mule and followed in the wake of his whirlwind mistress.

Chapter 2

The road was barely wide enough for Catherine and Mose to ride abreast, the banks on either side rising steeply above their heads. Far above, the trees intertwined their branches like skeletal fingers, so that in most places the dense foliage kept even the dim starlight from penetrating. The effect was an eerie one, for it seemed as if they rode through an all but lightless tunnel, one that might lead deep into the bowels of the earth instead of to Natchez.

Catherine glanced uneasily around her, trying to ignore the warning prickle that played along her nape. She stared at the dark walls rising on either side of them, at the blackened canopy overhead, and then at Mose, who was rendered nearly invisible . . .

He felt it too, Catherine realized, this sudden unease with their surroundings, this vague feeling that something was not right. But what was it? she wondered . . . and suddenly it came to her.

Just moments ago the night had been alive with sound, the serenade of the cicada in harmony with

a million tree frogs and crickets. Now there was
nothing to be heard ... not a single noise ... and
Catherine thought that it was as if a blanket of silence had settled over the land, smothering the
smallest indication of life. And through this vacant
landscape they must cautiously pick their way, the
throb of their own hearts a ceaseless roaring in
their ears.

Catherine strained to listen, becoming ever more
aware of her increasing tension so that Mose's
hand plucking at her coat sleeve caused her to
start violently. With a will, she fought down her
rising fear and whispered into the dark, "You feel
it too?"

"Yes'm, and I sure don't like it one bit. I expect
we should've stayed with those folks after all.
Maybe it ain't too late—"

Catherine might have agreed, but at that very
instant the quiet seemed to explode, raining chaos
all around them.

"Stand by there!" The hoarse cry rang through
the tunnellike passage, startling their mounts and
causing them to shy. A half dozen hulking black
forms appeared from the deep, concealing shadows, blocking the road before and behind them.

Catherine instinctively closed her fingers around
the worn grip of Andre's pistol, which protruded
from the waistband of her breeches.

The highwayman closest to her, a big man,
rushed up and roughly seized her bridle. Unused
to such handling, the bay gelding reared, pawing
the air precariously close to the robber's head,
while his rider clung tenaciously to the saddle.

Catherine's heart was pounding in her breast,

pumping fear and a terrible fury through her veins. Without even thinking, she leveled the pistol at the one who held the bridle and started to squeeze the trigger.

The sound of gunfire rang through the narrow, tree-lined passage, echoing into the night. It came not from Catherine's weapon, but from the outlaw leader's pistol. When she turned to face him, she saw that he held Mose before him as a shield, and while one rifle was trained upon her, two more shorter range weapons were fixed on her friend.

"If you care aught for your property and your life," the leader said, his tone surprisingly conversational, "then heed my warning, son, and throw your weapon aside."

Gritting her teeth in frustration, Catherine tossed the pistol into the weeds at the roadside. "I've thrown it down, now let him go," she said.

"All in good time," the leader drawled, stepping slowly forward. He was a tall, laconic-looking fellow with a thin face and lazy gap-toothed grin. Not even remotely did he resemble the image of the Black Lion which had formed in Catherine's mind over the past weeks. "We have a bit of business between us first. John," he called to the one who held her mount secured, "relieve this young bantam cock of his possessions."

The one called John reached for the leather satchels slung across the horse's withers.

Watching, Catherine felt a sudden fright. The few coins she carried were concealed in her left boot. The satchels held her clothing . . . a muslin gown, a lacy chemise, silk stockings, and small, heelless slippers. How could a boy of tender years hope to explain away such things?

"There is nothing of value in the satchels . . . letters only, from my mother!" Catherine said.

"Since we don't read anyhow, you won't mind if we just have a look-see," said the leader. He turned his head and spat a stream of spittle at his feet, then grinned again at her.

She saw John's huge hands close around the satchels. Her heart felt weighted down with dread. She now knew the cost of her arrogance in thinking that she and Mose could press on alone: discovery and cruel ravishment at the hands of these outlaws.

She swallowed hard and forced herself to think. There must be something she could do to prevent him from rifling through her things! Desperation rising, she dug her heel deep into the gelding's side just as John's thick fingers began to curl around the leather bags. The horse whinnied and pranced sharply to the right, dragging the satchels out of the outlaw's grasp. He cursed and lunged for the leather bags again, but the boot which was forcefully planted in his chest prevented him.

Catherine's mount sidled nervously, nearly treading on the toes of the outlaw's boots. The man spewed a fount of filthy epithets, purpling as laughter burst from his comrades.

"Perhaps we should recruit this puny lad into our small fraternity and leave John to fend for himself."

More laughter. It rumbled around the fringes of the small circle of bandits, low and vaguely ominous to Catherine's ears.

"Uppity little bastard!" John spat out, grappling for a hold on the offending boot. "I'll teach you not to sass your elders!" With that, he shoved hard, pushing over and up. . . .

Off balance, Catherine toppled through the air.

She hit the ground hard, knocking the wind from her lungs, and for a few seconds lay stunned. The rumbling sound she'd noticed before was growing louder; it filled her head, until the ground itself trembled. Then all at once it seemed to splinter into a confusing melee of shouts and screams and curses. Trying to gather her strength, she got to her knees and knelt there swaying, watching with disbelief the scene that was being played out and thinking surely this must be some sort of waking dream.

For through the very midst of her nightmare flew the Angel of Death.

She saw with wondering eyes the gap-toothed outlaw fall, trampled beneath the shining black hooves of a huge dark horse. With a thud the huge beast came to ground, plumes of smoke rising from its flared nostrils, its rider scowling as he kicked it forward again. But the remainder of his prey scattered in all directions, unwilling to stand before this terrifying apparition and risk being cut down like their leader.

In a matter of seconds all had vanished, and still he came steadily onward, bearing down on Catherine. Stunned with near-paralyzing fear, she could only stare in fascination at the spectral vision he made.

She surmised that he was a young man, for his ruffled hair was as black as jet. It was nearly shoulder length in back—longer than hers, she noticed with feminine chagrin—and his wild ride had mussed it so that some fell forward to frame his lean and hungry face. He stared at her with the most unsettling eyes she had ever seen.

Surely they could not be the eyes of a worldly being, she thought uneasily, for they seemed made of glass. Like pale mirrors set in his dark face, they caught and reflected the meager starlight that filtered through the leafy bower above, and were strangely at odds with his midnight hair and shadowed visage.

Just yards away, he reined in his mount with such force that it sat upon its great black haunches, forehooves striking the air before it settled to the earth and stood, trembling, eyes wild, as its master dismounted.

Struggling to her feet, Catherine slowly backed away. "Stay away from me!" she warned him, her voice rising with her fear. She clawed at her belt for Andre's pistol, then belatedly recalled that it was gone, lying somewhere in the weeds beyond him. There was only one method of protection left to her, and that was the thin-bladed Spanish knife which she carried tucked in the sheath in her right boot top. Desperate to halt his advance on her, she drew the knife and held it menacingly before her.

The man she had imagined to be the Angel of Death gave pause at the sight of the glittering blade. But to Catherine's dismay he did not give an inch of ground, just stood at his ease to consider her with those damnably pale eyes. "What will you do with your little knife, eh?" he wondered aloud. "Do you think to frighten me off? If so, you'll need to show me something more impressive."

"Just stay away from me," Catherine said again, her voice seeming to echo through her head. She turned a little, and his figure blurred and swam before righting itself. This sudden attack of vertigo caused her to sway slightly on her feet, and a rising wave of nausea momentarily threatened to overpower her.

He shrugged a little, his broad shoulders rippling the dark fabric of his coat, and his hard mouth turned slightly upward in what he must have considered a smile. Catherine was not in the least reassured by the change in his expression, for his eyes remained cold.

"Come now," he said in a smooth manner. "Let's be friendly for a moment. I didn't mean to startle you." He spread his hands, palms upward, and his smile deepened, revealing groovelike dimples in his cheeks. My God, he looked like one of Satan's imps! Catherine thought, finding the idea far from comforting as he continued. "It simply couldn't be avoided."

"Couldn't be avoided?" Catherine repeated, thoroughly amazed. "And I suppose you couldn't avoid riding down that poor beggar there. . . ." She nodded in the direction of the dead outlaw leader, her eyes never once leaving this enigmatic stranger who now threatened her.

"Sympathy for one who was about to rob you just moments ago!" he said with a derisive snort. "Your generosity of spirit astounds me." That intense pale gaze, so unsettling, traveled over her, causing her to shiver as though she'd been caressed by ice. "It's funny, but you don't have the look of a cleric."

Catherine had the distinct feeling that he could see right through her coat, shirt, breeches, and boots to the soft white skin beneath. A dull flush crept up her throat into her cheeks, and she wished fervently that he would go away.

The thought gave her further cause to fret, for she realized suddenly that she had not heard a sound from Mose. She had not even seen him since this madman had come thundering up on his devil's steed! She shot an anxious glance into the dark . . . and when she turned her gaze back upon the stranger, she saw that he had moved even closer.

She stepped backward a pace, felt dizziness sweep over her again, and groaned, putting her left hand to her throbbing brow. "I am not a cleric," Catherine said, "and I shall show no hesitancy in killing you if you come a step closer."

"Yes," the stranger said levelly, "I can see the light of viciousness shining in your eyes."

He was mocking her, and Catherine hated him in that moment. The scorn she felt for him did indeed shine in her eyes, caused her lips to curl in a sneer. "You are as much a bandit as those you chased away—worse! For you are even more cowardly. Like a damnable wolf you seek to wear me down, waiting until it is safe for you to rush in for the kill without risk to your own worthless hide!"

"I am the man who saved your life," he protested. "What makes you think I wish to kill you?"

Catherine's temples throbbed so that it was difficult to think. "You certainly look a brigand to me," she stated with no regard to tact. "And what manner of man goes galavanting 'round at night alone on this notorious road?"

What manner of man indeed, Jase St. Claire thought darkly. Aloud he said, "You do realize that I might also question your presence here?" His voice softened just a bit. "What manner of fool would travel this murderous road at midnight, with only a negro servant to protect him, hmm?" No reply was forthcoming from the callow youth, just a slight darkening of his earlier flush and a beading of sweat upon his pale brow. "Must I also remind you that looks are ofttimes deceiving?"

"Oh, just go away and leave me," the lad said. "None of this is your affair."

Jase's smile faded. *If only that were true.* "Fine then," he said. "I'll just go and leave you here alone, since that's your wish. The negro man is gone, your mount has run off, and it's forty miles on foot over hard terrain to Natchez. By the look of you, tomorrow's dawn will bring you fever. By sunset you may well be insensible. Perhaps that's for the best, though...."

The stranger's voice trailed away and he cocked his head as if listening. As if on cue, the eerie siren call of a wolf drifted to Catherine's ears. Her tormentor looked at her again and smiled wickedly. "If I were to hazard a guess, I'd say that you needn't worry. You won't be alone for long."

He was trying to frighten her, Catherine knew. And it was working.

The fine hairs on her arms and nape stood erect, and chills rippled down her spine. She was trying to decide which wolf posed the greatest threat to her safety, this grinning one who stood before her, or his distant canine cousin . . . when he struck.

His movement was so swift, so unexpected, that Catherine barely had time to parry the attack. She lunged to the left, dodging his lightning grab for her wrist, and brought her weapon slashing downward.

Jase felt the fabric of his skintight breeches part and looked down to see a long string of dark beads forming along the length of the thin cut which began a mere two inches from his groin. For an instant a wave of purely masculine horror washed over him . . . then anger rose to replace it.

"Do you see what you very nearly did to me?" he thundered. "You wicked little wretch! Why, I've a good mind to tan that scrawny backside of yours—"

He lunged again for the lad, who darted away, but not quickly enough, for Jase looped an arm around his neck and dragged him back against him.

As soon as Jase closed his hand around the slim wrist, the contest was decided. A tiny bit of pressure on the vulnerable tendons and the stiletto clattered to the ground.

"Villain! Release me now!"

"Not so damned fast, my fine young man," Jase mocked lightly. His suspicions had been confirmed as soon as he drew the "lad" against him . . . the only unanswered question was why. He started to turn her in his embrace so that she would be forced to meet his eyes when she thrust her hip hard against him, striking him full in the groin.

Catherine gained instant freedom.

Trying to ignore her pounding head, she burst into full flight, running as fast as her trembling limbs would carry her . . . down the road and into the concealing darkness.

But then she recalled the outlaw leader who had been ridden down by that monstrous horse! This new outlaw would mount and be after her as soon as he recovered. She couldn't hope to outrun the powerful horse, especially on these weak and quaking limbs! There was only one chance left to her, and that was to find a place to hide.

Her heart thundering in her ears, Catherine turned and scurried up the steep embankment. It took her several moments, moments that seemed to stretch into eternity, but at last she saw the lighter gray of the sky peeping through the trees.

Oh, please God! she prayed, one moment more! Gulping air into her searing lungs, she reached the top . . . at the same instant that a callused hand closed over the waistband of her breeches.

She could have cried. She was teetering on the very brink of freedom, and this dogged night-riding fiend was all that was standing in her way! She tried to kick at him, but to no avail, for he was steadily hauling her backward and off her feet.

In one last desperate bid for escape, Catherine twisted and thrust her shoulder low into his midsection. But instead of meeting soft and vulnerable tissue, she met with something akin to iron. The blow made no impression on him whatsoever, but her weight, suddenly thrown against him, caught him off balance, and without warning he fell, taking her with him.

Catherine screamed and clutched at him as they rolled end over end. When finally they came to a stop at the bottom of the ravine, her assailant lay sprawled atop her. Almost as stunned as she, he lifted his raven head and stared down into her furious face.

"You should have listened to me, you know," he said. "If you had, you could have saved yourself this humiliation."

"Thank you so much for pointing that out to me," Catherine said through clenched teeth. "Now get off of me, you damnable rogue!"

She pushed against his broad shoulders, but he was planted solidly atop her, and it was obvious he had no intention of removing himself anytime soon.

She was all too aware of his hard chest pressing against her soft breasts, his flat belly melding to hers, and his lean thigh riding so casually between her own. She felt his vital warmth envelop her, smelled the faint scent of cologne which mingled with the scents of horseflesh and leather, an intoxicating male perfume she found pleasing even amid her struggles.

Hot blood suffused her cheeks; it seemed to amuse him, for he grinned down at her. "Damnable rogue," he mused, repeating her earlier words. "Pretty vernacular for a little girl. Did you learn that at a convent school, my dear mademoiselle? Or have you made it a practice to hang around down on Silver Street?"

"What do you want from me?" she demanded. "Is it rape that you intend? For if it is, then kindly don't delay! I wish to have this detestable task over with swiftly!"

Catherine waited, fully expecting to feel those hard hands strip away her clothing, explore all the secret places never touched by any man, not even Alonzo, her fiancé. . . . Tensely she waited, hating this handsome rakehell with the translucent eyes.

But his only reply was clear, ringing laughter. It rippled from his throat, filling the night air with rich sound. It came from him powerfully; she felt him try to subdue it, felt his chest vibrate against her breasts until its force went clear through her.

Aside from humiliation that he found the idea of ravishing her so damnably funny, something stirred inside her, something totally female. She felt its warmth unfurl, reach toward him through her skin, and squirmed to stamp it out. "What is so amusing?" she cried. "Are you mad that you laugh at the idea of perpetrating such a heinous act?"

He leaned his forehead into the curve of her throat and sighed, his mirth at last subsiding. "It is just that your request struck me as ludicrous. You see, I prefer my women—" He searched for a way to explain. "Well, more like women. I'm sorry, but you just don't appeal to me . . . dressed as you are."

Catherine was mortified.

His words stung her to the quick. If he'd known what it had cost her to cut her long golden tresses, to leave her beautiful clothes behind! How dare he make sport of her when it was the search for justice that had brought her here! Tears sparkled in her eyes, dampened her long lashes. She turned her head so that he would not see how his words had wounded her.

"Request, you say, you arrogant beast! It was not a request but an attempt to get you off of me! Why, I would sooner bed down with the Black Lion himself than the likes of you!"

"Oh, you would, would you? Well, take care that you don't speak too loudly, mademoiselle, for these woods might well have ears, and this lion may well consider your boast an invitation."

She quieted for a second, and Jase gazed down at her, noting for the first time her damp lashes. The sight of her momentary vulnerability gave him pause. "What is this?" he said, his tone softer now. "After your defiance, your threats, your attempt to emasculate me—and a damned near successful one, I might add—you show me your tears?"

Uncomfortably, he stared down at her. In that moment she seemed a frail creature, part woman, part child. She was young and defenseless, tears making her lashes starry, yet there was something very old in her eyes. It was a certain look she gave him, as if she had viewed the world and found it lacking. It made him curious, that look, made him all the more determined to keep her from endangering herself until he could send her back to wherever it was that she belonged.

"I did not ask for any of this," she said in a tight voice. "I did not ask you to come thundering in on that devil horse of yours like some misplaced hero in a fairy tale."

"I am many things, mademoiselle," Jase answered softly, "but never have I felt the need to play the hero. Kindly do not portray me as one. My being here was purely coincidental and my interference unwelcome, obviously, since you have made it very clear that you would have rather risked death at the hands of those men than accept my help." He frowned. "Why? Why are you out here in the wilderness without a proper escort? And garbed like this?" He reached up and touched the golden hair that curled at her nape. "There is some reason behind this sacrilege, and if you wish me to release you, then you must first explain yourself."

"You would not understand," Catherine said, wishing that he would just disappear. Better to face the four-legged wolf alone than to look into those pale searching eyes and tell the truth. He would not accept it in any case. He would only roar with laughter at her audacity, at the very idea that she, a woman, had come in hopes of vanquishing a notorious renegade who for years had eluded capture. It was reason enough for Catherine to keep her silence.

"We can lie here like this all night if you wish," he said, "your soft form providing my mattress, or you can answer my questions."

Beneath him, she sighed. She was tired and feeling ill. She had fought him and lost. What point was there in further struggles? "If I tell you my reasons for being here, you must swear to release me."

"That's more like it."

"Swear!"

"You would accept my word?" he questioned with a twinge of mockery. "A heartless brigand, surely as bad as those men who stole your horse and your man, and would have taken your virtue as well if provided with the opportunity."

Catherine wished she could escape the warm muscular body that pinned her securely to the ground, but he was too heavy, and any movement might serve to increase his enjoyment. "As you have already pointed out, I have little choice in the matter. You, m'sieur, possess the upper hand."

"Very astute of you to realize it, and too bad that it took you so long."

Catherine bristled, longing for the stiletto lost up the trail. "Your word, m'sieur."

"My name is Jason St. Claire. I prefer Jase. And you have my word, such as it is."

Catherine took a deep, fortifying breath, which caused her breasts to press against the hard wall of his chest, sending a tingle of sensual awareness through her. "I am here on a mission of the greatest import. There is a man—an outlaw—who plies his lethal trade along this very road, and I have come to see him brought to justice."

"A tall order for so small a twit as you," Jase St. Claire remarked coolly, yet the keen light of interest shone in his eyes.

"Save your comments, m'sieur," Catherine said. "They mean nothing when compared with the task to which I must attend! My friend, Mose, and I were on our way to Natchez to meet with Governor Sargent when we were halted on the road. It is imperative that the governor take immediate action to stop the murderous activities of this outlaw before he kills again."

St. Claire was very still above her, and Catherine

could tell that she had caught his interest, that he was waiting for her to finish. She smiled inwardly, drawing out the moment for no other reason than to gain the tiniest, most insignificant revenge upon him.

"Well?" he said, growing impatient.

"His name is the Black Lion. Perhaps you have heard of him?"

Jase frowned at her. "It would be difficult indeed not to have heard him mentioned," he said dryly. "He seems to be a very popular fellow these days."

"Infamous!" she put in. "A blackhearted bastard who kills for wanton pleasure!"

Jase's frown deepened. It seemed his name was on everyone's lips these days, including those belonging to this disheveled beauty, and he had this impostor to thank for it.

"You have what you wanted, m'sieur. Now, kindly remove yourself so that I might be on my way!"

Her voice broke into Jase's musings, forcing him to face a more immediate concern. "You are in a hurry to leave me, mademoiselle." He traced his fingertips along her jaw, admiring its stubborn set, and noted that she shivered at his touch. "I still don't know your name, or what makes you think that an important man like Winthrop Sargent will rush to do your bidding."

"He will," she said with fervor. "The bounty for the Black Lion's capture still exists. There will be a fine feather in the cap of the man who captures him. Who would not wish to see this villain tried for his crimes?"

Who indeed? Jase wondered.

"He has been the cause of much hardship, heartache, and sorrow!" she concluded.

What would she know of hardship? Jase thought. The hands which strained against his chest were soft and white and bore no calluses. And though she was slim, her form was softly rounded; she had not known the deep and abiding hunger that had been his sole companion through that first hard winter with the Indians.

He didn't like to think of it . . . of how he'd been cast as a slave into the streets of the Seneca village where he was first taken as a captive, a half-starved lad of twelve who had to fight the village mongrels for scraps. . . .

Jase rose abruptly, bringing the girl to her feet as well. Saving her from that blasted outlaw Jack Lynch and his cohorts was bringing him no end of trouble. Jack had been no more than a petty thief who performed a job or two and retired to the taverns and brothels that lined Natchez's infamous Silver Street until his coin was depleted. He'd been too lacking in ambition to pretend to be the Black Lion. But now Jack lay sprawled in a lifeless heap, crushed under Sadist's hooves. Jase hadn't intended to kill him; it had been an accident caused in the confusion of the melee. But as Sadist had borne down on the hapless outlaw, the facade which Jase had spent four years carefully constructing had melted away beneath the old blood lust that had roared through his veins. For an instant he had once again been the Black Lion, a wild young man with ties to two worlds, one red, one white . . . belonging completely to neither. . . .

The sensation had been swift to die away, leaving Jase angry at himself, at Jack Lynch, at the young woman who had unwittingly precipitated such deadly events . . . and who represented a distinct threat to him.

He took the girl's arm and started off to where Sadist waited, dragging her along.

"Wait! What are you doing! You promised to let me go if I answered your questions!" She dug in her heels, but Jase pulled her along.

"I lied." Jase caught hold of Sadist's reins. "I'm taking you with me. I would be doing mankind a great disservice by leaving you to roam about at will, stirring up mischief. Besides, there are those who would do worse than relieve you of your purse and your servant, and I will not have your death on my conscience, such as it is."

He said nothing of his other motives, that he could ill afford to have her stirring up a veritable hornet's nest of trouble by running to the governor . . . or that he rather liked the way her softly curving derriere was so fetchingly displayed in her breeches.

She was as spirited as she was beautiful, and she intrigued him, despite her anonymity, or perhaps even because of it.

And there was still another reason, a reason that brought to life a certain dark discomfort inside Jase; he had already killed to keep her safe.

Surely that alone was reason enough to want to keep her from falling victim to the killer, who was now plying his bloody trade along this very highway.

Jase's stallion didn't like the unfamiliar scent of

this young woman. He pinned back his ears and reached forward to give her a punishing nip. Jase stopped him by pinching him hard beneath his jaw. "That will be enough of that," he told the animal.

"You don't expect me to ride that monster!" she cried softly.

Jase peered at her with an upraised brow. "Afraid of him, are you?"

There was something in the way he said it that made Catherine stiffen. "I am not afraid of him, or of you for that matter. It's just that he's very tall, this nag of yours, and I would prefer my own mount." There was no need to speak of what truly troubled her, that she was unnerved by the thought of sharing the beast's back with Jase St. Claire, of being pressed close to his hardened frame again!

"I've little doubt you would prefer your own horse," he said. "It would make escape so much more easy. No, you'll ride with me—would do so even if you were possessed of a mount. . . . I've no intention of our being parted so soon. Now, will you put that dainty boot of yours to stirrup, or shall I boost you up?"

Catherine saw no alternative but to admit defeat and hope for some miracle that would aid her in regaining her freedom. Until then, she would have to bear this man's noxious company as best she could. She stepped forward and grasped the pommel, then thrust her left boot into the stirrup. She tried to spring into the saddle, but the animal was simply too large for her to manage it. She made several false starts, swearing softly and breathing hard, when a calloused hand placed firmly beneath her derriere and another at her waist aided her ascent.

Jase ignored her outraged gasp and heated glare, and swung up behind her. But as he settled himself on the Spanish black, he found his lies winging back to flog him. For the truth was, despite her boyish locks and men's attire, he found this defiant slip of femininity desirable indeed. In fact, with her soft little rump pressed so close against his inner thighs, it might be deuced difficult to remember on the long trek to Rosemunde that he was her self-appointed savior.

Chapter 3

Night gave way to the next day's dawn with the greatest reluctance. The opaque blackness melted ever so slowly into the softer gray predawn, while out of the dense hollows a cottony mist rose up. It swirled eerily around the hooves of the Spanish black and, as horse and riders moved through it, bathed the hot skin of Catherine's face and throat. Yet she derived little comfort from its damp wash.

Feverish now, half dead with fatigue, she felt doomed to ride this devil's mount forever. Not even the first rays of the dawn, which slowly turned the blanketing mist to a gentle pink phosphorescence, lightened the foreboding that weighed upon her.

Since mounting this barbarous horse, her captor had not uttered a single syllable. Indeed, had it not been for the hard thighs which burned her own, and the sinewy arm which circled her waist, his hand resting on the pommel just inches from the apex of her thighs, Catherine would have thought herself alone. But he was there, damn his scoundrel's heart, and she had only to relax her stiff posture to feel that stalwart wall of iron-hard muscle bracing her back, the warm breath that stirred the tendrils at her temple . . . both of which she sought to avoid.

Jase St. Claire's touch was as unsettling as his probing stare. It sent queer sensation uncoiling from the source of contact, like strong fingers playing along the tautly drawn strings of her nerves to produce a deep, vibrating hum.

These strange sensations were as mysterious to Catherine as the man himself. Certainly Alonzo had never made her feel this way! Not even when he pressed his cool lips to her cheek and held her in his arms . . . and he was her fiancé!

Thinking of Alonzo fortified Catherine, and even though her aches and pains had become nearly intolerable, she managed to resist leaning into the strong support of her captor's chest.

Jase was aware of the girl's struggles to avoid him, and knew full well the price of her stubbornness. Any woman of his acquaintance would have long ago been wilting against him, begging with tear-filled eyes for whatever comfort he could provide—and complaining incessantly at whatever efforts he made to do so.

Jase had known many women. Yet, in all of his travels from Pennsylvania to the Great Lakes and down to Natchez, he had never encountered a woman with such fire as this one.

He permitted himself the luxury of surveying her stiff spine, and a grudging smile played about his stoic mouth, only to be replaced by a frown a moment later. His predictions had come to bear;

she was fast growing feverish. Heat radiated from her skin, and he knew that she must ache from the crown of her bright head to her smallest toenail. Still, she kept herself rigid before him, cringing away from his merest touch.

"We'll reach our destination by midday," Jase said, breaking the silence that had long stretched between them. "But you surely will not last so long, weak as you are." His astute observation won him a frigid look from her.

"I will last, just to spite you," she insisted.

"I have no doubt you'll try," he replied calmly, "but fever has a way of taking its toll on even the strongest. It will sap your strength quickly enough."

"You may keep your concern to yourself, m'sieur. I do not want it."

Jase shrugged. "I was only thinking of your comfort. Your muscles must be getting sore from sitting so stiffly."

"My muscles are just fine. In fact, they have never been better!"

"Indeed. You look as if you've a poker up your—" She looked daggers at him, but he went on. "Your seat is poor, even for a woman. Who taught you to ride, your grandmother?"

She clamped her jaws shut and refused to answer.

"You need to relax, otherwise you'll develop painful knots . . . here." He squeezed the area between her neck and shoulders, and saw her wince. "That feels good, eh?" he murmured near her ear. She had very nice ears, small and pearly pink, like the inside of a shell. He rotated his thumb at the base of her neck, brushing her short silken tresses with his knuckles. Her skin was very soft, like that of an infant, and it smelled sweetly of the out-of-doors, sunshine on tall meadow grass, and wild-flowers. . . . Unable to resist the urge, Jase nuzzled her hair, and using his arm at her waist, urged her gently backward. "Come, lean against me and rest. I think I can abide your closeness during this last leg of our journey."

"Abide me, can you? Why, how very generous of you, m'sieur," she rasped sarcastically, reaching up to force his hand away. "You must think me devoid of sense to accept such an offer. Well, let me tell you that though I am feverish, my wits are not so dulled that I cannot see through you. In short, I know what manner of man you are, and I know that such cooperation on my part is exactly what you want—indeed, what you crave! Why, I've an idea that thoughts are swirling in that swarthy head of yours at this very instant, and I wish you to know I think you a depraved individual." To stress her words, she stiffened her spine even more, though it cost her dearly in the way of comfort.

"Truly? What manner of man am I, mademoiselle?"

"A true bounder," she said. "A man without principle or restraint!"

Far from insulted, Jase displayed his even white teeth in a lupine grin. "Well, if I am as you say, then perhaps you should worry that I will give you cause to regret the insult." It was devilish to bait her, but he simply couldn't resist.

"The only thing I have cause to regret is that my

malady is not contagious," she retorted, "for I would have the greatest pleasure in passing it on to you!"

"Ah," Jase said. "You would like to see me burn for you!"

The bold comment made Catherine's cheeks blush with more than fever. "You are impossible!" she hissed at him. "A veritable roué!"

"You will receive no argument from me there," he said. "Indeed, I am that, and much, much more. You ran afoul of the very devil last night, whether you know it or not. Why, it pleases me to tell you that I haven't gobbled up a child in a distressing number of days, and therefore I was most happy when I happened upon you."

"Cease your babble, m'sieur," she said. "I liked you far better when you were silent."

"I humbly beg your pardon, mademoiselle. It was not my intention to bore you. Why don't you talk instead?" He paused a moment, as if in consideration, before adding casually, "Something entertaining to fill this dull interlude . . . ah, I have it! Why don't you tell me about yourself, who you are, and exactly what circumstance has made us such bosom friends?"

So, he was back to that again, was he? Catherine thought wearily. Little good it would do him, no matter how he tried to trick her, coax or cajole. She was not talking! His motives were surely far from pure. And not so many hours past he had shown his devious bent. He seemed to delight in his taunts, as a great black cat might toy with a small and defenseless mouse, allowing it a little freedom before sinking in its claws again. There was no telling what he intended, though no doubt it was far from holy. "I would hardly term our current situation 'friendly,' m'sieur," Catherine said wearily.

"Oh?" he replied, raising dark brows. "Surely after the events of last night, after I saved you from your own stupidity—"

Ears burning with this latest insult, Catherine swung her leg across the horse's withers and started a sliding descent. She would escape him one way or another, even at the risk of being trampled by those lethal hooves! But little good it did her, for in an instant her captor's sinewy arm swept out to grab her. Effortlessly, he dragged her back between his thighs and held her there. "Going somewhere?" he questioned darkly.

"Away from you!" she cried, panting from her slight exertion.

"Away from me?" he said. "But I am your rescuer, dear mademoiselle, and for that you should love me dearly."

"Love you, you great braying ass! I should like nothing better than to spill your blood upon this trail!"

To Catherine's further irritation, the grinning devil merely clucked his tongue. "Such vehemence is unbecoming to a woman. Now, be a good child and keep still, or I shall be forced to bind your hands and make you walk along behind me."

"I am not a child!"

Indeed, she was not, Jase thought, for her body was soft and oh so womanly. She fit against him perfectly. . . . His gaze moved over her flushed cheek and down her throat. At some time during

her travails the previous night, she had lost the
topmost button from her shirt. The throat of the
too-large garment now gapped open, providing
Jase with an enticing view of one generously
rounded breast. He could see the full inner ivory
curve, the pink crescent nipple. . . .

She was most definitely a woman, fully grown,
and the sight of her silken flesh warmed his loins.
It had been weeks since he'd been to Natchez, and
far longer since he'd spent a pleasurable night in
his mistress's bed. His abstinence, though unintentional, was beginning to wear heavily upon him.

"I am not a child!" she repeated.

Arching a brow at her insistent tone, Jase peered
down at her. "Oh?" he said lightly. "Your behavior
thus far has been far from that of a genteel young
lady. And I am guessing that you do come from
good family, for these rags you wear must have
cost their owner a pretty price indeed." Her
cheeks took on a deeper rose hue, and he knew
that he had struck upon the truth. "However, they
clash violently with your actions, and thus I can
only surmise that you stole these garments and
somehow persuaded that poor servant to accom-
pany you on this fool's errand. Hardly the every-
day pursuit of a genteel young woman, would
you not agree? Actions much more suited to a
headstrong child!"

He was most cruel to say these things to her
when she was defenseless against him! She
searched for something bad enough to use in reply, but no scornful words rushed to her defense,
and she had a niggling suspicion that she *had*
acted with a child's headstrong impulsiveness.

Still, she would not admit it. Not to him, not even to herself. Her cause was a noble one, one which she would not abandon. She had sacrificed much to see the Black Lion destroyed, and she fully meant to continue until her self-appointed task was done.

"Fool's errand, is it?" she rasped. "To seek vengeance for a grievous wrong?"

"The fever has you in its grip," her captor said, his pale blue eyes hooded. "It makes you babble."

She gave him a dark look that could have rivaled one of his own, arching one finely drawn brow and peering at him from fever-bright eyes. "Have you ever lost a loved one, m'sieur? Well, I have. And in the cruelest fashion. My brother was killed along this Trace, and I have come to find the man responsible and see justice done!"

"A monumental task for one so petite," he said. "Yet, I suppose one must laud you for your efforts."

"I will succeed!" she insisted. "I must!"

"How can you know that? Without proof, your claims are worthless—the mere suspicions of a grief-stricken woman."

He planted the seed of doubt in Catherine's fevered brain, but she stubbornly refused to let it take root. "I have proof, m'sieur. Proof that links the murderer to the crime."

"What kind of proof?" he asked, but she refused to answer. She was ill, but not delirious, and she was not going to jeopardize her chances of convincing Governor Sargent by revealing her secrets to this callous roué!

It seemed that her world was shrinking. Where

before there had been the wide, fog-shrouded landscape, there was now just the rocking sway of the horse beneath her and the stalwart support of the hard man at her back. She detested the gratitude she felt for this last, even while she grew more and more aware that he was the single force keeping her astride and upright. And no matter how great her show of bravado, the fact remained that she dreaded the thought of being abandoned along this terrible road.

She was ill, and growing more so by the moment. She began to shiver ... and with that first great shudder she found to her dismay that she could not stop. Soon she quaked so violently that her teeth chattered.

Through her fever-induced haze, Catherine heard the man behind her swear softly. His arm tightened about her ribs, just beneath her breasts, and without a word he settled her across his lap. She gathered her strength and raised her head just enough to send him a withering glare. But instead of shaking him, it only prompted his odd half smile. With hooded eyes he let his gaze roam freely over her person. She would reprimand him for it ... as soon as she could find the strength to do so.

"I see the fight has yet to leave you," he said. "Though foolishly you fight the wrong man."

"Y-you wish for me to t-trust you," Catherine said with clacking teeth. "T-that, m'sieur, would make me foolish!"

"Women!" he said derisively. "It is the greatest folly of your kind to fly in the face of plain logic and never to recognize when you are well off. Go on then, mademoiselle, and bite the hand that saved your scrawny hide! I should have left you to your fate last night!"

"M-my only folly was running af-foul of a blackguard like you." Catherine's voice sounded small, even to her own ears, but her words seemed to have a strong effect upon him. In a moment he brought the great beast which carried them to a halt and easily dismounted, taking her with him.

The world tilted crazily, righting itself for an instant so that she caught a glimpse of his stony visage, and she knew that she had angered him. "W-what are you d-doing?"

"I'm taking you into the house and putting you to bed," he said. "And there you will stay until you regain your senses."

"No. Put me d-down!"

Jase looked down at the slight form he cradled in his arms and his hard mouth softened. "Don't be ridiculous. You can't stand, let alone walk."

He strode quickly up a walkway, his boots loud upon the crushed shell that lined the footpath. The young woman in his arms had ceased to fight— had, in fact, given in to a sudden, overwhelming need to sleep.

For a long moment he stood before the wide steps of the palatial home that was Rosemunde, gazing down at this small bit of woman's flesh he held. In repose her face was angelic, and for an instant his searching gaze caressed the sweep of gilded lashes, resting now on flushed cheeks; the slim, pert nose; the perfect mouth . . . and lingered there. . . .

And in that fleeting instant, Jase St. Claire, renegade and ne'er-do-well, blackguard and inadvertent hero, was sorely tempted to test the pliancy of those ruby lips.

"Ridiculous," he muttered, in reference to himself and these unaccustomed urges he was experiencing. He was not a man given to irrational impulses, yet there was something about this particular female that aroused them in him. Had he not interfered in last night's raid on her behalf? And did he not, even now, bear her to a bedchamber in his own home, a place where he had never brought another woman . . . not even his mistress, Angela?

The thought gave him pause, and for a heartbeat he knew the same great unease he had experienced before. What was it about this young woman that provoked him into acting the hero? He considered the close-cropped golden curls nestled against his heart, the great turquoise eyes now shuttered behind fragile blue-veined lids . . . and snorted at his own folly.

He was a man as given to romanticism as the devil himself! The truth was that he'd brought her to Rosemunde out of necessity. She claimed to have evidence pertaining to her brother's killer. He needed to know if she was telling the truth, and if so, exactly what the evidence was. He needed to know more about her brother, to add whatever pieces she could provide to this intricate puzzle of the Black Lion that he was attempting to solve. Perhaps she could help, perhaps not. In any case, he could not afford to let her go to the governor.

He was getting old, Jase thought with a shake of

his dark head, too damned old to be cavorting about like some young buck, and raising unholy hell. As soon as he put a stop to the outlaw impersonating the Black Lion, his life would return to normal. What he needed most at this moment he could find in the library, enough to drown all coherent thought.

Bounding up the steps and crossing the gallery in three swift strides, Jase opened the great front door and bellowed, "Dora!"

A vague skittering sounded in the bowels of the manse, evolving into the sound of hurrying footsteps. A tall woman of middle years appeared, seeming out of breath. She was painfully thin, with angular face and large blue eyes that widened even more when she discerned what her employer was carrying.

"Sir!" she exclaimed, obviously unsure what conclusions to draw from this startling sight. "What on earth is this?" She peered intently into the girl's sleeping face. "Why, she's little more than a child!"

For some reason the housekeeper's observation made Jase impatient. "Hell, woman," he said, a muscle working in his taut cheek, "don't just stand there gawking. Turn down the bloody bed so that I can be rid of this burden."

Dora tightened her thin lips until they nearly disappeared, then hastened up the broad staircase. She reached the upstairs hall and turned to the right, where the master suite was located. Jase saw her pause and guessed at the cause of her indecision.

"Any bedchamber will do, Dora," he called, amused on some dark level. "All save mine."

Her hand fell upon the closest doorknob, the one adjoining the sitting room to the master suite, and she pushed the door wide, standing aside to allow Jase to enter, then coming forward to turn down the covers. She fussed about as he placed the girl on the bed and proceeded to remove her boots. One by one they dropped to the floor. Jase threw the covers across her shivering form, and then he stood back with arms folded, a black frown upon his face.

Dora screwed up her courage to question her formidable employer. "What shall I do with her, sir?"

"Do?" Jase repeated, trying not to show confusion. The very devil of a time he'd had, since meeting this tiresome little wench, trying to figure out that very same thing. "Do? Why the hell are you asking me? She's ill, knocked her head in a fall, and is running a fever. Do whatever is necessary to bring her out of it, then send for me when she is lucid." He moved toward the door.

"I'll do what I can for her, of course—"

"Well, what is it?" Jase demanded, halted by the taut look on her thin face.

Dora raised her eyes to his. "If she doesn't come 'round, sir? What shall I do then?"

Jase settled his gaze on the sleeping girl. "She'll come around, Dora," he promised. "Spitting and hissing, claws bared. And when she does, send for me immediately. I don't give a damn what time it is. I want to be here when she awakens. We have unfinished business, she and I. In the meantime, see that she has anything she requires, and if a word comes out of that lovely mouth, I wish to know what it is. Is that understood?"

Dora nodded.

Jase stepped into the hallway, pulling the door closed behind him.

Slowly he made his way downstairs and halted before the double doors of the library, his hand on the knob.

It was the only room at Rosemunde that was truly his. He had selected the books, the furnishings, even the carpet. The rest of the house still belonged to Maynard Dumonde, his friend and benefactor. The silk-draped walls, the opulent paintings, the candlesticks and silver had been Maynard's gifts to Jase.

But Maynard Dumonde had given him something of far greater value; he had given him another chance at life.

Dumonde had been a frequent visitor at Blue Jacket's Town, the Shawnee village where Jase had come to manhood. The Frenchman had often arrived in late summer, loaded down with trade goods, and with little persuasion had stayed with his Shawnee friends throughout the long winters. Dumonde had taken an interest in the white youth they called the Black Lion and had spoken with him often. Sometimes on quiet evenings they had shared a fire while Dumonde talked of Canada, of his sister and her fat merchant husband. Never once had Dumonde mentioned Rosemunde—or the land that in his absence had been overrun by the encroaching forest since then. Jase had often wondered if Maynard, like himself, had never felt at home here.

The house was a veritable palace with riches everywhere, but Jase St. Claire was not a prince. There was little evidence of himself within these walls. Not a single trace of the wild young man who had smoked and talked with the Frenchman beneath the dark night sky. . . .

Jase entered the library and closed the doors behind him. After Fallen Timbers there had been little left of his life with the Shawnee. Maynard had offered him employment, he had accepted, and he'd spent the next four years plying the Lakes Region in Maynard's great bateau, trading with the northern tribes. Jase acted as interpreter, helped with the traps, hunted and fished and labored. He had been richly and unexpectedly rewarded for his loyalty. In the early spring of 1798 Maynard Dumonde had succumbed to the spotted fever, otherwise known as smallpox. In his will he left Rosemunde to Jase.

Mississippi Territory was far removed from the Great Lakes and Quebec, and at Rosemunde Jase had never quite managed to banish the restlessness that had set in after the end of the wars. He'd thought that perhaps in Mississippi he would find the peace he was seeking and so far had been denied. . . .

He made his way to the desk and splashed whiskey into a glass, drank it down, and sighed. He found it puzzling, how some men seemed to go through life without experiencing hardship, while others struggled endlessly. But then, perhaps his struggle was recompense, an earthly penance for his many sins. . . .

He was not looking for salvation or even forgiveness, only a brief reprieve from his cares of the moment, which he found in the quiet room. Surrounded by sunlight and a thousand leather-bound volumes, he could take his ease without the need for caution, and perhaps keep the shadows of the past at bay . . . at least until the darkness fell and it was time to hunt again.

Chapter 4

That same evening Jase stood by the windows in the library, watching the sun go down. The vivid scarlet turned to deep maroon, and then to black . . . yet another bloody sunset.

Evenings such as this had been rare in the land of Jase's youth, just west of the Allegheny Mountains. There, in the wild river valley he'd once called home, the evening sky had leaned toward a gentler mien, with varying pastel shades, and ofttimes the days were chill and misty, even in summer. . . .

With an infinitesimal slowness the colors deepened and began to fade. Jase, listening with only half an ear to the droning voice of his factor, Alonzo Hart, was restlessly aware that it would soon be growing dark.

"It's bound to be a fine entertainment, with the elite of Natchez in attendance. It is rumored that Winthrop Sargent will attend." Alonzo paused. "Jason?" No response. "Jason!"

His host's dark head turned, and the pale aquamarine eyes focused on him.

"Are you feeling unwell?" Alonzo asked. "I hear there is fever in New Orleans."

Jase waved the statement aside. He hadn't meant to drift off, but there were times when he found Alonzo's company tedious. "There is always fever in New Orleans," he said. "And I don't know when I have felt better. If I appear distracted, I apologize. It is just that I'm in something of a quandary, and therefore preoccupied."

"A problem here at Rosemunde?" Alonzo said, praying he did not sound as hopeful as he felt.

"Nothing I can't manage."

"Perhaps if you explained, I could be of some assistance."

St. Claire's pale eyes shifted once more, pinning Alonzo, boring straight into his soul. Had he said something wrong? Had St. Claire taken offense? The man was so damnably hard to read! Nothing of his thoughts ever showed upon his face. Alonzo waited, feeling tension mount inside him.

For two years he'd acted as Jase St. Claire's factor, selling his cotton and seeing to the accounts, leaving Jase free to breed and sell his cherished horses.

During that time, Alonzo had managed to ingratiate himself with St. Claire, often dropping by the manse on some pretext of business and remaining for dinner and drinks. The master of Rosemunde Plantation played the perfect host, yet Alonzo knew that his civility, his generosity, were part of a facade.

Despite his efforts, St. Claire showed Alonzo little more than the nominal courtesy he would afford any guest who crossed his threshold. St.

Claire had proven himself a very difficult nut to crack, but Alonzo was determined. He meant to gain Jase's trust, and then much more than that!

"I wouldn't dream of boring you with my mundane concerns," St. Claire said. "Besides, it has nothing to do with Rosemunde's affairs, but my own. Now, I believe you mentioned the governor. . . ."

"Honestly, Jase," Alonzo said with exasperation, "sometimes I think I'm wasting my time trying to keep you abreast of local news. It's plain as the nose on my face that you don't give a damn."

"You are too hard on me, Alonzo. I do care about what's going on around me." Jase sat back in his chair and reached inside his coat for the long silver case which contained his tobacco. He flicked the lid open and politely offered Alonzo one of the long black cigars he favored. Alonzo declined, but Jase selected one, closed the case, and returned it to his pocket.

Alonzo looked on as Jase's butler, Leviticus, stepped forward with a sliver of wood which he touched to the candle's flame and then held to the end of the cigar. The old servant, his hair silver, his face round, was devoted to the master of Rosemunde plantation.

Blue smoke curled upward in graceful swirls, wreathing the raven head of Jason St. Claire and causing him to appear to Alonzo as Satan incarnate.

Leviticus resumed his station by the cherry sideboard, outwardly oblivious to his surroundings until such time as his services would again be required.

"I was just saying that old Tom Galliher is planning a soiree with Governor Sargent as his honored guest," Alonzo continued. "It's to take place in three weeks' time. I paid them a visit just two days past and the place was in a tizzy. Old Tom had taken himself off somewhere, and there was only poor, beleaguered Rebecca left to greet me."

Jase gave a short, humorless laugh. "As I recall, Rebecca Galliher is a vivacious creature, hardly to be pitied. Unless she has changed drastically since last I saw her."

Alonzo laughed, his black eyes twinkling in his boyish face. "I daresay she hasn't changed. She is just as fetching, and still piqued that you declined Tom's invitation to New Year's dinner last. But I wouldn't worry that you've discouraged her by your lack of interest, my friend. Far from it, actually, for she seems intrigued by your very reticence. She pointedly questioned me as to what keeps you all alone out here in the country. In fact, she hinted broadly that you might have a woman tucked away out here." Alonzo sipped his brandy, looking pointedly at Jase. "Of course I assured her that she was mistaken. . . . She was mistaken, was she not?"

Jase considered the glowing tip of his cheroot and deliberately delayed his answer. "A woman," he said after a prolonged pause, "what a novel idea."

"Novel, indeed." Alonzo snorted. "You really should get out more, my friend. It isn't healthy to stay ensconced in the country alone for months at a time . . . especially when Natchez is so close, and so full of delicious diversions." Alonzo drained his glass, then watched as Leviticus came forward from his post to refill it. "Why, I'd be willing to bet that even Leviticus agrees with me."

"Sir?" The manservant seemed nonplussed to be included in a matter that was clearly beyond the bounds of his position.

"I was simply proposing that your master should get out more," Alonzo stated. "His life is fast becoming singularly uninteresting, don't you agree?"

Leviticus cleared his throat in an attitude of disapproval, looking from his employer's bland face to Alonzo's expectant one. "I would not be so presumptuous, sir, as to dictate Mr. St. Claire's— uhhmm—*affairs*."

"You've very neatly sidestepped the issue, Leviticus," Alonzo said. "And I commend you for it."

"Thank you, sir." The manservant shifted his questioning gaze to Jase, who looked mildly amused. "Is there anything else you wish, sir?"

"That will be all, Leviticus," Jase replied. "Leave the decanter for Mr. Hart's pleasure, and you may go."

"Blind loyalty," Alonzo muttered as he watched the servant quit the room. "However do you manage it?"

"I expect nothing less than loyalty from those in my employ."

The remark was politely uttered but meant to cut. Alonzo stiffened slightly. "I suppose I must report back to Rebecca that you have declined the invitation. She will be greatly put out, you know, as will many others in attendance—"

"Yes," Jase said with derision, "opportunists all . . . looking for a husband. Thank you, no. I can do without an evening of fending off the advances of overeager matrons hot for the scent of a fortune for their flat-bosomed daughters. I've grown fond of my freedom."

Alonzo sighed again. It was clear that St. Claire would not be dissuaded. "I am sure that Rebecca will be heartbroken when she hears the news. Have you not an ounce of contrition in your soul?"

For the first time that evening, Jase smiled, though the expression was more knowing than friendly. "None. But I am sure that you will think of some inventive way to soothe her disappointment."

Placing one hand upon his shirtfront, Alonzo feigned surprise. "Surely you don't suggest that I—why, I'll have you know that my heart is already promised to another!"

Jase remained unconvinced. "Your heart may well be promised, but your hands and the rest of your anatomy remain unfettered. Oh, come now," he said, seeing the other man ruffle, "I may be ensconced in the country, but I'm neither deaf nor blind. And these things have a way of becoming known." He paused to sip his whiskey. "I wouldn't be overly concerned, were I you. I doubt such rumors would carry all the way to New Orleans to this Catherine . . . what was her name again?"

"Breaux," Alonzo supplied. "And I am deeply in love with her."

"Yes," Jase agreed dryly, " 'tis obvious you are."

Alonzo set his snifter upon the gleaming board and rose. "I suppose it is my duty as your representative to carry the ill news to Rebecca. I do hope she doesn't take it too hard." His thoughts leapt ahead to the coming interview, to Rebecca Galliher's wide brown eyes and generous hips.... If he hurried, he could stop by on his way back into Natchez. "I don't mind telling you, I'll feel much more at ease once I'm back in Natchez. It's getting so a man thinks twice before leaving his own house!"

Jase looked up sharply. "Is there news?"

"Nothing but rumors," Alonzo said. "Not that it surprises me. With a blackguard of the magnitude of this one, there are bound to be wild tales circulating. Folks are frightened, and I can't say that I blame them."

"Who do you think the killer is, Alonzo?" Jase asked.

The unexpected question pierced Alonzo's calm, and for a moment he felt his panic rise. There was no way St. Claire could have guessed, for if he had, he would not be calmly enjoying his tobacco, and he, Alonzo, would not be drawing breath.

Forcing down his fear, Alonzo gave a short laugh. "Well, dammit, Jase, how am I to know?" He shifted in his chair, seeking the obvious acceptable answer. "Some say the Black Lion has returned from Canada and is raising hell down this way. No other name leaps to mind, no one with such a bent for cruelty, so I can't dispute the claim."

Jase pinned Alonzo with his icy stare. "You think the Black Lion still lives?"

Alonzo shrugged, feeling ill at ease. "It's a distinct possibility. A man like that would need to be well skilled in the art of survival. Whoever brings him down will have to be very canny indeed." He took a deep breath, letting it out slowly. "What do you think? Has the Black Lion returned?"

Jase knocked the ash from his cheroot and took a leisurely draw, expelling a thin stream of blue smoke before replying. "I wouldn't begin to hazard a guess. I'm a farmer, a breeder of horses. What would I know of lawless renegades?"

What, indeed? thought Alonzo. "I'll bring those papers by next week for you to sign. But I must advise against your decision to use indentures over slaves. It's more costly in the long run, and you do realize that you stand to offend your neighbors with your unorthodox opinions."

"It is my money, and my decision. I won't be swayed on this, Alonzo." Jase knew his tone was curt, but he didn't care. The issue of slavery had been a sticking point between them since the very beginning. Alonzo missed no opportunity to point out that Rosemunde would produce more cotton and yield a higher profit if black slaves worked the fields.

Jase remained adamantly against the buying and selling of slaves. Time had not diminished the hatred he bore John White Elk, the Seneca warrior who had led him from the ruins of the small farm which had been his boyhood home. John White Elk had been cruel, his heart shrunken by hatred of the whites, his temper violent when he drank too much of the English rum. . . .

Jase touched the jagged white scar that scored

his temple and disappeared into his hairline, and frowned. Damn the profits, damn the bloody neighboring planters with whom he felt compelled to associate. No slaves would be forced to work his land.

The silence that stretched between Alonzo and Jase was far from companionable. The interview was over. Alonzo took up his hat and gloves, and left his host to his brooding.

In a moment Alonzo was cantering down the gravel drive, away from Rosemunde, with the burning satisfaction he always derived from dining with a man whom he detested.

His thin lips curved. It gave him a perverse sense of power, sitting at table with the eminent Jase St. Claire, swilling his brandy, surveying his rich surroundings ... and knowing that soon it would all belong to him.

A dainty ormolu clock sat upon the bedside table, its fragile hands shivering on the precipice of midnight.

For a breathless moment the hands held there, seeming indecisive, then hastened forward to proclaim with tiny chiming bells the changing of the old day into the new.

Seated comfortably in the large wing chair drawn up close by the invalid's bedside, her aging face haloed by the soft golden glow of a single taper placed upon the candlestand, Dora Hilliard nodded off, only to come straight up again with a jerk.

"Oh, sir!" she exclaimed softly. "You gave me a fright just now!"

"It wasn't my intention to startle you, Dora. I only thought perhaps—" Jase broke off, leaning a shoulder against the tall, carved support of the spindle bed, not sure himself exactly what he had anticipated in coming here.

Dora shook her head. "Nary a peep thus far. Sleeping like a babe, she is. The fever hasn't risen, so I fully expect she'll waken on the morrow. Just worn out, the poor little lamb."

"Poor little lamb, indeed," Jase said, but there was a note of irony in his tone.

For a long while he stood gazing down at the winsome face, now innocent and childlike in slumber. . . .

A fine deception, that.

He had serious doubts concerning her innocence; proper young ladies of gentle birth did not go running off unchaperoned through the countryside. And there was no doubt whatsoever about her maturity. Whoever this wild young miss was, she was no child.

But who was she? And what had compelled her to take such risks with her young life?

All through the interminable evening she had plagued him.

He had been relieved when Alonzo had finally departed, and he had turned straightaway toward the stairs. Yet he had stopped with one boot on the lowest tread. What manner of fool was he becoming? She was only a woman, and God alone knew he could have his pick of those! So why did he feel this yearning to stand beside her bed and play the mooncalf?

Disgusted by his own weakness, knowing it was

wiser to turn his thoughts to more important matters, Jase had immediately turned upon his heel and strode to the stable.

Mounted on Sadist's back, Jase had hunted the highway without success, the troublesome beauty never far from his thoughts. Now, hours later, here he stood, staring down at the woman he had been trying to forget.

It was exquisite torment . . . wanting to hold her soft form close again, to feel the heavy drugging passion pulsing through his veins . . . and all the while knowing he could not.

Running a hand over his bristled cheek, he turned away. "I shall summon Mary to watch," he said. "I shouldn't like to keep you from your rest."

But Dora would hear none of it. "Mary could sleep through the Second Coming," she said. "You go on, sir, and do not fret. I'll rest just fine right here, and if the young lady stirs, I'll be sure to hear. Do you still want me to summon you if she awakes? Or shall I wait until the morning?"

"Summon me, Dora," Jase said. "I wish to be here."

Dora nodded her compliance, then watched Jase meld once more into the shadows on the far side of the room. As soon as the door closed gently behind him, she settled back down to doze.

When the first soft snore issued from Dora's mouth, Catherine opened her eyes and glanced around the room. It was a spacious chamber, not unlike her own at Rivercrest, except that its appointments were far more luxurious than those at home. The furnishings were ornately carved, their highly polished surfaces gleaming even in the half-light. The canopy above the bed was hand tatted, the counterpane silken to the touch. Yards and yards of netting fell in folds to the floor, a gossamer cocoon touched by the candlelight which enclosed the bed and insulated her from these foreign surroundings.

Sighing, she closed her eyes again and turned her hot cheek into the pillow, feeling the cool caress of fine linen against her fevered skin. She prayed hard that this was all a fantastic dream, that tomorrow she would awaken to the sound of Andre's voice drifting up from the morning room where he took his coffee, that Mose's laughter would come to her from the yard.

During their youth Mose had been her and Andre's constant companion. Together the three of them romped and played, as wild as Indians, conjuring mischief among them . . . like the tiny garden snake they'd put in M'sieur Alamar's bed. M'sieur Alamar was the schoolmaster who had taught the twins their lessons, a sour old bachelor who'd jumped and screeched like a woman when he climbed into bed and discovered he wasn't alone. He'd looked very amusing as he hopped up and down, the snake curled around his bare ankle, his nightshirt flapping around his bony knees. The sight had sent the mischief-making trio into gales of giggles, which had in turn given their presence away.

Within minutes they had been summoned before a stern-visaged Girard Breaux, to whom M'sieur Alamar bitterly complained. The trio stood, heads bowed but unrepentant, while the judgment was handed down.

To this very day, Catherine considered the punishment unduly harsh—the forced disbanding of the young miscreants. Mose, whom Girard felt had too much idle time on his hands, was put to work helping Tom, the blacksmith; Andre went to Master Jean Castel's school in the city, which, his father hoped, would instill in him some badly needed discipline and prepare him for the young men's academy; and Catherine was banished to Aunt Thea's for the duration of the summer.

It had been difficult for her, a spirited girl of eleven, to be separated from her two compatriots. She'd missed Andre and Mose terribly, and each night of her exile she cried into her pillow . . . just as she did now.

Andre was gone, and poor Mose was missing! Oh, how she longed for everything to be as it once was . . . as it still would be if fate had left their lives untouched.

A single tear, shimmering silver, slid along her cheek and dropped onto her pillow.

No matter how fervently she wished it, Catherine knew that she would not awaken at Rivercrest, that she would never again hear the sweet sound of Andre's voice. These strange surroundings and the woman keeping vigil in the chair, for the handsome, enigmatic stranger who had so recently stood gazing down at her while she pretended to sleep, were her reality.

As grim as it was, she knew that she must face it squarely. But not now, not tonight, not while her head ached so intolerably.

Tonight she had no strength to withstand the barrage of questions that would surely come from her dark host. Tomorrow would be time enough to think of some way out of this predicament.

Tomorrow . . . when she was stronger.

The rich aroma of coffee teased Catherine from her dreams. She breathed deeply of it, allowing the pungent smell to fill her lungs, to set her mouth watering, but it was a full minute before she opened her eyes.

Sunlight was streaming through the windows, and from the angle of those slanting rays Catherine judged the hour to be well advanced toward noon.

She had slept long, yet she felt little better for it. Her muscles felt stiff and sore, and her temples still throbbed. Perhaps her headache would dissipate once she was up and moving about. With this in mind, she slowly sat up, dangling her legs over the side of the mattress.

"Charming." The single word was warmly uttered, rife with deeper meaning. Catherine recognized that resonant masculine voice and was swift to flash a look of irritation in Jase St. Claire's direction.

He was seated comfortably in a wing chair beside the bed, relaxed and confident, the very man who had ridden through her nightmares and carried her off to this place . . . except that this morning he looked civilized.

Garbed in black breeches that hugged his lean hips and long thighs, Hessian boots, and a loose-fitting white shirt which was carelessly fastened to reveal an embarrassing amount of smooth bronze skin, he presented the very picture of a gentleman.

Indeed, with his dark locks brushed back from his tanned face, his unnaturally pale eyes glinting with humor, Catherine found him extremely handsome. For the first time, she noticed the wicked scar that sliced at an angle across his brow. But instead of detracting from his good looks, it somehow added to them, giving him a slightly sinister air, an air of danger which she found attractive.

Noticing with rising ire how warm his gaze became as it traveled over her trim ankles and shapely calves, she drew herself back up onto the bed and gathered the covers securely around her. Someone had undressed her, for she was naked beneath the covers . . . and Jase St. Claire was very well aware of it.

It made her vulnerable; it made her suspicious. Was it possible that this pale-eyed rogue in gentleman's trappings had unbuttoned her shirt and slipped it from her body? Had peeled away her breeches and gazed upon her naked flesh?

"You might have warned me that you were sitting there," she snapped.

"I might have," Jase admitted, "but then I would have missed the expressions that flitted across your face just now. I find it amusing that you cannot hide what you are thinking. In fact, my dear mademoiselle, I found your thoughts of a moment ago quite flattering. I'm glad that you approve of what you see."

Catherine felt the heat of a blush creeping into her cheeks. "How dare you invade the sanctity of my boudoir to mock me!"

Jase chuckled softly. "*Your* boudoir, mademoiselle? Kindly look around you. Everything you see here is mine. Now, tell me, who is the trespasser here?"

"Trespasser?" Catherine said. "You kidnapped me! And I want you to know that I fully intend to see you brought to bear for your crime!"

Jase found her a joy to behold. With a will, he held back the smile that threatened, then, propping one booted foot upon the mattress, he leaned back in his chair and said, "I am trembling before your promise of reprisal, my dear mademoiselle." Raising the elegant china cup he held in one hand, he saluted her with it, then brought it to his lips and sipped the steaming brew.

Through slitted eyes, she watched him. The smell of coffee wafted to her, causing her stomach to complain loudly.

"Do forgive me," said the evil wretch, "I don't often have guests, and my manners are lax. Would you like some?" He lifted the silver pot and held it poised above a second cup.

Catherine hesitated. "I do not like to trust you, but I suppose in this case I have no recourse." Her stomach rumbled in agreement. "It is either that or slow starvation."

"A wise decision," he concurred. "The first of such you've made." He filled the cup and set aside the server. "How would you like it?"

It was an innocent question, surely, so why did Catherine feel that it carried a double meaning? She looked at him askance, but he returned that questioning glance with a bland expression. "Cream and sugar, please," she said at last.

He held the cup out to her, but did not rise to place it in her hand, so that she was forced to lean forward to reach it, bracing her weight with one hand upon the mattress. For an instant, the blankets slipped down, so that her soft white shoulders and the uppermost curve of her breasts were displayed above the wealth of silk and linen. Her fingers closed around the cup, brushing his before she snatched her hand away.

Catherine wasted little time in bringing the covers once more to their rightful place beneath her chin. She flashed him a cutting look, but it did little to chasten him, nor did it drown the sudden spark that had kindled in his pale blue eyes. Grudgingly, she thanked him, sipped the coffee, and sighed.

"Do you find it to your liking then?"

"Very much so," she admitted.

"Are you hungry?"

She nodded.

"Good," Jase said, seeming pleased at her admission. "A healthy appetite is a good sign. We'll have you up and around in no time."

"I can assure you, M'sieur St. Claire," Catherine said, "that nothing could please me more. I am eager to be about my business."

Rising from his chair, Jase went to the door and called for Dora. Upon resuming his seat, he said to Catherine, "I was hoping you would come to your senses. Now, if you will tell me your name and where you are from, I'll see that you are promptly returned to your family."

Catherine's cup was poised in midair. Her turquoise eyes turned smoky. "My *family*," she said tightly, "is no concern of yours, m'sieur. Just return my clothes and I'll be on my way."

"So soon? But you only just arrived."

"I have business to attend to," Catherine replied.

"Ah, yes. The Black Lion. I must admit, I thought your tale improbable." He saw her redden slightly and waved her protest aside before she had the chance to voice it. "Come now, a young woman of good family does not go off alone in search of a desperate renegade." He chuckled. "No. I think it more likely that you are a runaway. What happened, mademoiselle? Does your father disapprove of the young buck you've set your heart on? Oh, kindly do not relate the sordid details. I've no interest in your many *amours*, only in seeing you returned where you belong."

His disparaging speculations made Catherine's temper boil. "Have you nothing better to do than go about poking your arrogant nose into matters that are none of your concern?" she demanded.

Jase was unperturbed. "Must I remind you that had it not been for my meddling on the road night before last you wouldn't be alive right now to be angry with me? I killed a man on your behalf, and I have seen too much dying to take the matter lightly. In short, my dear mademoiselle, you owe me."

"Owe you? I did not ask for your interference!" Catherine cried. "Nor did I ask for you to ride down that bandit. You entered the fray of your own accord. And if the look on your face was any indication, I suspect that you enjoyed it!"

Jase rose out of his chair; her words like salt in a festering wound. He stood glowering down at her as he fought to maintain control.

Some dark part of him savored the wild night wind in his face, the thud of his heart heavy and hammerlike against his ribs. It was a savage exhilaration, forbidden, untamed, which he had fought to put behind him, to forget ... until this rebellious girl had brought it all back to him, forcing him to face it again.

She sat very still on the bed, looking small amid an ocean of ecru linen and lace, as he stood frowning down at her. Her eyes were large but defiant in her small face. They issued a challenge Jase couldn't resist. With cool deliberation, he placed a hand on either side of her hips and leaned down close to her face. "Little hoyden," he said silkily, "you had best sheath that rapier tongue of yours, lest you make me truly angry."

"I care very little for your anger," she said. Yet, in spite of her bravado, she had to repress a shiver when he raised his hand and lightly ran his fingertips along the gentle curve of her cheek.

His touch was like fire, and wherever those long, elegant fingers chanced to linger, Catherine burned.

"You are very much a woman when you blush," he said, very close to her mouth, "soft and pink and oh so delectable. An irresistible confection ... a tasty little morsel for a man like me. I could devour you in an instant ... and am quite capable of doing so ... if it suits my mood."

His lids came down slowly, the heavy black fringe of his lashes concealing the brittle gleam. "It would not be wise to provoke me...."

Catherine wished heartily to rise from the bed,

to quit the room. But without her clothing it was impossible.

Damn him. He had goaded her purposely, knowing she could not escape him. Heat suffused her cheeks; she averted her gaze.

"You cannot avoid me," he whispered, even while he closed the distance between them. His kiss was leisurely, seductive; it demanded a response that she was unwilling to give . . . yet helpless to withhold. Overcome by sweet sensation, she could only marvel at the incredible warmth of his mouth as it moved over hers, at the rich taste of coffee that lingered on his tongue.

Her lids grew heavy and her breathing slowed. All sense of urgency fled her being, and for the space of a heartbeat there was nothing in the world except Jason St. Claire and his dark, seductive powers.

Then ever so slowly Catherine's will returned, floating gradually upward through the deep well of her conscious mind like a swimmer pushing toward lifesaving air. It broke through her momentary lethargy, shattering her calm.

Jase remained blissfully unaware of the change in the woman he held. What had been meant as a subtle form of intimidation was quickly getting out of hand. She was so soft, so silken, so damnably desirable! And the instant he drew her into his embrace he was lost.

She was a temptress, truly, a woman perfectly fashioned for a man's bed. What the devil did it matter that she refused to give him her name? Her presence was all that counted, he quickly convinced himself, her acceptance of his mastery over her sweet, sweet flesh!

In a bold advance, his hand swept down her slim spine to the small of her back and beyond. Further deepening the kiss, Jase held her tightly against him and slowly pressed her back onto the mattress. He wanted to possess her, to feel her warm satin length against his bare skin. He wanted to lose himself inside her. He wanted it so badly that he lost all sense of time and place, all sense of anything except his own driving, burning need. . . .

Catherine saw what he was about and without hesitation sank her sharp teeth into the sensuous curve of his lower lip.

"Ouch! Dammit!" Jase pulled back and touched his smarting lip with a fingertip. It came away stained with red. "Damned unholy vixen!"

Catherine crouched, intending to bound naked from the bed, if need be, rather than suffer another mauling at his hands. "You deserved that, and much, much more," she said. "And if you wish to keep your anatomy intact, you'll stay away from me!"

Jase dabbed at his mouth with a clean kerchief. "You might have declined in a somewhat gentler fashion!"

Warily Catherine watched him, but when he didn't pounce upon her again, some of her natural hauteur returned. "You hardly seemed in a frame of mind to listen to my denials. Tell me, M'sieur St. Claire, do you treat all your guests in such a predatory fashion?"

"Only those who set my blood to boiling in my

veins," he admitted, then wondered why he had spoken so.

"We are fated to be enemies," Catherine told him. "It will be healthier for you if you simply allow me to leave. So, if you will just return my clothes and lend me a mount, I'll be on my way."

Jase stood glowering down at her. "I wouldn't dream of turning you loose *unkept* upon the world!"

Catherine felt a sudden wave of panic. "You cannot hope to keep me here indefinitely—a prisoner!"

He turned away, smiling, and walked to the door, where he paused with his hand upon the knob. "Tell me whom to contact, and I shall do so immediately. There must be someone who acts as your guardian—your father, an uncle, a lover?"

Her cheeks flamed anew, and there was a stubborn set to her jaw. "Governor Winthrop Sargent," she said.

"We're back to that again, are we?"

"I must see the governor, I must!"

Jase looked into her expectant face and saw his own dilemma: to let her take her chances upon the Trace, alone and unprotected, to take her to the governor himself and stand by while she pleaded for a noose to place about his own neck! Or to keep her here until whoever was posing as the Black Lion was caught and killed. . . .

"Take your time to mull it over," he said. "Take a week, if you feel so inclined—a month! It makes no bloody difference to me. For when you tire of holding your tongue, you'll seek me out." He swept her with his chilling glance, and in that instant Catherine felt as if the blankets concealing her nudity had been deftly peeled away. His smile grew wicked. "Who can say? If you stay long enough, you may not wish to leave at all."

Catherine hurled a pillow at the door and cried, "You cannot keep me here!" But Jase St. Claire was already gone.

Chapter 5

⟨ ∽⟩◯◯⟨∽ ⟩

Jase paused just beyond the closed door of the bedchamber. "Oh, can't I now?" he said very softly in answer to the rebellious young woman.

"Sir? Did you say something?" It was Dora, who had paused in the hallway, carrying his reluctant guest's freshly laundered breeches and shirt.

"What have we here?" Jase said. "The garments of our anonymous young harridan?"

"I was just about to return them to her," Dora explained.

"Why don't I do it for you?" Jase said. "I was just about to go back in to try and pacify the young lady. It seems that something I've said has offended her."

"But, Mr. St. Claire, it will take me but a moment—" Dora began, only to be cut off by her employer's charming smile.

"Nonsense," he said. "Performing this little task will give me the greatest pleasure. Besides, I need you to go to the kitchen and inform Aunt Sade that our young lady is awake and famished. Bring her a hearty breakfast, Dora. She will be needing her strength."

Without another word, Dora handed over Catherine's things and turned back down the hallway.

For a long moment Jase stood in the hall outside Catherine's door, savoring the sweet scent of victory. Then he strode down the corridor. It took him several moments to find what he needed for his intended task, but finally Jase located the tiny pair of scissors which Dora kept with her embroidery. He held them to the light and chuckled softly. *This was going to be such wicked fun!* He could barely wait to see the look of surprise on mademoiselle's face when she attempted her threatened leave-taking!

He took the scissors and the clothes to the library, and immediately set to work.

The shirt came first. He held the garment out before him. But instead of seeing the voluminous garment, he saw in his mind's eye how precisely it displayed its wearer's generous curves. She did look delicious dressed in breeks and boots, did his nameless little shrew. He flicked the topmost button of the shirt, which Dora had replaced—a wasted effort. Then, carefully, he snipped through the securing threads ... just enough so that the button was weakened, holding by a mere thread or two. To the remaining buttons he did the same, then folded the garment neatly and set it aside.

Next came the breeches. Jase paused long enough to sigh appreciatively. Her derriere looked wonderfully well encased in these. He *almost* felt regret for what he was about to do.

Patiently, he turned them inside out.

Snip, snip, snip. . . . It took several moments, but finally it was done. Righting the garment once again, he viewed his work with a satisfied grin, and privately considered that he hadn't felt this lighthearted in many years . . . not since the days of his youth in Castle Ford, before his world had been torn asunder for the first time.

That his current ebullient mood had everything to do with crossing swords with the spirited young female upstairs was not lost on Jase. That this same young woman who made him feel so incredibly alive might very well belong to someone else, he chose not to think about at all.

Dora returned some moments later with a tray, which she bore straightaway to the young lady's chamber. Outside the door was a neat pile of clothes which she immediately recognized as the same garments she had given to Mr. St. Claire at his request.

The housekeeper frowned. "Hhmmm, how very odd. He must have changed his mind." Shrugging off her questions, Dora struggled with the tray while attempting to open the door. . . . "Oh, dear," she said, and was on the verge of calling out for assistance when the door was unceremoniously jerked open by a sheet-swaddled Catherine.

"What do you want this time?" she demanded irritably, expecting to see Jase, then too late realizing her mistake.

"A bit of assistance with the door is all," came the older woman's cheerful reply. "I'm afraid my arms are full."

"I thought you were someone else." Catherine

moderated her tone, though it remained cool. She had yet to determine if the older woman was friend or foe.

"Yes, I'm afraid that much was obvious." The housekeeper entered, brushing past the girl only to stop in mid-stride. "Good heavens! What on earth happened here?" She surveyed the drawers of the bureau, which hung half open, contents tumbling out.

Catherine had the grace to flush, but her expression remained mutinous. "Someone has made off with my clothes, and I was searching for something to wear."

"Well, that someone was me. I only laundered them and saw that they were properly mended. No harm done, miss. I'll just set them aside for now, as you won't be needing them until you're feeling more yourself."

She was feeling just fine, Catherine thought, or would be, as soon as she got out of this house . . . *and far from Jason St. Claire!*

"I've brought you something else to wear in the meantime," said the housekeeper, shaking out a folded garment.

Catherine viewed the dark fabric with brows lowered. It was beautiful. Fashioned of midnight-blue silk, it looked suspiciously like a man's dressing gown.

The older woman seemed to know the direction of Catherine's thoughts. "You must wear something until you're feeling better, miss, and this will suit your current needs just fine."

"But surely he won't want me to wear his dressing gown," Catherine protested, though it was hardly his displeasure but the thought that this fabric had lain against his skin that she found unsettling.

"Nonsense!" the housekeeper countered. "Why, Mr. St. Claire has never even worn it. I don't believe a man like him has much use for such fripperies." And then, "Oh dear! I shouldn't say such things!" Her wrinkled face was cherry-red at her implication. "What I mean to say is that you are a guest here, and Mr. St. Claire did say that I was to attend to your every need."

Catherine sighed. She hadn't the stamina to fight both of them, and it seemed the sensible thing to capitulate on this one small point. She slipped into the robe, letting the sheet unwind from around her and fall to the floor at her feet.

"There, now," the housekeeper said as Catherine knotted the sash at her waist, "that's better, isn't it?" She carried the tray to a small piecrust table by the dainty wing chair. "I have brought you some breakfast. Mr. St. Claire is most concerned for your well-being. He says you should eat to keep up your strength, and I heartily concur." The housekeeper smiled. "My name is Dora, by the way, or Mrs. Hilliard, as you prefer. How might I call you?"

"My name is of no consequence," Catherine returned a little suspiciously. This might be a ploy of St. Claire's to pry from her what he so desired to know. He would like nothing more than to be rid of her, and though she certainly wanted to leave, she did not want Alonzo to be notified of what she'd been about. He might inform Aunt Este at Rivercrest, who would contact Aunt Thea, who would then descend upon Catherine and stop all her plans.

Aunt Este resided with Catherine at Rivercrest. She was a pleasant if flighty old lady much involved with the care of her garden and visits with friends. She had moved from town to the country just after Catherine's father's death to provide a steadying influence upon Catherine and Andre and act as a chaperone. At the time Catherine had been doubtful, but life had changed little upon her aunt's arrival; Aunt Este was biddable, negligent, and even somewhat dotty.

Este's sister, Thea, was another matter altogether, a large-bosomed termagant with hair of steely gray, who barreled through life bullying family and friends alike. She was the most headstrong and opinionated woman Catherine had ever known.

If Thea got wind of her niece's scandalous conduct, she would surely insist upon stationing herself at Rivercrest as Catherine's watchdog until Catherine was safely married. Her diligence was legendary; Catherine would not be permitted a single breath which Thea did not first allow her to take.

And while she dearly loved Aunt Thea, Catherine loved her freedom more. She could hardly bring the Black Lion to justice if she was being constantly watched at Rivercrest!

"Of no consequence!" Dora scolded, bringing Catherine back to the present. "But of course it is of consequence! We can't very well go about calling you 'miss' during the entire length of your stay. Besides, we are all friendly here at

Rosemunde, and no one means you harm. You have nothing to fear by giving your name to me."

Dora busied herself by uncovering the dishes on the tray. "Well, I suppose it will do no good to press you. Keep your name a secret then, if you so wish, but do come and have a bite to eat. Aunt Sade has fair outdone herself this day! Why, she's a prize in the kitchen, the best cook in the territory, Mr. St. Claire says."

"You think very highly of M'sieur St. Claire, don't you, Dora?" Even while her skepticism lingered, Catherine was being drawn by the seductive odors that teased her senses. Mother of God! It seemed forever since she had eaten a decent meal.

She picked up her utensils and cut into a strip of bacon. But as she brought it to her lips, she found she could not eat. Where was Mose? Did *he* have anything to eat, or was he lying someplace, bound and hungry?

Catherine experienced renewed sadness at the thought of her friend, and wished with all her heart that he were here to share this repast with her. What would become of him? Surely he was too valuable for the fleeing brigands to harm him!

It worried her to think of Mose, who had been her boon companion, being maltreated. Only the knowledge that depriving herself would not help him allowed her to sit down to this sumptuous fare. St. Claire was right about one thing; she needed to keep up her strength. Slowly she began to eat, and with each bite she vowed to find Mose as soon as she had met with Governor Sargent at Concord, his residence near Natchez.

While Catherine filled her empty belly, Dora set the room to rights, folding the misplaced linens and settling drawers into place. Covertly, Catherine watched her. The woman seemed friendly enough. Perhaps she could provide the information Catherine would need to take her leave. "What did you call this place?" she asked casually between bites.

"Why, this is Rosemunde."

"It is a lovely name, but I have not heard of it, nor of its owner."

"Well, that comes as no surprise, *miss*," Dora said, stressing the title in hopes of gaining some results. "Mr. St. Claire likes to keep to himself. He's not a social being."

"Why does that not surprise me?" Catherine muttered into her cup. "And just how far does Rosemunde lie from Natchez?"

"Oh, twenty miles perhaps, give or take a few. I'm afraid I'm no hand at figuring distances." Dora's brow crinkled. "You're not entertaining any foolish notions, are you, miss? Like setting off on foot for Natchez? It wouldn't be advisable, and I can say with the utmost certainty that Mr. St. Claire would take it much amiss if you were to try such a thing."

Catherine thought mutinously that she didn't care at all for the thoughts and feelings of Jason St. Claire. Indeed, she would love to tweak his arrogant nose! Unfortunately, she was in no condition to set out on such a rigorous journey just yet . . . unless, of course, it was on horseback.

To lend an appearance of innocence to her questions, she glanced about the room. "If this chamber is any indication, then Rosemunde must be very grand."

"Indeed, it is." Dora nodded. "Two thousand acres of prime land."

"Two thousand ... M'sieur St. Claire is very wealthy." The older woman nodded again. "And how does he manage his many acres?"

"Cotton is the cash crop here, but horses are his passion, miss. Mr. St. Claire has an eye for fine horseflesh. Buyers come from as far away as Carolina to purchase animals." Catherine was quick to note the pride in Dora's voice. She gave a secret smile. There were horses in plenty then. Surely St. Claire would not miss just one! If she could but escape the notice of his vigilant eye and locate the stables, she would be gone before he knew it. The anticipated taste of freedom was heady, and Catherine grew giddy just thinking of it. To cover her scheming silence, she murmured, "He must be a very busy man."

"Oh, yes indeed," Dora agreed. "He does far too much in a day's time, and now with all this night roaming ..." Dora sighed. "I worry about his health." The housekeeper pursed her lips, as if somehow angry with herself for this admission. "And now I've gone and said too much again. Certainly, I shouldn't be burdening you with my worries, so if there's nothing else that you require—"

Catherine's eyes took on the gleam of shining curiosity. It had always been the one facet of her personality over which she seemed to have no control ... that, and her impetuosity. Because of that unquenchable curiosity and her propensity for landing in one scrape after another, Andre had always called her "Cat."

"Then it was not a singular instance, Mr. St. Claire being so late upon the road that night," Catherine said. "Tell me, Dora, is he *often* abroad at night? Where does he go? What does he do?"

Dora became immediately flustered. "Why, yes—well, what I mean to say is that I'm not privy to the activities of Mr. St. Claire. Dear me, I've said too much! I will not trouble you further with this useless twaddle!" She turned to go, and this time Catherine did not attempt to stop her.

The older woman had given Catherine something to think about. Gathering the robe around her, she rose and walked to the bed. The hearty breakfast she had eaten had caused her drowsiness to return. Glancing once at the neat pile of clothing that still lay on the foot of the great bed, Catherine climbed back onto the mattress and sank down into its welcoming softness.

She could not simply walk from the manse in broad daylight and expect not to be noticed. Once the sun had set and the bustling activity of the plantation ceased, she would dress and make her way to the stables . . . and with any luck she could reach Natchez by dawn the next day.

Trying not to think about the outcome of her last evening spent upon the Chickasaw Trace, Catherine settled into sleep . . . to dream of a dashing rogue with hair like darkest night and eyes of pale blue crystal.

When Catherine woke again the sun was going down. Its red-gold glow filtered through the lace panels at the windows, pooled lazily on the richly patterned Turkey rug. Stretching languidly in her warm nest, she emitted a soft sigh. Soon it would be time to leave ... only this time she would set out alone.

For an instant, just an instant, she questioned the wisdom of her plan, and wondered if it would not be better to tell her host the truth. Likely, he would see her safely into Natchez, perhaps even deliver her into Alonzo's care.

St. Claire considered her a weak-kneed chit who could not act without his aid. But she was about to show him very clearly that he had erred in his thinking. He could not keep her here against her will, and she would not be returned to Alonzo like some unwanted waif in need of tending.

Catherine's doubts fled as she reached for the pile of clothing at the foot of the bed. She would show Jason St. Claire that she was not a woman to be bullied or manipulated, no matter how devilishly handsome he was.

Flipping back the covers, she climbed from the bed and took up her breeches at the same moment a knock sounded on the door. The rapping was too bold, too demanding, to come from Dora's fine-boned hand. "Just a moment!" she called out, dashing back into the comparative safety of the bed and dragging the covers up to her chin just as the door opened.

Jase stood in the doorway, one lean brown hand upon the frame, looking resplendent in a velvet coat of hunter green and snowy breeches. The latter fit his slim hips and muscled thighs in a way that seemed to Catherine totally devoid of shame.

Vastly irritated with herself for noticing how good he looked in his tight-fitting attire, she snapped, "Was there something you wished to say, or did you come simply to stare at me?"

Jase's expression was unchanging. He drank in his guest's disheveled beauty, the soft mussed curls the shade of pilfered doubloons, the sleep-bright eyes ... and wondered if she always woke looking so wondrously enticing. "I came to see if there is anything you need."

"You are leaving?"

Jase smiled slightly. "Don't sound so hopeful. I'll be back."

"But it's growing late, m'sieur. Too late an hour to be calling when decent folk will soon be in their beds." She shot him a look from under her long lashes, one of curiosity and suspicion. "But you are not going calling, are you?" She tapped a long, tapered finger against her cheek as she watched him. "You do not seem the type of man who would enjoy playing whist in some gentlewoman's parlor."

"How astute of you, my dear mademoiselle," Jase said. "As a matter of fact, I care little for such pastimes. I have never been one for idle socializing; indeed; I prefer my own company to that of most of my contemporaries."

"And why is that?"

"A lack of mutual interests," Jase said with a shrug. "Discomfort, perhaps."

"Discomfort? You?" Catherine sounded incredulous.

He inclined his head and his dark locks fell forward to reveal the wicked scar that marred his brow. "It surprises you that I should feel uncomfortable among virtual strangers? Men who neither share in nor understand my background any more than I understand theirs. . . ."

Catherine was surprised at this revelation. "Then you were not born to the South?"

He chuckled softly, and his pale eyes gleamed with a strange light which Catherine found intriguing. "Were you?"

"Yes," she admitted. "My home is very like this, though not half so large or so grand as your Rosemunde."

"And your family?"

He asked the question casually, but she sensed the trap. If she gave away too much he would notify her aunts, who would notify Alonzo, who would be very angry because she had defied him. "My mother died when I was ten, and my father a few years ago."

"You do not live alone?" He pinned her with his penetrating stare.

Instead of answering, she said, "You are going out again, aren't you? To roam the Trace?"

He did not reply directly. "If there is nothing else you require—"

"What are you doing out there?" she asked, unable to curb her curiosity. "What are you looking for, and why?"

"It is business, mademoiselle."

She frowned. "Business? What manner of business keeps you abroad night after night, alone? It seems to me you are a man who is looking for trouble!"

"It seems to me that I am a man who has found

it," he said, the light of humor in his eyes. "For someone who is unwilling to give even her name, you certainly ask a lot of questions. Perhaps we'll talk again in the morning. Good night, mademoiselle."

He turned on his booted heel, closing the door with a soft click. For a long moment Catherine continued to stare at the door. They wouldn't talk again, for she would not be here when he returned, and the mystery that surrounded him and his midnight rides would remain unsolved.

Chapter 6

Patience came devilish hard to one born to impetuosity, but Catherine somehow managed to conquer the impulse to dress immediately and tread close upon her host's richly booted heels. She was anxious to be on her way, to leave this gilded cage. But she knew that haste would only get her into trouble, and trouble was the one thing of which she always had too much. And so she forced herself to wait.

Dora arrived with her supper. There was a thick slice of ham, baked to tender perfection, potatoes in a rich cream sauce, and sugar peas laden with butter. Catherine hoped the housekeeper would set down the tray and leave. But she lowered her lanky frame into a nearby chair and began chatting amiably. Nerves had stolen Catherine's appetite, but she forced herself to eat, knowing that if she refused it might arouse Dora's suspicions. She was loyal to Jason St. Claire, and would no doubt fly to alert him if she thought aught was amiss in his household. The possibility that he might be close by at a neighboring plantation made Catherine doubly cautious.

When Catherine had consumed the last mouthful, Dora rose and collected the tray. "Well, I see your appetite's returned," she said, fixing Catherine with a fond look that made her inwardly wince. "It fairly warms my heart to see the bloom back in your cheeks. You frightened me a little, I must admit, when Mr. St. Claire carried you in all limp and wan. But he knew just what you needed, and never had a single moment's doubt for your recovery. I don't know why that should surprise me. He's a wise man, is Jason St. Claire . . . except when it comes to his own well-being, and then he displays the very worst traits of his gender, a fount of unending stubbornness."

Dora sniffed and tightened her thin lips. "I think it was a fine day when you came into our lives, miss. And I hope you'll not mind my saying so, but I hope that for all our sakes, you'll not be in a hurry to go."

"Thank you, Dora," Catherine answered, though she wasn't sure what the housekeeper meant by this strange comment. From the comfort of the wing chair, she watched as Dora took her leave with a warm wish for a good night's rest.

The sound of Dora's sprightly step became indistinct. Catherine removed the silk robe and donned her shirt and breeches. The buttons on the shirt seemed a trifle loose, but she shrugged off the notion and stepped into her boots.

She paced the floor for a little while, trying to tame the excitement that filled her breast, but to no avail. Victory was close, and the smell of it was oh so sweet!

Jason St. Claire could rant and rail to his heart's content, he could make his servants cower and scurry to escape his misguided wrath, but she would still be just as gone.

By this time tomorrow she would have already told her story to Winthrop Sargent, whom she felt sure would quickly catch the killer ... no thanks to Jason St. Claire.

Two nights before she had not known that St. Claire even existed, and after tonight she was unlikely to see him again.

For some inexplicable reason, the thought discomfited her. She let off her pacing to stand before the windows. The sun had long since disappeared, and a million stars graced the night sky. Their cool twinkling brought to mind a pair of ice-blue eyes framed by sooty lashes.

Curse the man! He preyed upon her thoughts more than she cared to admit, and certainly more than was proper for a woman who was betrothed!

But the harder Catherine tried to push him from her thoughts, the more insistent a presence he became. In her mind's eye, she saw him laugh at her feeble efforts to forget him. She imagined the brush of his silken hair against her cheek as he bore her slowly to the mattress ... felt the odd stirring deep inside conjured by his searing kiss. ...

"I will not think of it again," Catherine vowed, squeezing her eyes shut and pressing her fingers tightly to her temples in an attempt to drive the maddening images out. "This is insanity! It is Alonzo that I love!"

But did she truly love Alonzo Hart? Doubt, cold and discomforting, crept up her spine. *Have done with this way of thinking!* she ordered.

She forced herself to picture Alonzo's face, retracing each line of his boyishly handsome image, so unlike Jason St. Claire's hard bronze features. She began to calm down a little ... forced her thoughts back even further, to the first day she and Alonzo met.

Catherine saw the garden at Rivercrest as it had been that day, bright with summer sunshine. She saw her maman's roses blooming white upon the vine. She was on her knees pulling weeds the gardener had overlooked when Andre came through the gate with Alonzo following.

Dirt smudged her hands and cheeks; her gown was faded and frayed at the cuffs. Yet when Alonzo bowed before her, taking her hand in his, she forgot her dishevelment.

From that moment on, it was always that way with Alonzo. Since he had business dealings with Andre, he was often a guest at Rivercrest, and he frequently managed to find Catherine alone in the garden or walking on the lawn. His manner was always that of a gentleman, solicitous and kind. She grew fond of his rippling laughter, of the sparkle in his dark eyes.

Not long after her sixteenth birthday, Andre informed her that Alonzo had requested his permission to call upon her. Andre left the decision to her. He'd known Alonzo for several years; indeed, they had been introduced by a mutual friend, a young lawyer from Alonzo's native Tennessee named Andrew Jackson, who thought very highly of Alonzo. Andre made it clear that he would not contest the match, if it should come to that.

Catherine gave her assent. Two years later they were engaged, but their wedding had been postponed because of Andre's tragic death.

Alonzo's face wavered in her mind, turning darker, more sinister. The curling locks that framed his face straightened, then deepened to a midnight hue. A terrible scar showed white against his tan . . . and his pale eyes glinted, mocking her inability to answer truthfully if she loved her fiancé. Cool and aloof, he stood planted firmly.

Catherine turned away from the windows and the stalked to the door. If she were forced to spend another moment in this house, she would go utterly mad!

Carefully she edged the door open and stole a glance down the hallway. The tall case clock that graced the wide foyer counted the hour of ten. A single taper placed upon a candlestand feebly illuminated the passageway.

Catherine slipped from the chamber and headed for the stairwell.

When she reached the carved balustrade, she paused for a breathless second to listen.

The house was as silent as a tomb.

She peered over the carved handrail and into the wide foyer below, thinking that St. Claire might have ordered a sentinel to stand watch in his absence. But she saw no one. Taking a deep and steadying breath, she started her descent.

The stairwell treads were uncarpeted; her footsteps seemed to echo loudly. Treading as lightly as she could, she did not pause until she reached the shadows of the first landing.

Down the dimly lit hallway a doorknob rattled. Her heart in her throat, Catherine shrank back against the wall, wishing that the shadows would swallow her up. As she watched, an elderly man with silver hair emerged from the darkened room beyond the double doors. He sighed a little as he jerked on the hem of his waistcoat, straightening the fabric over his paunch, then made his halting way past Catherine without ever glancing up.

She straightened, releasing the breath that she'd been holding, then as quickly as she could, went down the remaining stairs. In a trice she had crossed the carpeted foyer and slipped into the night, keenly aware that the greatest test of all lay squarely in her path.

Flitting across the manicured lawn, Catherine kept to the shadows while skirting the manse, passed the brick kitchen, and there paused to get her bearings. At a little distance she could see a long, low building which she felt sure must be the stable.

The faint light of a sickle moon glinted off the small glass windows, but thankfully, not a glimmer shone from within. Taking a deep breath that did little to calm her, she pushed away from the concealing shadows and sprinted across the exposed stretch of lawn. In a moment she had reached the stable. She grasped the door handle and opened the door enough to slip inside.

She was instantly enfolded by an inky darkness

filled with warm and pungent horse smells. The atmosphere was a familiar one—she had ridden all her life, had spent much of her youth in the barn at Rivercrest—but the animals housed here were not known to her.

Had she thought to bring a light, choosing would not be so difficult ... or dangerous! But a light would have signaled her presence in the barn and possibly led to her discovery.

Catherine approached the first stall. To hesitate was foolish. She must have a horse and be on her way before Jason St. Claire returned. Her hand on the latch that held the stall closed, she heard a warning rumble and stumbled backward just in time to avoid Jase's stallion, which thrust its gleaming black head into the aisle. The equine lips were skinned back from huge square teeth, and the eyes showed white around.

"Ill-mannered brute," Catherine said as she hastened to move away. She shook her small fist at the beast. "If you were mine, by God, I'd see you gelded with a blunt knife and harnessed to a plow!"

The tall, lean figure of Jase St. Claire materialized from the impenetrable shadows, wringing a startled gasp from Catherine. "You *are* the bloodthirsty little wench," he said in an amused voice. "And I daresay Sadist is overwhelmingly grateful that he does not belong to you."

Catherine took a reflexive step backward. Her heart was beating frantically in her breast. A moment more and she would have gotten clean away. Instead, she'd been caught! "He is a beast!" she said, her voice rising with her frustration and ire. "He tried to bite me!"

Jase moved forward with a noiseless tread, pausing to stroke the gleaming black neck. "A love bite," he assured her, "and not at all malicious." As if to demonstrate, the mighty steed brought up its head and tugged at Jase's hair. "Here, now! Mind your manners or I might consider letting the petite mademoiselle have her revenge upon you!"

"Love bite. . . ." Catherine shook her head. "You belong together, the two of you. Two great oafs, is what you are, taking sheer delight in threats and bullying. You should be ashamed."

"We are alike, it's true." Jase patted Sadist's powerful neck, rumpling the blue-black mane, but his translucent gaze remained fixed on Catherine. "Each of us is much maligned by those who do not know us." He grinned slowly, and his shadowed countenance turned devilish.

"Your absence of remorse reveals a total lack of decency!"

"A good point, to be sure," Jase said smoothly. "Now, tell me, which mount have you decided upon?"

"What?" Catherine said, knowing full well what he was leading up to, and terribly aware that she had placed the noose about her own neck.

"You are here in the stables, are you not, alone and after dark?" Jase persisted. " 'Tis obvious you were about to take your leave unannounced. The only thing that remains unclear is which of my valuable animals you intend to steal."

When Catherine did not reply, Jase reached out and ran a hand up her arm. She flinched away . . .

a little too forcefully, for her topmost button departed her shirt and was lost in the straw-covered floor. The second hung suspended by a thread.

While she gazed down in amazement at the gaping garment, Jase examined her with a critical, if gleaming, eye. "Hmm," he said, stroking his lean jaw, "it seems you have a problem. Are you sure you wish to leave tonight? I'm sure Dora could mend your tattered garments and return them . . . in a day or two."

Matters always seemed to fall his way, Catherine thought with a frown. She pulled the shirt together with one hand and another of the buttons fell to the floor.

This was impossible! This was . . . sabotage! Deliberately she brushed the two last fastenings. They tumbled away. She stared openmouthed at the deep valley and the full inner curves of her breasts so wantonly displayed before pulling the edges of the wayward garment together with a jerk and holding them closed. She raised narrowed eyes to his. "You did this!"

Jase looked amazed; he looked innocent . . . an expression so foreign to his nature that it chased away her last remaining doubt. He placed a hand upon his shirtfront. "Me?"

"Oh! Of all the devious, underhanded . . . You did this on purpose! You planned it all! Your coming to my room, pretending you were going out, when all the while it was a pretense, a trap!" Catherine fairly seethed. Never had she stumbled upon a man so devoid of principles as Jason St. Claire! "I will see that you pay for this, m'sieur! That much I promise you!"

"Indeed?" he coolly questioned. "Will you sink your fangs into my flesh again, fair mademoiselle? Or perhaps you'll drag me to a magistrate and charge me formally there? But, pray, for what? Ruining your sainted rags?" He smiled a little. "Even if you were able to prove I caused this mishap, I doubt I would be punished for it. Rewarded, is more the like, for providing some randy old magistrate with a moment's sexual diversion.

"And then," Jase continued, his voice turning silky, "there is the matter of the stolen horse. Horse thieves are branded, and horse thieves are hung ... but if enough silver crosses the proper palm, the law will look the other way and allow a man to deal out his own brand of justice. Being a man of good standing in the territory ..."

There was no need for him to finish the thought. She understood well enough. Jase thought that perhaps he had intimidated her sufficiently to bend her to his way of thinking. Given a moment or two to consider her choices, she would jump at the chance to tell him her name and reveal what she knew about the murders, simply to escape him. The soul of patience, he waited.

"Name your price, you despicable bastard," she fairly spat out. "But make no mistake in thinking that I will enjoy a single moment in your noxious presence!"

"Spare the compliments for your loved ones' ears, mademoiselle, for you will soon be reunited with them. My 'price,' as you put it," Jase informed her, "is the same as it was before. You have but to tell me your name, and you will be free of me and sent safely home, where you belong."

"And if I refuse?"

In an instant he had seized her upper arm in steely fingers and was dragging her close to his lean length. His dark face was just inches away, and his pale eyes burned into hers. "Then you will remain with me, and we can test your theories concerning my 'total lack of decency' at our leisure."

For one dizzying moment Catherine swayed against him. He would kiss her now, she knew, and there was naught she could do to prevent his ruthless plundering of her senses. She felt her heartbeat quicken, her breath come fast and shallow, and hoped against all hope that he would not notice how his nearness affected her.

But Jase did notice. He saw the way her eyes seemed to glow. She was angry, furious, yet he suspected it was not her fury that prompted her to part her lips in this inviting fashion. He stared into her upturned face, wanting more than she would ever consent to give . . . certainly more than he deserved.

Something indefinable flitted over his shadowed countenance and then was swiftly gone. Something like regret.

Slowly he stepped back, releasing her arm. And in the next moment, while Catherine warily watched him, he did the unexpected. He removed his velvet coat and carefully placed it around her shoulders.

Catherine eyed him suspiciously. It puzzled her, this act of chivalry, but she hugged the rich garment to her, effectively covering her ruined shirt and saying nothing.

"Well?" he said at last. "Are you ready to surrender?"

She gave him a haughty look. "Not if you are intent upon calling it that."

"All right then," he said, more aware than ever that he could not seem to best her, no matter how clever or how devious the ploy. "Will you consent to sit with me at table in a civilized manner and discuss your situation honestly?"

Slowly sighing, Catherine said, "Yes. I will tell you what you wish to know."

"Good. You may begin with your name, and in exchange I will provide you with some decent attire."

Some of the tension that had coiled so tightly inside of her drained away. She hesitated only slightly. "My name is Catherine Blaise Breaux."

Jase went stiff. Breaux . . . Breaux! Alonzo's fiancée? He looked sharply down at her, but try as he might he could not picture her with Alonzo. Even more perplexing than the unsuitability of this supposed match were Hart's philandering ways. As he watched Catherine walk to the door, Jase wondered how Alonzo could betray her with a woman like Rebecca Galliher.

Catherine, he thought. Regal and strong. The name suited her. She was a woman who would carry herself with a queenly air while garbed in the poorest of rags, yet who would never quite shed all traces of the gamin, even draped in pearls and scarlet silk. She was irresistible, unreachable.

Perhaps that was why she so intrigued him, Jase

thought. And why he decided not to mention that he knew Alonzo Hart. He would keep his secret only for a while, he assured himself. He needed to know all about her before seeing that she was returned to New Orleans. A day or two at the most in which to gather information, to assure himself that she would abandon her plan to go to the governor.

A day or two could do no harm to either of them. There was little chance of Alonzo's discovering she was at Rosemunde, since he was not due to return for a week.

Surely Jase could abide her presence in the house that long. In the meantime he would continue his search for the impostor Black Lion. If he failed, then he would have no choice but to disappear again. The idea of leaving Rosemunde and starting over was unappealing, but not half so objectionable as ending his days as his grandfather James St. Claire had done, dancing a jig to the hangman's tune.

James had been a veritable rogue who for thirty years made his living on the fringes of the law. His luck had run out when he stole a horse from a lieutenant of the British dragoons. Cameron St. Claire, James's only son, was fourteen at the time, and witnessed his father's last moments.

James's roguish bent skipped a generation before resurfacing again. Jase couldn't help but wonder what James St. Claire would have done if he had been faced with the choices Jase had had to make in his youth.

Life was often cruel, as he had long ago discovered. He knew the course that he must follow to survive this debacle. But as Jase watched the gentle sway of Catherine Breaux's derriere beneath his coat, for one brief instant he wished that things were different.

Chapter 7

The silence that fell between Catherine and Jase upon leaving the stables was far from companionable.

As she entered the house, she brushed past the manservant who had opened the door and now stood awaiting his master's pleasure—the same man she had noticed earlier.

She cast a speculative glance at him in passing. The deep blue eyes that returned her brief scrutiny were devoid of deception. Set in a round face that was floridly Irish—and not so old as Catherine had first thought—they were eyes that bore a glimmer of kindness, and though he kept it buried deep, more than a hint of high good humor. Had circumstances been different, Catherine decided, she might have liked him.

"Leviticus, you will be glad to know that Mademoiselle Breaux has wisely chosen to postpone her journey and remain with us a while longer," Jase said. Catherine refrained from pointing out that she'd had no say in the matter. "Bring something from the kitchen, will you? Waylaying young ladies makes me deuced hungry. And something for mademoiselle."

"I have already eaten, thank you."

Jase inclined his raven head and his eyes took on a determined gleam. "Do you wish to offend me? A guest must eat what is offered, or at least make a pretense of doing so."

"What manner of host would insist that a guest overeat simply to satisfy his own rules of deportment? I don't know where you learned such eccentric behavior, m'sieur, but I can assure it is not the way in which we conduct ourselves in New Orleans."

Jase flushed dark beneath his tan. He let out a slow, impatient breath. She was correct. The intricacies of Shawnee etiquette did not extend to white society, though he privately thought the "civilized" world would benefit from adopting Indian ways.

Distracted by Catherine's presence, he had momentarily forgotten, and the mask he affected had slipped the smallest notch. He would have to be more careful in the future. "My apologies. However, although you needn't eat, I do require your presence in the dining room. Leviticus."

"Very good, sir." Leviticus seemed somehow pleased, though his placid expression never altered. He tugged at the hem of his waistcoat and asked, "Will that be all, sir?"

"Unless Mademoiselle Breaux requires something—"

Catherine opened her mouth to request some solitude when Dora came bounding down the stairs.

"Oh, thank heavens you've returned! I was near beside myself with worry—why, whatever has become of your clothes?" The older woman bent near and examined the garment above and below Catherine's hand, the only thing holding the garment together over her bosom.

"How very odd! I could have sworn the buttons were all in place when I returned it to you—" Dora closed her mouth with a snap as realization dawned and her widened eyes darted to Jase, then back again, her cheeks pinkening.

Leviticus harrumphed.

The master of Rosemunde folded his arms across his chest and looked mildly amused, but offered no explanation.

Catherine affixed Jase with a smoky look. "You promised decent attire. Do you intend to keep your word, or must I sit at table with you in these 'sainted rags'?"

"Dora, will you kindly assist Mademoiselle Breaux?" Jase gave Catherine a meaningful look. "I will expect to see you in the dining room in fifteen minutes. And do be prompt. I am sure you would not like me to come and fetch you."

Refusing to be intimidated, Catherine turned toward the stairs, Dora following. When both were out of earshot, Leviticus let his curious gaze fall upon his employer. "Sir . . . it is not my place to question you, but is it wise to have her staying here with . . . well, the Black Lion—" He broke off beneath the weight of Jase's stare.

"Indeed, it is not your place," Jase said, then relented. "There is considerably less danger in having her here than in letting her roam about out there, a prime target for murder. A murder that, I might remind you, would be attributed to me."

"Yes, sir."

The servant stood with eyes lowered, his round face carefully bland. His subservient posture irritated Jase. He could almost read the unspoken objections in Leviticus's cherubic face. "You do not think I *want* her here, do you? Because if you do, you are gravely mistaken! I take no pleasure in that woman's meddlesome presence in my household. My life has become complicated enough without adding to my present difficulties."

Jase frowned. He thought he sounded very convincing. So, why did he feel as if he was not being completely truthful, even with himself? He was losing his mind. Leviticus was in his employ, after all. There was no need to justify his actions to the servant, to explain Catherine's continued presence in the house.

"I have a right to have a guest if I so wish, do I not?"

"Why, most assuredly, sir!"

"And am I not a fair man in most things?"

"Why, without question, sir!"

"Good," Jase said, his irritation slowly fading. "Then I suggest you keep your opinions to yourself. Is that understood?"

"I believe I understand you completely, Master St. Claire." Leviticus remained absurdly unruffled. Indeed, he seemed to view Jase's menacing air as commonplace. "Unless there is something else you wish, I will attend to my duties."

"There is one more thing. Kindly refrain from calling me 'Master.' You know how I detest it."

"My most sincere apologies, sir." The servant bowed and hurried down the hallway.

Jase turned on a booted heel and strode into the library, where he snatched up the crystal decanter. He splashed a generous amount of whiskey into a tumbler and brought it to his lips.

Liquid fire, smooth as silk.

It slid down his throat and seared his belly, burning away some of his impatience. Jase tipped the glass and drank again, feeling no better for it. Things had gone his way this evening. He now knew who Catherine was, and to whom she rightfully belonged. But he was no closer to solving his difficulties.

He could send Catherine to Alonzo; Alonzo would keep her out of harm's way, prevent her from causing more mischief.

Tossing back the whiskey, Jase stared moodily at the empty glass. He *could* send her to Natchez, but he knew he wouldn't. Not now. Not yet. She claimed to know something about the killings, and he would not let her leave Rosemunde until he was certain he had pried from her every scrap of information she possessed.

Soon, Jase thought. Soon he would hand her over to Alonzo, and his life could return to normal.

He would find and kill the impostor, and people would forget. Memories were elusive things, impossible to hold forever. Like the mist that cloaked the early morning landscape, they slipped away. . . .

Aye, people would forget. *He* had forgotten,

hadn't he? He'd put the past behind him. Until Catherine Breaux had appeared. . . .

Jase set down the glass and leaned against the desk. He found it surprising, how swiftly it all came back . . . bringing confusion and regret.

He closed his eyes and pressed his fingertips against the jagged scar while the past flooded back, vivid bits of scenes. Flames leaping high into the blue summer sky . . . smoke, billowing and black . . . a farmer running to his burning cabin, an awkward scarecrow of a man . . . the farmer leveling a musket at Fire Hawk, Jase's adopted father. . . . As if in a dream, Jase saw his own hand gripping the war ax, felt the muscles of his arm coil and spring. . . . The weapon flew end over end and struck flesh and bone with a sickening thud, burying its blade in the farmer's chest. The farmer stared at the weapon buried deep, then at Jase, a stunned expression upon his face. And as he toppled forward, his woman screamed, and screamed again. . . .

That stricken cry echoed through Jase's memory, slow to fade away.

He rubbed his temple, willing away the past and the nagging throb which accompanied the unwelcome recollections.

Similar scenes had been played out during the final years of the fight for the Ohio Country. An equal number of Shawnee had lost their lives to marauding whites . . . not only warriors, but women and children as well.

Jase raked a hand through his hair. Fallen Timbers had brought peace to the Ohio Country, peace to him. Maynard Dumonde had offered him a hand in friendship and a way to make a living. Canada was still largely unspoiled, and did not hold the painful memories for Jase that Ohio did. He labored as a hunter and interpreter when Dumonde was among the northern tribes, and helped him with his trap lines. And when Dumonde went to Quebec to visit his sister and her husband, he took Jase with him.

It had seemed odd that he, the Black Lion, should be seated at table in civilized company, a glittering array of china and crystal and silver spread upon the board.

Dumonde had been instrumental in helping him adjust, and in time Jase found it all came back to him ... the white ways, the teachings of his early youth. But the white man's ways no longer penetrated his heart, his soul. The role he had assumed, bit by painful bit, was a facade. In some ways, *he* was more a fraud than the man for whom he searched night after night.

He did not belong in this house. The finery that surrounded him held no sentimental value, except that it had all once belonged to Maynard Dumonde. Perhaps, Jase thought wearily, he did not belong anywhere. He was firmly caught between two worlds, destined to remain in his own private purgatory.

Catherine had brought it all back, and whether he wished to admit it or not, the headlong tumble she had taken into his life had sent his world reeling off its already shaky axis.

"We'll need to hurry, Miss Catherine. We wouldn't want to test Mr. St. Claire's patience."

Dora went to the washstand and poured tepid water into the porcelain bowl.

More dutifully than she felt, Catherine bathed her face, hands, and throat. The water was refreshing, but didn't wash away the dread she felt for the coming interview, or the distasteful notion that *he* had won.

Well, she thought, blotting her damp skin with a soft linen towel, there was nothing for it now but to tell the truth and hope that Jason St. Claire would be reasonable.

She tossed aside the towel. "Now, if I only had something to replace this." She plucked at the gaping shirtfront with its missing buttons.

"It's all been taken care of, miss," Dora said with a small smile. She went to the wardrobe and came away with an exquisite gown of icy sea-green silk. It was fashioned with a deeply rounded décolletage and small puffed sleeves, and here and there it was artfully stitched with tiny rosebuds in silver thread. Finely wrought silver lace edged the neckline and sleeves.

"Dear heavens, Dora," Catherine gasped, "how did you come by this?" To Catherine's knowledge there were no females in the house except the housekeeper and herself.

Dora's smile deepened. "Why, Mr. St. Cl—" she began, but Catherine cut short her reply.

"Pray, do not tell me. M'sieur St. Claire, that worker of miracles, purchased the gown."

"Come along," Dora urged. "Slip out of those things and I'll help you into this lovely confection. I daresay you'll dazzle him dressed in this!"

But Catherine only shook her head. She did not

want to dazzle him. He was too free with his attentions already! To accept a gift of such great value would put her very squarely in Jason St. Claire's debt, the one place she didn't wish to be.

"I can't accept it. It isn't fitting. Go and bring me one of m'sieur's shirts. It will be far too large, of course, but surely it will cover me better than this one."

"But, miss!" Dora looked worried.

Catherine sighed and plopped into the nearest chair, at which time the seat of her breeches split down the middle. She closed her eyes, grinding her teeth in anger and frustration. She took a breath and expelled it slowly. "Dora, it seems that once again M'sieur St. Claire has found a way to assure my compliance. I will wear the gown."

Rosemunde had been constructed according to a simple plan. Spacious high-ceilinged rooms which were light and airy on the hottest of days opened onto a wide central hallway and grand staircase. Though Catherine was as yet a stranger to the house, she had no difficulty locating the dining room.

The walls were covered with silk moiré in a deep shade of mauve, and gilt-framed paintings provided the perfect accent. Two of these were portraits of a man and woman; the rest depicted hunting scenes and landscapes. The portraits briefly caught Catherine's attention. She searched the faces for any likeness to the present owner of Rosemunde, but alas, found not the slightest resemblance to the man now standing before the windows.

"You are late," Jase said, snapping closed the cover of his timepiece and returning it to his waistcoat pocket.

"I am here," Catherine contradicted.

He swept her with his unsettling glance, and though his expression showed not the slightest change, Catherine knew that her appearance pleased him. Her irritation with him rose, along with annoyance with herself for feeling a rush of feminine pleasure—and chagrin that she should value the opinions of this night-riding rogue! Heat swept over her, bringing a heightened color to her cheeks.

Jase moved forward, his steps deliberate, predatory. With a startled gasp, Catherine retreated. But he only paused by the table, holding out a chair for her. His mouth curled slightly at the corners and his eyes glinted ... or was that the reflected candlelight? The crystalline depths were so unclouded, it was difficult to tell.

"Will you sit?" Jase asked quietly. "Or does nervousness in my presence prevent you?"

He was issuing a challenge, damn him, knowing full well how his very nearness affected her. Catherine raised her chin and met his translucent stare levelly. "My nervousness? You mistake me for some weak and spineless female. I assure you, I am not afraid of you."

"I'm much relieved to hear it." Jase's smile deepened, his dimples showed. "Now, shall we?" He waited behind her chair.

Catherine watched him through slitted eyes, unsure what of make of him. One moment he played the rogue, the next he was the perfect gentleman. . . . She was unsure which side of him was real, which was only a facade. She only knew he was the most confounding man she had ever met. Moving forward, she sat down.

As Jase positioned her chair, he was afforded a brief glimpse of one rounded shoulder and the creamy bosom displayed enticingly above the sea-green gown.

He stepped away, his hands itching to caress those shoulders, to worship that bosom. . . . Surely this was torture, Jase thought as he slid into his own chair at the far end of the long table, willing the persistent vision of soft white skin to the back of his mind.

As if on cue, Leviticus appeared to serve the meal and pour the wine. He filled Catherine's glass and she thanked him with a smile, fully aware that Jase was watching the proceedings with a jaundiced eye. "Have you nothing to do?" he demanded of the servant once the meal was laid before them.

"Sir?" Leviticus raised questioning white brows.

"The lady and I require some privacy, so be off with you."

"Your pardon, sir, I did not realize." Avoiding Catherine's gaze, Leviticus took himself discreetly off.

The door closed softly, and Jase and Catherine were alone.

"You need not have been so rude," Catherine said. "He was not doing any harm by being here."

Jase considered her with something akin to disbelief. He was unaccustomed to explaining his actions to anyone, and did so now grudgingly.

"Leviticus is an employee. I pay him a goodly wage to carry out my bidding. His services were no longer required, and so I dismissed him. I fail to see how you can find fault with that."

"No longer required by you perhaps."

Jase's pale glaze kindled. "I begin to understand." He gestured toward the generously laden table with an elegant flick of his hand. "My lady fears the threat of ravishment here amidst the pigeon and sweet potatoes."

"Perhaps you are unaware that it is not proper for an unmarried woman to be alone with a man who is not her relative," Catherine said.

"It must be damned convenient, donning propriety's pristine cloak when it suits you and shedding it when it doesn't," he said.

"Think what you will," said Catherine, "but I do not wish to compromise my reputation with a stranger."

His mouth curved. "In order to compromise your reputation, someone must know that you are here. Thus far it remains a secret. Besides, you said you aren't afraid of me." He sliced his fowl, took a small sliver between his strong white teeth, and chewed thoughtfully. "It gives me cause to wonder just what you *are* afraid of."

Lightning, Catherine thought. Strong winds. Alligators. The way he caused her to feel when she was alone with him. The traitorous nature of her own heart. . . . Aloud she said, "I am afraid for my companion, Mose. I don't know where he is, or where to begin searching. I don't know what I will tell his mother when I return home."

"Tell her the truth," he suggested.

"You do not understand," Catherine said. "Mose is more than a servant. He is my friend. I can't just abandon him!"

"He means that much to you?"

"He does."

"I wonder if he knows what a fortunate man he is." Jase toyed with his wineglass, rolling the stem between his fingers. "Have you thought of posting a reward for his return?"

Catherine sighed. "How can I, when I am here?"

"If you like, I could do it in your stead," Jase said. "I am not without friends."

Catherine gazed at him. "You are offering to help me?"

He raised a sardonic brow. "You might try to hide your surprise, Catherine."

She smiled. "I did not expect you to—"

"To offer my help?" he asked mildly. "I have more money than I need to live comfortably. And if posting a reward for Mose makes you feel more at ease during your brief stay here, then I will consider the money well spent."

Catherine felt a slight chagrin in light of his generosity. She had had few kind thoughts concerning him since meeting him upon the road, and now she wondered if perhaps she had been too harsh. "Thank you, and on Mose's behalf, I accept your offer."

"Good. Now, tell me more about this 'mission' of yours to speak with Governor Sargent."

"You should not make light of it," Catherine chided.

"I wouldn't think of it. The murders occurring along the Trace are a serious matter indeed."

"Do you know much about them?"

"Not nearly enough, apparently." He paused to take a sip of wine, watching Catherine all the while, as a great black cat might watch a bird perched upon a limb. "I know that someone is killing travelers, and I know he enjoys what he is doing. A man who kills again and again in time of peace savors the thrill that comes with holding a life in one's hand and having the power to snuff it out in an instant. It is the ultimate power, Catherine. The only thing that can elevate man to the level of God."

"You sound as if you know the killer."

"I have known cruelty in my lifetime, and can recognize the love of destruction when I see it." Leviticus had left the wine on the sideboard. Jase got up and brought it to the table. "More wine?"

"Thank you, no." She watched as he sat down in the chair to her left, refilled his glass, and leaned back.

"And you, Catherine," he said. "Do *you* know him?"

She nodded. "He killed my brother, Andre, and he has killed two others since then. I have no doubt it is the Black Lion."

"That does seem to be a popular theory," Jase admitted. "But I am not convinced. I would need proof, and so, I should think, will the authorities. Accusations and suspicions count for nothing. You don't possess proof, do you, Catherine?"

He did not move a muscle, but she sensed a new tension in him, as though by watching her with those unsettling pale eyes he could force her next utterance. She held out her glass. "Perhaps I will have a bit more wine."

Jase poured the wine and tried another tack. "You said your brother lost his life upon the Trace. How did you find out about it?"

"Levi Colbert, from Colbert's Ferry up in the Chickasaw lands, sent a messenger to notify us at Rivercrest."

"All the way to New Orleans?"

Catherine looked up, instantly suspicious. "I never told you I lived near New Orleans."

The expression he affected was bland, but his pale eyes reflected the tiny flickering flames of the tapers. "You did indeed. You chided me for my manners and informed me that in New Orleans you do things differently."

She realized he was correct, and berated herself for her slip. She narrowed her eyes, her expression full of curiosity. "Who are you, really?"

"Who am I?" he repeated. "I had thought we were through with introductions and on to more interesting things. But since you insist—" He inclined his dark head, a habit he had, and his face changed subtly. There was something etched upon his hard Celtic features that she could not read, something disturbing. "Are you certain you wish to know . . . really?"

He leaned forward and caught her hand in his, bringing it to his lips . . . and all the while he watched her. Catherine felt a rush of warmth and a delicious shiver course up her spine. "Yes, I do wish to know. You make me curious, m'sieur. Certain ways you look, things you say. Your mannerisms are those of an American gentleman, but there is something about you—something I can't define."

"Something you do not like?" he said softly. "Or something you find intriguing? Something dark and unsettling, eh?"

"All of that," she admitted.

Jase laughed softly and raised his glass to his lips. "We should discuss the murders. It's a safer subject, I think."

"You admitted that you were not born to this wealth," Catherine said. "What were you born to, then? And where? Not here, surely, nor anywhere in the West."

"My, so many questions. May I claim a reward if I tell you what you wish to know?"

There was a wicked gleam in his eyes that Catherine wasn't sure she liked. Yet her breath came faster. "What manner of reward?"

He shrugged, a graceful lift of broad shoulders. "An exchange, shall we say? Information for information."

Catherine released the breath she'd been unconsciously holding. For a moment she'd thought he might demand a kiss ... and she wondered why she should feel disappointed that he hadn't. "Agreed."

"Your observations are correct," he said. "I am not from the West, but the East."

"And my other question, m'sieur?"

"Ah, yes," Jase said. "Mine was a humble birth. My father fought in the War for Independence, and was granted land for his services. He tilled the land to earn his bread, as I do now."

"Was? He is dead?"

"Another question," he murmured. "You will be heavily in my debt by the time your curiosity is satisfied. Since my own questions are few, I may be forced to make other demands." He smiled when she did not object. "Yes, my father is dead. As is my mother."

"There is one more question I would ask, m'sieur," she said, wetting her lips with the tip of her tongue. It would be a daring question, perhaps impolite, but she was burning to know the answer.

"Four questions? I cannot allow such flagrant abuse of my good nature," Jase said. "Unless, of course, you grant me a boon."

"Another?"

"A simple one that will cost you nothing. You must call me by my Christian name."

A small price to pay, Catherine thought. "All right, Jason. How did you come by that scar?"

If he was taken aback by her forwardness, he did not let it show. That same mysterious smile played about his firm lips, bringing Catherine's curiosity to an unbearable peak. She leaned forward slightly, her full breasts straining against the ice-green gown. She did not fail to note how Jase St. Claire caught his breath, nor where his pale gaze roamed.

Mesmerized, she watched as he touched the scar that sliced over his temple, gleaming starkly white in the candle's glow. "This was caused by a hatchet's blow," he said. "A tomahawk."

Her eyes widened. "But how?"

"His name was Captain John White Elk—"

"An Indian?"

"A Seneca warrior," Jase said with finality. He'd

already told her more than he'd intended. But she continued to lean forward, whether to purposely tease him or whether unaware of the fetching picture she made, he didn't know. He only knew that her fair white breasts were temptingly displayed, that the sparkle of interest in her eyes flattered him, rendering him bolder, more reckless than was prudent. She was so soft and alluring, it was damnably hard to deny her anything.

"You have not forgotten the Black Lion so quickly, have you?" he said. "Nor the strife that forged his reputation?"

"And were you involved in the conflict, Jason?"

He gave an inward grimace. "Few men of an age to fight were able to avoid the conflict west of the mountains. I myself played a modest role."

His answer was misleading, but true. There had been others of far greater stature than he . . . Little Turtle, great and wise chief of the Miami, who had led the tribes to defeat Arthur St. Clair on the Wabash River in 1791. And Blue Jacket, born Marmaduke Van Swearingen to white parents, who chose to live among the Shawnee and rose to great heights as a warrior.

Jase had fought alongside both men at Harmar's defeat, where they'd brought down the Indian fighter Josiah Harmar, and finally at Fallen Timbers. But he would admit nothing of that to this inquisitive young woman.

"Now, I have answered your questions, and your debt to me has steadily mounted. I am calling in the markers, Catherine. It's time to tell me of yourself."

Chapter 8

C atherine took a deep breath. "What do you wish to know?"

"Why, everything, of course. Details about your life before you left New Orleans. About your brother. The circumstances that brought you here...."

"I suppose my life varied little from that of any young woman of my class. I was not, as you say, of humble beginnings. My father's line is descended from Gerard de Sol Breaux, who fought for Charlemagne and won the Breauxes' ancestral lands near Lyons."

"Impressive."

"My grandfather came to Louisiana in 1745. He was a younger son, but ambitious. He built Rivercrest. It is not as large as your Rosemunde, but it has the grace that comes with age, and there is a haunting quality to the land. Andre loved it so...." Her voice trailed away. She sat quietly for a moment, her eyes suspiciously moist. Her small hand rested on the table, not far from Jase's own. He was tempted to take it, to offer whatever comfort it was in his power to give. She evoked strange urges within him, constantly pitting him against his better judgment.

He should not want to protect her. She was Alonzo's woman.

The battle for control was brief; Jase crushed his wild desires beneath his iron will.

"Andre and I were twins," she went on. "We were inseparable throughout our youth—and afterward. He was a good man, kind and generous to a fault. He didn't deserve to die, not that way!"

Tears spilled freely down her cheeks. Watching, Jase felt his iron will begin a slow disintegration, felt it turn to dust. He uttered a soft imprecation, seizing the small hand which had become a fist and drawing her up against him as he stood. "Ssshh, my love. Don't cry. Ssshh. It will be all right."

"Don't shush me as if I were a child, Jason!" she cried against his chest. "You don't understand! When the Black Lion killed Andre, he killed a part of me as well! It will not be all right until he is caught and made to pay for his crimes. I will not rest until I see him hanged!"

Above her head, Jase frowned. She had every right to be angry, every right to lust for revenge. Andre Breaux had died a cruel and unnecessary death. Months ago, Alonzo had related the details of how the young Frenchman had dared to try to defend himself against a greater adversary. If the story was accurate, then Breaux had kept a hideaway pistol in his boot, and had made an attempt on the outlaw leader's life. The gun had misfired, and the one masquerading as the Black Lion was spared. He could have killed Breaux instantly, but

he chose instead to make the man suffer. He slit
Breaux's wrists, deep, shot his horse, then bade
him walk the ten miles to Colbert's Ferry and salvation. With no way to bind the wounds, Andre
Breaux bled out his life's blood along the Trace.
Colbert found the dying Frenchman and listened
to his story, which was then conveyed to Hastings's and finally to Natchez.

Jase sighed against Catherine's hair, turning his
face into the shining locks. "I know you want justice, but you can't do it alone."

"Mose is gone," Catherine said against his shirt-
front. Beneath her cheek his heart beat strong and
steady. The arms that held her provided a steely
comfort . . . so warm, so safe! "There is no one else
to give me aid."

"There is . . . someone. . . ."

Catherine slowly raised her head and gazed up
into his face. His features had lost none of their
sinister cast, but he seemed less intimidating now.
He was not a villain as she had perceived, just a
man. The scar that marred his brow was just a
scar, not nearly as sinister as it was tragic. And
perhaps his motives were pure. "What are you
saying, Jason?"

"That I will lend my aid if you will accept it,"
he said. "A grave injustice has been done; it must
be rectified. The killings must stop."

"But what can you do against the Black Lion
and his men? And why would you want to help
me?"

He gazed steadily down at her. "Because in
helping you, I also help myself. I've been investi-

gating the murders. It's why I was on the Trace so late the night I came upon you."

So, it had not been a coincidence after all, Catherine thought. "But why?"

His expression became closed, and though he continued to hold her, she felt him pull away. "I have my reasons. Suffice it to say that I, like you, have a personal stake in the matter and am working to see it resolved. In a sense, I need your help as much as you need mine."

He gripped her shoulders. Catherine could feel the tension in his elegant fingers, could hear the eagerness in his deep voice. He wanted to capture the Black Lion as badly as she did. "How can I help you?" she asked.

"By telling me everything you know. What was Andre doing on the Trace that night? Did he make it his habit to travel alone? Exactly what did he tell Colbert? I want every detail, no matter how small or inconsequential it seems to you. And finally, the evidence you hinted at that first night—what is it, and how did you come by it?"

Catherine frowned. She had not expected this barrage of questions, but she did her best to answer. "Andre was coming home from Nashville. He had been away for several months, on business. And no, he did not make it a habit to travel alone. This was an isolated incident. As for the evidence, I'll get it for you now." She walked quickly from the room, but in a moment she was back, placing a small golden ring in Jase's hand. "I kept it hidden inside my coat. Andre told Colbert that when they struggled, he wrenched it from the Lion's hand and somehow managed to keep hold of it. When Levi Colbert's wife gave it to me, it was encrusted with blood. It is a woman's, obviously . . . too small to fit a man's hand, too finely wrought." Catherine glanced at Jase. He seemed transfixed by the ring that lay in his open palm. "Jason? What is it? What's wrong?"

He stared at her as though surprised she was still in the room. "I'd like to keep this for a while, if you don't mind." His hand closed over the ring, and then he bent slightly, touching his lips to her forehead in a chaste kiss. "We'll talk again tomorrow." With that he turned and walked away, leaving her to stare after him.

A thin wail pierced the stillness, penetrating the depths of the house but failing to waken the one who cried out. There were no hurried footsteps in answer, no reassuring voice to shatter the evil spell. Alonzo Hart was caught in the midst of a terror-filled dream without a prayer of release.

Stiff with fright, he tossed upon his sweat-dampened pillows, feeling more cries well up inside him. But none could escape his constricted throat.

The Indians were shouting, coming closer; he had to escape! Red faces leered, looming and retreating in a blur, hideous masks of streaked vermilion, white, and black. Beads of cold sweat appeared on his brow. He should run! But his legs seemed boneless things, incapable of movement. So he stood, rooted to the spot.

The shouting rose to unbearable levels as across the dusty way from where fifteen-year-old Alonzo stood, a red-haired woman of middle years emerged from the long log building that served as a council house. She was clutching the hand of a ten-year-old girl. The child seemed terrified to the point of insensibility. Alonzo watched them being herded off, his mother and his sister. His heart swelled against his ribs, floated up to clog his throat. To cry out was impossible.

He watched until they were out of sight, scalding tears racing down his thin cheeks. His family was gone now . . . beyond reclaim, his father shot down as he came running from the fields the day of the attack . . . his mother and sister presented as chattel to his father's killer, the fearless young warrior the Shawnee called the Black Lion, to do with as he saw fit. . . .

The subject of his thoughts stepped from the log council house. He was dressed in soft doeskin leggings gartered below the knee and a scarlet breechclout that covered his loins. He was tall and lean, but well muscled, with hair like jet and skin that was deeply tanned. Had it not been for his pale blue eyes, Alonzo would never have guessed that the man was white.

A white man turned savage. A soul without remorse. As Alonzo watched, the Black Lion passed on his way to join the contingent of waiting warriors, close enough to touch. The renegade's icy glance flickered briefly over Alonzo Hart's dirty face and matted hair, but his stoic features showed no recognition, no compassion, no willingness to help his own kind.

"Traitorous bastard!" Alonzo screamed, lunging for the Black Lion's throat. "I'll kill you for this! I'll kill you—" He came up in bed with a violent start, trembling uncontrollably as the shout died away.

It was only the dream.

Breath sobbing in his throat, Alonzo buried his face in his nightshirt sleeve and sought to collect his composure.

As the minutes ticked by, his panic gradually abated, the pounding of his pulse slowed, and Alonzo was able to breathe without gasping.

Again and again the nightmare had come over the years, yet never so frequent as in the two years since he had worked for Jason St. Claire.

With an unsteady hand, Alonzo snatched the brandy from the bedside commode, took the cork in his teeth, and spat it out upon the polished floor. He tipped the bottle and drank deeply, paused for breath and drank again.

It had been a fine coincidence, that the man Alonzo hated most in all the world had attended a political meeting at the house of Tom Galliher July before last. Alonzo could scarcely believe his eyes, but as Tom introduced Jason St. Claire, there was no doubt in his mind that he was being presented to the Black Lion, renegade, turncoat, abductor of women. . . . It took a Herculean effort, but Alonzo managed to keep his fury hidden and forestalled the urge to openly denounce the man.

That night the dream returned, more vividly frightening than ever before.

The following day Alonzo began making discreet inquiries into Jason St. Claire's background. Not suprisingly, there was little he could uncover concerning the man's origins—nothing, in fact, before the past two years. The consensus was that St.

Claire was as wealthy as sin, and with that kind of money, it hardly mattered where he came from.

Perhaps if St. Claire had been less charming, more questions would have been raised. But he had few detractors. He gambled skillfully and seldom lost, carried his liquor without succumbing to crude behavior. He was politely deferential to the ladies, and the horses he owned were without dispute the finest in the Territory. In short, he lived the life of the landed gentry as if born to it, and none but Alonzo could find fault with that.

Yet each allusion to the man's stellar character only fueled Alonzo's hatred. It seemed grossly unjust that the very man he blamed for his mother's premature death and his sister Finella's current precarious mental state should prosper. St. Claire had known nothing of Alonzo's struggles to repay his debts, to claw his way out of the depths of black despair and poverty he had suffered while trying to support his shattered family. The fact that St. Claire was living like a king at Rosemunde had become the proverbial thorn in Alonzo's side.

In the weeks immediately following his meeting with St. Claire, Alonzo seethed, dreaming up wild plans of desperate revenge and discarding them all for being too risky. He wanted his plan to be perfect. He wanted St. Claire to worry and fret and realize his loss before his untimely end . . . just as Alonzo had agonized over the fate of his mother and sister during the two years he had spent in captivity.

During that time, he had pretended to accept the Indians' ways, biding his time, but he had never forgotten his family's fate, and when the opportunity presented itself, he stole a horse and made his escape, returning to the settlements. Another year passed before word of his mother and Finella came to him. With the help of his friends, he was able to raise the money and purchase trade goods with which to ransom them. But nothing was ever the same.

Yes, he wanted St. Claire to suffer. It was the only way to quench this burning hatred which Alonzo kept hidden inside him.

Patience in this matter, along with a quiet surveillance, seemed to be the wisest approach.

And so Alonzo waited, scheming all the while to bring about St. Claire's downfall, yet undecided as to what plan of action might bring the most success.

Then, in the fall of 1798, his golden opportunity presented itself. He discovered that St. Claire was looking to employ a factor to handle some of his business interests while he devoted himself to managing the breeding stock at Rosemunde. Alonzo was nearly beside himself with joy when he learned of this. He immediately pressed Tom Galliher, a casual acquaintance of St. Claire's, to recommend him for the position.

One week later the summons arrived. The message was brief and written in a strong, unfaltering hand. Alonzo had been cordially invited into the Lion's den.

The man Alonzo met that day only faintly resembled the young warrior who still frequented his nightmares. For all the world he looked the gentleman, civilized and well mannered, if slightly taciturn. To look at Jason St. Claire, one would never guess that not so many years past he had strutted in breechclout and leggings, the terror of the unsettled frontier.

Only Alonzo knew that a murdering heathen lurked beneath that thin veneer of gentility. It was a secret he would clutch very close to his vengeful heart.

It had taken every ounce of self-control Alonzo Hart could muster to sit in the great library at Rosemunde, with its book-lined walls and massive desk, and not reveal his tumultuous thoughts. But Alonzo had managed it well enough to gain the desired position. From this day onward he would work closely with his enemy ... close enough to know the goings-on at Rosemunde ... and where best to strike the telling blow.

The answer had come about gradually, and Alonzo had taken great pleasure in putting the plan into action. Now, propped comfortably against his pillows, he reached again for the night table's single drawer. He withdrew a sheet of foolscap and smiled into the darkness.

The words that marched boldly across the page were indistinct, unreadable in the gloom, but Alonzo had no need to see them clearly. He knew them all by heart. In a voice honed sharp by the keen edge of his bitterness, he began to recite the contents.

"I, Jason Edward St. Claire, being of sound mind and body, do hereby declare this to be my last will and testament. . . ."

The bold hand was an exact copy of St. Claire's own. The months of painstaking practice would pay off handsomely. St. Claire had gone to great lengths to reconstruct his life, and with a few more night forays Alonzo would have done a great deal toward tearing it down.

He had taken special care to discover every evil deed attributed to the Black Lion. He now had only to duplicate them while wearing his Indian guise. As the incidents became more intolerable, the inhabitants of the countryside would raise a hue and cry against the outlaw. A choice word in a drunken ear, and suspicions would be raised.

Of course when the truth came out, he would be most aggrieved to learn that his esteemed employer had been a desperate outlaw. And after the Black Lion paid the price for his crimes and earned a pauper's grave, Alonzo would present the will.

His smile deepened. It would be so easy. The man had an abundance of acquaintances, but no close friends to speak of, no family . . . and not a soul in the world gave a tinker's damn if he lived or died.

Afterward there would be ample funds to bring Finella from Cincinnati. She would be happier at Rosemunde than she was in the hovel where she now stayed, looked after by a woman in Alonzo's employ.

Returning the paper to the drawer, Alonzo retrieved the bottle of brandy, tipped it, and drank, washing away every last vestige of the hated dream.

Chapter 9

It was misty and gray when Catherine woke the next morning, her eyes still feeling the scratch of an unfinished sleep. Curling on her side, she was snuggling deeper into the feather pillow and closing her eyes when it came again—a long, low whistle that originated from the yard below her window. Up the scale it quickly slid, warbling strangely.

Tossing back the covers, she slid from the bed and hurried to the window.

Carefully she parted the curtains and peered down at Jase St. Claire leading his huge black mount. He was dressed in the handsome velvet coat he'd worn the night before, but now the sleeve was torn, and his once snowy breeches were splattered liberally with mud. As she watched, he made his way across the lawn, his long strides seeming pained and awkward.

Halfway to the stables he was met by a burly man whom she had never seen before. For several minutes they stood in conversation, Jason gesturing in choppy motions with his right hand, then

136

pointing toward the northwest. His words were pitched too low to carry clearly, but they seemed strangely guttural, very unlike the smooth and cultured tones to which she was accustomed. In fact, he seemed to be speaking a different language altogether. Her curiosity was roused. She turned the latch that secured the window and pushed against the pane. It gave way with a rasping sound heard by both men, who turned questioning glances toward her.

She stepped back just in time, but stayed near the fluttering curtain. "Good work, Wools," she heard Jason say. "Have Bobby rub him down." He handed the black's reins to the big man, who led the animal away, giving it no more notice than he would a large and troublesome hound.

Jason cast a speculative glance at her window before making his way into the house. Belowstairs the front door opened and softly closed, and uneven footfalls sounded faintly in the foyer, soon ceasing altogether.

She returned to the comfort of her bed, but did not sleep again. Her mind was full of questions. Instead, she lay watching the changing light and listening to the melodious chimes of the ormolu clock that heralded the arrival of the hour of six.

He had been away all night. Had he been searching for the Black Lion, as he had said earlier? Where had he gone, and what if anything had he discovered? He certainly looked the worse for wear. What had happened upon the dark road? The man he was seeking was a murderous cutthroat; in tracking him, Jason St. Claire was putting himself in jeopardy.

For a few minutes she sat clutching the covers to her chest, questions and worries swirling in her head. Finally she yielded to impulse and made her way to the washstand.

The water in the pitcher was cool. She bathed her face and throat and brushed her short bright locks, donned the ice-green silk gown, then thrust her feet into the matching slippers and made her way from the room.

Downstairs, the sound of merry whistling issued from the rear of the manse, coming closer. Leviticus appeared in the shadowed hallway, bearing a deep basin of steaming water that required the use of both hands. "Good morning, miss," he said as he passed by, heading for the double doors of the library. There he paused, looking flustered at his inability to manage the knob.

Catherine hurried forward. She turned the knob and pushed the panel inward.

"Where the devil have you been?" The irate growl came from Jase, who realized too late that Leviticus was not alone. He was seated in the large leather wing chair behind his massive rosewood desk, but when he noticed Catherine in the doorway he struggled to his feet, impatience stamped upon his chisled features. "Catherine, I didn't realize you were there."

"That much, m'sieur, is readily apparent," she replied. "Leviticus was having difficulty with the door, and I was able to come to his aid." She watched as the manservant set the basin on the floor and placed a towel beside it.

"You may go," Jase said tersely.

Leviticus quietly left the room, closing the doors

behind him with a soft click. When Catherine made no move to follow, Jase raised a dark brow. "I'm surprised you stay. Can it be that you no longer fear for your reputation? You, an unmarried woman, left alone and unsupervised with a man who is not a relative and lacks the approval of your family?"

"Ordinarily I would not take the chance," she said. "But last night the stakes were raised, and I think it worth the risk."

"A woman willing to gamble. How intriguing." Jase sank into the chair, stifling a groan. "You'll pardon me, but you have come at an inconvenient time." He lowered his right leg into the water, sighing as the warmth penetrated his bruised and swollen ankle.

"I saw you from above," she said.

"Yes, I know." He saw the blush rise to her cheeks. She was beautiful when she blushed; her heightened color caused her eyes to sparkle like gems beneath her gilded lashes.

"Someone should see to your injury."

Jase waved aside her suggestion. "It's trifling."

"I'll just have Leviticus summon the physician." She turned to go, but Jase caught her hand, preventing her.

"No! No physician!"

"Dora is correct, m'sieur," Catherine said. "You are careless when it comes to your own well-being."

"Dora talks too much," Jase replied. Thank God there were others in his employ who did not share her dangerous tendency. "I shall have a word with her."

"She worries about you. And I am beginning to see that her fears are well founded. If you won't send for the physician, then I will see to it myself." Before Jase could protest, she sank to her knees on the carpet and plunged her hands into the water. "How did this happen?"

"Damn fool accident." Her fingers slid up his foot, over the arch to his ankle, probing, circling, gliding. *Sweet Christ.* She was leaning slightly forward, so that her breasts strained against the soft fabric of her gown, threatening to spill forth at any moment. He held his breath, his warming gaze riveted to that expanse of creamy white. What delicious pleasure he would derive from liberating her breasts, he thought, completely forgetting the throb of his injury because of the throb in his loins. He gave a long and shuddering sigh, which Catherine immediately misconstrued.

"It must be very painful for you," she murmured.

"At the moment I can barely feel it."

"What sort of accident was it?" She brought her fingers up his leg to his calf and slid them down again.

Jase felt his muscles tense. He gripped the arms of the chair, fighting back a primitive groan as up and down her slim fingers roamed, testing his flesh for signs of a broken bone. It seemed that she would linger forever on her knees before him, an instrument of exquisite torture.

"Jason?"

"Aye?"

"Your injury."

"Aye. I was—checking out a lead," Jase said.

"Some information came my way concerning a cabin northwest of here. My source heard it was used as a place of rendezvous."

"And was it?"

Jase shook his head. "Burned to the ground. I found the smoking ruins, and little else. It was situated in a secluded hollow with one way out. Someone was at the entrance when I was about to leave, a lone man on foot." He cautiously held back part of the information, that he felt sure the man was black. He hadn't gotten close enough to question him, and he didn't want to raise her hopes, but the man had looked suspiciously like Mose. "I gave chase, but Sadist balked when we came to a small stream and threw me. When I picked myself up, the man was gone. I spent an hour or two searching, but it was almost as if he had vanished into thin air."

"Do you think it was the Black Lion?" Catherine asked, pausing in her ministrations to look up at him.

Jase looked deep into her turquoise eyes and wondered why she did not feel the same strange longing that set his flesh on fire. Her small hands gripped his leg, and he could feel his ardor rising. Another dose of her attentions and he would take her here on the Turkey rug. "Catherine, please, I cannot bear it—" He winced at the raw edge in his voice, reaching into the water to take her hands in his. Lifting each in turn, he kissed her wet fingers. "It wasn't the Black Lion. I don't know who it was, the place was too damned dark to tell. But from the way he ran, I'd venture a guess that he knew something about what's been going on there."

Catherine sat for a moment, very still, and Jase could see the disappointment on her face. "Catherine, love, you must be patient," he said.

"It is difficult to sit by and do nothing when lives hang in the balance." She stood, and Jase released her hands, though reluctantly. "I vowed that I would put a stop to the killings, and I have done nothing."

"You have done something," Jase insisted. "You have placed your trust in me. I will settle it."

"Perhaps if I went to the governor—"

"No!"

The strength of his denial took her aback, and she stared at him before saying, "Surely you cannot apprehend the Black Lion all alone. It is too great a task for any one man."

"It is better that I do it myself. Calling out the bloody militia at this stage would only muddy the waters, make him all the more difficult to find. No. I'll go on alone, as I have been doing, and I want your solemn word that you will not interfere."

She raised her brows, about to protest, but Jase cut her off, softening his tone. "Three weeks is all I'm asking. Three weeks in which we go on just as we are now. There is a soiree in Natchez at the end of that time, which the governor is to attend. If you still wish to carry out your original plan then, I will escort you there myself so that you can speak with him."

"Three weeks," Catherine said. "But I cannot possibly remain in Natchez all that time."

"Natchez? No. But you can stay here with no one the wiser. You will find Leviticus, Dora, and me very discreet. Your every need shall be met. I will personally see to it." She hesitated, catching her full lower lip between her teeth. Jase watched the unconscious action, and felt an answering tug in his loins. Three weeks in which to know her better. "Not losing your nerve so soon, are you?" he prompted.

She took a deep breath. "I've come this far. I cannot give up now. All right. Three weeks, m'sieur, and I will take you at your word." She turned to leave, but paused. "Who was that man I saw you with this morning?"

"An old acquaintance who works for me from time to time."

"Someone from your past?"

"Yes," Jase said carefully. "Why do you ask?"

"You seemed different with him. I heard you speak."

"Did you?"

"You didn't speak English or French," Catherine said. "It sounded strange—savage."

Jase's mouth curled in a semblance of a smile. "Take care about eavesdropping, sweet mademoiselle. There's no telling what you might hear."

"I wasn't eavesdropping, not really. You roused my curiosity."

"And you will not be satisfied until I explain." Jase released a slow breath. He could lie to her now and perhaps sate her curiosity, or he could simply refuse to answer. Yet he found himself choosing a different course altogether, perhaps wishing to preserve the light of intrigue that shone in her lovely blue-green eyes. "I have a gift for languages, Catherine. During my youth I managed to learn several tongues, Seneca and Shawnee among others. Wools Burke, the man you saw me with this morning, was a captive of the Shawnee during his youth. That is the language you heard us speaking."

"Shawnee ... but the Black Lion is Shawnee," she said, a small frown forming between her fine brows.

Jase skillfully guided the conversation to less shaky ground. "So he is. It should prove useful, this bit of knowledge I possess. It will make my task a little easier."

She seemed to accept his explanation, yet he detected lingering suspicion in her eyes. "Take care with your ankle," she warned. "It would be best to keep your weight off it for a while." She turned and exited the room.

The doors closed. Jase was once again alone.

He stared into the tin of rapidly cooling water, feeling the insistent press of time. Three weeks until the gala ... three weeks in which to keep his inquisitive guest occupied, in which to catch a killer ... someone he was now convinced had somehow been a part of his past. Opening the topmost desk drawer, he took out the ring, the "evidence" Catherine had given him, and turned it up to the light so he could read the inscription.

R.S.C. from C.S.C. Forever.

His mother's wedding band.

John White Elk had cut it from her hand the day he killed her and her husband. Jase had seen the ring, had seen his brother's scalp as his captor stretched the flaxen curls over a birch rod hoop. His bitterness, his hatred that night had known no bounds, and he was careful to nurse those feelings all the long way north to the Seneca town where he became John White Elk's slave.

John White Elk had a fondness for the Englishman's rum, and his temper when he drank was murderous. He hated whites, and needed no excuse to beat the captive youth who slept outside the lodge with only a flea-ridden bearskin for warmth. The final beating Jase received nearly cost him his life.

Jase slipped the filigree band onto his smallest finger and sighed. The Seneca warrior had gotten drunk one day in early summer of 1786, and while he lay in a stupor Jase crept in and stole his mother's ring from the warrior's hand, concealing it inside his clothing. The following afternoon, when a visiting delegation of Shawnee came to the village, John White Elk discovered the theft. With a roar he knocked Jase down and drew his hatchet for the killing stroke.

Fire Hawk, a Shawnee chieftain and John White Elk's brother-in-law, deflected the blow, saving Jase's life. But the wound he received was a grievous one. For nearly a week he lay senseless. When he finally awakened, he was far from his enemy's lodge. Fire Hawk had traded for him, and from then on he was a willing member of Fire Hawk's Shawnee tribe.

Through the intervening years he'd managed to keep the ring with him . . . and then a year ago it had turned up missing. He'd thought he'd mislaid it. Now he knew differently. But who knew the significance of this small gold band? Who knew he was the Black Lion? And why had that person begun murdering travelers in the Black Lion's name?

Chapter 10

"I distinctly remember telling you that I wanted buttercup. This isn't buttercup, it's marigold, and it turns my hair to brass!"

Barbara Sawhill gritted her teeth as the whining voice droned on and on, increasing in volume and rising in pitch. She firmly held the pins between her lips and reminded herself that Rebecca Galliher was one of her wealthiest and most faithful customers. At the wane of this most difficult of days the effort to hold her retort in check was nearly more than she could manage. "Perhaps a bit of black silk braid would help make it more acceptable," she suggested.

Rebecca rounded on her. "Acceptable? If I wanted a gown that was merely acceptable, I would not be paying your exorbitant fees! Now help me out of this hideous misshapen blunder!"

Barbara reached out to help Rebecca extract her soft white body unscathed from the pin-saturated garment, but her fingers fairly itched to sink just one small pin into that plump white arm as recompense for the girl's cutting remarks. *Hideous*

147

misshapen blunder. She had worked half the night to have the gown ready for this afternoon's fitting, at Rebecca's insistence. And now she must begin anew.

"Would you hurry? I'm smothering in here!"

"One could only wish . . ." Barbara murmured.

Rebecca's hearing was sharper than most. She jerked slightly as the garment was drawn up over her arms. "Ouch! You horrid witch! You've stabbed me!"

"Miss Galliher, I assure you it was unintentional—" Barbara's apology was cut short by a resounding slap.

At the front of the dressmaker's shop, Angela Dane heard the ominous thunderclap and hurried from her inspection of a newly arrived bolt of China silk to head off any further escalation of the growing conflict between her niece and the harried seamstress. Angela arrived just in time to find the two combatants—Barbara with a scarlet handprint blooming on her ashen cheek and Rebecca a plump termagant in frothy pantalets and chemise—facing off in opposing corners of the tiny cubicle like two bristling cats.

Angela was swift to place herself between them. "Rebecca, this is most unbecoming."

"Unbecoming?" Rebecca's brown eyes snapped a warning to her aunt. "That *gown* is unbecoming!" She thrust a finger at the pile of yellow silk clutched to Barbara's bosom.

"This is the bolt of cloth she chose upon her last visit, Mrs. Dane, and the third time she has changed her mind," Barbara said in her own defense. "Now she insists that it doesn't suit. I do my level best to meet the requests of my customers, but Rebecca's demands are unceasing!"

Rebecca's face was a mottled red. "It is not the right shade!" She turned to Angela and her voice became wheedling. "My gown must be spectacular, Aunt Angela. It must!"

Angela sighed in capitulation. She suspected she knew the reason for Rebecca's desperation, and it had much to do with trying to impress a certain aloof and eligible gentleman. Of course, Rebecca was unaware that her youthful desires conflicted directly with those of her aunt, and Angela wished to keep it that way.

It would hardly do for her assignations with Jase St. Claire to become public knowledge. She was a married woman, after all, and her husband was not the sort of man to coolly play the cuckold . . . no matter that he was nearly twice Angela's age. Besides, she was sure that Rebecca's infatuation with the dark and enigmatic planter could come to nothing.

Taking hold of Rebecca's arm, Angela drew her aside and did her best to resolve the situation. "Of course the gown must be spectacular." She pressed the girl's arm affectionately. "I know how important the gala is to you. And I will be sure to impress that fact upon Mrs. Sawhill. Now be a good girl and finish dressing."

Rebecca sent the seamstress a final glare and took up her clothing, confident that her aunt would manage the woman. Angela dismissed Rebecca from her thoughts and turned to Barbara, who she could see was far from satisfied with the afternoon's outcome. "Mrs. Sawhill, might I have a word with you?"

The dressmaker inclined her head and bustled from the cubicle just as the small brass bell attached to the door of the shop jingled alarmingly. Barbara gave an exasperated sigh, wondering if this day would never end. "Will you excuse me, Mrs. Dane? I'll be but a moment."

Barbara hurried off to the front of the shop, and in an instant the murmur of voices reached Angela's ears. One voice was decidedly male. Curious, Angela strolled to the doorway.

Bobby Means, Jase St. Claire's stablehand, was leaving the shop. At the door he glanced back and caught sight of Angela. He tipped his disreputable-looking hat, gave her a lascivious wink, and grinned in his beard.

Angela gave no sign of acknowledgment, but she burned to know what had occasioned Jase's stablehand to visit Barbara Sawhill's shop. "Mrs. Sawhill, is everything all right?" Angela thought it best to pretend ignorance of Means's identity. "I couldn't help but notice that man just now—he wasn't bothering you, was he? If there is any problem, I could speak to my husband on your behalf—"

Barbara looked up from the missive she'd been reading. "No. No, It's quite all right. I've no need for assistance. It's business that brought him here, though I thank you kindly for your concern."

A spark of curiosity kindled in Angela's gray-green eyes. "Oh, please . . . after today it's the least I can do." Her glance slid to the shop door and back again. "And I can't help but wonder what business that rough-looking creature would have in a dressmaker's shop."

Barbara folded the single sheet of vellum Bobby had delivered and placed it in her apron pocket. "Well, I don't suppose there's any harm in telling you," she said, "so long as you vow that it will go no further."

"You will find me to be most discreet."

"Well," Barbara said, leaning slightly forward to take up and rewind a bolt of muslin lying on the counter. She placed it on the shelf and turned. "It really is the most interesting thing! Jase St. Claire has requested my presence at his residence before noon on the morrow, and he bids me bring a vast array of sample goods and come prepared to measure a young lady in residence."

"A young lady? Does he say she is a relative?" Angela's voice was carefully controlled. She gave her mind a thorough searching, but could not recall Jase ever having mentioned family. Angela belatedly realized that she had never given it more than a passing thought. It was the handsome planter, after all, who drew her attention. Surely that was the reason for the note—some distant cousin had come to call and Jase was inclined to show his generosity. Yet the cold lump in the pit of Angela's stomach refused to melt.

"The note is very clipped. It mentions no relationship . . . but one is free to guess. I've heard his name mentioned often, this Jase St. Claire—they say he is a very private man, mysterious and handsome as well! And I have heard that he lives like a king at Rosemunde, with house slaves who wear turbans and loincloths and slippers that curl at the toes. . . ."

Barbara rattled on, relating every tidbit concerning Jase St. Claire that had ever been uttered in her shop, no matter how inventive, but Angela was no longer listening. In her mind she reviewed the last night she and Jase had spent together, more than a month ago. Her husband, Harbridge, had been out of town on business for several days. Yet no amount of argument could persuade Jase to remain with her for more than a few hours. He had arrived at dusk and departed before the moon was fully risen.

Theirs had been an urgent coupling, lacking the remotest tenderness; throughout, Jase had been distracted. It came to Angela now with astounding clarity that he had been wrestling with some weighty problem . . . perhaps how to achieve a comfortable balance between bride and mistress. . . .

"Mrs. Dane?"

Angela came back to the present with a jolt. Barbara Sawhill was looking at her with obvious concern. "I'm sorry, Mrs. Sawhill, I'm not feeling quite myself—a migraine coming on, I think."

Rebecca emerged from the dressing room, her face still stormy, but Angela quickly hustled her off, assuring the girl that the gown would be sewn to her satisfaction in ample time for the gala, and wishing that her own problems were so easily solved.

The day dragged interminably for Catherine. She wandered the halls of the manse through the early afternoon, poking into corners where she had no business being, seeking some diversion to occupy her mind. The dinner hour came and went, but the house remained wrapped in silence.

Dora bustled in briefly to light the candelabra, her sunny disposition bringing a bit of brightness to an otherwise dull and dreary day.

"Mr. St. Claire sends his regrets, Miss Catherine, but he won't be joining you for dinner this evening."

Catherine glanced up sharply at the older woman, her golden brows furrowing. "Has his ankle worsened then? I warned him that he should summon a physician."

Dora hid her smile behind a gnarled hand. "I told him as much myself, but he is not a man to have a care about his own welfare. I've often thought that what he needs is a wife, someone to watch out for his own best interests when he's too proud or stubborn to do it himself."

"He doesn't need a wife," Catherine said. "He needs a keeper. Someone he cannot frighten into submission with his blusterings and growlings!" She calmed a little, a plan of action forming in her mind. "Where is he now? Still holed up in the library?"

"Why, no, miss. He was called to the barn not an hour ago."

For a moment Catherine was silent. She had no right to tell Jase St. Claire how to live his life, but she had seen his ankle, had been witness to his pain. It was foolish of him to further flirt with injury, and she intended to tell him so directly.

Not because she cared about the man himself, she assured herself, but because of the promises he had made to lend his aid and influence. He would be of precious little help to her if he were kept abed with some serious injury when it came time to meet with Governor Sargent.

If he wanted to act foolishly and tempt the turnings of fate, then he could very well have the decency to wait until he was no longer of any use to her!

"Miss Catherine, wherever are you going?" Dora followed her from the dining room into the hallway.

"I am going to berate that man for his utter foolishness and see that for once he listens!"

"Oh, but miss! You can't—I mean, it wouldn't be seemly at such a time as this!" Dora wrung her hands.

"I can think of no better time than now. Set another place at table, Dora," Catherine said with confidence. "Your master will be returning in my company."

She flung the door open and stalked across the portico and into the gathering storm.

Dora stood poised in the open doorway, hand at her mouth. "Miss!" she cried, but the wind flung her protest back in her face.

The interior of the stables was wrapped in soft dusk when Catherine entered . . . and much to her surprise the barn was empty. She stood in the hazy half-light and glanced around, girded for battle but with no one to fight. Had Dora been mistaken? Perhaps Jason had gone elsewhere. Frowning, Catherine turned to leave when muted voices, one familiar, one unknown to her, issued from the bowels of the barn.

Without thinking, she followed the sounds, down the wide aisle lined with stalls, through a small room containing a narrow pallet and hung with harness and bridles and bits . . . pausing only when she came to a solid oaken door which was open just a crack.

Light flooded through, and Jason's voice floated to her, low in tone and nearly indistinct. The stranger answered in a rumbling monosyllable that was punctuated by the unmistakable blow of a horse.

She knew that she should push the door wide and announce her presence. But something prompted her to stealth, some warning deep inside that bade her to spy out the owner of the unfamiliar voice before making herself known.

If she suddenly appeared, introductions would be in order, and there was a possibility that her name would carry into Natchez, to Alonzo, and cause no end of trouble. She was so close to speaking with the governor, and had scored a great boon in winning Jason's help and approval. She had no intention of giving up before her plan came to fruition.

Feeling conspicuous, she nevertheless stepped close to the door and pressed an eye to the crack.

The mellow light of an overhead lantern cast a golden circle in the large room beyond the door.

In the midst of that circle of light stood a dainty chestnut mare. Jase, naked to the waist, stood close by the horse's head, one hand holding the bridle. Catherine was shocked by the sight of him unclothed. She shifted positions and pressed her eye more securely to the crack.

He was as sleek as a tawny cat! Lithe and lean, without an ounce of flesh to spare. Her rebellious gaze seemed destined to wander, down across his shoulders to his tautly drawn pectorals, over his ribs and beyond. . . . His stomach was flat, his middle trim, and she noticed with awe that his skin was satin smooth, all of him, clean down to the waist band of his breeches.

Realizing just how far her gaze had wandered, Catherine pulled away from the door and started to leave when she heard Jase's stern command. "Hold her securely, I don't want her injured."

Catherine's curiosity got the better of her, and she put her eye to the crack once more. Jase was moving behind the tethered mare to a door on the opposite wall. His limping stride was painful to watch. Still she hung back, half hoping to catch Jase's attention and draw him off to the side where she might safely have a word with him.

In a moment he again appeared in the doorway, leading the Spanish black. The stallion flicked his ears back and gave a shrill whinny, sidling so that he nearly trod on Jase's booted foot.

Smothering a gasp, Catherine closed her eyes, then opened them again. Sadist needed little encouragement once he got wind of the mare's scent. He curled his lip in carnal appreciation and reared up, nearly dragging his master off his feet.

"Mother of God," Catherine breathed. The fool man was going to be trampled before her very eyes! But the black didn't come to earth at all; he eased down instead on the back of the mare, and

Catherine was presented with one mortifying glimpse of engorged male sex conquering female before she spun and, scarlet-faced, ran from the barn.

Shortly after midnight, the storm that had threatened in the late afternoon broke over the house. Catherine was still awake. Seated in a chair by the window, her feet tucked under the hem of the midnight-blue robe, she watched the sheets of wind-driven rain that lashed the panes, and tried to avoid the shameful thoughts that plagued her.

She should have heeded Dora's subtle warnings and stayed clear of the barn. By failing to listen, she had run headlong into trouble. Worst of all was the erotic path of her thoughts. Rebellious thoughts! Forbidden thoughts! Thoughts of sooty locks mingling with her own short golden tresses as Jase bent over her from behind, of brown skin like sun-warmed silk against ivory. . . .

Unbidden, thoughts of the stallion's excitement intruded, the docility of the mare . . . and Jase, looking both elegant and savage in the dusky lantern light . . . the very embodiment of virile male.

Impatient with the obsessive nature of her mind's meanderings, Catherine heaved a weighty sigh and shoved out of the chair. She paced a little. What she needed was something to distract her, to coax her wayward thoughts down more appropriate paths. She pondered the possibilities, and remembered the library and its endless shelves lined with books. Surely Jason wouldn't mind if she borrowed just one.

As she hurried from the room, she instantly felt her spirits rise.

On bare feet she padded down the stairs, and in less than a moment she was opening the door and slipping inside. Just beyond, she paused.

The room lay in darkness. Unfamiliar with its furnishings, she thought it best to allow her vision to adjust to the gloom before she initiated her search. With her back to the doors, she stood waiting, taking in the scents of vellum and leather.

The library exuded a quiet calm that was clearly evident even in this rousing storm.

She pushed away from the door, anxious to locate a suitable book and return to her room.

"Do watch your step. I would not like to see you bang your pretty shin."

His voice so took her by surprise that she started back, her hand flying to her throat. Lightning sizzled through the ebony sky, illuminating the room in blue-white light. For a brief space Jase was eerily cast in shimmering light and black shadow where he stood by the bank of windows, a sinister figure. Catherine was strangely glad when he spoke again, for the warmth of his voice ended the eeriness of the moment. "What brings you out of bed? Has the storm kept you awake?"

"No," she said, then shrugged a little. "I don't know. I find I'm ill at ease—I don't know why." She should turn and go. She was naked beneath the thin silk wrapper; the knowledge increased her feeling of uneasiness, of vulnerability. Jase was still a virtual stranger, and it was highly improper for her to remain.

"It is the house, I think," he answered. He came

away from the windows, moving slowly through the shadows toward a large leather chair. With a weary sigh, he sank down. "It has its share of restless spirits. It took me a long time to grow accustomed to it, and even longer until I began to think of it as home."

The remark was uncharacteristically revealing. Catherine found his candor intriguing. "Ghosts?" she asked.

His mouth quirked, not quite a smile. "Call it what you will. There is a sense of incompleteness about it, despite its luxurious appointments. There has been no real happiness here."

To stand in the eerie darkness, speaking of ghosts while garbed in nothing more than fragile silk, was scandalous. Yet Catherine made no move to leave. Last night he had intrigued her with his admissions; this morning he'd heightened her interest; tonight he seemed accessible and she couldn't resist pressing her advantage. "You mentioned before that you grew to manhood far from here. How did you come by this house, if you don't mind my asking?" Likely he would decline answering.

"It was—an inheritance of sorts," Jase said. "The original owner was a great friend to me—the best friend I have ever known. We were partners for a time. Maynard Dumonde was his name. He had no living heirs, and upon his death he bequeathed the place to me."

"He was indeed a good friend, and I'm sorry you lost him."

"Friends worthy of the title are difficult to come by, and I am not a man who lends himself easily

to others." Lightning flashed again, revealing the
stark set of his features, the livid white of the scar,
the melancholy in his eyes.

"Dumonde was a Frenchman?"

"Yes."

"How did you become friends?"

Something flickered in his pale eyes before he
replied. "He often came to the village where I
grew to manhood."

"He was your father's friend as well, then?"

"My," Jase said, "you *are* brimming with questions this evening."

"You intrigue me, m'sieur." Catherine bit her
lower lip. It was a dangerous admission to make,
but the truth.

Jase smiled darkly. "Do I?" he questioned in a
voice that was silky smooth. "Then we should
continue. I find I like the idea that I've managed to
capture your interest, and I am loath to let it go.
My father, Cameron St. Claire, never met Maynard
Dumonde. I was but twelve years old when he
was killed."

Catherine knew she should change the course of
their conversation out of simple courtesy. It was
inconsiderate to pry. And yet, there was something
about the way in which Jase replied that hinted at
a deeper, underlying meaning to his answers.

"How did your father die, Jason?"

His quiet voice contained an edge of steel. "Violently."

"I am sorry," she muttered hastily. "I should not
have pried into your personal affairs—"

"Your apologies are unnecessary. You asked a
question, and I answered. My father has been

dead for many years. It is not as painful for me now as it once was, and I've learned to accept his bloody legacy."

Catherine frowned. "Bloody legacy?" The words raised gooseflesh on her arms. "What do you mean by that?"

He sighed, leaning back against the leather chair. Lightning flashed beyond the rain-streaked panes, and the low roar of thunder caused the floor beneath Catherine's feet to tremble. "Are you sure you wish to hear it?"

She edged closer, chafing her arms against a sudden chill. "You are intentionally teasing me, making use of my inquisitiveness! You ought to be ashamed."

He gave a dark laugh. "I thought we had already established that I have no shame."

She stopped a few feet away. "Your legacy, sir," she prompted.

Jase lifted the trailing end of the robe's tie, lazily rubbing it between his fingers. He met Catherine's gaze and held it by sheer force of will. She felt something cold inside her begin to melt beneath that steady blue gaze.

"It began with James St. Claire, a Scottish rogue who emigrated in his twenty-first year. He left Scotland in something of hurry, a step or two ahead of the authorities, and came to the colonies. A new life, a new land . . . where a man might begin again. But James, it seems, had a bent toward lawlessness. Perhaps he knew no other way of life, perhaps he savored the thrill of living beyond the bounds of what was considered decent. Whatever the reason, he continued his wild ways.

"At twenty-five he married Katy Wellington, an Irish girl of good family, and they had three sons—James, Donald, and Cameron. James died at birth, Donald before his second year was out; Cameron alone survived long enough to carry on the line."

"What happened to James and to Katy?"

"James's luck ran out in '68. He stole a horse from a lieutenant of the British dragoons and was hanged for his pains. It had a profound effect on fourteen-year-old Cameron, who vowed to remain scrupulously honest and did so, until his death."

"And Katy?"

Jase's mouth turned grim. "Katy died of grief. She loved James deeply, despite his rascally ways."

"How did your father live? He was very young to be orphaned."

"A long-standing family tradition," Jase remarked. His sensual mouth twisted in a shadow of a smile. "My father never talked about those years, so I cannot answer you with anything more than supposition."

"And the legacy? How does it fit in?"

"Few St. Claire males live into old age. Death comes to us early, and in violent fashion. My grandfather was hanged, my father murdered, and—" He broke off. "Enough of that. I have answered your questions, and I grow tired, talking of myself. Tell me. How did you spend your evening in my absence?"

Catherine sought for something to say. She could not relate that she had gone to the barn. To think of it again was too unsettling, especially with Jase so near, still holding the ties of the robe in his strong fingers.

"I missed you at dinner." It was an impulsive admission and she was not sure where it came from. She only knew that his absence made a marked difference in her days and nights. Maddening he might be, imperious and ofttimes rude, but never was she bored in his company.

Jase shifted slightly in the chair, the leather creaking softly. It seemed natural to question her statement, but he held back, aware of the spell that seemed to surround them. Perhaps he almost feared to break it, to be thrust back into the role he had assumed since Fallen Timbers, the role of Jason St. Claire, landed gentleman, a man who out of necessity remained aloof from the world. Tonight he was weary of that role. And so he sat behind his desk, watching Catherine, letting the companionable silence stretch between them.

"There is sherry, if you would like," he said after a while, "and a chair if you care to sit out the storm."

Catherine knew she dared not stay. She eased the robe's belt from his grasp. "I only thought to borrow a book," she informed him. "I didn't think you'd mind."

"You enjoy reading, Catherine?"

She raised her brows. "You needn't sound surprised. My father was very modern in his beliefs. My education was well-rounded, despite the misfortune of my being born female."

"Then I applaud your father's wisdom," Jase said. "If there is one thing I cannot abide, it is an empty-headed woman . . . or one who pretends to be."

"I have neither time nor patience for artifice."

"Yes. A woman of purpose." Jase's gaze moved over her trim form, wrapped securely in his dressing gown. The robe was far too big for her small frame, and she appeared somewhat lost in its midnight-blue folds . . . but all the more beautiful for it, with her tawny hair softly rumpled. In a way, she *was* lost, Jase thought, a waif with no one left to care for her. She needed a strong hand to guide her, a man with a will to match her own. Someone to rein in her bent toward wildness, someone to love her well. . . .

Tenting his fingers, Jase continued to watch her with great concentration. "I am curious to know what comes after, Catherine."

"I don't know what you mean."

"What will you do once your task is finished and the Black Lion is dead?"

She was slow to answer. She did not wish to talk about the future, beyond the completion of her task, beyond the gaining of her just and due revenge. "I suppose," she answered, "that I will go home and pick up the threads of my life."

To this, Jase said nothing. A shattered life could be mended, but nothing was ever the same. "Is there a young man in your life?"

She stiffened. She did not wish to discuss Alonzo. "I have stayed too long," she said, moving toward the bookshelves. "I'll just take a book and go."

It was impossible to see the words printed on the leather spines, but it had ceased to matter what she selected. If it happened to be boring, then so much the better. Perhaps it would put her to sleep. She reached for a slim volume just above her head and was about to lift it down when Jase took it from her hands.

She stood stock-still. He had come up close behind her, so close she could feel his warmth, could smell the subtle sweet fragrance of tobacco that clung to his skin and clothes. It was such a manly smell, so oddly welcome. Closing her eyes, she slowly breathed it in, resisting the ridiculous urge to lean back against him. "Are you sure this is the book you want?" he asked, his breath stirring the tendrils that curled at her temple. "I can think of nothing more dull than Etruscan history."

"Hhmmm?" Catherine made a halfhearted attempt to wrest herself from her sudden, inexplicable lethargy. She knew that Jase represented a danger to her, and yet she did not seem to want to move away, to lose the unexpected comfort of his incredible warmth. It would have been heavenly just to turn and press herself against him, feel his strong arms enfold her. "Oh, yes, I suppose you're right. This one won't do."

Looking down at her, Jase was having many of the same thoughts. She seemed so sweet tonight, so wondrously pliable. He bent his head a little, the better to savor her fragrance. She smelled of sun-ripe meadow grass, of fallen leaves damp with dew. He drew a soft and ragged breath—the yearning to hold her against his heart was hard to resist. If only they could remain like this for a while longer. . . .

A futile hope.

Still, he could not completely suppress his mounting need. He replaced the book on the shelf and lowered his hand to her shoulder.

A soft touch, oddly questing.

Jase felt her tense, but she did not immediately resist him. Slowly, gently, he drew her back against him, until her soft curves were pressed against his hardened length. He wrapped her in his embrace, his lips finding the graceful curve of her throat. "Catherine, you are so beautiful, so warm and soft and ... Catherine ..."

She felt an alarming tingle in the shoulder Jase was nibbling. She caught her breath and arched her back, at the same time knowing that she should cut him with her scorn and turn away, run to her room, to safety. But lately she had known far too much loneliness and strife. Her life was off center—everything had been shouldered aside in her quest for revenge ... paled by her burning need to see the Black Lion's rein of terror brought to an end.

Now, quite suddenly, the emotion which had driven her for months, prompting her to take chances she would otherwise have shuddered at, was gently lulled to dormancy by this compelling desire for human contact.

Mother of God....

His hands slid down her back to her buttocks. His touch was hot and exciting. He groaned against her throat, his hands flexing as he urged her closer to him. With his right hand he continued to hold her tightly against him, while his left moved up and around, across her belly and ribs to her breast.

The tenderness of his hands and lips helped to salve Catherine's loneliness, to fill the aching void. He kissed her jaw, her cheek, her lowered lid, and sighed as he turned her. His hands fell to her shoulders, ever so slowly parting the robe and slipping it down her arms. The garment made a whispering sound as it fell and caught at her waist.

For a long and breathless moment Jase stood gazing down at Catherine revealed. She was perfect, her skin as smooth and flawless as heavy cream, the round globes of her breasts veined with blue and capped with gentle pink . . . delicate, pure succulence. . . .

"Jason . . ." she said softly, "we should not."

He said nothing, just lowered his raven head to taste the sweet offering before it was denied him. He was so weary of fighting against this forbidden flame that burned inside him, weary of resisting her piquant beauty. Tonight the world could go to Hell . . . he intended to give free rein to his senses, to revel in the pleasure that only Catherine could give.

"Mother of G—" She sucked in a swift breath, unable to finish her imprecation. Sensation, wild and new, coursed along her tautly drawn nerves. She felt Jase's mouth, hot and worshipful, as he suckled her breast. He was an expert at prolonging his special brand of torture with teeth and tongue, at extracting from her reactions she did not know were possible.

Something was wrong with her, she thought dazedly. She, Catherine Blaise Breaux, couldn't be standing here in a blackened room, allowing a man of questionable merits to take these shocking liberties! Yet here she stood, her arms looped around his broad shoulders, fingers threaded through his silken hair, head thrown back in ecstasy. . . .

She could not allow this to happen. There was no way of explaining away one's lack of purity to one's disappointed bridegroom on one's wedding night. She could not bring herself to hurt Alonzo by giving in to her desire for Jason St. Claire.

And Catherine did desire him. He was dark and dangerous, a man who refused to be bested. He defied understanding, and everything about him spoke of innate sensuality. Catherine looked down at his rapt face. It pained her immensely to admit that she did not *want* to stop him—she had to. Yet before she could speak the words of protest, he sank to one knee before her and took up the ends of the belted tie that held the robe secure at her waist. Slowly he began to slip the neatly done bow . . .

"No." The single word drew Jase's immediate attention. He paused and gazed up at her.

"No?" he said, his face cast first in harsh blue-white light, then in darkness. Only his eyes continued to glimmer through the stygian gloom, lit by some strange inner fire. "Catherine," he began, "you're only frightened."

"Yes," she admitted, "I am, but not for the reasons you think. I cannot do this, Jason."

He laughed wickedly. "You can. I'll show you." In one fluid move he came to his feet again, reached to take her and pull her against him, to kiss away her reticence.

"You must listen to me!" She shoved at him, struggling to right the dressing gown.

"Very well, I will listen." Catching at her hand, he drew her to the great chair behind his desk. "Sit with me and we will talk."

Clearly, if she sat with him in the way he had in mind, they would not do much actual speaking. The image of the stallion mounting the mare flashed through her mind, causing her to strain away. "I cannot sit with you, Jason. I cannot *be* here with you!"

He frowned, not liking her urgent tones. He sensed that this was more than just a virgin's jitters.

"I am betrothed."

Instead of the chilly withdrawal Catherine expected, Jase chuckled. "Betrothed." He came forward and drew her against him so that Catherine could feel his arousal. "Knowing you're promised to another man does little to eradicate this hunger I feel for you."

"It is *your* hunger, m'sieur," Catherine reminded him haughtily. "And I hardly think it my place to assuage it for you." She spun on a heel and padded to the door, righting the robe as she went.

"Catherine, wait!"

She paused at the door. "If you find yourself in dire straits, I am sure there are women in Natchez willing to soothe your baser needs for a bauble or two. As for me, I'm going to bed, alone."

The door closed behind her, eliciting a low growl of frustration from Jase. His thoughts were wild. If he followed, would she continue to resist? He felt almost desperate enough to do it, and only

Catherine's words tumbling back upon him kept him from crossing the room and making his way to the stairs.

She was going to marry Alonzo.

Expelling a pained breath, Jase tipped back his head, closed his eyes, and forced himself to calm. The exercise did little to ease the aching fullness in his loins.

He had never forced a woman. Yet at this moment the idea of force had its merits.

With a snort of disgust he strode to the French windows, flung them wide, and stepped into the deluge.

Wind-driven rain stung his face and swiftly plastered his clothes to his skin. The heavens were roiling. Churning clouds were revealed by each flash of lightning. But Jase did not return to the safety of the house, standing instead with his baleful gaze piercing the violent night sky.

Chapter 11

At half past eleven the next morning Catherine made her way from her chamber and crept to the balustrade, peering down at the wide hall below. The library doors were open, a good indication that Jase was elsewhere. Leviticus and Dora were nowhere in sight; her timing was perfect.

Smiling to herself, she moved quickly down the stairs, her stocking feet noiseless on the bare treads. Jase had sent Dora to her room an hour ago with the summons. She was to meet him in the library promptly at twelve. A guest was coming and her presence was required.

Catherine had no idea what he could be thinking, and she was not anxious to find out! No one knew that she was a guest at Rosemunde; she wished to keep it that way. Outside, the sun was shining; the air after the rain would be fresh and clean-smelling. A perfect time to take a stroll and view Jason's estate for herself.

With that purpose in mind, she had donned her shirt and breeches, leaving the ice-green gown

171

hanging in the wardrobe, taken up her boots, and stolen from the room.

Jase might be angry because she ignored his request, but not half as angry as Alonzo would be if he discovered her comfortably ensconced in the handsome bachelor's household.

She was taking a chance just being here, and had it not been for Jase's promise to help her bring the Black Lion to justice, she would not have stayed another moment.

Catherine stepped from the last tread, casting a cautious glance down the dimly lit hallway that led to the rear of the manse. Assured she was alone, she hurried toward the front entrance.

She walked quickly past the open library doors. Jase was standing at his desk and happened to glance up just as she passed.

"There you are!" His deep voice stopped her in her tracks. She squeezed her eyes shut, muttering a soft curse at her ill luck. He came into the hallway and took her arm, propelling her toward the library. "How good of you to join us!"

She dug in her heels and hissed at him. "Stop it. Are you mad? I can't go in there!"

"Of course you can," he said. "I have made all the arrangements."

He dragged her to the door, but she dropped her boots and caught the sill, clinging to it as if it were a lifeline. Jase stood back, hands on hips, and looked down at her as if she were an errant child. "You are being silly and childish."

Her cheeks grew hot. "Silly and childish, m'sieur? You gave me your word that no one would know about our arrangement! And now you invite a guest to your home and order me to appear? Have you given any thought to my position? No," she said, not waiting for his reply. "It is clear you have not!"

"So, that's what this is about." Jase smiled. "Allay your fears, Catherine. Your secret is safe."

"Do not be so cavalier! I have my future to consider! And I assure you, my fiancé would not take it lightly were he to discover me here with you!"

"Mr. St. Claire? Is something amiss?"

Jase stepped to the doorway and offered his guest his most charming smile. "It's a slight misunderstanding, Mrs. Sawhill. If you will excuse us, I need to have a word with my betrothed."

He pulled the doors closed with a firm click as Catherine exploded. "Betrothed! You truly are mad!"

"Lower your voice," Jase commanded. "Unless, of course, you *wish* for Mrs. Sawhill to suspect that something scandalous is going on here at Rosemunde."

Catherine stared at him accusingly. "Oh, Jason, how could you invite someone here? How could you tell her that we are to be married?"

"It was not as difficult as I thought it would be," Jase answered. "You must have clothes, Catherine. Can you think of a better way to get them than by hiring a seamstress?"

"I cannot accept clothing from you," she protested. "It wouldn't be proper."

"You worry too much about propriety."

"One of us must!"

Jase smiled sardonically. "Well, I *could* send her away . . . if you insist. I rather like the way you look in this." He brushed his hand down her shirt-front, releasing buttons as he did so, as if by magic.

Catherine gasped, batting his hand away. "You are an insufferable man!"

He crossed his arms over his chest and grinned wolfishly down at her. "Yes, I am that. I am also generous, so why not accept my largess quietly and with dignity? You cannot win against me, you know."

Catherine shook her head, knowing he was right. He was too strong, too forceful a personality, for her to resist. "All right," she said. "I will go along with this scheme of yours, on one condition."

"And what is that, sweetheart?" His voice was suspiciously warm and caressing.

She glared at him, but it did not seem to chasten him in the least. "You must swear that woman to secrecy! I will not have word of my presence carried into Natchez. I will not have my reputation ruined!"

Ruined, Jase thought, was an exaggeration. For the life of him, he could not fathom what she saw in Alonzo Hart. He only knew that he rather liked the idea of dressing her to suit his tastes, and so he readily agreed.

That night Jase saddled Sadist and led him from the barn, glancing up at Catherine's window as he passed the house. He half expected her to be there, peering suspiciously down at him as she had been the previous morning. But the window was dark and empty; she must be fast asleep.

What would she think if she discovered that he was the infamous Black Lion? he wondered. Would she give him a chance to explain? Or would she hurry to betray him?

There was a bounty of five hundred dollars for his return to Cincinnati, of which Catherine was aware. Despite the passing of more than half a decade, people's hatred of him had not dimmed. There were some who would push for his trial and execution. . . .

The wars had come to an end six years ago . . . but not for him. He must always be wary, ready to take to his heels if need be. And he found it a heavy and inescapable irony that when he most wanted peace, all he seemed to find was more turmoil.

And then there was Catherine, who seethed for his head in a noose one moment and melted in his arms the next. He thought of the previous night, of how she had softened, become pliant, willing and warm up to a point. He hadn't planned to seduce her, but he found her charms impossible to resist. They were well suited; it was unfortunate that Alonzo Hart had come upon her first.

The thought that Catherine was rightfully Alonzo's should have turned Jase's thoughts in another direction. But her fiery spirit was difficult to dispell. He wanted her in his bed. Having her there would complicate matters for her, but quite possibly simplify them for him. The closer they became, the less likely she would be to turn against him if she stumbled upon the truth about his past.

He was smiling as he reached the drive and swung into the saddle. Seduction had its advantages, and thoughts of it did not leave his mind completely until a rutted lane appeared to his left.

Jase drew rein and watched as the great black bulk of an ancient live oak tree seemed to split in two and the dark shape of a man stepped into the road. He was large and lumbering, half a head taller than Jase and twice his girth. Wools Burke's size and appearance had earned him the name "Muga" from the Shawnee word for bear.

"Meshepeshe," the big man said, addressing Jase as "Lion."

"What have you learned?"

Wools grunted. "The killer keeps his distance. But there's talk that he's a great man from Natchez."

"From on the hill?" Jase asked. *"Nethowwe?"*

"If I knew who he was, I'd kill him myself and have done with it." Wools snorted. "He's a crafty bastard. Worse than any Iroquois I ever saw! This bunch he's put together are cutthroats. They make me seem a pew-sitter by comparison. Ain't a one o' 'em that'll trust me enough to say 'Boo.' " He hawked and spat in disgust. "Seems like I'll have to get my hands dirty before they'll trust me enough to talk, and you know I don't like that."

Jase sighed. "It's gone too far already. There has to be another way." He sat for a moment, absorbed in thought. "What about Hastings?"

"Be headed up that way directly. Fella by the name of Willie Ames is stayin' over on his way down to Natchez. Little man, big talker. Wears an eye patch. Claims he saw the Lion up in the Chickasaw Lands. Thought maybe you'd want to amble on up and see Ames yourself."

"If Ames saw the Lion, he may be able to help identify him," Jase said. "Someone must have gotten a look at him." He turned the black's head back toward the Trace, saying over his shoulder, "Wools—"

"Yeah, I know. If that son of a bitch Black Lion so much as farts and I get wind of it, I'll get word to you right away."

Jase spurred the black, pushing him to his limits. Shortly before midnight he entered Hastings's establishment. Despite the lateness of the hour, the place was bustling. Leo Hastings recognized him and hurried over. "Whiskey, sir?"

"Just bring the bottle and a clean glass, if you have one."

Leo brought the requested liquor and took the coin Jase offered, depositing it in the deep pocket of his grimy breeches before he turned away.

Jase found Willie Ames easily. He had the size and disposition of a bantam cock, and was currently haranguing a fellow patron who quickly got his fill of the smaller man's strident Irish voice and stumbled away to claim a quiet corner. "Ungrateful beggar," Willie said. He looked up as Jase placed the unopened bottle on the table and sat down.

"You look thirsty, friend," Jase said. He didn't wait for Ames to reply, but splashed the amber liquid into the Irishman's glass then half filled his own.

"That's bloody generous of you, mister." Ames hitched up his breeches before he resumed his seat. "Some folks are glad to share a glass with Willie Ames!" he said loudly, directing the com-

ment to the corner where the other man had retreated.

Jase leaned back in his chair and watched the
Irishman toss back the whiskey. As soon as the
glass was empty, Jase refilled it. "I'm surprised to
find a man of your caliber staying here."

"Better here than out there," Willie said with a
sniff. "They told me this bloody place was halfway
civilized. I should ha' listened to my ma and
stayed in Boston. 'Tis safer there."

"You sound as though you've had a bad experience," Jase said, hoping Ames would need no further encouragement.

Willie held out his glass for more whiskey, and
as Jase filled it to the rim, his hopes were realized.
"I narrowly missed being scalped by an Indian!"
Ames shot back, running anxious fingers through
his thick shock of reddish hair. "Happened two
nights ago, a few miles north of here. Come at me
like thunder out of the night, he did, a-screechin'
his awful war cry! I near messed my pants, I did!
Willie Ames'll fight any Christian man and not
back down, but when it comes to savages—" He
shook his head.

"Did you see this Indian?"

Ames nodded. "I seen him, all right. He looked
me right in the eye and said as how he'd kill me."

"A big man, was he?"

"Bigger than me. Aye, a big man—like you. Tall
and not too heavy."

"What about his face?"

"Hideous. Half red, half black. And his eyes
stared out of his mask like hot coals."

Jase digested this information. A man of his approximate height and build, a man who knew his war insignia and had copied it. "Dark eyes?" he questioned.

"Black as bloody sin."

"Black eyes," Jase murmured. He looked at Willie Ames, wondering what else the Irishman knew. "You said he spoke to you. How?"

"How—"

"Was he Irish, Scottish, French?"

"None of those," said Willie, scratching his head. He brightened. "Gentry! He talked like gentry. Softer in tone than you, I think. Drew his words out, and no burr to his *r*'s—no harsh sound at all. Slurred like, almost."

A drawling, gentle voice. A native Southerner. A gentleman, or someone who affected the mannerisms of one. Things a man would not think to hide, mannerisms so ingrained he would not think that anyone would notice.

It was a start.

Jase got to his feet, leaving the bottle. "Mr. Ames, it has been a pleasure."

Over the course of the next few days the battle to dress Catherine was waged, and it was difficult even for the participants to tell who was winning. Much to Catherine's disgruntlement, Jase St. Claire was present through most of the measurings and fittings, freely giving his unwanted opinions while she seethed behind an ornate dressing screen. He ordered more gowns than she deemed proper or intended to accept . . . and seemingly nothing could stop him. As the days passed, she grew more aware that he intended to have his way in the matter of her wardrobe, and he went about getting it with all the delicacy and tact of a tyrant.

Each bolt of fabric was presented for his inspection before it was shown to Catherine. But what rankled deepest was the growing awareness that she could find no fault with his selections. His taste ran toward soft and sinuous fabrics, silks and satins, cottons and muslins, and velvets for damp, chilly days ... goods that would feel wonderfully well against her skin, drape flatteringly over her lithe form. The selections he made seemed limitless, a wardrobe more suited for a real bride than a temporary houseguest.

Had it been Alonzo who sat so casually by the bed, sipping coffee and lavishly spending an inordinate amount of money to see her outfitted in fine new feathers, Catherine would have been ecstatic. That it was Jase St. Claire involving himself in her life annoyed her to no end.

Alonzo would not have watched her with eyes alight, would not have taken such obvious relish in selecting the delicate lawn and imported lace which would now comprise her underthings! Why, it was most unseemly—and yet not surprising—that Jason would know of such dainty things, that he would speak of them to Barbara Sawhill with such casual authority. Catherine blushed bright pink to think that he would now know what manner of garments she wore beneath her gowns!

She hardly knew Jase. She had asked him questions, and he had answered, yet she realized now that he revealed each tidbit of information reluctantly. He told what he felt was prudent to tell, and nothing more.

"A few more moments and we'll be finished for the day." Barbara Sawhill whisked the final garment from her large valise and held it out for Catherine's inspection. "I never would have chosen this color, but Mr. St. Claire instinctively knew what would be best for you. He said it would bring out the tiny flecks of silver in your eyes, and I do believe he was correct. Here, let's try it on and see."

"He said that?" Catherine dutifully slipped the gown over her head and gently pulled it into place.

"He did indeed," Barbara affirmed with a self-satisfied nod.

"What else did Jason say?" Catherine wondered. It made her feel strange, all quivery and warmly feminine, that he would freely make observations about her person to Barbara, and complimentary ones at that. Even the thought that he might simply have been acting the part of her financé for the seamstress's benefit did not lessen her curiosity.

"Only that you were to have the very best, and that expense was not to be a consideration." Barbara adjusted the sleeve of the gown, not looking at Catherine. "You are indeed fortunate to have found Mr. St. Claire."

"Ummm . . . yes. I suppose any woman would be happy to wed him." It was the only comment she could trust herself to make. She was not unaware that her feelings toward Jason were gradually changing, yet she didn't comprehend exactly *what* she felt for him. She only knew that his presence kept her in a constant state of confusion.

The man was a study in contrasts . . . darkness and light; goodness and evil. . . . And the only thing of which she remained certain was that she found him virtually impossible to ignore. Her thoughts full of Jase, she slowly turned toward the cheval glass.

The half-finished gown was made of silk that ranged in shade from amethyst to violet-blue to deepest purple. The vibrant color made her eyes look huge and luminous. She smiled at her image, noting how her eyes seemed to spark with silver, then caught at her lower lip as she turned her gaze to Barbara. "Do you think this one will be ready soon?" She was thinking of the gala and, rebelliously, of the look of approval in Jase's eyes when he saw her wearing his gown.

"Why, yes," Barbara said. "It will be completed by the end of the week, along with the rest of the gowns and dainty things Mr. St. Claire has ordered."

Catherine frowned at her reflection and smoothed the skirt with her hands. The night of the gala would surely be the last one she and Jase spent together. Once she met with the governor, there would be nothing to keep her here at Rosemunde, no reason for her ever to see Jason again. The realization brought her a queer little jolt.

Soon they would return to pursuing their individual lives. She would go back to New Orleans, to Rivercrest, to Alonzo . . . and Jason could return to his life of well-ordered solitude, with Dora and

Leviticus to look after him as much as his stubborn nature would permit.

The very thought that her ordeal would soon be over should have brought her vast relief, yet Catherine experienced a strange emptiness which she could neither fathom nor banish. It stayed with her long after Barbara Sawhill repacked her satchel and took herself off to Natchez to finish the gowns.

Chapter 12

Jase finished reading the documents spread before him on the desk, then reached for a pen which he dipped into the inkwell. He pressed the point against the inner rim of the glass bottle to release any excess, and wrote his name across the bottom pages with clean, bold strokes. The documents were indenture papers to be signed by immigrants willing to work off the cost of their passage. Jase would take responsibility for their debt of transportation, feed and clothe them for a period of four years. In exchange, he would obtain a crew of laborers, free men, who after their term of indenture would collect a sum of fifty dollars and fifty acres of land provided by Jase.

Alonzo Hart sat forward in his own chair, watching with a professional eye. "That should just about do it, at least for now." He took up the papers and prepared to leave. "You heard about Sandler and his wife and son. Terrible shame. Imagine, cut down like that on their own land. Poor beggars never had a chance. Seems that simple robbery didn't sate the Black Lion's lust for

184

blood. Hope to God they find him. That's one hanging I'll gladly attend!"

Jase clenched his fist until his knuckles creaked under the pressure. Alonzo's voice droned on and on. He seemed to derive a perverse pleasure from relating the details of the most recent murders. But Jase didn't need enlightening; he'd been on his way back to Rosemunde before dawn that morning when he'd glimpsed the reddened sky, the sparks that danced high above the trees.

He had spurred Sadist off the Trace and along the winding path that led to Edgar Sandler's modest cabin. He had arrived too late. Sandler and his wife, Molly, lay in the dooryard, murdered and scalped . . . and ten-year-old Samuel lay sprawled a few yards away, a look of fear frozen forever on his thin face. . . .

"Pure meanness," Alonzo said, shaking his head. "Savagery, with no reason for it."

Jase looked at Alonzo, but said nothing. In 1790 he had participated in a raid on a settlement called Sandler's Station near the Big Sandy in Kentucky. A man named Josh Evans was killed in the fighting, his wife captured. Edgar Sandler . . . Sandler's Station. Was it just a macabre coincidence?

He had made a quick circuit of the area around the Sandler cabin, searching for signs, and had found four sets of tracks, one made by a horse with a split hind hoof.

He had left Sandler's place feeling dissatisfied. He was no closer to finding his enemy, and his frustration was building.

The impostor was both cruel and clever, a man who knew Jase's history intimately and bore him a grudge, a Southerner with black eyes. . . . But who was he, and where would he strike next? Alonzo had black eyes, was a native of the South, and a gentleman. But he was also heavily involved in business, and had been with Jase on at least one occasion when a crime attributed to the Black Lion was being committed. Besides, he was Catherine's fiancé. And if Jase found that fact hard to accept, he found it harder still to imagine Alonzo Hart impersonating the Black Lion and committing all sorts of hideous crimes. He was capable of lying, even of infidelity, but murder? Jase dismissed the notion.

"It may take time to find indentures hearty enough to suit your purposes," Alonzo was saying. "Are you sure you won't change your mind? With a hundred slaves and a good foreman—"

Jase stood abruptly, making his way to the French windows, where he stood contemplating the gathering dusk.

A discreet tapping sounded at the library doors. Jase called out for entrance. The panels swung inward; Leviticus hesitated in the doorway.

"Yes, what is it?" Jase inquired coolly.

The manservant hesitated. "Sir," he harrumphed, "miss wishes to know if she should begin dinner without you this evening, or will you be joining her directly?"

Jase saw Alonzo's knowing grin, but chose to ignore it. "You may tell my lady that I will be joining her shortly if she cares to wait. And if she does not, she may start without me."

"Very good, sir." Leviticus exited the room.

" 'My lady,' is it? Then I must assume that the

rumors concerning your engagement flitting round the parlors of Natchez are true." Alonzo waited, but Jase just shot him an annoyed glance, saying nothing. "Well, where is this mysterious female? I should like to have a look at her, to see the type of woman to finally snare the most eligible man in the territory, a man who not two weeks past vowed in this very room that he meant to savor his freedom."

"Another time, perhaps," Jase said. Apparently Barbara Sawhill had wasted precious little time in spreading the news of his supposed engagement. It was just one more irritant to rub his patience raw.

Alonzo let the matter go, albeit reluctantly. She was a snag in his perfect plan, this woman who had materialized from thin air, but a small snag if handled correctly. He took up his coat and walked to the door. "I would imagine that Rebecca is beside herself with grief."

Jase gave a careless shrug. "Rebecca has no claim on me, nor has she ever had one."

Alonzo shook his head. "Two women vying for the privilege of sharing your bed," he said with amazement. "I wonder what the future Mrs. St. Claire will say when she learns of her potential rival."

"Jason?"

Catherine's voice barely penetrated Jase's musings. Since Alonzo's departure, he'd been unable to shake the image of Sandler's cabin, and consequently his mood had plummeted. It took a concentrated effort to give his full attention to the golden creature peering down the table at him with a frown of concern. Before him, his plate was generously laden with the bounty of his table, and conspicuously untouched. "Something is wrong," she said flatly. "What is it?"

"Indeed?" Jase said tersely. "And why must something be wrong? Why can a man not simply sit at his own bloody table and choose not to eat if it suits him?"

"You stare and you scowl and you say nothing, even when spoken to. I shouldn't wonder that by now you've given yourself a fine case of the stomach complaint."

Jase cursed softly and threw down his still-folded napkin, his pale eyes glittering in his dark face. "I thank you for your concern, Mademoiselle Breaux, but I assure you it is neither wanted nor needed. I have been taking care of myself since the tender age of twelve without the nagging influence of a woman." He shifted in his chair, painfully aware that his sore temper was digging him a huge black hole where Catherine was concerned, yet somehow he had difficulty stilling his unwise tongue. "You sound suspiciously like a wife. Must I remind you we are not in reality betrothed? You are a guest in this household, and as such you overstep your bounds."

Catherine fell ominously still. "Are you quite through, M'sieur St. Claire," she asked with terrible calm, "or is there some insult which you wish to add to your venomous diatribe?"

Jase passed a hand over his face. "Catherine . . ."

"Do not 'Catherine' me!" she said, her voice rising as she came to her feet. "I have had enough of your bullying for one evening, but before I leave you to your own sullen company, let me tell you this: If the worst brigand on earth held a gun to my head and attempted to force me into accepting you as a husband, I would fall to my knees before him and beg to be shot! To live out my days as your wife would be a torment beyond recounting, abominable, disgusting, an endless trial of my patience."

Jase looked hard at her, his expression thunderous. "Disgusting? What in hell do you mean by disgusting? I insist that you explain yourself."

Elevating her small chin in elegant refusal, Catherine turned and sailed gracefully from the room and down the hallway. Bootheels rang against the shining puncheons as Jase followed.

"Catherine, wait!"

"Why should I? Do you wish to growl and snap at me some more?"

"What I wish is for us to sit down and finish our meal."

"I have had my fill, thank you." She swept him with a cool glance that clearly indicated she wasn't referring to the fare at his table. "I need some air."

"You cannot go out."

"I can and I shall," she said. She reached for the door, but Jase stepped quickly to bar the portal. "Have you lost all semblance of sanity? Stand back and let me pass!"

Jase muttered a vile curse, raking a hand through his hair. "You cannot go out alone. There has been another murder. This time nearby."

The statement, though uttered in a low voice, lashed Catherine like the meanest whip. Her small face went ashen, and she began to tremble. Jase reached out to steady her, but she quickly, nervously, moved out of reach. "Another ... while I dally here with new clothes and silly, meaningless things!" She caught her breath, fighting for composure. "What happened?"

"A family was killed not far from here."

"How?" When he hesitated, she cried, "Tell me!"

A muscle jerked in Jase's jaw. He didn't want to say the words. Yet he could not keep the truth from her. "It was made to look like an Indian raid."

"No! Oh, God no!" She put her small fist to her mouth, as if she would force back the emotional storm that threatened by sheer force of will.

"There is nothing you could have done to prevent it," Jase said, searching for words of comfort that would put the fire back into her eyes, the color into her cheeks.

My God, how he longed to hold her, to keep her safe. But he was the Black Lion, a man she despised. And this was an impossibly complicated situation made worse by the fact that he was coming to care very deeply about her.

There it was, out in the open and all too true for Jase to ignore. *He did care for Catherine* ... as he had never cared for anyone in his life. And no matter how much he argued inwardly that it was wrong to feel as he did, he seemed powerless to stop it. Perhaps she was right after all, perhaps he was losing his mind. . . .

As he watched, she wrung her small hands, and in doing so she wrung Jase's callous heart. God help him . . . she was crying. In that instant, when the sorrow welled up in her beautiful turquoise eyes, he would have given anything to alleviate her pain, to stop the hot flow of agony that now poured from her. His mind full of Catherine, he drew her into his arms, the only secure barrier against the cruel outside world he had to offer.

Not knowing what else to do, he rocked her as she cried, murmuring mindless endearments into her shell-like ear. "Sweet Catherine . . . my fearless little Catherine . . . how very brave you are, how lovely."

For a while she sobbed, then gradually she quieted in his embrace. But instead of pushing immediately away as he expected, she simply stood, her small hands splayed beneath his superfine coat and against his shirtfront, her dampened cheek resting softly against his heart. Jase was keenly aware of the warmth of her small hands, the gentle rise and fall of her breasts with each breath she took. "Darling," he said softly, dropping a light kiss upon her sunlit curls, the urge to bury his face in the short, silky mass nearly overwhelming. He reached into his coat and produced a clean, folded handkerchief, which he used to gently dry her tears.

He hugged her close and kissed her curls again, wanting so much more from her.

Catherine pulled back just enough to raise luminous eyes to his, eyes with damp and starry lashes, eyes in which a man could easily lose himself. "When did it happen? When did the Black Lion strike?"

"Last night."

"Last night, while you were abroad, searching."

"Yes. I saw the fire from the Trace and went to investigate. The cabin was beginning to give way to the flames. It had been burning for a while."

"And the Black Lion?"

Jase gave an inward grimace. "Whoever was responsible was gone when I arrived."

"He roams free," she said, sounding angry and forlorn. "Free to kill again!" She pushed away, but not out of his arms, for Jase would not let her go. Her expression was taut, and there was a look of desperation in her eyes. "I must get to Natchez now, tonight! I must meet with the governor, Jason. Put an end to this!"

His expression was carefully closed. He drew her against his side and guided her toward the library doors. "I can't let you do that, Catherine. Not yet. I understand your feelings—"

"I don't believe you do," she said. "The killings are the sole reason for my being here! I lost my brother to that heartless savage! And until you yourself have known that kind of loss, you cannot understand it!"

They entered the library. Jase kicked the doors closed and poured brandy into a snifter, pressing it into her hands. "Drink it; it will steady your nerves."

"Spirits cannot wash away the pain, Jason, nor absolve me of guilt."

"You are not the only one who has experienced loss, Catherine. When I say that I understand what you are feeling, I don't do so lightly. I too had a brother, and I lost him, just like you lost Andre."

She raised her eyes to Jase's face. "Why did you not mention it before?"

"It happened long ago, when I was just a lad." Jase leaned against the desk and sighed. "I have never spoken of it to anyone. It hurt too much at first, and afterward—well, there was no one to tell, and little point in talking about it."

"It may help you to speak of it," she suggested. She reached out and touched his hand tentatively.

He smiled without warmth. "Help me, you say? Help me how, exactly? It cannot take away the pain, can it? Nor help to ease the horror of the memory." He turned the hand she touched palm upward, flexing his fingers and lacing them with hers. "Will it help to bring us closer?" he asked, his voice softening. "If it will, then I will tell you everything."

Catherine's heart fluttered in her breast. He was a strange mixture, hard-bitten yet capable of great tenderness, even of compassion. Capable of being hurt. "Tell me, please. I want to know."

He brought her hand to his mouth, kissing each knuckle in turn, then her wrist. His lips were warm and vibrant, his tongue rough against her sensitive skin. Catherine shivered.

"Why am I unable to deny you?" he asked. "You demand and I give, no matter the cost. It doesn't matter that I sense the danger in giving you all, or that I already fear the price I may pay in the end."

"You, afraid?" Catherine said incredulously.

"Why are you surprised? Do you think me less than human? Less a man than your fiancé?"

"No," she replied too quickly. "No, it isn't that.

I don't think of you in the same way as I think of my betrothed." Indeed, she thought with chagrin, she hadn't given much thought to Alonzo at all in these past few days. "You just seem so—invulnerable. So strong."

"Steel is strong," Jase said simply. "But to become that way it must be tempered with fire."

"And, like steel, you have been tempered by fire. You have known much hardship, haven't you, Jason?" She wanted to hear of his brother; she wanted to know it all. Perhaps then the attraction she felt toward him would lessen, this unquenchable yearning in her breast would burn away. He said there was danger in giving her what she requested, but there was danger in his touch as well.

He held her hand in both of his, and Catherine let him, enjoying the warmth of his nearness. He looked at her and she felt all warm and golden, as if a fire had kindled deep in her belly; a simple touch fueled the blaze to frightening heights; a kiss and she would melt. No man had ever caused her to feel so helpless.

This was dangerous. He was dangerous.

But at this moment, Catherine didn't care.

"Will you tell me about your brother, Jason?"

He raised his eyes to hers. "Will you keep your word to me and postpone going to the governor? Will you give me the time I need?"

"Time to get yourself killed?" She shook her head. "I should not have made that promise—"

"But you did make it," Jase reminded her. "And I mean to hold you to it. You placed your trust in me. Surely you will not withdraw it now?"

Catherine gave a shaky little laugh. "How can I trust you? I barely know you."

"I have given more of myself to you than I have ever given to anyone, certainly more than I have ever given any woman to come before you."

There seemed to be something else he wished to say. Catherine wondered what it could be. For a wild moment she thought he might be on the verge of declaring his feelings for her, but he tipped back his dark head instead and massaged his neck with his free hand, sighing with resignation. "My brother's name was Eben. He was several years younger than I at the time of his death, a good lad with winning ways and an even temper. He was very like our mother in looks—fairhaired—whereas I favored our father. . . ."

He was quiet for a moment, caught up in his reverie. When he continued his tone was softer, and Catherine had to strain to hear. "I have told you about my past, but I have not told you everything. There are things, Catherine, aspects of my life in which I take no pride."

"Surely everyone has some regrets," she said, trying to smooth the way for his confession.

He only smiled a little sadly and lightly chafed the hand he held. "My God. To be so young and innocent. How can I expect you to understand?"

"What does this have to do with Eben?"

"Everything," he said. "And nothing. It has to do with the way he died, and my parents, and my life after that tragic day. Do you remember my grandfather's legacy?" She nodded. "Well, I did not term it 'bloody' for dramatic effect. My parents, you see, were murdered by a Seneca raiding party in 1784. I was twelve years old at the time, and my world was torn asunder before my very eyes. I was in the clearing when the first shot rang out. I heard my mother scream and saw her fall. My father had been busy that morning making repairs to the spring that supplied our water. He heard the scream too, and made the short dash from the spring to the cabin dooryard. I watched him approach with my heart in my throat. I could not even cry out, I was so terrified. The look on his face—" Jase shook his head. "Such horror, such anguish. It is a look I will remember the rest of my days, one I hoped never to see again, but I have many times since. He ran directly into the arms of death, and because my mother was dying, I think he was glad to embrace it."

Tears had gathered in Catherine's eyes. "I am sorry," she said. Jase seemed not to hear. His grip on her hand was painful, but she could not bring herself to withdraw from him.

"He was cut down before he could reach her. The ball took him through the heart." He gazed down at their hands, still entwined, and seemed unaware that his other hand had clenched into a fist on his thigh. "With her dying breath, my mother called out his name . . . and strained to touch his lifeless hand. . . ."

Catherine's tears flowed freely now, coursing down her cheeks. Jase smoothed them away. "You must be wondering how it was that I escaped with carnage and destruction all around me. The fact is that I did not. The man who killed my mother was the same Captain John White Elk I spoke of briefly before. I tried to run, but he knocked me down and bound my hands behind me so that I couldn't fight. Then with a rawhide tether 'round my neck they took their plunder and marched me off toward New York."

"And Eben?"

He shook his head. "I was insensible for hours. For the life of me, I do not recall leaving the valley where we lived. I remember only the noose tightening when I fell behind; I had lost all feeling in my hands. Most of my energy was directed at just keeping up the pace they set. I put one foot before the other and thought of nothing else until nightfall, when we stopped to eat in a thick stand of pines. They were afraid of pursuit, so we had no fire that night. It was April, and spring in Pennsylvania is sometimes bitterly cold.

"The second day's march was even more arduous than the first, and John White Elk seemed to take peculiar delight in pulling tight that damnable tether. I consoled myself by plotting his death, and with the hope that Eben had somehow managed to escape. He had been playing by the creek the morning of the raid, and I felt there was a good chance he still lived.

"My hopes were dashed that night when the warriors made camp. I had eaten precious little for two days, nothing more than a handful of pemmican, a mixture of dried meat and berries ground fine together and mixed with fat. I was watching John White Elk, who sat close to the small fire, and wishing for some sort of weapon I could use against him, when he produced the trophy. He raised it high and shook it out so that the flaxen curls caught the ruddy glow of the fire. Then he set about stretching it over a birch rod hoop. It would have been hard not to recognize my brother's scalp. In that moment I had no more hope for Eben."

"How long were you a captive?" Catherine asked.

"I remained with John White Elk for almost two years. He had no compassion for the sullen white lad he had taken captive. One day he grew angry and tried to kill me, but his brother-in-law stepped in to prevent it, deflecting the blow. I lay unconscious for nearly a week. When I finally came to myself and began to recover, it was at Blue Jacket's Town, far from the Seneca village where I had been a captive. My new owner was Fire Hawk, a good man. He showed me kindness when I was friendless, and in turn I gave him my loyalty."

It all made sense. For the first time Catherine understood the subtle differences about Jase which had puzzled her. His noiseless tread, the guttural language he sometimes spoke, his allusions to a dark past ... "Why do you seek to hide your past?" Catherine asked. "Why do you keep the truth concealed behind a brittle facade?"

Jase uttered a soft, derisive snort. "You think I am some hard shell concealing a soft and liquid center, but you could not be more wrong." He straightened, turning slowly toward her as he touched his fist to his chest, speaking with silken savagery. "Inside this smooth skin lurks a wolf."

She did not flinch, did not hurry to put distance between them. She only stood before him, gazing at him with a curious half smile, completely undaunted by his cryptic pronouncement.

He had given her an intriguing glimpse into the

real Jase St. Claire. What she saw did not frighten her; it only made her long to sort through the many contradictions he displayed to find the truth, to understand the conflict within him. Slowly, she raised her hand and touched his weathered cheek. "Even wolves can be tamed, Jason."

He looked down into her small upturned face and knew that she had no idea of the effect she had upon him. Her touch was like a heated blade passing slowly through his flesh. It seared him, and the burning spread, seeping through his skin, dancing along his veins. . . .

Drawing a slow breath, he covered her hand with his. "What would you know of untamed things? You are an unsuspecting innocent. You haven't the courage to follow your heart, to set aside old alliances and forge new ones. You have propriety to consider, eh, mademoiselle of the prim and proper? A financé whom you adore."

She stiffened and withdrew. Jase released her hand, grinning cynically. Better that she recoil from him now, before it was too late. "You find it more palatable to remain the cold-fleshed virgin, true to your sainted love, than to dare something wild." He walked to the windows and folded his arms across his chest. When next he glanced at her, his control had tightened once more, and he was again aristocratic, arrogant, and aloof. "Your choice is wise, Catherine, for both of us. Your flesh is chill; I like my women warm."

His words hurt. "You fault me for respecting the pledge that binds me to another man! You are jealous, m'sieur, a dog in the manger."

Jase's answer was coldly calm. His gaze raked her trim form, lingering a little too long on the rapid rise and fall of her breasts. "I see you as being bound to no one. You were alone on the Trace the night I found you. Pray, tell me, mademoiselle, what manner of man lets his lady go off alone to battle the lion in his stead? If you're bound at all, then I'm bloody well certain you've bound yourself to a coward."

Catherine reacted before she could think. With all her might she slapped the very cheek she had a moment before caressed. "You think to label my fiancé a coward and thereby put yourself above him, you who freely admit to being a disreputable wolf. At least Alonzo Hart has nothing to hide! While you, m'sieur, slink and stalk and ride about doing the devil's work!"

In one fluid motion Jase closed the distance between them and stood towering over her. She could tell by his expression that he was sorely vexed, but her own anger was running high, and it swept her to new acts of daring. She stood toe to toe with him, returning glare for glare, not even showing surprise when his hands closed around her upper arms and she was crushed against him. "Were I your mate, you would never stray far from my side," he growled, "and never would you stray at all from my bed!"

Her defiance swiftly drove every ounce of mercy from him, and the kiss that Jase bestowed upon her tender lips was ruthless.

With lips and tongue and teeth he thoroughly ravaged her, stealing the breath from her lungs, subduing her once indomitable will. Catherine felt herself weakening; she was powerless against his seductive onslaught. Passion seeped druglike through her veins, sluggish and warm, heightening her senses, causing the world to rapidly retreat . . . until there was nothing in her awareness, nothing at all but Jase. . . .

Slowly, his mouth not giving an instant's reprieve, Jase bore Catherine backward, not pausing until her thighs came up against his desk . . . and then he was gradually pressing her down so that she lay among his scattered papers . . . edging up her skirts . . . worshiping her breasts with fervent ardor. . . .

"Mother of God," she breathed. He was a demon, an unholy seducer totally lacking in remorse, and he set her flesh to burning with a desire such as she had never before experienced. Alonzo had ceased to exist for her the moment Jason laid hands on her. There was no barrier remaining to keep them apart, no more resistance . . . nothing, save for the sharp little tugs he made at her breast, the taut need of her nipples.

Unable to bear Jase's attentions without responding, Catherine touched him. She entangled her hands in his hair—how silken it was!—pulling him closer, urging him onward. Down her hands roamed, marveling at the breadth of his shoulders, the sheer power contained in the corded muscles that flexed under her fingers. In Catherine's mind flashed unbidden that day a week ago when she watched him in the stables. She remembered how sleek he had appeared, how satiny his skin. She ached to touch him intimately, to run her fingers across his hard-muscled chest and feel his small erect nipples abrade the sensitive skin of her palms.

Mindless of anything but her sudden impulsive need, she moved her hands around to his shirt-front and began the painstaking business of unfastening his fine linen shirt. Gradually the creamy shirt parted, revealed his collarbone, his breast-bone, one finely contoured pectoral.

While Jase looked down in wonder, Catherine's pink tongue crept out to moisten her lips. She was lying prone beneath him, her skirts hiked up to mid-thigh, and she resembled more a lush sacrifice to his starved senses than what she was in actuality: a tumbled virgin, unaware of what was about to transpire between them and the changes their actions would bring about. She was so different from Angela, who was cool and controlled, even in bed.

Catherine was bright and impetuous and volatile, totally enchanting, utterly maddening. She pushed him beyond the bounds dictated by wisdom, then pushed him again. Her every utterance, every glance ... hell! Every breath she drew demanded a reaction from him. He was the gunpowder and she was a flaming brand.

Watching her face as she pulled his shirt free, Jase felt the pressure building in his loins increase. The pain of resisting her was quickly becoming unbearable. He ceased even to breathe as small, tingling sparks electrified his skin, as his muscles contracted of their own accord.

His rigid control swiftly evaporated.

At first he had intended to carry her off to his bed, to devote the night to making her shudder and sigh, but that had changed the moment she placed her small, deft hands upon him. His skin, famished for human touch, drank up the sensations she aroused and clamored for more. Jase closed his eyes and breathed harshly again, pulled himself up just enough to brush aside her skirts, to loosen his belt and his breeches.

The desk would do just fine. The unyielding wooden surface lacked the comforts provided by a large feather bed, but driven by his fierce need to possess her, Jase was beyond caring. It mattered little where he took her, so long as he did, so long as he could bury this passion-born ache deep inside her.

Caught beneath Jase's lean, muscular frame, Catherine was only half aware of what was happening. As soon as he had claimed her lips, reality had receded, leaving a strange languor which she didn't care to shake. It sharpened her senses and honed her needs, while dulling her inhibitions. In that dreamy state she felt her skirts being drawn up over her hips, felt the heat of his hand as it slid slowly up her inner thigh.

Her skin prickled deliciously beneath his questing touch. Somewhere deep inside she knew that she should stop him from caressing her so intimately. It was the same stubborn part of her that sought to hold Alonzo as her ideal, despite her undeniable attraction for Jase, but it was not strong enough to withstand his unique method of persuasion. One by one, her objections sank beneath the waves of carnal pleasure.

Jase was not Alonzo. There was nothing safe about him. But instead of frightening Catherine, the knowledge increased her excitement. Through her lashes she watched as her dangerous lover lifted her hips and brought her to him, his dark face a mask of tension. . . . He was going to mount her, as Sadist had the mare. A wonderfully wicked thrill chased through her, causing her to catch her breath.

An urgent rapping shattered the intimacy of the moment. "Sir! Master St. Claire, sir. There is someone to see you."

With a small cry, Catherine struggled up, rearranging her skirts and tugging her bodice back into place. Crimson-faced, she slid off the desk and went to stand before the bookshelves, pretending interest in the wide range of titles, her back to the door.

With angry jerks, Jase refastened his trousers and slipped into his shirt, cursing low and violently as he did so. Finally he stalked to the doors and threw them wide. "What the devil is so important?" he demanded.

Leviticus spoke rapidly in a low voice. Catherine heard the tone, but was too embarrassed to listen carefully. She stood very still, her back rigid, horribly aware of what had almost happened and fervently wishing that she possessed the power to disappear. Jase's reply was a low growl. "Tell Mrs. Dane I am indisposed."

Jase would have closed the door in Leviticus's face had Catherine not intervened. "No, wait! Please, m'sieur," she said without looking at Jase, "see to your company. Our discussion is over in any case, and I'm afraid I've suddenly taken ill."

Avoiding the servant's knowing glance, she fled

the room. She went swiftly, gathering her wrinkled skirts above her ankles and hardly sparing a second's glance toward the strikingly attractive brunette who calmly observed the scene.

By the time Catherine reached the sanctity of her chamber, her legs were trembling and would no longer support her weight. With the solid door at her back, she slid to the floor and covered her burning face with her hands.

Chapter 13

Moments after the girl's flight, Jase entered the parlor. The brief delay gave Angela time to compose her thoughts and decide upon the tack to take with her recalcitrant lover.

She sensed that feigned indignation or jealous demands would in no way bring about a satisfactory arrangement between them, for Jase was not a man to be manipulated by feminine wiles or swayed by a show of tears. Truth to tell, she had no secure ground on which to stand, and she knew it.

Their affair had been brief and purely physical, an assuagement of mutual needs. When they had chanced to talk at all, it had been of inconsequential things, never of Angela's husband or Jase's life. Indeed, during the seven months of their involvement, Jase had never shared a morsel of himself beyond his sexual prowess—he had guarded his thoughts and dreams as jealously as a miser guards his gold.

Not that it mattered to Angela. She was content in her marriage to Harbridge Dane. Harbridge remained a good provider, gave her security, a fine home, powerful alliances, worshiped her youthful beauty. . . . Only one element was lacking in their marriage, and it was something that Jase could easily provide.

The ring of bootheels alerted Angela to Jase's arrival. Taking a fortifying breath, she turned away, pretending to admire a small figurine on the mantel.

"Angela," Jase greeted her coolly, firmly closing the door. "What brings you to Rosemunde? Some trouble at home?"

She turned and offered him a knowing smile. He was wondering if Harbridge had gotten wind of their relationship. "Nothing so grave as all that, Jase. Actually, I came to congratulate you on your betrothal. It seems that my timing is somewhat faulty, for 'tis obvious that my visit has disrupted your evening." She shrugged and gave a lazy smile. "I can't say that I'm sorry for it though. I've had a glimpse of your bride and doubt I'd have been given the opportunity otherwise. She is lovely, Jase. By the by, when is the wedding?"

Jase went to the sideboard and poured a generous glass of whiskey for himself and a half glass of sherry for his guest. Her presence was an annoyance on this, of all evenings, but he held his irritation in check, even forced a stilted civility into his manner. Until this moment, he'd had no intention of breaking it off with Angela. The arrangement was much to his liking—there were no attachments or expectations, no guilt. Angela was lush and eager, a vessel in which to funnel his pent-up desires when they troubled him too greatly, and if that vessel had been oft-used by others, then so much the better. Virgins posed endless problems, a fact of which Jase was at this moment most painfully aware.

Offering the sherry to Angela, he went to lean one shoulder against the mantel, bolting his whiskey before making a reply. "I expect the whole matter to be resolved very soon." A pretty evasion of the facts.

"You do not sound eager," Angela said, keeping all but the faintest hope from entering her voice.

"Don't I?" He tipped back his dark head in a futile effort to release the tension which throbbed in his neck and shoulders. "I suppose I am weary, Angela. It's been a damnably trying day."

She set aside her glass and moved to where he stood, her skirts making a sensuous swish as the fabric brushed against her shapely limbs. "Perhaps I can help," she said quietly, running her finely boned hands up his spine to his shoulders.

His knotted muscles felt like granite, unyielding to the touch. Slowly Angela began to work them, an easy kneading exercise which before long would soothe what ailed them both. She felt rather than heard his sigh, but his tension did not seem to lessen. In a moment he turned and gently forced down her hands, moved impatiently away. "Not tonight, Angela."

"My," she said, "you really *are* tired."

Tired of the pretense, Jase thought. Tired of being vigilant lest someone see something telling in his mannerism, as Catherine had, some vestige of the Black Lion in the man he was today. "Another time," he said in an effort to put her off.

"Yes, of course." She forced a smile, but dread closed 'round her. She had erred in coming here tonight. Something cataclysmic had occurred between Jase and his enchanting slip of a bride, something that had affected him more deeply than a simple quarrel. There was only one possible explanation, and that notion turned her cold. He was in love with her.

"It would be foolish of me to expect you to come to me again, wouldn't it, Jase?" She saw him frown and hurried on. "Oh, you don't have to answer. I can see it in your eyes."

Jase downed the last swallow of his whiskey and stood frowning into the empty glass. What was wrong with him? he wondered. Angela was here, and she had it in her power to ease his torment.

Yet here he stood, embracing the very rack upon which he daily received a fine measure of torture . . . for even the suffering was exquisite where Catherine was concerned.

"Go home, Angela," he said. "I have neither the time nor the patience to be sociable this evening."

"If that's what you wish, I'll go." But instead of making her exit, she put her small hands against the flat of his belly and moved them downward as she gazed steadily into his wintry eyes. "I'll go," she said. "But first I ask you to remember what it was like between us." She strained to her toes and, fitting her lush form fully against him, kissed him long and languorously.

Jase remained curiously detached. Where was the raging lust that had beleaguered his senses in the library this very night? he wondered. His mind was quick to answer.

All of his longing, all of his desires, had traveled with Catherine up the long curving stairway to her silken boudoir.

Knowing the truth was cold consolation.

Angela ended her vain attempt at seduction, lowered her hands to her sides, and made to step away, but not before Jase caught her fingers and raised them to his lips, lightly kissing each in turn.

She remained dry-eyed despite her bitter disappointment, still the practiced courtesan she'd always been. "Take care, won't you, Jase, not to fall in love with your little bride. Love has no place in a marriage. It distracts the mind and wrings an unbearable anguish from the unwary heart." She smiled up at him, perhaps a bit wryly. "That's why I've sought so hard to avoid it in my own marriage."

"I'll send word to my stablehand to see you home," Jase said.

"I would rather you didn't," Angela said. "I came with a heavily armed guard. Harbridge insisted."

"Harbridge knew you were coming here?"

Angela squeezed his hands. "You need not worry," she said. "Our secret is safe. He thinks I'm bound for Tom's, which I am, roundabout. Rebecca is still in a tizzy over an altercation she had with Barbara Sawhill, and I thought I could help." She saw Jase's grimace at the mention of Rebecca's name and laughed lightly. "Yes, I know. Rebecca is spirited. But she is also my brother's only child."

Jase walked with her to the front entrance, accepting her peck on his cheek with his usual gravity. "Should you change your mind, I'll be waiting," she said.

"I'll remember. Good night, Angela."

When she was gone, Jase raised his eyes to the stairwell and thought of going to Catherine. . . .

But what would he say?

That he desired her, lusted after her, needed her as he had never needed anyone? That much she already knew. And to tell her that he loved her would be absurd.

What the devil was love anyway except a heavy dose of misery? He wasn't altogether sure he'd not rather have the French pox. He stood for a brief interval at the foot of the stairs, torn between his desires and cold logic. Yet the only revelation that came to him was that his restraint was wearing precariously thin.

He had to leave, to get out of the house!

If he stayed another minute, he would likely do something he would regret.

Reentering the library, he tried hard not to think of what had occurred there earlier in the evening. Carelessly, he rifled through his desk. In the second drawer was a brace of pistols which he removed and thrust through his belt. As he took up his coat, Leviticus came to hover in the doorway. "Will you be going out tonight, sir?"

Jase met the other man's eyes. "Aye. And I may be gone for several days. I'm to rendezvous with Wools Burke just north of here, then I'm headed for the Sandler place. I've a nagging suspicion there is something I may have overlooked. After that—well, I can't say."

"What shall I say to Miss Catherine, should she inquire after you?"

"I expect she will be relieved to hear of my absence," Jase said flatly. "However, I give you leave to tell her whatever you like, Leviticus—so long as it's not the truth." Slipping on his coat, Jase left the house without a backward glance.

Leviticus doused the candle flames one by one, then slowly made his way to the back of the house and the small rooms that served as his quarters. "Rest assured, sir," he said softly to himself, "you may depend upon Dora and me."

Catherine wasn't sure how long she stayed crouched miserably on the floor, except that by the time her sobs had ceased and she regained the strength to rise and make her way to the bed, the house had grown quiet. Not even bothering to disrobe, she flung herself on the bed, burying her tear-ravaged face in her pillow and trying not to think about what had so nearly occurred in the library.

It proved impossible, however, to forget how Jase had made her feel . . . a fact that compounded her guilt.

It had been inadvisable to enter his lair. She recognized that now. Foolish in the extreme to accept from him a single shred of solace.

Something was happening to her, something unlike anything she had experienced in her lifetime, and it frightened her. She had persuaded him to reveal facets of his life she had no right to know. He had admitted having done things in which he took no pride. That single admission should have warned her away, yet it didn't seem to matter. Nothing mattered when she was with him. It was almost as if the outside world ceased to exist ... leaving only Jason's dark good looks ... his sensual mystery ... his triumph over his tragic beginnings. ...

She had no right to care about him; but she did care, and deeply. The way he touched her, the things he said, his kindness and his callousness, all heightened her awareness of him, added to her confusion.

What was to become of her? She was engaged to one man, and falling in love with another.

And that other was a man, she was certain, who did not love her. He wanted to possess her, to slake his passion in her arms as he would with any willing woman, with no thought of honor or decency. He would ruin her if she allowed it, and what frightened her most of all was the niggling suspicion that some dark part of her might rejoice at that ruination if it meant belonging to Jase St. Claire even for a little while.

Despite the warmth of the evening, Catherine shuddered.

The thought of how perilously close she had come to betraying Alonzo brought on a fresh flow of tears. Dear, unsuspecting Alonzo! She had forgotten him the instant Jase's mouth covered her own.

What manner of man sends his lady out alone to do battle with the lion? Jase's words lashed her already lacerated feelings. A man who'd been duped, lied to! A man she'd sorely betrayed. ...

A moment more and she would have let Jase

abscond with that which rightfully belonged to
Alonzo. And what would have followed his thiev-
ery? Boldly Jase had stated that if she were his,
she would not venture far from his side, and not
at all from his bed. Now, lying full length on her
own feather bed, Catherine stiffened at the implication in those words. Not once had the word *marriage* passed his hedonistic lips. And had she been
foolish enough to question him on it, he likely
would have laughed in her face.

What he had promised was far less binding than
marriage, and totally unacceptable to her. Yet had
it not been for the timely arrival of his guest, she
would have awoken tomorrow in his bed, and in
disgrace.

She thought of the strikingly beautiful brunette
and wondered who she was, about her relationship to Jason St. Claire. She owed that woman a
debt of gratitude for having saved her from herself.

All along she had known it was wrong to remain at Rosemunde, and yet something had kept
her here against her better judgment. Now she
had no choice but to leave. It was the one way to
thwart the disaster she saw looming. And so, with
characteristic impetuosity, she seized what she
viewed as salvation with both hands.

The breeches and shirt she had worn when
starting out with Mose were tucked away in the
wardrobe, carefully mended by Dora. Catherine
plucked them up and jerked them on, anxious to
be on her way.

From outside came the sound of a carriage pulling down the gravel drive, and she surmised that

the lately arrived guest must now be leaving. Following close upon the coach was the strange warbling call that she had heard on the morning that Jase had come home injured. Breeches and shirt hastily fastened, Catherine sped to the window in time to see the mysterious master of Rosemunde Plantation standing on the lawn beneath her very window. He was bathed in the silvery light of the incandescent moon; its bright beams reflected softly off his midnight mane, cast a deep black slash beneath his high cheekbones, shone like pale starlight in his translucent eyes.

Quicksilver and shadow he was, at once beautiful and lethal.

A shiver crept up Catherine's spine, causing her to hug her upper arms. She knew she should look away, but at this moment that simple act was beyond her power.

Out on the lawn, a hulking figure materialized from the shadow cast by the live oak trees which overhung the stables. It was Jase's groom leading the Spanish black. The two men met a short distance from the house and for a moment they stood in intense conversation. Their voices floated to Catherine on the soft night wind, Jase's a low and indistinguishable murmur, the big man's a rumble like distant thunder.

"Should be damn good night for what ye're about," the groom said. "A bonny big moon to light yer way."

Jase said something in reply that made his companion turn his head and spit derisively.

"Cunning bastard leaves a bloody trail behind him. Almost seems to be begging to be caught."

He patted the stallion's shining black neck and handed the reins to Jase, who vaulted into the saddle with savage grace.

"Good hunting, sir!" the groom called out.

Standing at the window, concealed in shadow, Catherine watched the Spanish black lunge forward.

She remained by the window until the horse and rider were no longer visible. To become further embroiled in Jase's life was to court certain disaster. Leaving would be difficult, and she already felt a pang that she would not see the shy and likable Dora again, nor the stalwart Leviticus. She had purposely become a buffer between master and servant, and she could not help but wonder how they would fare in her absence.

But it was none of her concern, and not reason enough to remain.

Catherine looked around the room, then, tucking the ice-green gown under her arm, she hurriedly left before she could reconsider.

Chapter 14

Compared with her first aborted attempt at escape, this time Catherine's departure from Rosemunde was incredibly easy.

This time there was no Leviticus traversing the hallway, and out on the grounds the moon shone bright. Haste last time had led to her downfall; now she was more cautious.

Remembering the big man who had brought the stallion to Jase, she crept quietly to the stable's westernmost wall, where she melted into the shadows and paused to regulate her breathing, listening all the while to the soft rustling noises coming from inside the building. Finally she made her stealthy way to the small window set high in the stable wall.

The wavering light of a tallow lamp flooded from the window, pooling weakly on the grass at her booted feet. Cautiously, she edged forward to peer inside.

The groom was slumped on a pallet of moldering straw, his powerful legs stretched out before him and crossed at the ankles. In his hand, all but hidden by his meaty fist, was a small brown bottle. By the looks of it, it was already half empty.

As Catherine continued to watch, he tipped back his head and belched, then drank again. Each time he tilted the bottle, his posture slumped a little more, until finally her patience was rewarded and he slid sideways down the wall. As Catherine crept away from the wall, she heard him utter the first of what proved to be prodigious snores.

The noise seemed loud enough to rattle the rafters, and certainly sufficient to block out any slight stirring she might cause among the animals.

Satisfied now that her efforts would be met with success, she crossed to the entrance and ducked inside the barn.

Windows were considered an extravagance in a stable, but Jason St. Claire could well afford them. Moonlight screamed in through the wavy glass, turning the shadows to a penetrable gray. For two swift strokes of her heart, Catherine stood just inside the door, looking carefully around. Her quick search yielded no raven-haired satyr with pale eyes that shone like moonbeams, no maddening grin prompted by her inability to outmaneuver him . . . only stall upon stall of warm and smelly horseflesh. . . .

Near the middle of the long room she found what she was seeking, a doe-eyed little bay mare who poked her nose over the boards to nudge Catherine's sleeve.

She stroked the velvet muzzle, reaching up to scratch behind the horse's ears. The animal remained docile, standing patiently as the stall door was opened, a halter was slipped over her head,

and then she biddably followed Catherine from
the barn.

. To lift the heavy saddles stored in the barn
seemed too great an effort, and too risky. Each
minute that ticked by made discovery more likely
. . . gave her another opportunity to reconsider
what she was doing . . . to weigh the dangers of
the road against the danger of Jase's touch.

She led the mare to a mounting block in the
stableyard and hopped up on its broad back.
Then, with the ice-green gown held firmly between her thighs, she clucked to the animal and
started off down the long and winding drive.

As luck would have it, the journey into town
was entirely uneventful. Only once did she
glimpse another traveler, a lone man on horseback. She heard him long before she saw him, for
he was whistling as he rode along. It provided her
the opportunity to guide her mount off the path
behind a clump of bushes. Through the sparse
branches she watched his black-coated figure pass
by, but she remained in hiding until he was a good
distance away.

By half past eight the next morning she was
standing on Franklin Street in Natchez, gazing up
at the black-lacquered door of Alonzo Hart's
house, well aware that behind that gleaming door
lay her future.

Catching her bottom lip between her teeth, she
tried to rid herself of the unsettling notion that
once she passed through that portal, there could
be no turning back. She shook her head to clear it,
certain that this queer feeling of trepidation would
pass as soon as she saw Alonzo's face.

Tying the reins to the wrought iron gate, Catherine took a deep breath and mounted the steps.

She raised the brass knocker and let it fall three times. Doubts about her decision crowded in on her. Perhaps Alonzo was not even home. She turned and started down the steps toward the waiting mare when the door was suddenly jerked open.

"What in Christ's name is so important!" Alonzo stood in the doorway, clad only in breeches and stockings, a towel draped over one shoulder. His lower face was lathered with soap, and Catherine surmised that he must have been shaving. He looked hard at her, then his brows shot up as realization dawned. "My God ... Cathy?"

His voice held not the slightest trace of warmth or welcome. She tried to put it down to the shock of finding her disheveled on his doorstep, coated with a layer of reddish dust, the golden hair which had once brushed her hips now shorn to a point just above her rapidly pinkening ears.

Hugging the wrinkled ice-green gown to her breast, she fought down her rising disappointment. Whatever reaction she had expected from him, it was not this. But the hope that she had made the right decision in coming refused to die. "Alonzo," she said, forcing a stiff smile onto her lips, "will you ask me in, or shall I take my ease here on the stoop?"

Alonzo blinked, and it seemed as if a veil settled over his sharp black eyes. His initial amazement, his expression of mild distaste, at once vanished. "Of course, Cathy, come in!" He grasped her by the arm and pulled her past him through the door, then hurriedly closed it. Holding her at arm's length, he looked her over, his critical gaze lingering on her shorn locks. "What has happened to you, and what on earth are you doing here?"

Catherine was tired beyond belief, and his questions nettled her. "Had I anticipated the reception I would receive from you, after six weeks of separation, I would have gone elsewhere. Belatedly, I recognize my mistake in coming here, but that is easily rectified."

Catherine spun on her booted heel and started for the door, bringing Alonzo to his senses. He had worked too hard to secure his future to allow it to slip away. "Cathy, please. I didn't mean it the way it must have sounded. Come in, dear heart, and tell me how you are." He guided her toward the parlor, to a pale green brocade settee where he urged her down and into his arms. He kissed her, trying to ignore the sandy grit on her lips and the pungent odor of horse that clung to her clothing.

Closing her eyes as her fiancé's cool lips were pressed to hers, she waited for the sweet languor she had experienced in Jase's arms to steal through her veins ... Patiently, she waited for the rest of the world to recede, leaving only the two of them, locked together in passion's wild embrace.

It did not happen.

Alonzo's mouth pressed hers tightly, yet Catherine remained acutely aware of all that went on around her. The rhythmic tick of the mantel clock seemed extraordinarily loud in the otherwise quiet room. Outside, a carriage rattled by and two young women called greetings to each other.

Distracted, feeling strangely unsettled of a sudden, Catherine pushed Alonzo away and stood up.

He chuckled. "Yes, of course," he said, "you will be wanting to freshen up, won't you? And there will be plenty of time for us to become reacquainted later. I'll ring for Clara, and she'll heat water for your bath. Afterward, you can explain." He went to the parlor doorway and tugged sharply on the satin bell rope which summoned the housekeeper.

In a moment a great lump of a woman with a sour expression on her sagging face showed herself in the doorway. She said nothing, just waited for instructions. Catherine disliked her instantly, and as the woman's piggy eyes traveled over Catherine's outlandish garb and short hair, she was certain the sentiment was fully returned.

Catherine thought quite suddenly of timid and friendly Dora, who by now would have noted her departure, and hoped Jase's housekeeper was not too upset at finding her gone. She listened to Alonzo instructing the woman to arrange a bath for the future Mrs. Hart in the guest room. "Now," he said, once Clara had departed, "perhaps you'll explain how you come to be so far from your Aunt Thea's in Mobile, and dressed like the worst sort of urchin."

Catherine drew a deep breath before answering. It seemed that Alonzo and Jase shared at least one thing—an intense aversion to her choice of attire. Thinking of Jase brought him instantly to mind, and it was with that dark, sardonic face flickering in her thoughts that Catherine related a partially fabricated tale of robbery and Mose's kidnapping, careful to avoid any mention of her rescuer.

"It happened two weeks ago," she said in conclusion. "I took a bump on the head and awoke in the care of a farmer and his wife. They were kind enough to lend me a horse and these clothes so that I might reach Natchez." She paused, trying to gauge Alonzo's reaction. He seemed to accept the story at face value. Pray God he did not question her.

"Then you lost your baggage?" he said after a moment.

"Yes," she replied, glancing down and remembering the ice-green gown balled in her lap. "All except this. The farmer's wife found it lying near the place where I fell."

"How very fortuitous," Alonzo observed, "for you not to have lost everything to these desperate robbers." As he took Catherine's hand in his, he thought of all he would have lost had she been killed and her fortune reverted to Thea Alvarez. "Indeed," he said, squeezing the dainty but dusty appendage, "we both have much to be thankful for."

Something in his manner caused Catherine's spine to prickle. It was nothing she could lay a finger on, just the odd impression that his words held some unguessed at double meaning.

Later, while soaking in a warm tub, she tried to determine if the feeling was real or simply imagined. Her mind, however, lulled by the relaxation of the scented bath, refused to cooperate, and turned instead in a direction she would rather have avoided.

In a few hours the sun would be setting on the white columns of Rosemunde. Had its owner returned yet to find her gone? How would he react? Had he railed at poor Dora and sent her scurrying for cover? Was he even now threatening Leviticus with the loss of his job? Or was he simply relieved to find she was gone from his house, from his life?

Leaning back, Catherine closed her eyes and tried to picture Jase in anger, yet all she could see was the way he had looked the night before, his handsome features taut with need.

Jase met Wools Burke at half past midnight on the moon-dappled path that was their usual rendezvous point, then rode directly to the Sandler farm.

An eerie quiet prevailed over the clearing. He stood for a while, staring at the charred remains of Sandler's modest home, the three fresh mounds of earth and stone that comprised the victims' graves, and felt the old feelings of rage and grief well up inside him. For an instant he was transported back to his boyhood home in Castle Ford, where another smoking sentinel stood stark and black against a blue morning sky.

Now, the wooded hills and vales of the Ohio Country for which he'd fought rang with the song of the ax and the laughter of children instead of Indian war cries and musket fire; the mighty voice of the eastern tribes was still. The Choctaw and Chickasaw, whose settlements made up the heart of the Mississippi Territory, were at peace with the whites.

Jase stared down at the smallest grave. He had

never made war upon women and children, but someone had, gleefully. Turning away from the fresh mounds of earth, Jase pushed down the anger, the bitter regret, the memory of the smoldering remains of that other cabin flanked by the smoky blue Allegheny hills. He forced himself to think logically.

There had been five killings so far. Elias Drake had been the first to fall prey to the impostor. Drake had been shot and mortally wounded not far from Natchez, but like Andre Breaux, he'd lived long enough to relate his tale of robbery and murder.

As the Black Lion, Jase had helped lay siege to the Drake blockhouse on the Scioto River. But that had been long ago, and far from here, and so he had at first dismissed the connection as mere coincidence.

Andre Breaux was the next to die. The young Frenchman's death had seemed a random killing. But was it? Jase now wondered. If, as Catherine claimed, it had been committed by the man impersonating the Black Lion, then there must be some link to his past which he failed to see.

He dismissed it for the moment, returning to the obvious.

The Sandlers' farm had been carefully chosen as a target, a deliberate taunt that prodded at Jase's anger. Wools, who had infiltrated the group, said there had been three men beside himself; they had not worked independently, but had awaited the arrival of the leader at a prearranged time and place. Clearly Jase was dealing with a coldly calculating mind, not a madman. The strikes were following an emerging pattern; by closely examining events of the past, he might be able to determine where the outlaw would strike next ... and be there waiting.

He felt hopeful as he walked toward the ruined cabin.

There was little remaining of the mean dwelling. The roof was gone, the walls partially burned away. Charred beams lay scattered on the scorched grass. Jase searched the smoking remains with care; nothing had been touched, it seemed, nothing stolen.

He finished quickly and ducked through an uneven hole framed by a sagging beam, glad for the clean night air that helped to erase the stench of smoke from his lungs.

His search the previous day had been cursory. He'd been there only moments when Tom Galliher had arrived, and there had been the burials to see to. He'd been wary of arousing suspicion. No one but Catherine knew that he was searching for the killer; he wanted to keep it that way.

If the killer felt safe from capture, he would be more likely to make a mistake.

As Jase rounded the corner, something moved in the deep shadows of the building. He pulled a pistol from his belt. "Step away from there, into the moonlight."

A tall man, painfully thin, materialized. His hair was lank and black, and whiskers dusted his hollow cheeks and bony chin. "Sir," he said in a deep, resonant voice, "you would not harm the Lord's messenger."

Jase kept the pistol trained on the figure, but

eased his stance a bit. "Who are you? And what business have you here?"

"I might ask those very questions of you, good sir," the man replied. "Since you are armed, and I am not, whose motives are more suspect?" When the pistol didn't waver, he chuckled dryly. "All right then, since you insist. I am the Reverend Hezekiah Rose, at your service. As for my business here, I have come to bless the dead. No Christian soul should be denied the benefit of God's Word to speed his passage unto the Kingdom of Heaven."

Hezekiah Rose looked at Jase with eyes so dark that no pupils showed. "And you, good sir?" he said. "You have yet to state your business. Although, since you come bearing weapons, I might guess you do other than the Lord's work. Hath no one told you that he who liveth by the sword shall die by the sword also?"

"One can only hope so, Reverend." Jase indicated the shell of the house with a nod. "What do you know of this? Are you a friend of the Sandlers?"

"You are full of questions, friend," Hezekiah answered. He hesitated a moment, then asked, "Are *you* a friend? It does not seem likely."

Jase lowered the pistol, thrusting it into his belt, though his hand didn't stray from the worn walnut grip.

Hezekiah went on reluctantly. "Edgar Sandler was one of my flock, a good man whom I trust has gone to his reward, along with his beloved wife and son. I often shared a meal with them while en route to Natchez. As it happens, I was here just last night."

"Indeed?" Jase said. "And how did you leave them, Reverend?"

"I left them at dusk, good sir. In good health and pure of spirit."

"Do you often travel the Trace?"

"I do. It is my mission to carry God's Truth into dens of iniquity and spread the Light wherever I go." He looked hard at Jase, and a ghost of a smile played over his thin lips. "What are you searching for?"

"Good night, Reverend." Jase turned to go, but Rose called him back.

"Are you on the side of Right? Or bent upon destruction?"

"I haven't time for your pious mouthings, Reverend Rose. There are matters which demand my attention." Jase strode across the level ground to the copse where Sadist waited. He led the stallion into the open and swung easily into the saddle.

Hezekiah Rose had followed, and reached out to grasp the black's bridle "Wait. This animal, have you had him long?"

Jase frowned. Hezekiah Rose's black eyes shone with keen interest. "Why do you wish to know?"

"Have faith, sir," Hezekiah answered. "When did you come by him?"

"Two years past."

"You were in the shallow draw just northwest of here a few nights ago, where a cabin was burned. You chased a man on foot until this animal refused to cross a stream and threw you."

There was but one way for Rose to know the

events of that evening. But the scarecrow figure in black coat and breeches did not fit the image of the man Jase remembered. "How do you know of it?"

Hezekiah's smile broadened. "Verily, sir. God is good! I think I may be able to help you." He fished inside his long black coat and produced a small ball of light-colored cloth, which he offered to Jase.

It was a kerchief of faded blue; the inner crease was stained vermilion, and it was similar to the kerchief he had worn during his days as the Black Lion to conceal the livid red scar on his brow. With time the scar had faded and Jase grew accustomed to the imperfection. But someone had remembered. Someone linked to his violent past. "How did you come by this?" he asked at last.

"It was given to me by a friend who finds himself in a most uncomfortable position. He was the one you chased that night."

"Why did he run?"

"Put yourself in his position, friend. A sinister stranger on a huge steed charging after you. Would you stand your ground and risk death?"

Jase snorted. "I meant only to question him."

Hezekiah spread his hands. "He knows not whom to trust."

"Was he a witness to one of the murders attributed to the Black Lion?" Jase demanded.

Hezekiah nodded gravely.

"Then you must bring him to me."

"I am afraid that is impossible. He is ill, unable to ride. Even if he could, I cannot in good conscience deliver him up to you. I must be vigilant.

Satan ofttimes cloaks himself in the guise of good to fool the unwary."

There was nothing unwary about this itinerant man of the cloth, Jase thought. But time was running out, and he had gained little ground this night. He pocketed the kerchief, and speaking low to Sadist, nudged the stallion into a slow walk. "Speak to your friend, Reverend. Soon."

"I will indeed," Hezekiah said in his ringing voice. "You might come to me in Natchez, sir. We will speak again. I am venturing to that Babylon, Silver Street. Why, the very name leaves a vile taste upon my tongue!"

Chapter 15

By midmorning the next day, Jase returned to Rosemunde. Nearly ten hours on horseback and the meeting with Hezekiah Rose had left him in a curious frame of mind. If Rose was telling the truth, then he was harboring a witness to one of the killings . . . the black man Jase had tried to apprehend near the outlaws' rendezvous, the man he thought might be Mose Aubrey, Catherine's friend.

He had no proof yet, but if the servant had holed up somewhere with the aid of Hezekiah Rose, it would certainly explain why Jase had been unable to turn up any clues concerning Mose's whereabouts.

Jase would give Rose a little time in which to convince his "friend" to share the information he possessed, and would speak with the reverend again in a day or two. In the meantime he needed to rest and prepare for this evening's ride.

Joshua MacLeemer's farm was not far from Bayou Pierre. Going there to watch and wait was a gamble, but one Jase felt he had to make. It fit the pattern, being fairly isolated ... and the name was familiar. There had been a MacLeemer's Landing on the western Pennsylvania border which had been put to the torch in 1792 by a Shawnee raiding party. Two men had been killed and one wounded, and several captives had been taken who were later ransomed back by their families.

He could be mistaken about the connection, Jase thought, but it was too obvious to ignore.

Soon this long ordeal would be over. He would resume the peaceful existence he had built here at Rosemunde, and Catherine would ... Catherine would what? Go back to Alonzo?

The idea brought a scowl to Jase's face. He couldn't imagine what she saw in Alonzo Hart to make her want to marry him. He was a womanizing bastard who would give her no end of grief.

If she married him. She was determined to do so, but Jase knew she'd be better off if the anticipated marriage never took place. Her infatuation with Alonzo would pass in time. Jase remained convinced that that was all it was, an infatuation. Had she loved Alonzo, she would not have come so close to making love with him last night.

He glanced up at Catherine's window. She would be performing her toilette in preparation for breakfast. In his mind's eye he saw her soft and curvy form draped in the dark silk dressing gown, saw the garment part and fall away to pool around her slender feet.

The mental image quickened his steps as he led Sadist to the stable. She would be eager to learn about the events of last night, or at least the portions he could safely relate to her, and it would be cruel to make her wait until breakfast.

Bobby Means came from the stable; Jase handed the reins into his keeping. "Walk him a bit to cool him down," Jase said. "He's had a hard run these last few miles."

Means accepted the reins, but ducked his head and didn't meet Jase's eyes. "There's somethin' you ought to know before you go in, sir."

Jase frowned. Means's manner gave him a hollow feeling in the pit of his stomach.

"The new mare is missing, sir," Means said. "Gone from her stall."

"Missing? How the hell could she be missing?" Before the words had left Jase's mouth, he knew the answer. Swearing softly, he turned toward the house.

His angry strides carried him down the hall and up the stairs in a trice. He went directly to Catherine's door and, not bothering to knock, flung it open, knowing very well what he would find yet hoping he was wrong.

The room was in perfect order. The counterpane was neatly spread over the large feather bed, which had not been slept in.

His mood becoming blacker by the moment, Jase stalked across the room and threw wide the wardrobe doors, scowling at the contents. The gowns which he had commissioned from Barbara Sawhill were neatly hung inside, vying for space with frilly chemises, stockings, slippers, and hair ribbons. She had taken nothing with her.

"Those bloody breeches," Jase muttered darkly

to himself. "I should have burned them while I had the chance."

A soft sniffle sounded from the hallway, interrupting his inspection. Jase looked up to see Dora standing in the doorway. Her eyes and nose were red from crying, and a wrinkled handkerchief was wadded up in one fist. "When did she leave, Dora?"

"Last night, sir. I came to rouse her this morning and knew ... Oh, Mr. St. Claire, you don't think she has met with some calamity, do you? Leviticus and I have been beside ourselves with worry!"

Jase closed the wardrobe doors, saying nothing. He doubted Catherine had come to harm upon the fleet-footed mare. But the possibility did exist.

"Sir?" Dora urged in her naturally hesitant manner.

Jase met her gaze. "No," he said, "I don't think she's come to harm." He sighed and raked an agitated hand through his hair, remembering with sickening clarity Catherine's insistence just last night upon seeing Governor Sargent. Was she even now raising a hue and cry for his own capture? There must be a way to prevent her from creating more mischief.

"Is there aught for us to do, sir? Shouldn't we search for her?"

Dora was mercilessly wringing her handkerchief into a tight ropelike strand—not unlike a noose, to Jase's mind. "I'll see to it myself, Dora. Instruct Leviticus to bring a bath up for me, and see if there's anything in Aunt Sade's kitchen to save a man from starvation."

Dora bustled off, her fading sniffles marking her progress through the house.

Jase wandered to the foot of the bed to lean against the bedpost. The wood was cool against his skin, and brought to mind another night when he had stood at the foot of this very bed, watching its occupant sleep. Matters had been less complicated then, his only goal to keep Catherine out of the way long enough to find the person responsible for the recent rash of murders along the Trace. But that was before she opened her eyes and began to weave her magic spell around him.

Her beauty and her spirit had bewitched him; without her he was lost.

His hand tightening around the post, Jase saw again a tumbled Catherine lying prone across the paper-littered surface of his desk, lips parted and breath coming in swift gasps.

The way she returned his kisses, the manner in which she slid her fingers across his bare skin, told Jase more surely than words that she desired him. And it came to him that had Angela not interrupted, Catherine would be here with him now. But Angela *had* interrupted, and Catherine had been given time to think about the consequences of making love with him.

He raked a hand through his tousled hair. She was always worrying over her reputation, what was proper and what was not. What had she felt last night? Anger at his insistence? Panic because she had yielded so easily? Guilt because she had nearly betrayed her fiancé?

Distracted, Jase left the room and went downstairs to the dining room, where Dora was fussing about the table, positioning his plate and laying the napkin and utensils. He thanked her and sat down in his usual place.

The chair at the other end of the table was conspicuously empty.

Jase turned his attention to his food—cold breast of chicken in a honey glaze, minced potatoes and chives, and a slice of Aunt Sade's spiced apple pie. But the sumptuous fare could not stop him from wondering at the incredible silence of the manse. Never before had the house seemed so large and tomblike. And quiet, without Catherine's lively chatter to enliven it, without her sharp replies to challenge him.

Jase set aside his utensils and, with a weary sigh, rose from his chair and dragged himself back up the stairs.

Who would have thought that a mere slip of a girl could bring a spark of life into their lives that had been sorely missing? Certainly, Jase had never suspected the extent of the havoc which she would wreak on his well-ordered existence, or he might have been more inclined to abandon her on the road that first night.

In the master bedchamber the tub waited. Steam rose in a cloud from the silken surface. Jase removed his shirt and boots, stockings and breeches, then stepped over the rim and sank down, sighing as the warmth seeped into his aching muscles. Leaning his head back against the high rim, he let his mind drift.

Idly, he wondered what Catherine was doing at this moment. Not exactly a safe subject, for it was difficult to picture her without the irritating specter of Alonzo rising up to haunt his thoughts.

Thinking of Alonzo Hart putting his slender hands upon Catherine's soft white skin conjured up an anger that was surprising in its ferocity.

Imagining Catherine, her golden head tossed back in ecstatic response, hands other than his caressing her flesh, caused Jase's pulse to throb. Wild thoughts filled his head, thoughts that would never have occurred to him a month past. In an effort to drown the clamoring din, he sank beneath the water, remaining there until his body's need for air blocked out all else.

Rising slowly, he filled his lungs and frowned through the curtain of water sluicing over his face and down his bronze torso. He felt a little calmer now. Only one thought remained, steadfastly refusing to be dislodged. It nagged him relentlessly as he crawled between scented sheets and tried to sleep.

At last he stopped fighting it and dragged himself naked from the bed, spurred into action.

A lifetime of experience had rendered him something of an expert on lost causes. He had learned early on when to fight, and when it was wisest to cut and run, or simply to call for quarter. And so he recognized that any further battle waged against his own desires was a pointless one, one which he could not hope to win.

So why not just admit it?

He wanted Catherine . . . here, at Rosemunde . . . *where she belonged.* Despite Alonzo Hart, despite her own objections.

He would say anything, do anything, to have her back.

Once she returned, it would not be difficult to keep her here. Marriage vows were binding, and Jase felt it within his power to persuade her to marry him. She worried over propriety, did she? Well, he would properly wed her and properly bed her as soon as he gained her consent. It was the perfect solution to keeping in check her zeal to catch the Black Lion, and he could not imagine why he had not considered it sooner.

But first he would have to find her. It was unlikely that she would return to New Orleans without her goals fulfilled, and there were just two other places he could think to look. The first was Alonzo's brick residence on Franklin Street; the second was Concord, the governor's mansion. He would begin with Alonzo's home. It was closer than Concord, and Jase had no real desire to meet with Winthrop Sargent.

Later that same afternoon, at the handsome brick house on Franklin Street in Natchez, Catherine was preparing to go downstairs to dinner when the sound of approaching hoofbeats drew her to the window. Alonzo had left early that morning on business and was expected home at any moment. Parting the curtains, she looked down in time to see Jase step from the saddle, a long and unwieldy box tucked under one arm.

Watching him tie off Sadist's reins and come through the gate gave Catherine the oddest feeling, a sort of giddiness which left her breathless and weak ... which kept her stationed at the window the entire time that Jase remained in sight.

Her hungry gaze eagerly drank in the picture he made striding up the walk, the very figure of unshakable male confidence in close-fitting buff breeches and a dark blue coat. His face and hands were very bronze in the afternoon sunlight, a perfect contrast to his pale aquamarine eyes.

Something caused him to glance up to where she stood. Catherine had the giddy notion that he had heard the gentle acceleration of her heart. In her mind flashed the image of that shining head pressed close to her breast, the searing flame that leapt from his mouth to her yearning flesh. ...

She drew a startled breath and jerked back inside, bumping her head on the sill. But her retreat was not swift enough to miss the break in his stride as he saw her, nor the gallant bow he sketched on the uneven walkway.

Whatever his faults, he cut a dashing figure. A wayward lock of jet-black hair fell across his forehead, but he did not bother to brush it back. Instead, he stood with booted legs in a casual stance, grinning devilishly up at her.

"Good day to you, fair mademoiselle," he said in a voice that was clearly meant to carry. "I trust your journey into Natchez was without incident."

Catherine leaned out the open casement and whispered, "What do you mean by coming here, m'sieur? I insist that you leave at once!"

"Will you not invite me in?" Jase inquired politely. "It's the least you might do, considering all that we've been to each other."

Down the way, a matronly woman poked her

curious face from her parlor window and peered at them. Catherine turned a lovely shade of magenta as Jase exchanged salutatory nods with the nosy woman, cheerfully bidding her good-day before returning his attention to Catherine.

"You are making a spectacle of yourself!" she accused.

"Yes," Jase readily agreed, "and I will continue to do so until you come down here and open the door."

He waggled the package to entice her, a suspiciously large box with a scarlet bow. A dressmaker's box, Catherine thought suspiciously. She narrowed her eyes at him, slamming the window closed. But the wavy glass and bright flowered curtain proved insufficient to block out the ringing sound of his laughter.

Impatient as always, and determined to have his own way despite the consequences, the ill-mannered rogue made shameless use of the brass knocker. Catherine winced as she flew down the stairs and across the foyer, sternly informing Clara that nothing was amiss that she could not handle personally. Clara stumped back down the hallway, but Catherine was certain the woman would be lurking close by to listen. She reached the door and jerked it open, an imprecation ready on her lips, when the box was thrust into her arms. She gasped and stepped backward, allowing Jase to step into the house and firmly close the door.

"Will you open it now or later?" he asked, his gaze traveling slowly over her. She seemed none the worse for wear, and he surmised she had met with no difficulty on her journey to Natchez. He relaxed a little, resigned to the current situation. He disliked the idea of Catherine's being here in this house, so close to his rival. Yet there was no justification for hunting him down and killing him either.

As he watched, Catherine struggled with the box, finally opting to stand it on end in the corner, though he suspected her fingers itched to pull the bright ribbon. The face she turned to him was suitably stern. "What are you doing here?" she demanded.

He smiled. "Why, I'm here to see Alonzo, of course. It's a business matter concerning Rosemunde."

Catherine paled slightly. "You have business . . . with Alonzo?"

His smile turned devilish. "Did I neglect to mention that Alonzo works for me? He's my factor, and has been for two years."

"You knew! All the while you kept me there at Rosemunde—" Catherine shook her head. She was furious with him. "Why did you keep it from me?"

"I saw no reason to bore you with the mundane affairs of managing Rosemunde."

"But Alonzo might have suspected!" she said. "It was a terrible thing to do!"

"Yes, terribly selfish," Jase said. "But I'm not sorry. Indeed, Catherine, I would do it again just to have you near me. I miss you. Dora misses you. She is driving me mad with her weeping. And Leviticus has been impossible. Even Sadist misses you. Rosemunde isn't the same with you gone."

Catherine suppressed the urge to laugh. He was

an outrageous rogue, and charming in a devilish way when he wished to be. But this was no time for levity. She had one man to whom she was betrothed and owed her loyalty, and one who seemed bent upon stealing her heart. "You are impossible, and you must leave now! I can't return to Rosemunde. I belong here, with Alonzo."

Jase snorted derisively. "You don't belong with Alonzo, Cathcrine. You belong with me. Why are you so afraid to admit it?"

The creaking of a board in the hallway gave Catherine pause. She clamped her jaws shut and grabbed his arm, pushing him into the parlor and shutting the door with force. "Noxious old toad," she said.

"Now see here," Jase said with mock severity, "I well understand your upset, finding your lover on your fiancé's doorstep, but there is no need to defame my character. 'Tis shredded often enough these days."

"Not you," Catherine grumbled, then smiled in spite of herself. "I meant the servant, Clara. She's given to eavesdropping."

The humor slowly faded from Jase's hard features. He raised a hand and ran a fingertip across her peach-colored cheek. He'd never come across such lovely skin, not in all his travels, and each time he touched her, its softness struck him anew. "I'm all for giving the withered old bat an earful," he said softly.

Catherine stepped back and turned away, hands tightly clasped before her. "If you've come to see Alonzo—"

"He can wait."

She looked down at her hands. "Jason, please—"

"Why did you leave?"

"Because I could not do otherwise." She drew a fortifying breath that caused her pearly breasts to swell above the daring décolletage. "To remain after you nearly seduced me would have been woefully wrong."

"You put yourself in jeopardy, leaving as you did," he said. "You might have come to serious harm."

She raised her gaze to his. "I would have come to serious harm if I'd stayed. This attraction between us isn't right!"

He seized her hands, his grasp warm and sure. Catherine felt an answering flutter in her breast. "I'll make it right," he said fervently.

"You can't!" she cried. "Don't you see? I am promised to Alonzo. My brother gave his pledge, and I am bound by honor to uphold it."

"That's damnably cold-blooded," Jase said. "I should think that Andre wanted more for you than to see you wed to a man for whom you feel nothing more than misplaced loyalty!"

Catherine pulled from his grasp, but the sensation of his touch lingered. "My feelings for Alonzo are not your concern!"

"Do you love him?"

Her reticence to reply was answer enough. Jase snorted. "I thought as much. It was not any overweening fondness for Hart that caused you to flee Rosemunde, but fear of what almost happened between us." He gave a dark laugh. "You are terrified by what you feel for me."

She glared at him. "I was preserving my honor!"

"At the price of your heart, your happiness."

"Oh, you are incorrigible!"

"So I have been told." His mouth quirked. "There are other ways to salvage your honor, you know, without sacrificing your desires."

His dark head came down, and Catherine knew he would kiss her. Despite her denials, despite her anger, she tipped up her chin and her lips parted in sweet anticipation. She felt the warmth of his lips briefly on hers. But at the sound of hurrying footsteps outside, Jase broke the kiss. "What damnably perfect timing," he remarked, turning a face gone purposely bland toward the parlor door.

Catherine hastened to put some space between them and had just enough time to seat herself in a chair before the door was opened. Her heart was still beating heavily in her throat, and the face she turned to Alonzo was suffused with heat.

The look of surprise on his youthful visage quickly turned to wariness. His dark glance moved from Catherine to Jase and back again before he finally spoke. "Cathy," he said, "what is going on here?"

It was Jase who answered. "A lively and vastly interesting discourse on New Orleans. Your bride-to-be was kind enough to keep me entertained while we awaited your return." A simple lie, but told with such convincing ennui that Catherine was impressed. "Mademoiselle Breaux is ravishing, Alonzo," Jase said with a flash of white teeth. "I compliment your taste in females, and must admit to being consumed with envy over your good fortune."

Catherine flushed anew, and silently cursed him for flirting with danger in so casual a manner. It was obvious he didn't give a damn for his life, or for her future, for that matter. Alonzo's temper was explosive, and there was no telling what he might do if provoked.

Alonzo missed Catherine's blush. He was too busy frowning at Jase. "That's a strange remark, coming from a man who's himself about to be wed."

"Ah, well. There's a bit of bad luck, I'm afraid. The wench quite suddenly decided against the match."

Alonzo's interest was piqued. "Oh?"

"Yes. Though it pains me considerably to say so, I fear I may have frightened her off. She left without so much as an explanation." Jase turned his gaze full force upon Catherine. "Perhaps Mademoiselle Breaux would be so kind as to give me some advice. I'm afraid I've a difficulty dealing with creatures more timid than myself."

"It might be helpful if you were to keep your mouth shut, m'sieur," Catherine supplied readily, a sweet smile on her lips. "At times your manner is exceedingly abrasive."

Alonzo stared at Catherine, unsure of what to say. He looked suddenly to Jase and attempted to judge his reaction. "Cathy, sweetness, I beg you, be kind to our guest. Jase is not only a friend, he is also my employer."

Catherine arched her golden brows. "I *was* being kind," she said. "The word *overbearing* also applies to M'sieur St. Claire's character, but I gracefully chose not to use it."

Alonzo gave a nervous laugh. "Listen, Jase, would you wait for me in the study? I'll come in directly."

"As you will," Jase said. But instead of exiting the room immediately, he went to stand before Catherine. He bowed low and caught her hand to hold it imprisoned in his warm grasp while he bade her farewell. "Mademoiselle, I hope that we shall meet again very soon," he said. "I relish the chance to change your opinion of my poor, much maligned character. Perhaps you'll attend the Gallihers' gala with Alonzo on Saturday. I am sure he is most eager to show you off to his friends, and I hear that the governor is to be there as well."

"I will assuredly be there," Catherine said softly. "As to my opinion of you, I doubt it will alter." She snatched her hand from his grasp, but not before he brought it to his lips.

Long after his dry chuckle faded, after Alonzo's admonishment for her to be civil had gone from Catherine's thoughts and she had retreated to her room, the feel of Jase's gentle nip on the tender flesh of her palm still tingled. She rubbed the skin and tried to be angry—but couldn't. He was such an irrepressible blackguard, a rogue with a dark charm that was impossible to resist.

Feeling confused and strangely excited, she paced by the side of the bed. Saturday was three days hence . . . the day of the gala . . . and she had nothing to wear. It was then that she remembered the box, and grew alarmed. What if Alonzo found it? How could she explain? He would surely deduce that Jason had brought the gift, and whatever Alonzo's shortcomings, she had no wish to wound him unnecessarily.

He had been kind to her since Andre's death. Whatever she decided to do after she met with Governor Sargent, Alonzo must not learn of her time at Rosemunde.

To this end she crept downstairs, past Alonzo's chamber. She found the box where she and Jase had left it, just inside the door.

Safe in her room again, with no prying eyes to witness her suddenly rapt expression, she placed the long box atop the bed. With fingers that trembled slightly, she pulled the ends of the scarlet ribbon, releasing the perfect bow, and lifted the lid.

Inside was the amethyst gown, Catherine's favorite. Atop the garment was a long velvet box, with a note written in a bold hand.

A ransom against your return to Rosemunde....

It was signed simply, "Jason."

Catherine felt suddenly breathless. For a moment she just sat, staring down at the long velvet box clutched tight in her hands. When at last she summoned the courage to lift the lid, she was stunned. A glittering chain of finely wrought gold, studded here and there with tiny diamonds, glittered upon a field of black. Suspended on the chain was a medallion.

With trembling fingers, she lifted the piece from its velvet nest and held it up to the light, seeing as she did so the great leonine head embossed on the gold.

The lion . . . symbol of her struggles, her private travail . . . Through a misty veil of tears, she saw the sparkle of the perfect gems refracted into a thousand points of blue-white light.

Chapter 16

A lonzo's manner at dinner that evening was reserved, and from the smug look on Clara's normally dour countenance, Catherine was given cause to suspect that the housekeeper had eagerly imparted to him all that had occurred between Catherine and Jase St. Claire that same afternoon.

Just how much the eavesdropping Clara had managed to hear was a matter of speculation, and hardly mattered in any case. The fact remained that one's intended bride did not entertain a gentleman in the absence of her bridegroom ... and most certainly not behind closed doors.

Watching Alonzo from her place at table, Catherine knew that he was vastly displeased with her actions. But instead of confronting her openly, as Jase would have done, he sulked.

Catherine did her best to ignore his anger in the hope that it would pass. She paid close attention to her meal, thinking often of Jase and hoping that her expression did not betray her thoughts. Jase had said that he wanted her to return with him to Rosemunde; he had said that he missed her. His

manner had been very different this afternoon—
determined, she thought—and the memory
brought a subtle heat to her cheeks. To hide her
blush, she took a sip of tea and grimaced.

Alonzo was swift to notice. "The tea is not to
your liking?"

Catherine shrugged. "You know I prefer coffee."

"There is no coffee in the pantry. There is only
tea. As it so happens, I was not expecting a guest.
Therefore, I am unprepared. I'm a man of modest
means, Cathy, and I must depend upon my wits to
make a living. Unlike some men, I have no fortune
to fall back upon."

Catherine stiffened. "It's plain that you are angry, but I do not intend to sit here quietly and allow you to ruin my evening with your ill temper,
Alonzo." She calmly plied her napkin and stood.
"I shall be in my room, resting."

"Resting," Alonzo said mockingly. "I shouldn't
wonder that you would need to rest *after your recent ordeal.*" He vigorously stabbed at his meat
with his knife. "In fact, I wish to send some token
of my appreciation to the farmer and his wife who
helped you. It was very generous of them to take
you in—selfless, you might say. What were their
names again?"

Catherine looked at Alonzo. He knew that she
had been at Rosemunde. She could see the truth in
his eyes. She thought of inventing some falsehood
that would sound plausible, just to placate him,
but then decided against it. This situation, after all,
was partly his doing. If he had gone with her to
Buzzard's Roost, none of this would have ever

happened. She lifted her chin. "I didn't say their names."

"And precisely why is that, Cathy?" Alonzo asked. "Could it be that you knew the name of your benefactor would upset me greatly?"

Catherine stared at him, her jaw set stubbornly. "We can discuss this when you are sufficiently calm."

"We will discuss it now!" When the outburst had died away he shook his head. "You must think me gullible indeed. You were with St. Claire at Rosemunde these two weeks, weren't you? *You* were the woman he was passing off as his fiancée. And all this time I believed you had gone to Thea's!" He tossed down his napkin in disgust. "I thought that damnable mare looked familiar, but it was not until I came home and found *him* here that it struck me. Why, Cathy? Why did you lie to me!"

"I had no choice!" she shot back. "Don't you see? I had to come. I was desperate to know about Andre. His death was a terrible blow, Alonzo! Do you know how it feels to lose someone you love in that way?"

"I know how it feels to be betrayed." The passion seeped from his voice, leaving it flat, emotionless.

"It was not like that!" Catherine cried. "Jason saved my life! Part of what I told you was true. I was about to be robbed when Jason came along. I lost my mount, and lost Mose, and Jason helped me."

"By taking you back to his lair and keeping you there."

"You should be grateful to him! He saved my life!"

"Grateful?" Alonzo snarled. For an instant his face was an ugly mask, twisted with malevolence. Catherine took an involuntary step backward. But he quickly gained control over his seething passions. Quietly, and with terrible calm, he continued, "You will not see him again. Do you understand me? I will not have you consorting with him."

"Consorting?" Heat crept up Catherine's throat. "Exactly what are you implying?"

"I am telling you that Jase St. Claire is no gentleman, and I do not wish him to defile my doorstep, let alone come sniffing 'round the woman I am to wed like some lascivious hound!"

"How dare you say such things!"

Alonzo came out of his chair and quickly stepped forward, towering over Catherine. She could see the suppressed fury in his black eyes, but he did not attempt to touch her. "If you defy me again, Cathy, you will learn just how much I dare!"

He gave her no opportunity to reply, but spun on a booted heel and exited the room and then the house, slamming doors behind him.

Catherine stood for a long moment, listening to a silence that was broken only by the sound of hoofbeats as Alonzo rode away.

He had every right to be angry, but his vehemence was uncharacteristic, and therefore very upsetting. In all the time they had known each other, they had quarreled only once, and that had been after Andre's death, when she had insisted on investigating the murder. Never until this moment had he threatened her.

His manner confused and repulsed her. He had spoken Jase's name as though the taste of it was vile upon his tongue ... and yet he continued to serve him in business, to take his monetary due. He hated Jason, of that she had no doubt.

How could he be so false? she wondered ... and did his propensity toward deception extend to other relationships as well?

She thought back to the morning when he had opened the door to find her. His manner had not been that of an eager bridegroom finding his love arrived unexpectedly. He had been shocked and cool and questioning, but there had been no warmth, no affection in his manner.

Her thoughts were troubling. She'd been feeling disloyal to Alonzo for falling in love with Jason St. Claire, but as she went slowly up the stairs to bed, she wondered if those feelings were justified. She had fled Rosemunde without a word of farewell, or a note of explanation, a fact that must have worried Jase. And yet he had not come with mean recriminations, accusations, threats; he had come with gifts, with his warm touch, with sentiment, admitting how much he missed her.

Once the door was locked, Catherine made her way to the bed. To avoid the housekeeper's prying eyes, she had placed the large box with its gay scarlet ribbons beneath the bed. Now she removed it and lifted the lid, finding the jeweler's box she sought. Just now she desperately needed solace, and strangely enough she found it in Jase's gift. Once clasped about her throat, the gold medallion nestled securely in the valley between her breasts, a tangible reminder that there was *someone* who believed in her.

He had not planned to hit MacLeemer's farm so soon, but coming home that afternoon to discover Jase St. Claire alone with Catherine had given rise to a towering rage within Alonzo, a rage that cried out for an immediate release. Against the eventuality of the next strike, he had sent word for Ned Rails and Tom Kenny to come, and to bring the new man, Wools Burke. It was time to break him in.

By the time Alonzo reached their scheduled place of rendezvous a mile from Joshua MacLeemer's farm, all traces of Alonzo Hart, gentleman of Natchez and factor to some of the wealthiest planters in Spanish Louisiana and Mississippi Territory, had been wiped away.

He'd purchased the clothes he wore from a hunter in the markets of New Orleans. When not in use, they were hidden in the stable loft behind the house on Franklin Street. The buckskin was old and rank with the sweat and grease of its previous owner; in no way did it compare to the soft tan leather Jase had worn as the son of a Shawnee chieftain, but it provided the effect Alonzo wanted. The black wig he sported was shoulder length, kept in place by the pale blue bandanna tied across his brow. He took special care with his paint. The left side of his face was vermilion, the right black, each with rings of the alternating color around the eye, black on red and red on black, Jase's war insignia. Mounted on a big roan gelding which he kept stabled just outside of town, he cut a terrifying figure indeed, especially when seen by the light of a blazing house.

Alonzo drew rein by a great sycamore that had been struck by lightning long ago. Beneath its bone-white skeletal limbs he sat his mount and waited, watching the shifting shadows cast by the fitful moon. The gelding shifted uneasily beneath him, pricking his ears and giving a low whicker.

Something moved in the deep ebony shadows several hundred yards to the north.

Alonzo glanced behind him, cocking his head to listen. Where were the others? He had sent the message for them to meet him here. He glanced over his shoulder again, looked again to the north, and saw that the black mass was moving closer.

The nape of Alonzo's neck prickled, but he fought down the urge to turn and run, despite the fact that he was without the security of the others at his back. "Stand by!" he called out in ringing tones.

No reply came, just a low equine rumble and the muted thunder of hoofs churning earth.

For an instant Alonzo sat electrified as horse and rider seemed to take flight. Steam rose from the great beast's nostrils; but it was his rider who was the embodiment of Alonzo's nightmares ... pistol drawn as he raced toward him. . . .

Alonzo's shock lasted for the space of a heartbeat. He clawed at his own weapon, which he had thrust into his belt, and squeezed off a shot at Jase, then wheeled his mount and spurred it on toward Natchez.

Alonzo dug his heels into the roan's heaving

sides, cursing viciously. He could not hope to out-run the Spanish black on the open road.

And Jase St. Claire would show him no mercy once he knew the truth.

A shot whined past Alonzo's ear. He felt its painful kiss and yelped, pressing a hand to his neck just below his jaw. His fingers came away warm and sticky. He bent lower over the roan's neck. His heart was racing; it felt as if at any moment it would burst free from the confines of his chest. The surge of his blood was an unrelenting roar in his ears.

Just ahead was MacLeemer's Cove, a small creek that wound into the Mississippi. If only he could manage to keep a length ahead, he would jump the bank and hope Jase didn't follow. The hope seemed futile, but he clung to it anyway, his only chance now of avoiding discovery, of cheating death.

From the corner of his eye, Alonzo saw the black edge closer, heard the stallion's labored breathing. Almost caught! He cursed and cried out, urging his mount to greater exertions. The roan began to pull away, but not quickly enough to avoid the punishing teeth of the Spanish black nipping at its flank.

The blood left Alonzo's ears in a rush. With star-tling clarity he heard the harsh Shawnee command uttered by his pursuer, heard the whinny of his terrified mount as the devil black lunged against the roan, using its broad, muscled breast like a battering ram.

The roan gelding stumbled and fell; Alonzo lost his seat and tumbled headlong into the road at the

very moment a trio of riders appeared in the road-
way yards to the south.

Angry shouts and shots rang out. Confusion
ruled the moment.

One of the riders broke from the others and
came to the aid of their of their fallen leader. He
was dressed in the same tattered buckskin and
braided wig, though his shirt appeared to be cal-
ico. He charged directly at Jase, who wheeled his
mount and leveled the second pistol, drawing a
bead on the outlaw's chest. He squeezed the trigger and the piece bucked and roared, spurting fire
and lead.

The charging outlaw seemed to leap in the saddle, then toppled slowly backward from his perch
until his boot caught in the stirrup and he was
dragged several score feet before his mount came
to a nervous halt.

Jase turned back to where the leader of the outlaw band had fallen.

He cursed and gnashed his teeth. The miscreant
was gone.

Down the way, Wools Burke fought for possession of a sword with the single remaining combat-
ant. As Jase touched his heels to Sadist's flank and
urged him forward, he saw Wools wrench the
weapon away from the smaller outlaw and bring
it up for a killing stroke. "Muga!" Jase shouted. "I
want him alive!"

The days passed slowly for Catherine, but at last
that of the gala arrived. It dawned sunny, but as
the morning wore on, a solid bank of clouds
moved in from the west and a drizzling rain began

to fall. By early afternoon it had turned into a deluge, running in thick ribbons down both sides of the street, churning the center of the thoroughfare into a thick mire.

From the parlor window, Catherine watched the steady downpour pelting the streets and the occasional passing carriage, thinking the weather appropriate for her mood.

Alonzo had not returned to the house that night after their argument, but had remained away until very late the following night. He had come down to breakfast this morning looking staunchly correct in his high collar and immaculate stock, which rose to a point just beneath his chin. Catherine had questioned him as to his whereabouts, but she had received only a coolly hostile stare in answer. It was obvious that he was still piqued over Jase's visit, and stubbornly, Catherine made no further attempt to correct his assumption that she had betrayed him. If he wished to believe her a faithless jade, then let him.

She sighed, feeling a little apprehensive. Jase had said that he would be attending the gala. What was he likely to do or say? Would he try again to persuade her to leave Alonzo? Could she resist if he did?

It was becoming more difficult to think of Alonzo as her betrothed, the man with whom she would spend the rest of her days. She had begun to realize that she had erred in accepting his suit.

Taking the medallion from her bodice, she gazed wistfully down at it. The gold shone softly; it was warm against her cool palm.

"Ahhemm." The sound issued from the parlor

doorway. Glancing up, Catherine saw Clara's bulk filling the doorframe. "If ye don't mind, I'd like to tidy up in here. Per'aps ye'd be more at ease in yer room."

It was a less-than-subtle reminder that Catherine did not belong there. She raised an elegant brow in inquiry. "Tidy the room to your heart's content, Clara. You will not be disturbing my comfort." She turned back to her contemplation of the medallion that still nestled in her palm, pointedly dismissing the woman. "When you are finished here, you may prepare my bath. I wish to be ready when M'sieur Hart returns to take me to the gala."

Clara gave a rude snort. "What ye wish and what ye get'll be two different things, Miss High-and-Mighty!" She waited, knowing that the younger woman would question her.

The look Catherine presented to Clara was cool and unruffled, though her heartbeat had ceased its normal rhythm and was executing short, stiff thuds that presaged a slight feeling of nausea. "If you've something to say to me, then kindly come to the point."

"Aye, and I'll be happy to do just that!" Clara said, eyes gleaming with malice. "You thought to betray the master in his own ruddy household with that good-for-nothing blackguard, and now ye'll be payin' for yer sinful ways! Pretty is as pretty does, I always says! An' ye'll be settin' your pretty arse at home tonight, not going to some fancy shindig, like you think! Mark my words!"

Catherine glared at the woman. "You ancient hag, you don't know what you're talking about."

"Don't I?" taunted Clara. "Well, ye're the fool if

ye think for a minute the master'd take you somewhere's that rascally St. Claire's bound to be! Ye're
stayin' here, and I'm to watch ye so as ye don't get
into no mischief, nor do nothin' that might shame
the master."

"Alonzo set you to spy on me?" Catherine came
slowly off the divan and advanced upon the
housekeeper, her soft voice full of malice, stopping
only when the older woman's back was pressed
up against the hearth. The smell of sweat which
rose from the housekeeper's person assailed Catherine's senses, but she did not retreat an inch. Eyes
aglow, she said, "Answer me, or I swear that I will
stuff you up the chimneypiece."

Clara was not easily cowed, but the fierce light
in the younger woman's eyes convinced her that
she was not indulging in idle threats. "Aye," she
said quickly, "but it was no more'n ye deserve, ye
sinful little witch. For shame!"

"The only shame that I can see is that Alonzo
thought you equal to the task of preventing me
from attending the Gallihers' gala," Catherine
said. "I came all the way from New Orleans to see
the governor, and by God, I will see him ... despite you, despite Alonzo! Now get out!"

Clara's gaze fastened on the poker that stood
just out of reach, a weapon equal to the task of
forcing this wicked hoyden into her chamber,
where she could be secured until the master returned and took the situation in hand.

Chubby sausagelike fingers twitching, the older
woman made a dive for the weapon. But Catherine proved swifter, and tore the wrought iron im-

plement from its stand, flinging it with all her might across the parlor.

End over end it flew, striking the window with considerable force. Glass shattered, sparkling nearly as bright as the diamond-studded chain that glittered against Catherine's heaving breast. "Get out!" she cried again, trembling with the force of her fury.

Her face crumpling suddenly with fear, Clara turned and fled.

Catherine let out a slow breath, feeling the tremors that coursed through her slight frame gradually lessen, and wondering what to do next. Outside, the rain was a relentless drum on the rooftop. It lashed the windows left intact, and howled through the panes she had broken.

There was a slight sound on the portico. Her head snapped up and she cried aloud in relief ... for Jase was there, framed by the casement containing only a few shards of broken glass.

He looked bemused as he studied the poker in his gloved hands, then glanced up at her. "It's obvious my timing is opportune ... a moment sooner and you might have skewered me." He handed the poker through the glassless sash to Catherine. "Your weapon, mademoiselle," he said, bowing slightly. "Will you open the door, or shall I enter by my own inventive means?" He indicated the window with a slight incline of his head.

She hurried to open the door and, seizing his arm, pulled him inside.

"Anxious to see me, are you?" Jase said, still amused. "Now there's a definite first." He looked again at the window and his teeth showed white in his dark face. "A pretty piece of work, my love. I compliment your pluckish spirit, but I somehow doubt that Alonzo is going to appreciate it."

"Alonzo Hart can go to the devil for all I care!" Catherine shot back.

Jase's sensuous mouth curled slightly. "Is it the same wondrous Alonzo, of whom you've so often spoken, to whom you now refer—that shining example of moral correctness? His offense must be grievous indeed to have brought about this sudden dearth of affection where not long ago there was an endless wellspring." He affected a grave demeanor, but his pale eyes glinted. "Would it please my lady, I would be happy to call him out. I'm a good hand with pistols, you know."

"This isn't amusing, Jason," Catherine said. "You know how important it is for me to speak with the governor. I have anticipated this evening for weeks, but now that it has finally arrived and I have my chance to see the Black Lion pay for his crimes, I find myself abandoned!"

A look of mild surprise crossed Jase's features. "He refused to escort you?" He glanced around. "Where is he, by the by?"

"It is worse than that. He left his morning and has not returned. There was no warning, no explanation, no honesty. . . ." Her voice quavered on the last word, and she found she had to pause before going on. "He simply left me here to languish, with that fat spider of a housekeeper to guard me!"

"What will you do?" Jase asked cautiously. It would not do to appear too pleased with Alonzo's stupidity.

The eyes she turned on him then nearly made him wince. They were wide and childlike, and oh so trusting. "Oh, Jason, I must go to the gala! I must speak with Governor Sargent—for all our sakes! Will you take me with you?"

He looked down into that piquant little face and bit back the urge to tell her what he was thinking, that he would take her to the ends of the earth if she but asked him ... or beyond, if it were in his power. Instead he traced a fingertip down one gently curved cheek. "It means that much to you to see the Black Lion brought down?"

She didn't answer, just continued to stare at him with those huge and luminous eyes ... eyes which mirrored her newly found trust in him.

Feeling more at war with himself than he ever had before, Jase carefully formed his reply. "If it pleases you, then I will take you to the Gallihers' ... and Alonzo Hart be damned."

"Thank you! Oh, thank you!" Catherine flung herself against him and hugged him tight, stretching up on her toes to press a grateful kiss upon his cheek. Jase had the fleeting sensation of feminine warmth, but before he could move to close his arms about her, to savor it more fully, she was gone, flitting up the stairs with a bright little laugh.

When she was out of sight and earshot, he sank down in a nearby chair and let out a slow breath. "Though it may in the end cost me my life, I will take you ... if only to call you my own for a little while."

Part 2

Bride of the Black Lion

Chapter 17

While he awaited Catherine's return, Jase casually wandered around the room, mindlessly studying the few paintings hung on the pale green walls. Two were landscapes, poorly done, but the third caught his interest. It was a portrait depicting an adolescent girl with plaited brown hair and a nervous smile. A youth on the threshold of manhood stood stiffly behind her chair, a protective hand upon her shoulder. The young man's unruly brown curls had been coaxed into a queue and his attire was not as fashionable as today, but Jase recognized the young man as Alonzo.

For a long moment Jase studied the youthful face. There was nothing in the boyish countenance to trigger a memory, nothing that suggested Alonzo as tied to Jase's past.

His gaze fell again upon the woman. Who was she? he wondered. Alonzo's sister? His cousin? There was little resemblance, yet Jase did notice certain shared physical characteristics.

Both had light brown hair and dark eyes. Both

were fair-complected . . . and there was a vulnerability in the set of the mouth and jaw that appeared inherent.

Jase lifted a hand to his temple and rubbed the scar. It sometimes troubled him in bad weather. But the girl in the portrait troubled him as well. He had the nagging notion that he had seen her somewhere before. . . .

He pondered the possibilities for a moment or two before dismissing the notion. If indeed he had met her, then he would eventually remember, but for now he turned his attention to the small wooden shelf positioned below the portrait and the ornate box sitting there.

He had never seen anything like it. It was made of teakwood, intricately carved with trailing vines and cherubs, and about as large as a man's hand. Curious as to what it might contain, Jase lifted the lid.

But the box was empty.

A board creaked in the upstairs hallway. Jase replaced the lid and put the teakwood box back just as he had found it, turning as Catherine came into sight. And in that instant the portrait and the box were both forgotten.

She looked a vision, a rare and glittering gem, this woman who had wrought such enormous changes in his life . . . and so far removed from that ragtag little wretch he had rescued from brigands on the Chickasaw Trace that Jase could barely believe they were one and the same.

Standing in the parlor doorway, he watched her slow descent, feeling the muscles in his stomach contract. More than anything he wanted to sweep her into his arms and carry her, protesting or not, back up those very stairs, to dispense with the barrier which her innocence posed in whatever bed was handy. . . .

Oh, how he wanted to . . . and yet he could not.

His illusions were not so grand that he believed the shine in Catherine's turquoise eyes was solely for him. She was electric with anticipation—the very air surrounding her crackled with it—for her long-sought goal was about to be reached, and she was certain that the Black Lion would soon be caught.

It stung Jase more than a little to realize that the blush on her cheek, the lush red of her sweet lips, was put there not by his presence but by a fervent desire to bring about his own untimely demise.

Ruefully, he conceded that the knowledge that she would even now gleefully knot the hangman's rope which would end his days did not lessen the keen desire she kindled in his soul to make her his.

He burned to possess this golden woman who came to stand before him, pliant lips smiling with ill-concealed delight . . . and possess her he would, before this night was out.

Taking her small hands in his, Jase stepped back a little, just enough to allow his ravenous gaze to devour her. "You are indeed a miracle in the guise of woman," he said in a voice both warm and low, "and for me there exists no one to equal your golden beauty."

Catherine was warmed considerably by his open admiration. "I am glad you came by this evening, Jason. Aside from the obvious reason that you are lending your aid in my time of need—I haven't had the chance to thank you properly for your gift." She quickly came up on her toes and pressed her lips to his, experiencing his vibrant warmth as a brief but pleasurable jolt which was destined to linger long after the contact was broken.

Quickly, she stepped back and out of his arms, feeling suddenly and inexplicably nervous in his presence. She lowered her gaze to the medallion, touching it with reverent fingers. "It has a very special meaning to me, and you may be certain that I will cherish it always."

Better still that you should cherish the giver, Jase thought.

For a moment he stood looking down at her, his face carefully devoid of expression. He had already lived out three lifetimes, first as the son of Cameron St. Claire, and then as the Black Lion. . . .

Each time a phase of his life had ended, the fates had seemed to smile upon him, and he was presented with the opportunity to begin anew, to put the past and all its pain behind him.

He had been swift to seize opportunity in both fists, lest it be cruelly wrested away, but as he gazed down into Catherine's lovely visage and plotted how best to bring her around to his way of thinking, he wondered if perhaps this time he was asking for too much.

His dark face not revealing any of the doubts that plagued him, Jase reached out and slipped his hand under the bright chain. Gently, he slid his fingers along its length, allowing his knuckles to brush against the bare skin of her chest, right down to the pearly swell of her breasts, so enchantingly displayed above the bodice of her gown. With exquisite care, he lifted the golden circlet from its warm and fragrant nest.

"Take care, Catherine," he said softly, his pale eyes shadowed by the thick ebony fringe of his lashes, "lest you give me cause to hope."

The Galliher home was situated on Orleans Street, near the high bluffs that overlooked the rambling white house seemed to Catherine a huge apearl aglow in the soft white light of a harvest moon, though in reality the illumination camrambling white house seemed to Catherine a huge pearl aglow in the soft white light of a harvest moon, though in reality the illumination came not from the moon but from the flambeaux strategically positioned along the circular drive and brick walkway leading up to the house.

By the time their conveyance pulled to a stop in front of the walkway, the driving rain had lessened to a mere drizzle. Yet the air was heavy with dampness, and a definite chill pervaded the evening, making Catherine grateful for the black velvet cloak which Jase had thoughtfully provided before departing the house.

Once, she had considered him selfish, but now she saw that all he did and all he said—even his ordering her about—was designed to protect her, to shield her from harm, to provide her with greater comfort.

There was nothing she could fault in the man who alighted from the coach, then turned to hand her down.

Roguish he might appear, wicked at times, and
even ungodly. But never was he petty or mean-
spirited. His anger was swift and fierce, but never
coldly calculating, as Alonzo's had proven to be.

Thinking of Alonzo made Catherine's eyes kin-
dle with renewed wrath as she placed her small
hand in the crook of Jase's steely arm. She would
have a choice word or two to say to her former
fiancé when she saw him this evening, and she
doubted that he would enjoy hearing any of it.

Inside the house, Alonzo retrieved two glasses
of chilled wine from a servant and offered one to
Angela Dane before allowing his gaze to shift to
the gay figures who preened and pranced in the
center of the ballroom floor. Now and then,
Alonzo would catch a glimpse of the fat saffron
curls piled high atop Rebecca's head, before she
was lost once again in the bright whirl of broad-
cloth and silk.

"I wonder ofttimes why you continue to pursue
her, Alonzo, fickle little creature that she is. Can it
be that you've allowed your heart to become entangled with Rebecca?"

Alonzo cast a sidelong glance at Angela. "If I
didn't know you better, I would think that your
query was born out of concern."

"Rebecca is my brother's child, in case you have
forgotten," she said, prickling slightly at his tone.
"It is only natural that I don't wish to see her hurt
in any way."

Alonzo sipped his wine, still watching the subject of their conversation. "A sudden show of loyalty, my dear Mrs. Dane? It's just the slightest bit

out of character, don't you think?" He knew his comment rankled, for he saw Angela stiffen her spine. "Surely you know by now that you needn't play the prude in my presence. I'm aware of your dalliance with St. Claire ... as is half the town, I daresay. But you needn't worry that I'll let that knowledge slip to your husband. I wouldn't think of causing you difficulties ... just as I'm sure you wouldn't consider interfering in matters that are none of your concern."

Angela's smooth countenance did not betray her thoughts. She knew that Alonzo would run to Harbridge in a moment if it would suit his purposes to do so. And though she was kin to Rebecca, she was not so fond of the girl that she would jeopardize her marriage to protect her. Still, she could not help being curious, or wishing that Jase shared a little in Alonzo's lack of scruples about being faithful to a fiancée, present or otherwise. Giving an easy shrug that rippled the pale blue satin over her breasts, Angela smiled. "Rebecca's affairs are of no great consequence to me. And yet, I can't help wonder why you bother with her. Did you not tell me before that you were to marry the Breaux girl, from New Orleans?"

"What has one woman to do with the other?" Alonzo said. "Your niece is but a dalliance, something with which to amuse myself while I'm in Natchez. While Catherine—"

Angela looked at Alonzo, who stared open-mouthed at the newly arrived couple who stood just inside the door to the ballroom. His face was chalk-white, but his cheeks blazed with two spots of vivid red. "It's obvious that you've met Jase's intended bride," she said. "Tell me, what is she like?"

The eyes which Alonzo fixed on Angela burned like bright coals in his bloodless face. "Lovely," he said stiffly, "but spoiled and impossibly head-strong."

"Indeed?" Angela said sweetly. "That surprises me; but perhaps it also explains her manner when I saw her at Rosemundo." Angela ignored Alonzo's strangled curse and continued. "I went by the house one night to offer my congratulations to Jase upon his impending nuptials and saw her there. They were closeted in the library when I arrived. I've no idea what transpired between them, but whatever it was, she was mightily upset by it. When Leviticus announced my arrival, she sped from the room and up the stairs, and I had the impression that she was precariously close to tears."

Angela gave a wistful sigh. "Still, there's no de-nying her beauty, no matter that it pains me to ad-mit it. I suppose I can see why Jase is so taken with her."

Alonzo barely heard Angela's comment. His en-tire being was focused on the strikingly handsome couple.

Even from this distance, he could see that they were creating a stir. Jase was richly garbed in coat and breeches of deepest blue, with tall black Hes-sian boots. The snowy linen which contrasted viv-idly with his dark skin, and the waistcoat of silver and blue displayed beneath the coat, remained his only concessions to the festive mood which sur-rounded him. Indeed, he had the grave demeanor of one attending a funeral mass . . . until Catherine pressed his arm and gazed up at him with trusting eyes, speaking softly so that he was forced to bend near to catch her words. And then that stony expression was transformed, that unyielding mouth curving ever so slightly into a rare smile, his icy gaze glowing with the fierceness of his longing ... and Jase St. Claire, the Black Lion, became a man with wants and needs and human passions ... very like Alonzo.

The change that came over that lean visage doubled the force of the rage that boiled up inside of the watching Alonzo. This was the man who had razed his life, leaving the cold gray ash of ruin in its wake ... and now he plotted to take the last thing of value Alonzo had left. . . .

Catherine.

She was being wooed relentlessly away from him ... her loyalties were subtly shifting. In the course of the past few days she had lied to him, defied him again and again, and if what he suspected proved true, she had betrayed him in the most vile fashion. Alonzo watched with glowing eyes the hand of his enemy openly caressing the velvety cheek of *his* woman ... the woman with whom Alonzo planned to build a dynasty.

The scorching blade of unreasoning hatred which had been lodged in his vitals for countless years was given a cruel twist.

Catherine had always been willful, but never had she given him cause to doubt her fidelity—until this moment, when she smiled up into those hated eyes with the beguiling face of a fallen angel.

Never had she looked at Alonzo with such rapt

attention. But then, neither was he the practiced deceiver that he knew Jason St. Claire to be. And given the dark magnetic pull of the man's personality, Catherine could only be partially blamed for what was occurring.

She was a mere woman, after all, coddled by a family who had adored her and had never suffered hardship; and as such, she was susceptible to a seductive word or burning look. She was weak by nature ... defenseless against the unrelenting evil of Alonzo's archrival.

And in desperate need of someone to save her from certain destruction, to save her from herself.

With a pale face and glowing eyes, Alonzo started off through the crowd just as Rebecca, breathless from her turn about the floor, caught his arm.

Her generous bosom pressed wantonly against his sleeve, threatening to overflow her yellow dress. "Alonzo Hart," she said, fluttering her lashes at him, "you promised me a dance!"

"Becca, I'd love nothing more, but first there is something I must do."

"Something more important than pleasing me?" Rebecca looked like an overripe sunflower in her bright yellow dress, but her brown eyes were hard.

Glancing from her to Catherine, Alonzo seethed. Damn his ill luck! Damn Jase for bringing Catherine here!

Across the room, Tom Galliher was hailing Jase, bearing down upon the couple, haranguing them with his jovial sallies. . . . Tom was long-winded; it appeared that Catherine was well occupied for the moment. Alonzo turned back to Rebecca, his face suddenly alight with a charming smile. "It is business, I assure you, Becca. But no business is so important that it takes precedence over you."

Rebecca's plump face shone with pleasure. "Perhaps we should find a place to rest a little. I find I am overexcited from all this activity."

She did indeed appear excited, Alonzo noted. "Perhaps we *should* find a place," he said. "A private place, where you might recover ... undisturbed."

With one final furtive glance in Catherine's direction, Alonzo guided Rebecca through the crowd toward a curtained alcove. She was not Catherine, but past experience had told him she *was* a willing partner, and she offered a much-needed release for the tension that gripped him.

He would find a way to deal with Catherine later.

"You've brought about a miraculous change in this young man, Miss Breaux. But then, I suppose I shouldn't wonder at that. A beautiful woman wields great influence over a man and can sway him as nothing else can. I suppose Jase is no more immune to the allure of feminine charms than the rest of his fellows ... though until recently he has done admirably well in eluding those who would have caught him." Tom Galliher chuckled at his own wit and winked at Catherine. "Including my own Becky, who led the pack pursuing this wily fox. She was sorely vexed at the news of your betrothal."

Jase merely looked dubious.

"Luckily, the lass bounces back with amazing alacrity and is already in pursuit of her next quarry. My own disappointment, however, was not so easily salved." Tom's brown eyes twinkled at Catherine as he explained. "Jase's stables are the finest in the territory, without question, and it would have been quite the feather in my cap to claim him as a son-in-law. I suppose my loss is your good fortune."

"Indeed," Catherine murmured noncommittally. Jase was watching her with an unreadable expression, and she wondered what he was thinking. She met his penetrating stare with a sidelong glance cast from beneath her lashes, and for a long moment, their gazes locked.

"On the contrary," Jase murmured, his mouth curving in a slow smile that sent shivers along Catherine's spine. "It was my good fortune to have found Catherine when I did. And I shall move heaven and earth to keep her in my life."

Looking up into that dark and handsome visage, Catherine forgot to breathe. Mother of God. . . . His statement was no fabrication meant to pacify the curiosity of his hosts, but a bold declaration of his intent.

The thought that Jase wanted her caused a trembling weakness in her limbs, which she prayed he could not see. "If you are sincere, m'sieur, then I suggest you remember your promise."

One corner of Jase's mouth turned down imperceptibly. "Ah, yes," he said, "the governor. Catherine is eager to make his acquaintance, and I did promise to use what little influence I have to gain her an audience with him."

"Well, I'm sure that can be easily arranged." Tom frowned and looked around the room. "Hmmmp. He was here a minute ago ... talking with George Restwier and Albert Falsey." Tom shook his graying head. "Most likely he's besieged in a secluded corner by someone seeking favor. Listen, why don't I go and effect a rescue? You can wait in the blue room across the hall. That way you will be assured of a few moments of uninterrupted discourse. Jase knows the way."

Tom melted into the crowd, and Catherine was once again alone with Jase. She was keenly aware of his presence, of the looks of envy being cast in their direction by many of the young women as he guided her from the room and down the wide central hallway. In an effort to break the heavy silence that had fallen between them, Catherine put voice to her thoughts. "Tom is right, you know. You could have wed any one of them, doubling your lands and improving your fortunes. And yet you remained unwed. Why is that?"

Jase gazed down at her, a strange half smile on his lips. "Because the woman I wed will need be a woman of fire, to match my steel ... not some vapid creature who indulges in fits of the vapors to have her way."

"What of Rebecca?" Catherine asked. Her heart was beating rapidly, suffusing her cheeks with a gentle pink heat.

Raising a brow, Jase presented her with a sardonic look. "Fie, Catherine," he said, "I have already answered you. Despite Tom's wishes to the contrary, Rebecca means nothing to me."

Glancing around, she caught sight of a familiar

face, the woman who had visited Rosemunde late upon her last night there. She was standing in conversation with an elderly gentleman, not far away, and when Catherine met her gaze, the woman quickly looked away, taking great pains to appear casual. But not before Catherine saw the look of longing in her gray-green eyes. "There is no one in your life?" she asked pointedly.

Jase followed the direction of her gaze, but his expression revealed nothing of his feelings for Angela Dane. When he looked again to Catherine, his pale eyes were glinting. "If I didn't know differently, I would think you were jealous."

"Jealous?" Catherine tried to appear affronted, but her rapidly deepening blush gave her away. "I am not jealous!"

His wolfish grin appeared to taunt her. "I am glad to hear it, for I believe I've already found my woman of fire . . . therefore your jealousy would be wasted."

Catherine stared up into his dark countenance in wordless wonder, trying to think of something to say that would urge him to clarify his last statement without revealing the true nature of her feelings for him. Yet nothing clever came to her, and so she continued to gaze at him, heart lodged high in her throat.

Jase seemed not to notice her dilemma. He took her hand in both of his and brought it to his lips. "Since you took your departure from Rosemunde, I have had much time to think, to consider the future. A man should not live out his days alone. It isn't as nature intended."

Catherine smiled slightly. "Exactly what are you saying, Jason?"

"I am saying that I have come to some conclusions about my life, which for me were not easy to accept." He paused, chafing her hand lightly. "Hell," he said. "I don't know why this must be so difficult."

His manner amused Catherine. He seemed prepared to make some grave confession, yet appeared unable to form the words. "Jason, is something wrong?"

"Yes, dammit! Everything is wrong. The house, my life! Nothing has been the same since you left! Catherine, I—"

"St. Claire? I say, is that you?" Jase turned, frowning at the man who interrupted, unsure if he should bless or curse him.

"By God, yes, it is you!" the fellow continued. "I'd know you anywhere—but you don't recognize me, do you? It's Timothy Gladwyn, sir! From Nashville! Do you not recall? I visited your place early last year and purchased that fine two-year-old from your stables. Handsome piece of horseflesh he is, too! Shows a great deal of promise. . . ." Gladwyn leaned forward. "Listen, do you suppose I could steal you away? There is someone you must meet."

"Mr. Gladwyn, in other circumstances I would gladly comply, but I fear I am engaged at the moment—"

"Oh, but it will take only a moment of your time, sir, and I'm sure the young lady won't mind." Timothy Gladwyn beamed at Catherine.

"But of course I don't mind," she said readily,

catching sight of Jase's pained grimace. "Whatever it was M'sieur St. Claire was about to say can surely wait. Perhaps with time it will come more easily."

"Splendid!" Timothy Gladwyn said, taking hold of Jase's arm. But Jase pulled out of the man's grasp with a look of irritation and turned once more to Catherine.

"It seems to me that this matter between us has waited long enough, and begs to be resolved!"

"Oh?" she asked innocently. "And which matter is that?"

Jase's expression grew dark. "The matter of our future, if you must have it spelled out for you. I would have it out with you—set things to rights—if only I could manage a bit of privacy without the whole damnable territory plaguing me for a moment of my blessed time!"

Raking an impatient hand through his raven locks, he fairly glared.

Watching him, Catherine could not suppress a giggle.

"You dare to laugh, madam?" he demanded.

She did indeed dare, and in reply, laughed again. Behind Jase, Timothy Gladwyn coughed discreetly. "Go and have done with it," Catherine suggested with a lingering half smile.

"It seems I've little choice." Jase shot an angry glance over his shoulder at the pesky Mr. Gladwyn, then sighed through clenched teeth. "Wait for me here," he said to her. "And don't be wandering off. I'll be back momentarily, and if I find you gone, I won't be at all pleased."

"I'll wait," she promised, knowing that she

would not have considered doing otherwise. Tom Galliher was to bring the governor here so that she could meet with him, and all of Satan's imps could not have driven her from the spot.

While Jase was being led down the hallway by an eager Timothy Gladwyn, Catherine entered the room and closed the door.

Concealed by the shadows of the curtained alcove just across the hall, Alonzo watched the two men until they were out of sight, then, smiling, he parted the curtains and stepped into the hall.

Chapter 18

"You never learn, do you, Cathy?"

The words were sneered, laced with a venom Catherine found surprising coming from Alonzo. She'd been standing by the bank of windows, looking out at the torchlit front lawn, and thinking of Jase. Alonzo Hart had barely entered her thoughts since her arrival at the Gallihers'— but now she turned to face him. "Learn, m'sieur?" she said icily. "You sound as if you are addressing a child instead of a woman, fully grown."

"Oh, but you are a child. A very spoiled, willful child who badly needs chastising! That much is obvious from your actions! Why did you do it, Cathy? Why did you disobey me and come here with him, when I specifically said that you weren't to see him again?"

Until this moment the fires of Catherine's anger had remained carefully banked within her breast, but suddenly they flared up, scorching Alonzo with a heat to which he was unaccustomed. "You *dare* to question me? You, who would have kept me locked away like some felon, with that razor-tongued harpy acting as a jailer!"

"I did it to protect you," he replied. "But I don't expect your gratitude, Cathy—not while you are under the influence of that damnable black-hearted rogue!"

"I want you to leave, Alonzo."

"St. Claire has you mesmerized. So much so that you can't even recognize that you're making a fool of yourself! You'll see, though, once you're away from Natchez ... and then you'll come to your senses."

"I believe that at last I *have* come to my senses, Alonzo," Catherine replied. Never had she imagined that she would defend Jase St. Claire against Alonzo, but hearing Jase maligned by one who had so recently proven himself to be calculating and petty incensed her beyond all reason.

Her eyes, a smoldering blue-green, burned into Alonzo's. "I find it ironic indeed that the very one you name a damnable blackhearted rogue was the one who rescued me from your spiteful scheming. You are petty and vicious and small, Alonzo, and I will never forgive your actions this night! I only wish to God I'd had the wisdom to see you before now for what you truly are. Thankfully, it is not too late. I am not your wife, and never will be. I want you out of my life; the engagement is off!"

Alonzo laughed. "You faithless bitch, you have no idea what you're talking about. If you had any idea who your lover is, you would shudder and beg my forgiveness." Alonzo stopped and seemed to collect himself. He straightened his shoulders, tugged his sleeves down, and let out a patient breath. "You will need to change your ways, Cathy ... in effect, prove yourself worthy of my affections after your tumble into disgrace. But I know you will be more amenable when removed from his influence. St. Claire is to blame for your waywardness, to blame for everything."

"Beg, you say?" Catherine said with a terrible calm. "You self-centered, arrogant bastard. I will beg you to take yourself from my sight before I scream this house down!"

She opened her mouth to fulfill her threat, but before she could utter more than an outraged squeak Alonzo covered her mouth with a hand. Inches from her face, he snarled, "I am going, my dear, but you are coming with me! I hope you have fond memories of Jase St. Claire, Cathy, for they will need suffice ... you won't be seeing him again in this lifetime!"

Alonzo jerked Catherine to him with such force that her head snapped back; for the barest instant the moist palm covering her mouth slipped. She opened her mouth and clamped down with all her might on the soft flesh of his palm, wringing a yelp of pain from her captor. "You uncouth ass! Let go of me this instant, or I swear I'll make you rue this day!"

She struck out with all her might and her fist caught Alonzo squarely on the chin, causing him to curse and sputter and dab at his tongue. His fingers came away bloody; the sight seemed to fuel his anger, and before she could break away he brought back his hand and struck her a vicious blow that rocked her head back on her neck.

The room spun crazily. In a blur Catherine saw

Alonzo's face—saw the look of dawning horror which came over him as he gazed up at the man who haunted his life and his dreams—and then her legs folded beneath her and she was sitting down hard on the carpet. . . .

Jase lunged at Alonzo. Locking his hands around the younger man's throat, he knocked him to the floor, planted one knee in the center of Alonzo's chest, and slowly, deliberately, began to squeeze the life from him.

All of Jase's fury, all of his being, was focused on the mark that showed just above his left hand. It was a shallow crease in the flesh of Alonzo's neck, not healed as yet and still livid red around the dark scab.

Jase's fingers tightened convulsively around Alonzo's throat. When he'd caught the roan gelding two nights ago, he'd stroked the gleaming neck to calm the animal. His hand had come away sticky and red. The outlaw leader had been wounded, though not seriously enough to prevent his escape. . . .

Alonzo.

The one man he would never have suspected, because he was so close at hand. Too close, Jase thought. He'd had access to Rosemunde. Jase had accepted him as an associate, if not a friend. And all along Alonzo had been the one creating such anguish for Jase—and such grief throughout the territory.

Reality intruded. Catherine was tugging desperately on his arm. "Oh, Jason, no! Please, don't hurt him. For my sake, please!"

Jase stared at his factor's mottled face. "I'll kill

you for this, and slowly," he promised in a near whisper.

"Jason! Oh, God, please! You must listen!"

The frantic note in Catherine's voice penetrated Jase's rage. He looked up at her, pale eyes cold as ice shards, and slowly relaxed his deadly grip.

He had to get hold of himself. He could not end this here, in this fashion. Too many questions would be raised. Neither could he denounce Alonzo without bringing suspicion to bear upon himself. He was in a damned awkward position, and Alonzo knew it. Jase could see the light of satisfaction burning in his enemy's dark eyes.

They would settle it; of that there was no doubt. But not here, not tonight . . . not until Jase had the answers to some nagging questions.

Jase released Alonzo and got to his feet.

Alonzo choked and wheezed, struggling to recover.

"If you value your life, you will stay away from her," Jase warned.

Alonzo straightened his clothes with angry jerks, bringing the high stock he wore into place so that it once again concealed the wound on his throat. "What right have you to interfere?" he rasped. "Cathy is to be my wife."

The wolfish grin Jase displayed was decidedly unpleasant. "Is she now?" He flicked an icy glance her way. "Perhaps she should speak for herself. I, for one, am most interested in hearing what she has to say. Catherine?"

"We had a quarrel, is all!" Alonzo insisted. "It was nothing serious . . . nothing that required an outsider's unwelcome interference." He was breathing easier now, regaining his slightly bruised confidence. "She is headstrong beyond belief—stubborn and full of sass—"

"I agree wholeheartedly," Jase interjected, looking at Catherine, who stiffened and huffed indignantly. "But a little willfulness is hardly cause for a beating."

"I told you—" Alonzo began.

"I heard you quite clearly."

"Then there is no need for further discussion. Cathy and I will be leaving—"

"Not just yet." Jase spoke softly, but there was something in his voice that caused her to shiver. While she watched him, his gaze moved from Alonzo to her, and the intensity of that stare pierced her to her very heart. She swallowed, hearing his words with dread anticipation. He said, "I am unconvinced that you speak for Catherine, and I wish to hear it from her own lips." He slowly extended his hand, palm upward, in her direction. "Catherine . . . choose."

She drew a shaky breath. She felt as if she were standing high on a cloud-shrouded precipice. Behind her lay the unhappy past, ahead an uncertain future. If she stepped from the edge, she might tumble endlessly downward, into the abyss . . . or she might find a firmer footing than she had previously known.

Whatever her faults, she could not be accused of cowardice. Catching her bottom lip in her teeth, she gazed up into Jase's beloved blue eyes and stepped from the precipice . . . placing her small hand into his keeping.

His gaze never once left her face, but his words

were for Alonzo. "Your presence is no longer welcome, Hart. Get you gone while you still can."

Alonzo hesitated. He stood, hands clenching and unclenching at his sides. His face was mottled with rage, and there was a dark ring of bruised flesh circling his throat. "This isn't finished, Cathy, so don't grow too comfortable in his bed. You won't be there for long."

Jase started to break away from Catherine, a dangerous glint in his eyes, but the hand Catherine placed upon his arm gave him pause. For a brief moment their eyes met, then Jase shifted his hard gaze to Alonzo, inclining his head just slightly. "Leave this house now, or by my life you'll be carried out."

Alonzo's mouth thinned to a grim line. It required all the self-control he possessed to stride quickly past and make his way from the room. He knew St. Claire suspected that he was the outlaw ravaging the countryside . . . he had seen it in his rival's expression. But St. Claire couldn't prove anything. And without proof there was nothing he could do but wait and wonder if and where and how Alonzo would strike again.

He had come very close to disaster this night, Alonzo thought. But perhaps, after all, it had been worth it.

St. Claire might think that this was the end. But Alonzo knew it was just the beginning.

Winthrop Sargent, governor of Mississippi Territory, sat quietly as he listened to Catherine relate the details of Andre's murder, and all that had occurred since. When she finished speaking, she sat, hands folded demurely in her violet silk lap, waiting for him to make some pronouncement that would magically stop the violence occurring almost daily along the Chickasaw Trace.

The governor sighed heavily, pushing back in his chair. His expression was one of regret.

"Miss Breaux, your story greatly saddens me, and I truly wish I could grant your request to put an end to this senseless butchery. The fact, however distressing it may be, remains that the Black Lion is but one among many miscreants who plague our byways. Daily, tales such as yours filter in, and now and then an outlaw *is* taken. Yet for each one brought to justice two arise to take his place ... and thus the savagery continues.... I fear the lawlessness will continue to reign until this country is settled in truth. May God help us all until that day is realized."

"Then you will not help me find the Black Lion?" Catherine said, the keen edge of disappointment in her voice.

"I could send forth a party to search," Sargent said wearily, "but to what end? If indeed the Black Lion is actively marauding along the Trace—and I am not wholly convinced that he is—then I must assume that a renegade of that magnitude would take it upon himself to attain an intimate knowledge of the area. There are hundreds of places where he could hide, and a mere handful of men could not hope to find his lair."

Jase's hand, resting on Catherine's shoulder throughout the long discourse, was a comfort for her. Now, he gave her a gentle squeeze when she would have argued against the governor's decision. Instead, she sat silently, disillusionment weighing heavily upon her.

It hurt her deeply to think that she had failed Andre and failed Mose, who by now might also be dead.

Her thoughts drifted as Governor Sargent stood, murmuring his regrets, shaking Jase's hand and clapping his shoulder in friendly fashion. In a moment, he was gone . . . and Catherine's futile hopes for a swift justice were gone with him.

The Black Lion would remain free to rampage and kill.

Looking down at Catherine's small face, Jase could almost read her thoughts. Her lovely countenance was a mirror to her disappointment. Her eyes looked huge, and were swiftly filling with tears.

"Catherine," Jase said, pulling her up and into his arms. He held her close as she wept, feeling a foreign tightness in his own throat . . . a mute reply to her pain. For the thousandth time, Jase wished that it were within his power to wipe away his past . . . and Catherine's. It was not. And from here they could only go on.

To that end, he vowed to do his utmost to protect her, and there was only one way to make certain she would be safe.

"Darling," he said softly, brushing the curling golden tendrils from her temple, "this evening you have given me your trust. I wonder, can you give me your heart as well?"

Sniffing loudly, she raised her great blue-green eyes to consider him. "What did you say?"

Jase gazed down into her small upturned face

and smiled. Her lashes were damp and clung together, and her nose was mottled red, but he thought she was the most endearing bit of womanhood he had ever beheld. "Sweet, fiery Catherine," he said softly, "I want you for my wife. I have been trying to tell you all evening, to ask if you will consent. We are alone now, and I'm laying my heart before you. My darling Catherine, will you marry me? Will you share my life, my wealth, my home, my bed?"

She stared at Jase for a long moment while he held his breath, and slowly her lips curved up in a smile. "Yes, Jason. I'll take your heart, and gladly give you mine. I'll share your life . . . your home, and your bed."

Catherine was blushing as she came into Jase's arms. He barely noticed. He was too busy marveling at his good fortune.

Chapter 19

The following evening was well advanced when the master of Rosemunde Plantation arrived home with his intended bride. Tom Galliher's gala had lasted until the predawn hours, and because the subject of horses had been introduced among the gentlemen, Jase had been pressured to stay.

Arrangements had been made for the gentlemen, and Catherine had been led to a sumptuous guest chamber where she spent the night.

Tom Galliher took scandalous advantage of Jase's presence that morning, insisting that he view the stable and tour the fields before their departure, so that dusk was almost upon them when Jase and Catherine finally bade their host and hostess farewell and set off for Rosemunde.

From the moment Catherine entered the great house it became apparent that Jase had anticipated the evening's outcome. Dora and Leviticus were waiting in the foyer upon their arrival, and Catherine had no more than shrugged out of the black velvet cloak than she was swiftly ushered into the library.

Though the hour was late, the room was brilliant with candlelight and a fire had been kindled in the grate to banish the chill. Its cheery glow seemed to fascinate the scarecrow's figure who awaited their arrival. He turned as they entered and gave a solemn nod of acknowledgment. In his right hand was a well-worn Bible.

Catherine turned to Jase with a look of amazement.

His hard mouth curled slightly at the corners. "Patience has always eluded me," he said. "And I would have our marriage made fact before you change your mind."

"How could you know that I would be willing?" she wondered. Surely he could not have known her better than she knew herself!

Jase merely shrugged. "It was a gamble, and well worth the risk." He took her hand in his and brought her close to his side, then turned and gave his full attention to the Reverend Hezekiah Rose.

With half an ear, Catherine listened to the man's ringing voice while he extolled the virtues of matrimony. Outside, a storm was venting its fury against the French windows. A gusting wind moaned mournfully about the eaves, adding to the strange dreamlike quality of the scene slowly unfolding before them.

The mantel clock counted down the hour of midnight, the final dulcet note fading away just as the vows were spoken that would bind Catherine to Jase for all eternity.

"I, Jason Edward St. Claire, take thee Catherine—"

He sounded so sure, so unfaltering, vowing to love and to cherish her for his lifetime. . . .

Catherine's mind was reeling.

It was all happening so quickly. When she had accepted his proposal, she had assumed that she would be granted a small reprieve, a little time in which to come to know Jase better. She should have known that, as in all things, Jase would masterfully turn events to his own liking, never content for matters to run their natural leisurely course.

By his own admission he was an impatient man, and Catherine wondered with mounting concern if he would bring that same impatience into the privacy of their marriage bed.

Looking up into his grave visage, she shivered.

At that same instant Hezekiah Rose turned his intense gaze upon her. "Catherine Blaise Breaux—"

She listened to the words with all the joy of a funeral dirge. Her heart was beating wildly. If she answered, she would be pledging to bear Jase's weight in bed, to bear his babes . . . and he, a relative stranger.

This very night she had learned a hard lesson. She had thought she'd known Alonzo Hart, a friend to her family for years, only to discover that all she had known of him was what he had wanted her to see.

Would it be the same with Jase? Would she awaken some day to discover that he had duped her and was in reality altogether different from the man she had at first thought him to be?

It was a question seemingly without answer. Only passing time would reveal the consequences of tonight's impetuosity.

Hezekiah queried Catherine, breaking into her troubled musings, and everyone in the room held their breath.

Jase said nothing as he looked down into her small, frightened countenance, but he caught her hand in his.

Somewhere in the background, Dora sniffed.

The warmth, the strength, the tenderness in Jase's grasp was the deciding factor for Catherine. It opened up her heart and the words came pouring out. She swore before God and these witnesses to love, to honor, and to cherish him. Only when it came to the word *obey* did she falter.

Hezekiah looked sternly down his nose at her. "This is most irregular," he said. "God's Word says—"

Watching his bride closely, Jase saw her small chin elevate a notch and, knowing she was girding herself for battle, quickly intervened. "It is enough, Rose, and I am satisfied. I don't intend to stand here all bloody night while you test the depth of my lady's stubbornness. Get on with it."

Hezekiah harrumphed to show his disapproval, but nonetheless proceeded with the ceremony.

Again Catherine willingly placed her hand into Jase's keeping, this time in marriage. With a swelling heart, she watched as he slipped the golden band onto her finger, brightly shining proof that she now belonged to him. "With this ring, I thee

wed . . . and with all my worldly goods I thee en-
dow. . . ."

He had promised her his world, and she had accepted.

It was done, and there remained no reason for
Catherine to deny him. As Jase drew her against
his lean hard length, she caught her breath, but no
protest was forthcoming. Whatever restraint was
left within her melted away as ice beneath the hot
caress of the delta sun, the moment his lips met
hers.

With eagerness Jase claimed her, unashamedly
unleashing the passion he had so long held in
check, seemingly oblivious to those who looked
on, smiling.

At first Catherine made to pull away, but in a
moment she forgot Dora, forgot Leviticus, forgot
the Reverend Hezekiah Rose, and wound her arms
around her husband's neck.

When at last the kiss was broken, Jase smiled
down into her heavy-lidded eyes and gave her
into Dora's keeping. "It's been a long day," he
murmured against her cheek. "Go with Dora and
prepare for bed, and I'll join you in a little while."

Feeling strangely compliant, Catherine gave the
briefest of nods and followed Dora from the room.

Jase had apparently thought of everything, for
when Catherine entered the master bedchamber
she found that a fire had been laid in the hearth
and a steaming tub was positioned cozily before it.
For a few moments, she stood uncertainly near the
door while Dora bustled about, placing the clean
towels, a washcloth, and several bars of soap

within easy reach of the tub. Catherine avoided looking at the huge bed which dominated not only the room but her thoughts as well.

All too soon, Dora was finished and turned to go. "If there's nothing else I can do then, madam, I'll just say good night."

Catherine searched her mind for some flimsy excuse to detain the housekeeper . . . and found none. "Good night, Dora—and thank you."

"Rest well, madam."

"I'm sure I will," she said, then privately wondered if she would rest at all. The door closed quietly, and she glanced around the room she would be sharing with her husband, the one room in the manse that she had never seen.

The chamber was richly but plainly appointed, with no adornment on the jade silk walls. The only furnishings were the big bed, a spacious wardrobe containing his clothing, and two wing-backed chairs covered in the same gold brocade that comprised the bed hangings.

It all seemed impersonal to Catherine, and she could find nothing of her husband's character in any of it.

Sighing, she began to disrobe, carefully laying her amethyst gown over one of the chairs, then her chemise and stockings. She went to the tub and stepped over the rim, sinking down. The delicious warmth of the silken water slowly seeped into her taut flesh, soothing her nerves as she settled back for a moment's relaxation. . . .

That was when her gaze lit upon a rifle, ancient in appearance and in such disrepair as to appear worthless, mounted over the mantel. Even from this distance, she could see that the stock was split lengthwise and had been bound together by a crudely fashioned leather sling. Positioned carefully upon wooden pegs above the blazing hearth, the weapon seemed at odds with the rich surroundings, a strange keepsake for a landed gentleman.

Perhaps, like the portraits which hung in the dining room, the rifle was some relic left by the former owner, and had nothing at all to do with her husband.

Husband. . . .

How very peculiar it felt to call him that, Catherine thought, looking down at the golden band encircling the third finger of her left hand. It was the very ring that she had given him two weeks ago, the ring that Andre had clutched in his hand during his last moments. It was ironic that Jase had used this particular ring to bind them together . . . but then, perhaps there had been no opportunity to purchase another ring. She stared, fascinated by the way the gold glinted in the fire's glow. Was it a rich promise for the future? Or a cold metallic wink at the turnings of capricious fate?

Only time would tell, she thought, picking up a linen cloth and testing the fragrance of each bar of soap. One had a floral scent, reminiscent of her mother's flower garden on a warm day in spring. The second was a woodsy scent, musk and moss and fresh green ferns. The third smelled of spice and something exotic, undefinable.

Each was equally pleasing, but which one would Jase prefer?

Catherine pondered the question long—too long, she soon discovered, for the door opened and closed quietly, and when she raised her startled gaze, Jase was standing just inside the door, his hand resting on the knob.

For a moment he just stood, his pale eyes warming as they traveled over her, seeming to penetrate the shadowy waters that hid her nakedness from view.

Catherine felt the heat of a slow blush rise into her cheeks, but she made no move to shield her body from his hungry gaze. She only lowered her lids, so that her lashes masked the uncertainty she was feeling, and waited. . . .

Slowly, he moved to one of the brocade chairs. Slipping off his coat, he slung it across the chair back, then pulled his shirttail from his breeches. Catherine's breathing quickened as she watched him, fascinated.

His hands were beautiful, undeniably masculine, but elegantly formed, with long supple fingers burned brown by the sun. They possessed such a quiet strength, those hands, and she couldn't help but wonder what tasks they had performed before his coming to Rosemunde. Much of his life was a mystery, but perhaps tonight would clear away some of her questions.

"Why do you tarry, madam?" His voice startled her, and she looked up at him with an expression of complete candor.

"I was wondering which soap you would like," she said, "and then again, wondering about you."

Jase smiled a little. "I rather like the smell of *you*, Catherine, so suit your own fancy as to fragrance." Pointedly, he ignored the second half of her admission.

She, however, was undaunted by his obvious reluctance to reply immediately. She picked up the bar of soap smelling of ferns and moss and began to lather her cloth, watching him all the while. "Will you tell me something of yourself?" she said. "I still know very little of you, aside from your beginnings, and I should like to know the man I married, the father of my children." She fought back the blush that crept into her cheeks and looked levelly at him. "If there are to be children of this union, they have a right to know their father." Almost shyly, she added, "You want children, don't you, Jason? Sons to carry on your name?"

With a sigh, he looked away. He unbuttoned his shirt and slid it off, placing it over the coat on the chair back. "Until now I hadn't considered the possibility," he admitted.

Glancing at her again, he noticed that she looked somewhat crestfallen. He frowned, feeling the chafe of his impatience. He hadn't come up here to launch some lengthy discussion but to hold her and love her as he'd dreamed so long of doing. But first he would have to extract her from that damnable tub.

Rising from the chair, Jase went to the tub and knelt down. Reaching out a hand to cup her chin, he tipped up her face and gently touched his lips to hers. The kiss was tentative, tender in the extreme. It displayed more clearly than words how he felt about her, and he only regretted that it was not enough.

When he sat back upon his booted heels, she still wore that perplexed little frown. "It never occurred to me that you wouldn't want children," she said. "I thought that every man—"

Jase stilled her words with another kiss, this one longer, warmer, less tender than the last. His loins ached with wanting her. "*I want you*, Catherine," he said against her lips, "and if there are children, then I will accept them. But pray God they are not sons to tread the paths that I have walked. It would be a fitting punishment indeed for my many transgressions." He smiled a little. "Daughters would be more to my liking. Yes," he said emphatically, "little girls with flaxen tresses and smiling lips and temperaments sweeter than that of their firebrand mother."

He kissed her again, leaning forward until he was partially immersed in the water himself, and gathered her into his arms. It mattered not at all if she was finished with her bath, for Jase lifted her and carried her dripping to the bed, where he lay her down.

"You are a wicked man, Jason St. Claire," she declared breathlessly.

"Never doubt it," he said.

"And you've likely just ruined the counterpane!"

"I never liked it anyway."

He pressed her onto the feather mattress, kissing her deeply. She opened her mouth to his tongue's silken invasion, tasting the slight tang of whiskey, welcoming him in. With the eagerness of innocence, she toyed with him, rubbing against him, gently drawing him farther into her mouth until she heard his low and anguished groan.

But Jase was in no mood to rush. And not until he had fully explored her sweetness did he move on, raining kisses along her jaw, down her throat.

Growing ever bolder, Catherine put her arms around him, touching him as she had done only once before, and then so briefly. Now she had every right to do so, and she indulged the privilege, curling her fingers into the long hair at his nape, running her hands over the corded muscles of his shoulders and back, conducting her own exploration. . . .

How satin-smooth his skin was, how warm, how wondrous to touch! From his nape to his ribs to his waistband and beyond. . . . She plunged her fingers into the restricting breeches, sighing heavily when her palms sought and found the muscular swells of his buttocks.

She heard him gasp, felt the sharp little pang as he gently sank his teeth into her shoulder, and gasped herself. Pleasurable shock waves radiated outward, along the tendon that joined her neck to shoulder. "Oh, Jason!"

He barely heard her cry. He was moving downward, sampling the sweetness of her breasts. Christ, but she was lovely, so virginal and pure. Her skin was still damp; it glistened like liquid pearls in the firelight. Lowering his head, he took her nipple into his mouth, feeling it come erect under the worshipful ministrations of his teeth and tongue.

Beneath him, Catherine softly moaned, her small hands pressing against his shoulders. She rolled her head against the mattress and called his name.

"Oh, Jason, please. . . ." Her flesh was on fire, and in the midst of the exquisite torture which Jase was practicing upon her, all of her questions about his past were forgotten.

The only thing remaining in her universe was the white-hot need which centered in her lower belly. At once it was terrible and wonderful, an ache and a fantastic longing . . . an emptiness which Jase alone could fill.

With feverish hands, she urged him upward again, to communicate her desires, but he was moving at cross-purposes, lower, ever lower, homing in on the very center of her desire.

When he first touched the ache, she cried aloud. She could not help it.

The lavish kisses he bestowed upon her woman's flesh were hot and searing, kisses that were excruciatingly intimate, which left little doubt that he meant to possess her wholly. And when this night was over, there would not be an inch of flesh he had not thoroughly pleasured, or a darkened corner of her soul his penetrating gaze had not plumbed.

Possess her he would, undeniably and completely, and Catherine could only bow before his iron will.

His breath was hot against her womanhood. She could feel the roughness of his beard stubble brush her inner thighs. And his exploring tongue . . . so insistent and so knowledgeable in carnal matters . . . instructed her in the secret ways of man and woman that had until this moment remained a dark and erotic mystery.

Deep in the untouched recesses of her being passion bloomed like an exotic night flower unfolding. Velvet petals unfurled beneath his practiced seduction, stretching outward toward the rising sun that was her lover, her husband.

Catherine's tension was mounting. Restlessly, she tossed upon the dampened counterpane, wanting an end to the madness which gripped her ... wanting it to continue forever. A sob of anguish escaped her throat in the form of Jase's name ... and then he was there, covering her quaking, burning body with one that was strong and invincible ... and she was drowning in his kisses, breathing Jase, lifting her hips instinctively to press against his maleness.

At the crucial moment when he claimed her, Jase St. Claire looked down at his bride. With her golden tresses in sweet disarray around a face gone taut with yearning, she appeared a disheveled angel, and he paused to wonder how a man such as he had chanced to win the heart of a woman like Catherine. She was perfect in every way imaginable, and, God help them both, she seemed to love him.

The fates had indeed been kind.

With exquisite care Jase took her, kissing away the soft cry she uttered as he pierced her maidenhead, murmuring her name again and again ... as if to remind himself that she truly was real and that nothing could wrest her from him after this night.

Slowly he began to move, seeking the age-old

rhythm of life and continuance, of love and physical union. Catherine learned swiftly, meeting his every thrust with hips poised high, tightening her muscles to hold him deep inside, releasing him for his withdrawal only with the greatest reluctance.

Every ounce of Jase's will was now employed to keep his wild response in check, to prevent his filling her prematurely with his seed.

Sweet Mother of Christ! Her hot sheath gripped him like a molten glove. There seemed no end to the ecstatic waves that swelled and swelled and then suddenly crashed against his senses ... too powerful to be contained.

Bending his dark head, Jase closed his eyes and dragged her tightly against him, feeling the shuddering release that shook her small frame, closely mirroring his own. ...

Catherine cried out as the shattering climax claimed her, one surging wave after another, before they faded to pleasurable ripples. So this was what it meant to love a man. It was incredible, wondrous! She uttered a soul-deep sigh of contentment and tangled her fingers in his hair, pressing a tender kiss to the jagged white scar at his temple. "Never will I love you more than I do at this moment," she whispered, then kissed the scar again.

"Nor I you," Jase answered. "Nor I you."

Long after the blaze of passion had burned away, leaving only glowing embers, Catherine lay curled trustingly against Jase's side and slept, her small hand resting in the center of his chest, close against his heart.

One by one the candles guttered out, until the

room was left in darkness. Yet plagued by the words of Hezekiah Rose, Jase couldn't sleep.

He frowned into the dark. And as Catherine sighed contentedly in her sleep, snuggling closer, he retraced in his mind the events of the evening.

He'd spoken with Reverend Rose following the nuptials, but their talk had done little to confirm his suspicions about Alonzo. Rose had reported to Jase his discussion with the man who had witnessed a murder along the Trace. "You must understand his position, friend," Rose had said to Jase. "He has seen firsthand the cruelty of the killer, and he fears reprisals."

"I should think he would want to help put an end to the killing," Jase said. "Surely the risk to his own skin is minimal."

Hezekiah sighed, a doleful sound, shaking his head. "A man of color speaking out against a wealthy white man. Tell me, friend, is there one person in the territory, besides you and I, who would believe him? You must understand. Perhaps when this is over . . ."

Jase understood, but he didn't like the situation. He had a witness who could identify the killer, but was too fearful to come forward. He had suspicions, but no proof. It was his word against Alonzo's, and in light of his past, he himself could not afford to go to the authorities. He had far too much to lose.

His only consolation lay snuggled close beside him in the big feather bed. Catherine was safe. Alonzo could not touch her, could not taint her with his madness.

Holding Catherine close, Jase watched the darkness gradually fade into the drab gray of predawn. Water dripped lazily from the eaves, plopping softly to the ground far below. The rain had ceased, but the world outside this room still seemed dull and uninteresting ... while the soft and naked body of his wife beckoned to his rising needs.

Setting aside his cares, Jase turned to Catherine, pulling her against his long length and kissing her awake. He pressed his mouth to her cheek, her ear, her neck ... all the while telling her in his own wordless fashion how very dear she was to him.

With an abandon that surprised them both, she responded. All restraints had been torn asunder the previous night. She was shameless as she pressed him back into the pillows, smiling coyly down into his dark and handsome face. "Are there not many ways to share in each other?" she questioned, her voice soft with sleep.

"There are," Jase said with mounting interest.

"And as your wife, I am permitted to try my hand? To take control?"

Raising a suspicious brow, Jase peered at her. "So long as that dainty hand does not wield a stiletto, madam, you are indeed permitted."

He made to rise, but she pressed him back again, bending to run her small pink tongue in a leisurely path from his neck to his breastbone. She felt the answering leap of his pulse and laughed wickedly. "Not afraid, are you, M'sieur Husband?"

Jase grabbed for her, but she caught his hands and pressed them down as she moved to kneel between his thighs. Bending low, she allowed her curls to slide along his flat belly, taking perverse pleasure in the way he flinched and glared at her. But the hot light shining in those beloved pale eyes had nothing to do with anger, and everything to do with passion.

Mercilessly, she teased him, watching him intently as he reclined against the pillows . . . biting here and licking there, running her fingers down his inner thighs and back again. When at last she took him into her mouth, mimicking the kisses he had bestowed upon her last night, he closed his eyes and threw back his raven head, letting loose a savage growl.

Catherine laughed. She could not help it. And tried to silence him between giggles.

"They'll think I am killing you!" she admonished. She ran her tongue round the tip of his maleness and took him again into her mouth. He tasted of male musk and her . . . not at all unpleasant.

"I swear you are," he rasped. "But thunderation, I'll die a deliriously happy man." He would have made the sound again, except that Catherine, swiftly covered his mouth with her hand, then bent once again to her torture.

Chapter 20

Breakfast the following morning was a leisurely affair. Jase had risen early, as was his habit, and had already been to the stable to confer with Bobby Means concerning a mare that was ready to foal. Now, he sat perusing a newspaper while he sipped his coffee.

Down the long and gleaming board, Catherine toyed with her food, pushing to-and-fro the pile of fluffy scrambled eggs and casting frequent, furtive glances at the newspaper which all but hid Jase from view.

Several moments passed before the silence was punctuated by yet another feminine sigh and the rattle of the paper as Jase lowered it to peer at her. "What is it that plagues you this morning, Catherine? You've been looking at me as if I've grown horns and a tail."

She folded her hands in her lap. "I was thinking of last night."

"Oh?" His hard mouth curled at the corners, and he relaxed a little. "Was there something in

particular about last night which sticks in your
thoughts, or was it last night in general?"

He was wicked to tease her, Catherine thought.
"I was referring to our discussion, and how neatly
you avoided the issue at hand." She gave him no
opportunity to guide the conversation in some
safer, more desirable direction. "I am your wife,"
she pointed out, "yet I know very little about
you."

Jase watched her for a long moment before
forming his reply. There was a tentative warmth in
her manner, a gentle caring light deep in her turquoise eyes ... both of which would wither and
die if he told her of his past. And for the life of
him, he could not wantonly destroy this tentative
beginning they had forged between them.

The bond that held them together was new and
fragile. It needed time to strengthen—though,
even as he thought it, he knew that a hundred
years spent in perfect harmony would not soften
the blow that Catherine would sustain upon discovering that she had unwittingly married the
Black Lion.

Jase was undeniably selfish. He had his heart's
desire; he was not prepared to give her up, to
watch her affection turn to hatred.

Perhaps he never would be.

"Yes," he slowly said, "you are my wife ... and
with all my heart and all my strength I will ensure
that you remain exactly that. I have vowed to
share my life from this day onward with you, to
give you my unrelenting devotion. Everything I
own is yours, Catherine. . . ."

"I do not dispute your generosity," she countered. "But I did not marry you for your wealth."

"Indeed?" He raised his brows, his expression turning devilish. He tossed aside the paper and pushed back his chair, patting his thigh. "Why don't you come over here and tell me just why you married me."

A flush of pleasure washed over Catherine, but she refused to be dissuaded. She recognized his tactics. Each time she raised questions about his past he did not wish to answer, he deftly turned the topic, ignored the question, or otherwise diverted her attention, thereby delaying the inevitable. "What is it you are hiding, m'sieur?"

"Hiding, madam?"

He looked innocent, Catherine thought. In fact, his expression was very like the one he had affected that night in the stable when she'd accused him of sabotaging her clothing. "Jason St. Claire," she said, "you cannot elude this issue forever."

"You are looking for confessions, are you?"

"I am looking for the truth."

Jase sighed heavily. The look of innocence was gone; his expression was guarded. "I haven't lied to you, Catherine. Each time you have asked questions, I have answered. I cannot for the life of me imagine what else you wish to know!"

His sharp tone wounded her. She twisted the wedding band on her finger, feeling suddenly and inexplicably vulnerable. The ring reminded her of Andre, of Jase's promise to help her find the killer, of the fact that he still roamed free. . . . It seemed a good place to begin.

"The night I gave you this ring you were open

with me. You offered your aid in my search for
Andre's killer. You even admitted that you too
were searching for the Black Lion, long before you
came upon Mose and me that first night. You said
your reasons were personal, Jason, but you did not
explain. I am asking you now, as your wife and
your helpmate, to share them with me. What is
your interest in this matter? Surely your motive
must be a strong one to drive you into searching
so relentlessly."

Jase raked a hand through his hair and stood,
walking slowly to the windows. The tension that
gripped him was palpable. "Suffice it to say that I
do not like what has been occurring in this vicinity
any more than you."

Another evasion. She frowned. "This time that
will *not* suffice, Jason."

"Then kindly tell me what *will* suffice, madam,"
he grated, his patience quickly eroding beneath
her cool persistence. "What can I say that will put
an end to your damnable inquiries?"

"Why won't you discuss this? We are wed, Jason! There can be no secrets between us!" Rising
from the table, she went to him, placing a hand on
his shoulder. It was like touching living stone,
warm but unyielding. "It hurts me to see you like
this. Why won't you tell me what is wrong?"

He turned slowly to face her, and the gaze he
fixed upon her chilled her to the marrow. "This
time you ask too much of me," he said. "What you
want, I cannot give."

"Jason," Catherine said, her voice trembling,
"you are frightening me. I am your wi—"

He seized her by the upper arms, his fingers biting into her soft flesh. "Yes, you are my wife! And that is reason enough for you to not press me on this matter!"

The moment he said the words he wished to call them back. Staring into her upturned face, he saw her blink, and her look of bewilderment quickly changed to one of hurt, anger. She looked at him as if she did not know him, and it hurt Jase all the more because it was the truth. *She did not know him. She had seen only the portion of him he had allowed her to see.* "Catherine," he said lamely.

"Let go of me."

She was pale and trembling. Jase would not let her go. He relaxed his grip without releasing her, but when he attempted to draw her against him, she wrenched away. "Catherine, please, you must listen—"

"Listen," she said. "Yes, I will listen—when you are ready to tell me the truth, but not before. I want no more of your evasions, Jason, no more of your denials. You are keeping something from me, some part of your life which you are unwilling to share. I want to know why that is."

He reached out to her, but she moved away, out of his reach, hugging her arms as though they pained her. She had every right to be defensive, he thought, but they had to get past this, to get back the closeness, the intimacy of last night.

"I am no mongrel hound to whom you can throw the scraps of your life which you feel free to give," she said. "I am a selfish woman, Jason. I will have all of you, or I will have none. In this I will not compromise."

"You pledged your love," he said. "I am asking for your trust."

"You dare to ask for trust—you, who will not give it!"

Jase's fingers curled inward, hardening to un-yielding fists which he lowered to his sides. Damn her curiosity! Damn her dogged nature! Damn ca-pricious fate for giving with one hand and wrenching away with the other!

How could he give what she was asking when two nights ago she had stood before the territorial governor and prettily begged for the Black Lion's head upon a platter? How could he possibly give her his trust?

How could he not?

His blood turned cold in his veins and every painful beat of his heart seemed to push her a lit-tle farther out of his reach. "Perhaps someday I can do what you ask," he said. "But not now. There is too much at stake. I cannot take the chance."

"When, Jason? When will you open up to me? When will you allow me to be your wife in truth? After a year has gone by? Two or ten? Or never. . . ." She shook her head and produced a sad smile. "I am sorry, but it is not enough. You must realize that it takes more than sharing a bed and board to sustain a marriage. There must be trust as well. You vowed last night to share your life and lot with me. Today, you close yourself off. I do not understand you, Jason. And what is infi-nitely worse, I fear I never shall."

Before he could reply, she brushed past him and ran from the room. He listened to her sobs as she hurried up the stairs to the master bedchamber, and then the door slammed and there was silence.

Jase turned back to the windows, rubbing the knotted muscles in his neck and shoulders, and sighed. "There may come a day very soon," he said softly, "when you wish to Christ you had not asked."

Catherine dressed carefully for dinner that evening. The gown she chose was fashioned of apricot silk shot through with golden threads, one of Jase's favorites. She had had all afternoon to think, and she had decided that what could not be achieved on demand might well be gained through seduction.

She was feeling confident when she entered the dining room. But Jase was not waiting by the sideboard, whiskey in hand. Her confidence was beginning to dwindle as she turned to Dora, who was laying a single place setting. "Is Jason in the library, Dora?"

Dora looked flustered. "Mr. St. Claire sends his regrets, Miss Catherine. He won't be supping at home this evening."

"Oh, I see." She tried not to let her disappointment show. "Did he say where he was going?"

"No, madam. Only that something important came up, and for you not to wait up. He may not be returning this evening."

Catherine said nothing. She took her solitary place at the end of the long table and picked at her food while the painted faces in the portraits gazed sourly down at her. Then, when she could bear the silence no longer, she retired to the master bed-chamber and prepared for bed.

Leviticus had kindled a fire in the grate to dispel the dampness that had invaded the house after the prolonged rain. She curled in the large wing chair by the fireside, her feet drawn up beneath her fine lawn night rail and blue silk robe. A book lay open in her lap, but she had spared it no more than a glance or two. Her thoughts, her heart, were elsewhere.

Sighing heavily, she stared at the ring Jase had placed on her left hand. She had been wed for less than a day, and already she was miserable. She thought of Jase, of the way he had been that morning, and her heart grew heavy with a painful, yearning ache as persistent as her troubling thoughts.

Where was Jase now? What business had called him away? Nothing legitimate, she was certain. He was searching for Andre's killer, and at this very moment he could be locked in violent confrontation with the outlaw. She lowered her face, and a single tear fell onto the open page. He could be hurt, or dying, while she sat and pretended to read.

This waiting was unbearable. She closed the book, stood, and walked to the windows, holding the tome clutched close to her breast. Outside, the rain had ended, but the sky was furrowed with clouds. She gazed at the distant trees, beyond which lay the Chickasaw Trace. With trembling fingers, she touched the cold glass pane; the ring upon her hand shone brightly as she whispered, "Please, God, keep him safe."

* * *

The brick residence on Franklin Street in Natchez was dark and silent. Across the way, concealed by the deep shadows of a ramshackle structure, Jase watched and waited.

"Deserted," Wools Burke said. "Been that way since the night of Galliher's shindig." He glanced at Jase. "You don't suppose he's cut and run, do you?"

"Any rational man would have, given his position. But I'm not so sure Alonzo's rational." Jase was quiet for a moment before continuing. "No, I don't think he's even considered leaving. He seems to have the crazy notion that he can hide behind the Black Lion and not be touched by what he does."

Wools snorted. "Maybe it's not so crazy, eh, *Meshepeshe?* He's picked a hell of a scapegoat for his villainy. There aren't many who would pass up the chance to nail your hide to the barn door."

Jase grunted. "Keep watch. I'm going to head up Hastings's way. I doubt Alonzo will like working alone. He may be recruiting fellow outlaws."

The same moon that lighted Jase's way from Natchez turned the garden at the rear of the Galliher mansion to a lush forest awash in silver and black. The cloaked figure moving silently along the gravel path to the garden gate did not pause to admire the night in all its glory ... just hurried on, its single-minded purpose apparent in its quick, furtive movements.

Just ahead, a huge mulberry tree shaded the path, casting it in deepest shadow. The scurrying

figure slowed, and Rebecca turned her hooded
head for a final look at the house before plunging
headlong into the darkness. Almost immediately,
she was seized by the arm and dragged several
steps backward. The sharp cry she would have uttered was stifled by the hand which clamped
across her mouth.

"I can't imagine why you've dragged me over
here," her captor rasped beside her ear, "but I
gather it must be urgent."

Rebecca stilled, recognizing Alonzo's voice instantly. He moved his hand from her mouth,
bringing it to rest at the curve of her throat. "It is,
or I would not have summoned you. I'm late," she
blurted out. "My cycle should have begun two
weeks ago, and I want to know what you intend
to do about it."

Alonzo did not reply immediately, but his caressing hand was suddenly still. She strained to
see his expression, to fathom his reception of this
unexpected news, but the shadows prevented her.
"You know you were the first," she said, hoping to
provoke some response. "And Papa won't take it
kindly if you run out on me."

"Becca . . ." There was a slight warning note in
the sibilant tones. "What have you done?"

"Nothing . . . yet," she admitted. "But I can't
wait forever for you to do right by me. And you
can't have everything your way. You'll have to set
aside your intended, Alonzo, and marry me."

He looked down at the pale oval of Rebecca's
face. He did indeed intend to have everything his
way. Drawing Rebecca back even farther into the
concealing shadows, he darted a swift glance at

the house before bending to kiss her. In an instant she was more pliant, and raised no objection as he led her toward the garden gate where his horse was waiting.

Chapter 21

The next morning Catherine breakfasted alone. Leviticus stood sentinel by the door, as always, attentive to her every need. But even he seemed subdued this morning, the lines in his cherubic face a little more apparent.

Catherine sighed. She seemed incapable of lifting her sagging spirits above the tops of her dainty slippers.

The pastry Aunt Sade had prepared for breakfast smelled delicious, yet Catherine didn't eat. She simply sat, sighing at frequent intervals and sipping her coffee.

Jase had not returned home last night.

For a long while she had waited, and finally she had fallen asleep in the wing chair. At half past four she had wakened with a painful crick in her neck. At first she had listened for his footsteps, expecting him to materialize from the shadows and coax her to bed. But the stultifying silence had remained unbroken except for the rhythmic tick of the mantel clock.

Disappointment weighing heavily upon her,

Catherine had gone to bed alone, and had found the large rice bed cold and empty without Jase's warmth. She'd tossed and turned, seeking a comfort she was not destined to find ... and toward dawn had drifted off to sleep, dreaming unsettling nightmares of Jase being confronted by bandits as he tried to reach her ... of the Black Lion wreaking havoc on her life yet again. ...

A few hours later she had risen, filled with a strange foreboding which refused to be dislodged. Even now, she could not shake the feeling that something wasn't right.

It was ridiculous to worry, of course, for Jase was more than capable of taking care of himself. Though she had thought the same thing of Andre, shortly before his death. ...

Catherine placed her cup on its saucer and strained to listen. Had she heard the sound of hoofbeats?

She glanced at Leviticus, who was freshening her coffee, and asked, "Did Jason leave any instructions before he departed last evening?"

Leviticus looked uncomfortable. "None, madam."

She felt deflated. She would have liked to question him further, suspecting that little went on at Rosemunde that escaped Leviticus's watchful eye but pride prevented her from asking if he knew where Jase was and what kept him from home so long. To admit that her husband did not see fit to discuss his plans with her was humiliating enough. She would not grill Jase's servant concerning his whereabouts.

Besides, there was a part of her which shied

from delving too deeply into Jase's activities for fear of what she might find.

She thought of the woman, Angela Dane, whom she suspected had been Jase's mistress, and there was a horrible moment when she considered the possibility that their affair had not ended, that he might have devised a way to keep both wife and mistress, that through the years ahead there would be many nights as empty as the one just passed.

The possibility was disconcerting.

"Is there anything else I can get for you, mum?" Leviticus asked.

Catherine offered him a sad smile. "No," she said, "I'm fine." But the words sounded wooden.

Silence stretched between them, broken at last by the sound of the front door being opened and closed, and then by Jase's familiar footfalls.

Catherine tried to appear unruffled. Relief washed over her that he was home, but she felt anger and resentment also as she looked him up and down.

He cut a rakish figure as he strode into the dining room, and she could understand the attraction he must hold for Mrs. Dane. His shining black hair had been mussed by the wind and fell forward to frame a face drawn with fatigue.

Striding directly to Catherine's chair, he bent down to kiss her cheek, murmuring a casual salutation before taking his accustomed seat at the opposite end of the table.

Leviticus hurried to serve him, but Jase waved him away. "Just coffee," he said.

With a jaundiced eye, Catherine watched him

lean back in his chair, brushing back the tousled locks caught on the rough stubble of his beard.

The unconscious action bared his left cheek to her gaze.

Three livid furrows, dark with dried blood, scored his lean cheek diagonally, looking very much as if they had been bestowed by a feminine hand.

Catherine's heart squeezed painfully in her breast. Quite suddenly she felt ill. It took her a moment to find her voice, and when she did, the calm with which she spoke surprised her. "How did you find Natchez?"

"Disappointingly uneventful," he answered. "I am afraid I did not accomplish what I set out to do."

"Indeed?" she questioned coolly, wondering what sort of business a man could have in Natchez that would rake savagely at his face and leave him looking worn and exhausted. She could think of only one.

The chill in the room was not lost on Jase. He slowly raised his head to regard her. She was sitting stiffly, as though ready to spring to her feet and flee his presence. It was apparent she was still angry with him, and doubtless the fact that he had stayed out all night had not helped matters.

There was an argument coming, which he could think of no way to avoid. Still, he longed to put it all behind them—selfishly, perhaps—to find what comfort he could in their relationship, to have her once more warm and pliant in his bed. There must be some way to rectify matters between them, to get what he wanted from her without giving all she demanded . . . but just now, when he was feeling tired and sore from long hours in the saddle, he lacked the patience to sort it all out.

He wanted nothing more than to sleep an hour or two before he once again took up the task before him. But it was easy to see from the light in her eyes that Catherine would not permit it, and so he sighed and mentally prepared for the coming confrontation.

"Indeed," he said flatly. "Now, perhaps you'd like to explain that icy tone you've taken."

Catherine's turquoise eyes turned smoky. All of her anger, her worry, her fear came boiling to the surface. "Explain, m'sieur?" she said. "*I* am not the one coming home looking as if he is returning from a night of debauchery, and therefore not the one owing an explanation."

Jase's hard mouth turned grim. He swallowed the last draft of the cooling coffee and set down his cup with a clatter. Had he not been so damnably weary, he might have laughed. "Debauchery?" he said quietly. "Is that what you think?"

Elevating her stubborn chin, Catherine met his burning gaze. "What I think is that you did not go to Natchez on business, as Dora told me. The scratches on your face give the truth of the matter more clearly than words. I already know there is much you haven't told me. Perhaps you would like to tell me now, beginning with Mrs. Dane."

Jase observed Catherine sitting so rigid in her chair. She was waiting for the ax to fall . . . for him to admit that he had betrayed her in the arms of another woman. . . .

If only it were that simple.

"What I would like is to sleep undisturbed," he said at last, absently touching his fingertips to the furrows that slashed across his cheek, and frowning. "You may join me if you like, but only if you leave your shrewish ways outside the bedroom door."

Catherine bristled. "You need not worry, M'sieur St. Claire. My 'shrewish ways' will not intrude upon your rest, and neither shall I. Indeed, I hope you drown in your damnable solitude!" She rose from her chair and stalked to the doorway, summoning Dora.

Dora emerged from the rear of the manse. "Yes, madam?"

"I shall need your assistance in removing my things from the master suite, and I wish to do so at once!"

Dora's face crumbled. "Oh dear!" she said, looking immediately to Jase, whose expression was growing darker.

"I am your husband, and the head of this household, and by the thunder, your possessions will remain in *our* chamber." He turned his stormy gaze on Dora. "There will be no need of your services at this time, Dora. *Mrs. St. Claire* is going nowhere."

Catherine glared at Jase. "I will do as I please! And you cannot stop me!"

Jase's look was dangerous. "I can and I will, and I would advise you not to push this argument further, for I am in no mood to coddle your hellish temper!"

"*My* hellish temper?" she demanded. "I am not the one who acts like some ungrateful cur, snarling and snapping and growling at everyone who crosses my path!"

Tears filled her eyes, pooling up so that Jase's black scowl wavered and swam before her. With an anguished groan, she turned away, hating her weakness in loving this black-hearted rogue. "You go out at night and return long after dawn, your face savaged . . . worn to the bone. . . . Do you expect me to accept that without question, Jason? If you do, then you think very little of me."

He ground his teeth and raked a hand through his tangled hair. There was little that he could say to ease her worries. His stern gaze shifted to Dora. "Be gone," he told her. "I want a word alone with my wife."

The housekeeper scurried from the room, closing the door behind her.

When they were alone, Jase took Catherine by the shoulders, turning her slowly to face him.

Christ help him, why must she weep?

Her tears wrung his heart. But there was nothing he could say that wouldn't turn her away from him. "Catherine," he began, "it's not what you think."

She lifted lashes sparkling bright with liquid hurt and looked up into the rugged face she loved so well. "Then what is it, Jason? Where were you last night and how did this happen?" She touched the angry welts on his face with gentle fingers. "What are you doing out there, and why? There is a certain desperation in your search that terrifies me!"

His expression grew closed, and it seemed as if that steely curtain he sometimes employed to keep the world at bay had swept down once again, shutting her out of his thoughts ... his life.

He said nothing.

"Why?" she repeated slowly, tears streaming down her cheeks. "Why did you marry me?"

Jase's expression did not soften, but he touched her face with weary reverence. "Because I love you, Catherine. ... I didn't think it was possible for anyone to reach my heart, cloistered away these many years as it has been. But you did."

Catherine's heart beat painfully in her chest. How she had longed to hear those words from him! And now that she had, she found them inadequate in satisfying this burning need to know the truth.

"You profess to love me," she said, "and yet you ride abroad at night, leaving me alone."

His answer was carefully worded. "I have not been with Angela Dane."

"Then tell me who you have been with."

He sighed wearily. He still held her gently by the shoulders. Her skin felt warm and the fragrance of meadow grass and wildflowers warmed by a summer sun rose from her silken tresses to tease his senses. How he wanted to be done with all of this ... to carry her up the stairs and into sweet oblivion. ...

He shook his head. "I cannot tell you, Catherine—not now—and if you care for me at all, you will not ask again."

She *did* care for him. Far too much, her aching heart professed. And because she cared she could not turn a blind eye to whatever was coming between them.

Squaring her shoulders, she stepped back and out of his grasp.

Jase seemed to hesitate. He opened his mouth to speak, and for an instant she thought that he would draw her back, telling her again that he loved her, and beg her understanding.

"I am asking," Catherine said, "because I want to help you. Because I want to understand."

"Help me, madam!" Jase laughed low and without the smallest trace of humor. "If you wanted to help me, then by God you would let this matter lie!"

With a muttered curse, he turned on his booted heel and left the room. His impatient strides bypassed the stairwell and continued down the hall toward the foyer. The library doors were jerked open and forcefully closed.

"Stubborn wretch!" Catherine grumbled. He had made his position abundantly clear. She, Catherine, was to be permitted limited access to his life. And he would not be a willing participant in any further discussion.

For the remainder of the morning Catherine seethed. How dare Jason declare that he loved her, then refuse to permit her behind the barrier of steel he'd erected around his life! Why, he was acting suspiciously like a man who had something to hide, and the more she considered it in this light, the more convinced she became. But the question as to what that "something" was seemed doomed to remain unanswered.

Feeling restless, she changed into a gown of pale blue muslin with a deep blue velvet sash and a matching long-sleeved spencer jacket, brushed her unruly locks, and made her way from the house. As she swept past the library doors, she cast them a withering glare.

Outside, the day was lovely and bright, with a winter sun's pale yellow rays peeking through breaks in the soft gray clouds. Catherine had the strange notion that if she could capture the shifting beams and shine them into Jase's life, she would banish forever the grim shadows that always came between them.

It was a childish notion at best, a foolish fancy. And their present difficulties were all too real to be glossed over so easily.

And as she strolled across the sweeping lawn, she was at a loss as how to solve them. Jason was stubborn, unbelievably so, and unlikely to willingly yield whatever secret he was keeping.

Chapter 22

The box was neatly wrapped in tissue and tied with scarlet ribbon, just as the dressmaker's box which had contained Catherine's amethyst gown had been. It sat conspicuously upon the table in the foyer, and drew her attention the moment she came through the entrance. Her frown began to soften, melting slowly into a wistful smile, and all the unkind things she had been thinking about Jase faded into nothingness.

The small tag attached to the bow had her name scrawled upon it, and it occurred to her that Jason must have purchased something for her in Natchez, perhaps hoping to mend their recent quarrel. It was a thoughtful gesture, and surely not the action of a man just home from his mistress.

Perhaps she had judged him too harshly.

Catherine took up the package, and with shining eyes hastened up the stairs to the master suite.

Jase was nowhere to be seen.

Catching her lower lip between her teeth, she sat down on the bed with her foot tucked beneath her, and with a feeling of anticipation, gently pulled loose the trailing ribbon.

The scarlet streamers came away with a soft hiss and lay in bright contrast to her blue muslin lap. Slowly the paper was unfolding, the gift revealed to Catherine's wondering gaze.

It was a lovely teakwood box, ornately carved with nymphs and trailing vines, and surely exceedingly rare. She had never seen anything like it, and could only guess at what it contained.

Feeling her heart swell in her breast to painful proportions, she slipped the tiny golden catch that held it closed and slowly lifted the lid ... her expression changing to one of puzzlement.

The beautifully carved box contained a wadded bit of kidskin, badly used and covered with drying mud. She picked it up, examining it more closely, her brow creased with growing perplexity.

It was a lady's heelless slipper! And clinging to the mud-encrusted sole was a small slip of foolscap, neatly folded. Gingerly extracting the note, she opened it, and as she read she began to tremble.

To the Bride of the Black Lion

Her hands felt cold and numb, her fingers stiff; the foolscap escaped her nerveless grasp and fluttered to the carpet unnoticed.

The Black Lion. ... Squeezing her eyes shut, she willed away the vision of Andre's lonely wilderness grave that leapt suddenly to mind.

This was some sort of macabre joke; it had to be! But who would do such a terrible thing?

Not Jase surely! He was well aware of how much the Black Lion had cost her. Indeed, he alone had supported her failed attempt to bring about the outlaw's capture, to stop the reign of terror along the Chickasaw Trace. Why, the very suggestion that *he* could be the legendary renegade was ridiculous, unthinkable, beyond the realm of possibility!

Wasn't it?

In one swift motion, she leapt from the bed she shared with Jase by right of wedlock, uncaring that the teakwood box tumbled to the floor. Slowly, she backed away, a low moan rising from deep within her tortured soul.

"Nooo!" She shook her head until her curls danced. "No, it cannot be true. He is my husband!"

And he was just as much a mystery today as he had been the night he rescued her on the Trace. Indeed, what little she knew about Jase's past she had pried from him by sheer dint of will. He remained close-mouthed, reticent . . . like a man with a terrible secret would be. . . .

No! She refused even to think it! Yet despite her firm resolve, something deep within her seemed to grasp the notion, refusing to relinquish it to the absurd as she vehemently wished to do.

Uncertainty, chill, and dread crept along the edges of her mind, conjuring up reluctant recollections, beginning with that first night on the Chickasaw Trace.

Jase had seemed to appear out of nowhere, a spectral figure with a lethal air about him, a man of boldness and daring that was uncommon in ordinary men. Handling the huge Sadist with savage grace, he had cut a wide swath, subduing all who stood in his path . . . including Catherine.

But what was the real reason he was on the road that night, and at so late an hour? He said later he'd been searching for the Black Lion, but that could have been a lie. . . .

Suddenly it all made sense, the fact that he shunned society, his life with the Shawnee, the odd way he sometimes spoke, his midnight forays into the countryside. Why hadn't she considered it before?

Because she'd been blinded, she thought with a pang. Blinded by her love for him. The yearning of her heart had clouded her judgment, and now she was trapped.

Her desperate thoughts were interrupted by the sound of voices in the foyer below. Listening to her husband's strident tones, her heartbeat quickened alarmingly, and for one long and anxious moment, she thought she would be ill. Turning to face the French windows that overlooked the front lawn and curving drive, she forced herself to take deep breaths until the feeling passed.

Out on the lawn the hulking figure of Bobby Means loped toward the stable, but Catherine's mind refused to register the urgency in the big man's stride.

Jase's visage was grim when he entered the chamber a moment later. He glanced at her as she stood rigidly by the windows. Her face was partially averted, but even from this distance he could tell she wore a stricken look.

Did she know about Rebecca? It hardly seemed

possible, since he had only just been notified himself.

Still, some terrible shock had turned her cheek waxen, had brought that haunted look into her eye. His frown deepening, Jase approached her. There was ample time to change his attire before Tom Galliher arrived.

"Catherine," he said, "what has happened? You look as if you've glimpsed the devil lurking in some corner."

Slowly, she turned to face him, lovely turquoise gaze seeming to judge him. "Perhaps I have," she said.

Jase felt a chill crawl up his spine. "Will you explain that remark, or must I guess at its meaning?"

"I have been thinking about our conversation yesterday," she said shakily. "Indeed, about every conversation we have had concerning your past. I find it very strange that every time I broach the subject you turn it aside. Yesterday I asked what you were hiding, and you refused to discuss it. You said that if I cared for you at all, I would not ask again."

"Where is this leading, Catherine?"

"It is leading to you, Jason," she replied. "That night in the library when we almost made love, you told me of your parents, of how they died and what came after. You told me you were taken to New York, where you remained for two years, and from there you went to Blue Jacket's Town. But there was much you didn't tell me, wasn't there?"

Jase was very still. The mingled hurt and hope in her eyes was impossible to miss. She suspected the truth, but desperately needed a lie.

"Catherine," Jase said in grave tones, "you must *listen* to me."

"Listen!" she cried frantically. "Listen to whom? The Black Lion, the man who raped and pillaged with no regard and no compassion, the man who betrayed his own kind?"

Jase scowled blackly. "It was never like that," he said, but his words were lost in her tirade.

"Or perhaps I should listen to my husband instead," Catherine suggested, tears racing down her pale cheeks, "the man who wed me, knowing full well that he was my most hated enemy, my brother's executioner, the very one I came here to see hanged!" Sobs racked her, lending a desperate edge to her demands. "How could you! How could you practice such a cruel deception!"

"I did not kill Andre."

"You deceived me! How can I believe you?"

"Catherine." Jase reached for her, intending to calm her, but she flinched away. The muscle in his cheek worked. When his voice came again, it sounded soft and scornful. "You wish to know why I was less than eager to rush to you with the truth, do you? Well, you need only look to yourself for your answer. From the first you have slavered to see me mounting the gallows stair. Only a madman would gleefully offer you the noose to place about his own bloody neck!"

Catherine was too distraught to hear. She brushed past him and would have run from the room had he not seized her and forcibly dragged her back. "You wanted an explanation, you wanted the truth, and by God, you will listen until

I am through with you! As my wife, you owe me
that much."

"I owe you nothing!" She struggled in his grasp,
trying to escape the steely hands that cut into her
upper arms. But as he dragged her roughly up
against his hardened length, she immediately
stilled, gazing in alarm into the dark and furious
visage which inhabitants of the frontier had regarded with dread a decade before.

"You are my wife," he ground out. "And by the
Saints, you will remain that. Now, unless you wish
to test the strength of my husbandly ardor, I suggest you sit."

Jase released her, then watched as she skirted
the bed, choosing a chair near the hearth. She
perched upon the edge, prepared to take instant
flight. She seemed an exotic little bird, but Jase
knew how deceptive that impression was. There
was no flightiness, no timidity in Catherine; and
she was more catamount than canary.

Making his way in silence to the hearth, he
reached up and took the broken rifle from its sup-
porting pegs to place it in her hands. "Look
closely at it, then tell me what you see."

She stared at him as if he'd lost his senses. "I see
no reason—"

"You will," he put in coldly. "Now, do me this
one courtesy. What price would you place upon
this trinket?"

She examined the gun in her hands, thinking to
have this done with as quickly as possible. It was
in terrible condition. The lock was rusted and
would not hold a flint, and as she'd previously
noted, the stock had split lengthwise through its

center and was bound together with rough strips of rawhide. "Very little. No one with half an eye and fondness for his coin would pay you a picayune for this pitiful excuse of a rifle."

"Then you would not deem this a fitting trade for the life of a young lad?"

Her head came up and she regarded Jase, lips parted in surprise. Her eyes, brimming with tears moments ago, now seemed huge and luminous.

How lovely she was. . . . It hurt Jase to look upon her . . . or perhaps it was the knowledge that he would lose her now that filled his chest with this dull ache.

"Some of my unwillingness to share my past with you stems from habit. I have never spoken of it to anyone."

He sighed, tipping back his head. His muscles were taut with painful knots, and he would prefer to be anywhere at this moment than where he was, making an ineffectual attempt to convince his bride that he was a man worthy of love, instead of the snarling monster she believed him to be.

Only with the greatest reluctance did he begin the telling, surprised that the words flowed past the lump of dread in his throat.

"All that I have told you is true, the account of my parents' deaths and Eben's, the scar and the way I came to live at Blue Jacket's Town. I did not lie to you, Catherine. My sin was one of omission. This time I will omit nothing; you shall have what you wish; you shall have it all.

"I was an unruly lad, quick-tempered and at times ungovernable. John White Elk tried to take that out of me during the first year of my captivity. He was brutal when he drank, which was often; he abandoned all pretense of humanity and vented his spleen on me. The beatings were sometimes severe." He noted her expression and snorted softly. "Don't look so shocked, Catherine. It was permitted; I was his slave, you see, and he could do with me as he wished. For two years I endured his abuse. My hatred alone kept me alive ... that, and the fact that he had something I wanted, something that was very precious to me."

He paused and reached out to take her left hand, not permitting her to withdraw from him. He didn't hold it tenderly within his grasp, but took hold of the wedding band that circled her third finger. "*This* was my mother's wedding band. John White Elk took it from her the day of the raid. He had to cut off her finger to get to it. He didn't give a damn that she was still alive."

He released her hand, frowning at the memory, and rubbed impatiently at the scar John White Elk had given him. "I waited and I watched for a very long time. I had planned to run away, but I was not about to leave Mother's ring with that bloody bastard. He was very drunk when I crept into the lodge and took the ring from his smallest finger. For a long while I stood staring at his skinning knife. I wanted badly to cut off his finger as he'd done to Mother, but in doing so I would have sealed my own fate. And so, I settled for the ring, concealing it on my person. I planned to depart the village that evening, but before I could make good my escape, John White Elk awakened.

"He intercepted me outside the council house. Immediately a crowd gathered, including several members of the visiting Shawnee delegation. He caught me by the scruff of the neck, like one might take hold of an unruly hound. I maintained my defiance, despite the hatchet which came arcing down . . . and then there was nothing until I awoke in Blue Jacket's Town.

"It was in the Ohio Country, not far from the Miami River, a place of unsurpassed beauty. My years with Fire Hawk and Co-o-nah, his wife, were relatively happy ones. Co-o-nah nursed me back to health. She saw that I had clothes to cover my nakedness, skins to keep me warm, and always a place by the fire. For the first time in two years my belly was full and I did not have to fight the village dogs for scraps."

The statement was uttered so softly that Catherine had to strain to hear it. Her heart was sore, but it still went out to the lad he once had been. The sympathy she felt, coupled with an unsettled yearning to rise and comfort him, only added to her confusion.

He was her husband!

He was her enemy!

She frowned, steeling herself to listen, berating her heart for not remaining detached. "Why did you keep the rifle?"

He took a deep and shuddering breath, releasing it slowly. "That rifle signifies the lowest point in my existence. It was used to barter for my life, along with a pair of bone dice and some glass beads. Fire Hawk offered them to John White Elk, who accepted to save face before his powerful brother-in-law. Many years would pass before it reverted to my possession by way of Maynard Dumonde, who had witnessed the exchange."

Catherine watched him, imagining what it must have been like for the proud and arrogant youth to endure the humiliation of bondage.

Caught up in his journey across the years, Jase missed the fleeting expression of tenderness which kindled in Catherine's gaze and was instantly squelched. "The Shawnee were kind to me," he said. "My own family was dead, and I was alone in the world. When Fire Hawk adopted me, he was bestowing upon an orphaned lad a great honor. He took my father's place, not in my heart but in my life, and the tribe became my extended family. My life was good. I hunted with the warriors and displayed great skill with a rifle, for which I was lavishly praised. With the passing of another year, I was joining in the forays against the whites—"

"Against your own, Jason! How could you?"

"It was war," he said flatly. "We were protecting our homeland!"

"That does not make it right!"

"No," he said, "it does not make it right. But tell me, was it right for the militia to march on our villages when the warriors were away? To murder the old and the young, the women and the children? To burn the fields so that we would starve in winter? To lay waste to everything?" He ran a hand over his face, forcing himself to calm. "No. It does not make it right. And the responsibility for the destruction that occurred during those difficult years does not belong exclusively to me. *It was war, Catherine.*"

She remained ominously silent, her face a pale mask. Jase's gaze was cold and piercing. "Upon what little honor I possess, I swear to you that I have never slain innocents, nor have I taken a woman against her will. If I am guilty of anything, then it must be ambition. I fought bravely, and because of it I rose to prominence in the waning days of the war. I was the slave of John White Elk no longer. I had become the Black Lion, a name given to me upon the day of my adoption. My voice was often heard in council, and when I could, I intervened on the behalf of white hostages. I can imagine *that* is something that you have never heard in connection with the Black Lion . . . but it is true. You would know only of St. Clair's defeat, of Fallen Timbers, the evil deeds of a soulless renegade."

"And because you stand here now and confess all this to me, I am expected to believe you?" Catherine said. "You will understand if, in the face of your many lies, I find your avowed innocence hard to accept!"

Jase's pale eyes glittered. "You mistake me, madam. I never claimed to be an innocent."

Averting her face, she refused to look at him. Indeed, it was her own impetuosity which had pried the lid from this Pandora's box. Oh, how she wished that she had left that damnable package in the foyer! "Are you quite through?"

Jase's hard mouth curled in his strange half smile. "Eager to escape my dangerous company, eh, my little wife?" He reached down and with one strong brown finger tipped up her chin, forcing her to meet his gaze. "No, I am not through. You must know the end of the story. You must know how I lost my family a second time, Co-o-nah to smallpox, and Fire Hawk at Fallen Timbers. You will be interested, I am sure, in hearing how after the battle we sought help from our allies the British, and they turned a deaf ear to our pleas. They would not open the gates of the fort to our wounded. Those of us who were able took the wounded and dead and went away. The treaty was signed soon after; we lost our land.

"After Fallen Timbers there was little left for me. My family was gone, the land was gone, the tribes were scattered. I could not have returned to Castle Ford if I had wanted to. A man with a price on his head, a white skin, a red soul. Where could I go and what could I do? My situation seemed hopeless—until I met up with Maynard Dumonde."

He sighed and placed his hands upon his hips. "I told you that he took me in, gave me work, this place. But in truth he gave me back my life. He took a wild young man and tamed him—at least on the outside. He is responsible for the grand facade, the Jase St. Claire who is master of Rosemunde Plantation, your husband. But Maynard was not completely successful, and he often chafed at the fact that he could create no more than a thin veneer of gentility where I was concerned. I kept the part of me that was the Black Lion locked away; that is, until you came along. For some reason you bring out the worst in me."

Jase watched her for a moment, trying to gauge her reaction. Her trembling had subsided; her fury had lessened, but there was still a look of resentment in her lovely blue-green eyes. "So," he said, "you have your precious truth at last. I did not kill your brother, nor did I have anything to do with the other recent murders. The man claiming to be the Black Lion today is an impostor."

"Are you suggesting that my brother would lie about such a thing on his deathbed?" she demanded.

Jase answered with a question. "How did you come by this information?"

"You know very well that Mose and I traveled to Buzzard's Roost in the Chickasaw Lands!" she snapped. "Andre told Colbert's wife of how the masked brigand bragged to him of his identity before he left Andre on the Trace to die!"

Jase was unconvinced. "Indisputable evidence, to be sure. But perhaps you can tell me this: why would a renegade with a price on his head, who went to great lengths to disappear for six years, commit such a foolish blunder as to announce his identity?"

It was a question Catherine could not answer.

Reaching out, Jase cupped her chin, thoroughly searching her gaze. "Do you really think that I have lived so long by being foolish?" he questioned softly. "Or can it be that the man responsible for Andre's death wished to have his deeds attributed to me, one whose evil reputation would not afford him the lowliest defense against charges brought against him?"

Catherine pushed his hand away. His touch confused her, made her remember the long and languid night they had shared in the huge feather bed, made her horribly aware of how traitorous her body could be. She wrenched the ring from her finger and held it out to him; he would not take it. "How do you explain this? How could Andre possibly have come by your mother's wedding ring unless he took it from your own hand?"

"It was stolen from me, from this very house, six months ago."

Catherine was incredulous. "By whom?"

"By the one man who had access to this house, a man I trusted, a man who has worked closely with me to manage the plantation so that I could devote my time to breeding the horses."

When it dawned on Catherine to whom he referred, she shook her head. "No. Not Alonzo. It isn't possible."

"My thoughts exactly, until I met him on the Trace several nights ago. Wools Burke, the man you saw me conferring with on the lawn, has been my eyes and my ears for weeks. His connection to me is known only by you and the members of my staff. He could go where I could not, without being recognized, and thus provide me with information. He managed to infiltrate Alonzo's band and together we figured that MacLeemer's farm would be the next strike. I went there, and I waited, hoping to confront my enemy at last. I was not disappointed. He came, dressed Indian fashion and wearing my war insignia painted on his face. I didn't know it was Alonzo that night. We clashed, and I managed to graze his neck with a ball and knock him to the ground, but his band made a timely appearance and he got away. One of his men wasn't as fortunate. Wools Burke and I caught him that night on the road. He didn't know the impostor's name. But he had sent messages to a house on Franklin Street."

"Then you have no proof."

"At the gala, when we fought, I saw the wound, here." He indicated his neck just below the jawline.

Catherine's mind was reeling. Here before her stood the Black Lion, the renegade she had long despised, the man whose passionate embrace left her weak with longing ... and he was accusing her former fiancé of the very crimes she had attributed to him.

Feeling shaken, she rose and made her way to the windows. "But why would he want to harm you? It makes no sense. You were his employer."

Jase sighed and ran a hand through his hair. "For months I have asked myself those same questions, and I can only think that Alonzo knows who I am and is seeking some warped revenge. Perhaps, like you, he simply guessed the truth."

She looked at him with dawning horror. "*I* did not guess the truth, Jason. Indeed, had it not been for the gift, I would not have had the slightest notion."

"What gift?"

Rushing forward, she gathered up the teakwood box, forgotten on the floor, the slipper and note, and lay the items on the bed. "I thought you'd brought me something home from Natchez," she admitted. "It was not until I opened it that I realized it was not from you."

Jase reached for the slipper. "Where did you get this?"

"In the foyer—Jason, what is wrong?"

He picked up the mud-stained slipper. His reply was slow in coming. "This belongs to Rebecca Galliher. Bobby Means found her shortly before I came in. She was in the tall weeds by the end of the lane. She'd been strangled."

Jase's words seemed to come from far away, nearly drowned by the loud buzz in Catherine's ears. Her knees buckled beneath her, and Jase was there, lifting her and carrying her to the bed. He gently lowered her to the mattress, pressing her back when she struggled to rise. "Stay where you are. I'll summon Dora to sit with you." He went to the door and called for the housekeeper.

"No, I'm all right," Catherine said. "It is a shock to think—the slipper." She shuddered to think that it had been removed from Rebecca's lifeless body. She raised her eyes to her husband's dark, enigmatic face. "What happens now, Jason?"

"Now, I must find him. He must be stopped."

Chapter 23

⌒◯◯⌒

The early winter's eve descended slowly, painting the western sky with gentle pastel hues which faded gradually into a violet dusk.

Standing by the windows, Catherine watched the purple shadows deepen, the subtle blending of day into night. Twilight was a peaceful time, a few moments during which every living thing gave pause and the very world seemed to hold its breath.

And yet she felt no peace this night.

Coming away from the window, she sat down on the bed, the same one she had occupied when she was first at Rosemunde. How small the chamber seemed now. How devoid of life and energy— without Jase to fill it.

Sitting with knees drawn up and arms wrapped around them, she found herself listening for his impatient footsteps, the beloved sound of his voice ... and yet the morose silence that gripped the house remained unbroken.

Despite the warmth of the quilts drawn over her lap, she shivered, unsettlingly aware that by attempting to find Rebecca's killer Jase was gambling with his life.

She still could not believe it was Alonzo. It simply made no sense. What reason could he have for wanting to hurt Jason? There must be some mistake. And then there was Andre. He and Alonzo had been business associates, friends. Why would Alonzo wish to kill him? Of all people, Alonzo would have known how difficult the loss of her brother would be for her to bear.

If Jason's suspicions proved true, then Alonzo must be mad. It was the only reasonable explanation, and it turned her blood to ice. The chill crept up the inside of her ribs, stretching cold fingers out to brush along her heart.

It hardly mattered who Jason was seeking, when in his search for the killer he could be hurt or killed.

He'd been gone all afternoon, but she'd heard him return a while before. She should go to him; ask him to give up the search. Surely he would listen! But even as she thought it, she knew that she would not approach him, could not bring herself to face him just now.

She might have lost her innocence this day, but she retained her tattered pride.

Jase had duped her, tricked her, and deceived her from the first. But despite all his scheming, she loved him still.

Burying her face in her folded arms, she groaned aloud. "Why must things be so complicated?"

"Life is never easy, ma'am. Not even when you're old and gray." Dora stood in the partially open doorway, a candlestick in her hand. The halo of golden light that wreathed her mob-capped head made her appear a wizened angel. "You should not sit in the dark, child. You'll ruin your eyes."

"What does it matter after what's happened?" Catherine said. "My world has crumbled, and there is nothing left."

Dora entered the room and set the candlestick on the high bureau. "Silly child," she chided gently, abandoning all but the faintest traces of her hesitation in speaking so directly to her mistress.

Perching gingerly on the edge of the bed, she asked, "What exactly do you feel you have lost? You have a warm and comfortable home, friends to confide in . . . a husband who loves you."

"What does Jason know of love?" Catherine demanded, unwilling to admit that Dora's words echoed what her heart was already saying. "He has betrayed me, Dora."

Dora reached out and took Catherine's hand, patting it gently. "Perhaps you feel that way now—"

Catherine slowly shook her head. "I shall never forgive him for what he has done."

"Forgive him what, dear? For loving you?" Dora clucked her tongue. "There surely is no sin in that! Or perhaps you can't forgive his stubbornness? It's a quality in which you yourself seem to abound." She paused, smiling, and her next words were softly spoken. "As I see it, Mr. St. Claire is guilty only of being a man, and men are often foolish when it comes to their own hearts. For some reason they can't seem to accept the fact that they feel love, pain, and even joy, and therefore they go 'round trying to hide it all behind a bluff facade, or stony silence. It's silly, isn't it? To deny what's in our hearts?"

On some level, Catherine knew that the housekeeper was right, but that knowledge was threatening to unseat her anger . . . the one thing which enabled her to keep her formidable husband at arm's length. She was not yet prepared to let go of her hurt. Not yet . . . and perhaps she never would be. "I fail to see what any of this has to do with Jason," Catherine said at last.

"It has everything to do with Mr. St. Claire," Dora countered. "Do you know what I see when I look at him? I see a man who has been bumped and bruised by life, but who has risen to his feet again each time fate knocks him flat and carried on with the simple business of living. And I suspect that most of those who fault him for his past actions do so out of envy, for they know within their hearts that they would have lacked the courage to survive if placed in similar circumstances. Mr. St. Claire has known much tragedy in his life, more than those who stand in judgment of him can ever know. And yet, he has been unfailingly kind to Leviticus, Bobby Means, and me . . . despite all his dark grumblings."

And to you, ma'am.

The unspoken words hung in the air between them. Catherine felt her guilt stir to life, and frowned at her companion. "Is that what you think? That I am judging him?"

Her tone was strident, but Dora, accustomed to her employer's emotional thunderstorms, remained unruffled. "Aren't you?" she asked. "It seems to me that you are more willing to listen to rumors than to the man himself. My God, child, Mr. St. Claire loves you! Recognize how precious and rare that is and forget the outright lies and half-truths you may have heard."

Catherine shook her head again, swallowing back a sudden hot rush of tears. She was weary of crying, but she seemed to lack the power to hold her tears in check. "I am not altogether sure I can, Dora."

"Then truly I am sorry for you, miss. For you are clinging to a fairy tale for the sake of your pride."

Rising from the bed, she smoothed her skirts and went to the door. There, she paused to regard with shining eyes the bewildered young woman on the bed. "There is no Black Lion, miss," she said softly. "It is only a myth . . . a wild tale spun from hearthside to hearthside to enliven long winter nights—and, I suspect, lavishly embroidered by many a wagging tongue. There has been just Jason St. Claire, a man who has managed to survive a trial by fire that would have vanquished lesser men . . . and possessed the audacity to flourish. Who among us can fault him for that?"

Who indeed?

Long after the housekeeper made her exit and the house settled once more into waiting silence, Catherine pondered what Dora had said. Was the older woman correct? Was she throwing away her life, her love, and her happiness for the sake of her pride?

What would she have for her pains in the end?

A cold and brittle chalice where her brimming heart once had been, an endless succession of days in a life that was lonely and dull? Would she awake one day when she was Dora's age, a bitter old woman filled with regret?

It seemed a very real possibility, and Catherine was surprised that she found it a far grimmer prospect than the sacrifice of her pride.

Jase reached into the second drawer and removed the pair of pistols, placing them carefully on the desk beside the teakwood box ... the final clue in a mystery which had been plaguing him for months. It was the same ornate box he had seen on the shelf below the portraits at the brick residence on Franklin Street the night of Tom Galliher's gala.

His mouth turning grim, he thought of how blind he had been. For months the search for the killer had consumed his life. Waking and sleeping, he had racked his brain for some way to stop the slaughter ... and all those midnight rides! combing the bloody countryside for a faceless enemy ... when all that time the one responsible had been right beneath his very nose!

Thinking of Alonzo, Jase ground his teeth. What a fool he had been not to realize it. And yet, even now, with the evidence before him, the notion that Alonzo Hart was responsible for the reprehensible acts committed in the name of the Black Lion seemed nothing less than preposterous.

As Jase methodically loaded and primed the pistols, Alonzo's face rose up before him, a vision of boyish charm. Who would have suspected that behind that appealing countenance and youthful smile lurked the scheming mind of a murderer?

The only remaining question in Jase's mind was why.

Why would Alonzo concoct this elaborate scheme to exact revenge upon him? A thorough search of his mind brought forth no memories of the man beyond their first meeting that day in July, two years ago at Tom Galliher's. Had Jase met him before, he surely would have remembered.

And what of the luckless Rebecca?

Tom Galliher would soon arrive to take her body home. Until then, a servant kept the vigil of the deathwatch, staying with the body through the night.

How did Rebecca fit into Alonzo's maniacal plan? Had she been a pawn in his game? Marked for death since the beginning? Or was it simply a quirk of fate that had brought about her demise? It seemed not to fit the pattern of the other killings, all carefully planned, with nothing to connect Alonzo Hart to any of them.

Perhaps most perplexing of all was the question of Andre Breaux, Catherine's brother. What possible motive could Alonzo have had for killing the brother of his betrothed? What could he hope to gain?

Jase became very still, and the hand that gripped the powder horn showed white at the knuckles.

Rivercrest.

With Andre Breaux in his grave, there was no one to stand in his way. Catherine would inherit, and by right of marriage the holdings would fall to Alonzo's control.

Christ, how it must have galled him to know that Catherine had slipped through his grasp, linking her future with that of his enemy! It was the motive behind the teakwood box, the murdered girl's slipper, the note. . . .

Alonzo had sought to drive a wedge between him and Catherine. And he had succeeded. Their all-too-brief happiness was shattered, and Jase was not sure that he possessed the power to bridge the yawning gap which lay between them.

The pistols were primed and ready. Jase thrust them into his belt at the same moment a soft knocking sounded at the door. Slipping into his coat, he called out an entry.

Leviticus appeared in the doorway, his face lined with worry. "Sir," he said, "all is just as you requested. Wools has arrived and is stationed at the rear of the house, Bobby Means at the side, and I myself will guard the front. Do you really think that Mr. Hart will come this way?"

Jase had no ready answer. It had been his difficulty all along, trying to outguess an adversary possessed of an insane cunning. "I think it more likely that he is waiting for me to come to him. But with Catherine here, I will not take unnecessary chances. I'm going to ride toward Natchez. If he decides to run, he'll stop by his house first to gather his belongings. I think it's worth a try."

"May God go with you, sir," Leviticus said. But too late, for Jase St. Claire, master of Rosemunde Plantation and the Black Lion of legend, had already gone.

* * *

The Spanish black was surely the devil's mount. With uncanny grace it moved across the broad lawns, its dark mane swept by a silent wind, its hooves striking sparks against the gravel drive. Secure in his place of hiding, Alonzo Hart shuddered with the force of his loathing. Unblinkingly, he continued to watch until horse and rider were far down the drive and out of sight, headed in the direction of distant Natchez.

Then and only then did Alonzo crawl from the dark recesses of the dovecote and turn his feverish gaze upon the house.

Dora's words had the desired effect upon Catherine. Somehow the older woman's directness managed to penetrate the great wall of her stubbornness, pierce her wounded pride, and touch her heart.

Unable to bear the solitude of her chamber any longer, Catherine rose from the bed and passed through the connecting door to the sitting room that adjoined the master bedchamber.

She had to speak with Jase, to tell him that the past no longer mattered, that nothing was more important than their life together. . . .

She had to tell him that she loved him, again and again until he would listen, until he believed her sincere. Desperately, Catherine needed to feel his arms so strong about her, to look into his wintry eyes and watch them thaw beneath passion's rising sun.

Her heart in her throat, Catherine threw open

the bedchamber door. But the room was dark and empty. Jase was not there, nor had he been.

Disheartened, she went again into the hallway, and that was when she heard something, the tinkle of falling glass.

The sound came from downstairs.

Making her way to the balustrade, she peered over the carved rail.

In the foyer below all was still. The servants had apparently retired for the evening and the only sign of life was the ribbon of buttery light edging the floor by the library doors.

Jase must still be there, preparing for the night to come.

Swiftly, she went down the stairs, her bare feet skimming the floor as she ran to the great double doors of her husband's private sanctuary. Pausing just long enough to utter a breathless prayer, she threw wide the doors.

"Jason?"

The candelabrum cast the room's lone occupant in its brilliant light, while throwing a huge shadow across the wall with sinister effect. At the sound of her voice he raised his head, and Catherine nearly screamed.

Lank black hair hung from beneath a faded blue bandanna, framing a terrifying visage of scarlet and black. His eyes were ringed around with the contrasting color, seeming to glow with an unearthly light. Catherine caught the doorframe, and for an instant she thought her legs would fold beneath her. It was then she realized that the black hair was a wig, and that the features beneath the hideous mask belonged to Alonzo Hart. His clothing was disreputable, greasy ill-fitting leather, so different from his usual dapper attire. Indeed, there was no lingering trace of the Alonzo Hart she knew and had planned to marry in the man standing before her now.

Her heart was racing, yet she managed to sound calm. "What are you doing here, Alonzo?"

He flicked his hand at the desk, which he had been rifling. Papers were strewn over the surface, chair, and carpet. He ignored them, and leaving a drawer hanging open, started forward. "I'm here to collect what is rightfully mine. I'm so glad you've come to me, Cathy. It makes things so much easier. You see, I thought I would have to come and find you."

Seeing the odd glint which had entered his black eyes, Catherine felt a tingle of fear. It originated in the pit of her belly and shot upward and outward, along her limbs to her fingertips and toes, a tingling sensation that warned of imminent danger. And yet something made her stand her ground.

"Easier, m'sieur?" she said. "Unless you turn and leave this instant, your life will become unbearably complicated. Jason is—"

"Out there searching for me," Alonzo supplied. "I watched him leave, you see. Indeed, I've been watching the house since Becca's accident . . . waiting for the best time to come to you."

"Rebecca Galliher? But she was murdered. . . ." Her words trailed away into silence. With a sickening clarity, she was beginning to see.

"She was going to ruin it for us, Cathy," Alonzo said. "I had to do something. The stupid, insipid little bitch was pregnant. She was threatening to go to her father. I couldn't let a slattern like Becca come between us, not after everything I'd done to make things perfect."

"Mother of God," Catherine breathed. "It was you all along. You really *are* the one Jason has been hunting, the one who murdered in the name of the Black Lion. You killed that poor girl and sent me her slipper . . . and you killed Andre! And you tried to blame it all on Jason." She shook her bright head, trying to absorb it, reeling from the shock and revulsion which swept over her. "Oh, Alonzo! How could you? What could you possibly have to gain by the taking of innocent lives?"

Alonzo spread his hands wide and answered with startling calm. "Why, everything. Everything he has would have been mine, had you only listened to me and stayed in New Orleans. But you didn't listen, did you, Cathy? Why do you never listen!" As his shout died away, he straightened. "My plans have changed," he said stiltedly, "but I will still exact my pound of flesh for what he has taken from me."

"You are mad even to think such a thing."

Alonzo shook his head. "No, I am not mad. My sister, Finella, is mad, and the Black Lion is to blame."

"There is no Black Lion," Catherine said, employing the same logic Dora had used to make her see. "It is all a myth, a tale that has run wild and been blown far beyond the truth."

But her strategy failed to work with Alonzo. Indeed, it seemed to enrage him. "You don't understand. I *saw* him! I stood and I watched as he led my mother and Finella away ... *a white man*, and he betrayed us! Damn his black soul! He never lifted a hand to help us!"

The rage seemed to build within Alonzo even as Catherine watched, and for one long and terrifying instant she looked into his burning black eyes and thought she saw her death.

"That savage took my world from me," he said, "and now I will have his in payment."

"What about Andre?" she cried. "What did he take from you?"

Alonzo laughed maniacally. "You want to know about Andre, do you? Well, you'll be relieved to know that his death wasn't planned, Cathy. He stumbled onto us one night shortly after the first murder, the perfect victim. By getting rid of Andre, there was no one to stand in our way. Rivercrest is yours now, and you've only to share it with me. You really should thank me for clearing the way for you to inherit. You love the place more than Andre ever did."

"You murdering cur!" Catherine screamed. "I shall see you hanged for this!"

While she spoke, she had been cautiously backing toward the large double doors, intent upon escape, and now she spun on her heels and dashed the few remaining feet to her goal, Alonzo close upon her heels.

Her fingers closed over the doorknobs. And then Alonzo was there, dragging her back as she kicked and clawed and heaped vile promises of a certain retribution on his head.

"Jason will kill you for this!" she told him, even as he flung her forcibly into a large leather chair and, taking out a stout piece of cord, began to bind her wrists. Catherine, struggling against him, managing to free one hand just long enough to ball her fist and strike him in the face with every ounce of strength she possessed.

The blow caught Alonzo squarely in the nose; blood spurted.

For an instant he seemed mesmerized by the spatters of bright crimson dotting his buckskin shirt, but then the shock wore off and he gave the wrist he still held a vicious twist, causing Catherine to cry out in pain. At the same time he brought back his hand and slapped her hard.

Her head rocked back, her vision swam, and for a moment she thought that she would faint.

"You always were the bloodthirsty little bitch," Alonzo said, ignoring her murderous glare. "But never fear, Cathy, your sanguine appetite will very soon abate." With a final cruel jerk he secured her wrists, making her wince. "I'm going to make a widow of you, and you will be there to witness the monumental occasion that will be the Black Lion's downfall."

"You sound very sure of this night's outcome," she said, trying to undermine his confidence. "What makes you think you are man enough to destroy the Black Lion, when all of those who tried before you failed?"

Alonzo mopped his face with his kerchief, then grinned. "I have something the others didn't have, Cathy," he told her. "I have you."

She felt sudden nausea. Her heart began to flutter. He intended to use her as bait to trap Jase, and very likely his plan would work. "He will not come," she said, feeling suddenly desperate.

But Alonzo only laughed. "You forget that I know Jase St. Claire, better even than you. He doesn't give up so easily." As she watched, an expression of cunning came over his face. "I can see that you doubt me, and so I will just summon him on your behalf."

With sickening dread, she watched Alonzo grab up the candelabrum and hold it to the curtains at the French windows. In less time than it took her to gasp in horror, he moved to the other windows and followed suit, and soon the room was ablaze.

Ravenous flames surged up the fragile batiste to lick at the ceiling. The smell of blistering paint was thick in the air, and the smoke caused Catherine's eyes to water. She stumbled up from the chair, shielding her face with her upraised hands, and made her way to the doors. And then Alonzo was opening the closed portals and pushing her through.

"Tell me, Cathy," he said with a smile, "do you still doubt that he will come?"

Chapter 24

A half mile to the south along the Chickasaw Trace, Jase reined in the black and, turning in the saddle, glanced back the way he had just come.

The night was undisturbed, but above the trees to the west, the sky glowed a sullen red. Without an instant's hesitation, he wheeled his mount and dug his heels into its shining flanks, sending the stallion flying back down the Trace, back toward the house . . . and Catherine.

Rosemunde was burning.

That thought pushed all others from Jase's mind.

The way was dark, the foliage overhead too dense for the moonlight to penetrate. Sadist galloped through the black void, his powerful strides eating up the distance—but not quickly enough for Jase.

It seemed an eternity before they reached the drive and Jase caught the stench of smoke and destruction borne on the night wind. Spurring the black onward with a hoarse cry, he cut across the lawn. *Catherine ... oh, God, Catherine!* The words beat relentlessly against his skull. Just ahead, several figures huddled in a grieving knot. Jase recognized Dora, Leviticus, and the aged Aunt Sade. Bobby Means lay a short distance away, unconscious.

The one he ached to see most was terrifyingly absent.

As he approached, Dora lifted pleading eyes to his and pointed to the house, but her words were lost to Jase as he sped past, kicking up great chunks of sod, taking the gravel drive at a single bound. Onward he urged his mount, directly toward the burning structure, for all the world as if the devil himself was hot upon his heels.

The fire was spreading rapidly. Greedy flames consumed costly leather and raced along the Turkey carpet, advancing into the foyer toward Catherine and Alonzo. They stood near the staircase, Alonzo gripping Catherine's arm as he watched the licking flames in fascination. Inside the library, the windows exploded with a deafening noise. Shards of razor-sharp glass rained throughout the room and into the foyer.

Catherine fell to the floor, shielding her face with her forearms.

Beside her, Alonzo cursed and struggled to his feet, pulling her up by the arm. He started off through the house, dragging her beside him ... but away from the front entrance and the safety of the night.

Tears of frustration streaming down her cheeks, Catherine begged him to release her. "Alonzo,

please! We must get out or we both will perish!"
She tried to wrench away from his insane grasp,
straining back toward the front entrance. Smoke,
thick and black, billowed into the foyer and
poured down the hallway where he seemed intent
on taking her. That corridor was long, and any attempt to traverse its smoke-filled length would be
like climbing up a chimney.

"Alonzo, please, I am begging you!" Catherine
tugged against his hold, but was soon pulled up
against him. His eyes were wild. "You think me
mad!" he screamed at her. "*He* is waiting out
there! And I won't walk docilely into his trap!"

"There is no trap!" she cried in anguish, but
Alonzo only snarled and redoubled his efforts to
drag her toward certain destruction.

Fire inched its way into the foyer, slithering in
orange, snakelike ribbons across the carpet, then
rushing forward. It crackled gleefully, seeming to
mock Catherine's plight.

Somewhere out there in the chill damp night
was Jase. She thought of him as she'd last seen
him, wishing with all her heart for one last chance
to make things right between them. "Alonzo,
please, let me go and save yourself! You can be
away from here to safety within minutes!"

"Not without you. Damn it, Cathy! Stop fighting
me!"

With her last ounce of strength, she battled her
tormentor, employing every trick she could think
of to gain her release. Desperation made her wild.
Her elbow caught him in the midsection; she managed to gain an instant's release, dashed for the

front door, but was brought up short when Alonzo's fingers caught in her hair.

He jerked her cruelly backward, bringing her face up to his. "Why can't you see that I'm trying to protect you from him?"

The hand in her hair twisted harder. Catherine cried out in pain and despair. She was sobbing uncontrollably now, drawing more of the hot smoky air into her lungs. Each searing breath caused the dull ache in her chest to grow more acute, until she felt as if she were breathing pure fire.

Beyond the low wall of flames the great front door shivered and burst inward.

Gripping Catherine's arms, Alonzo stumbled backward.

With a hideous scream, the Spanish black reared up outside the opening, squatting on his huge black haunches. Smoke swirled around the churning hooves and seemed to stream from the flared nostrils.

Alonzo shrank back as the animal came to ground and dashed off the portico, conspicuously without his rider.

Jerking Catherine up before him, Alonzo put his arm around her neck. With his right hand, he reached into his coat and withdrew a pistol, and he pressed it tightly to her throat just below her ear.

At that very instant, Jase emerged from the curtain of smoke, a sinister figure silhouetted against the bright backdrop of flames.

"Come closer and I swear I'll kill her." To emphasize his intent, Alonzo pressed the cold steel of the barrel harder into the delicate curve of Catherine's neck.

Cautiously, Jase advanced. "Then put your arm 'round death's bony shoulders, Hart, and draw him near, for he's about to become your closest friend."

"Jason, please, get out of here now!" Catherine's plea ended in a strangled fit of coughing.

Jase, however, did not listen. Through the smoke his pale eyes glittered. "You wanted your revenge," he said, "and you shall have it. But only after you release my wife."

Alonzo's look was ghastly. His eyes bulged from his hideous mask and his mouth was twisted in a feral snarl. Clearly, he was wavering on the edge of hysteria. "You would say anything to gain her freedom!"

"I offer you a life for a life!"

At that moment, Alonzo teetered over the edge into utter madness, and turned, scrambling up the stairs. He dragged Catherine as far as the second landing, where her struggles slowed his progress so that he finally flung her from him, leveling his pistol at Jase.

Caught off balance, hands still bound before her, Catherine toppled backward down the stairs. At the same time, Jase lunged forward in an abortive attempt to break her fall, and unwittingly presented the perfect target for Alonzo's bullet.

Grinning a death's-head grin, Alonzo jerked on the trigger. The piece bucked in his hand and spat fire. Jase St. Claire wavered slightly on his feet, but did not fall. Blood welled from the wound in his right shoulder, soaking his coat sleeve and blooming dark upon his breast . . . and in his eyes was murder.

Dread surged up inside Alonzo. He had gambled and lost. If he descended the stair, St. Claire would kill him.

In desperation he turned and began to climb, unaware that at that moment Jase was reaching for his own pistol. At the top of the stair Alonzo paused to glance over the balustrade . . . and into the gaping black bore of Jase's weapon.

The shot took Alonzo through the left breast. For an instant his fingers tightened spasmodically on the railing, then he slowly folded forward.

Jase turned away from the crumpled form of his enemy, to Catherine, and kneeling, covered her face with his coat, gathered her into his arms, and hurried into the hallway, the only way to exit the burning house.

The fire was racing along the passageway, consuming the carpet, lapping in waves at the western wall. Jase plunged into the inferno with his precious burden, and was quickly blinded by the acrid smoke. His eyes watered uncontrollably; the salt of his tears was like acid on his burning skin . . . but still he kept on, bending low as he sought to escape the black pall of smoke roiling halfway down from the ceiling, his wounded shoulder an agony that was matched only by the searing fire in his lungs.

None of it mattered now. The pain, the past, the future. Nothing compared with his struggle to reach the open air so Catherine could live! He could not lose her now.

He was rapidly weakening. The smoke in his

lungs robbed him of life-sustaining air. His head spun crazily. Each step was torment, too little ground gained, too damnably slow. His limbs felt boneless, too weak to support him any longer. Unable to go on, he fell heavily to his knees.

Holding Catherine's unconscious form tightly to him, he let the racking cough claim him.

Muffled shouts sounded nearby. Jase passed a hand over his burning eyes. Through the swirling smoke and bright yellow glare he saw the gaping doorway, a mere six feet in front of him. He braced a shoulder against the eastern wall and struggled up . . . and a gush of cool wind rushed to him, fanning the hungry blaze to a deafening roar. Wools Burke plunged through the opening and helped Jase through the door and into the cool night air.

Outside on the lawn the crowd was growing. Tom Galliher was there, with Angela and a few neighboring planters who had seen the flames and hurried to lend their aid. They formed an uneasy circle around Jase, who sat on his heels, Catherine clutched against his chest. He severed the bonds that secured her wrists, but he would not let her go. The only one who possessed the courage to try to convince him to relinquish her was Dora. She laid a gentle hand upon his shoulder. "Sir, the doctor's come."

Jase looked up into Dora's face, his pale eyes filled with anguish. "I will not let her go, Dora. What would I do without her? She is my life." His voice broke upon the last word and he buried his face in Catherine's throat while silent sobs shook him.

She was slipping away from him. He could feel it, yet he was powerless to stop it. "Catherine," he said. "Come back to me. I need you in my life. I need your love . . . Catherine. . . ."

The strength of Jase's sorrow penetrated her unconscious mind when mere words could not. The salt of tears stung her burning cheeks and throat. In his arms she stirred, struggling up from the depths of the black abyss into which she had plummeted. The way was difficult, her strength depleted; she felt unequal to the task. Had it not been for Jason, who anxiously awaited her on the other side, she would have given up the fight. For him, she struggled onward, toward the light, and though it took her several moments, she finished the climb and opened her eyes.

The broad canopy of the night sky above was filled with stars, each one seeming to beckon to her. Yet she knew that they paled in comparison to what she had here on earth.

Her arms were leaden, yet she managed to enfold Jase in her loving embrace. Tightly, she held him, stroking his hair.

"Stay with me," he said brokenly. "You are my strength, my all, and I cannot bear the thought of losing you."

"I am here," she replied softly. "I am here."

Raising his head, he gazed deeply into her eyes, and something of his old facade returned. "I need your bright presence, madam, to dispel the shadows of this lonely existence."

Catherine smiled up at Jase. "I am becoming passing good at dispelling shadows."

"Will you consent to stay, then, knowing my many dark secrets? Can you live with what I am?"

He held his breath, waiting for her answer. It seemed an eternity before it came, and in the interim the roof of the house gave way with the sound of thunder and a shower of red-orange sparks flew high in the night sky.

Catherine touched Jase's soot-dark face. His skin had been reddened by the heat of the fire and his hair was singed. Flashes of images from the hour just past flickered behind her eyes. He had braved the fires of Hell to save her, and in light of his selflessness, the words she spoke seemed woefully inadequate. "You are my husband, my lover, my heart's desire . . . all the rest counts for nothing."

Jase thought that simple declaration the dearest words ever spoken, and needed no encouragement but bent to claim her lips in a reverent kiss . . . the first sure step toward this, his final new beginning.

Epilogue

The great white house that once capped the gently rising knoll lay in ruins. Nothing remained save for the portico and a single pillar, charred and askew against the pale sky of evening.

The crowds had dissipated; Dora, Leviticus, and Bobby Means had been taken to the home of Tom Galliher, to stay until other arrangements could be made. Jase St. Claire, looking ragged, his face and clothing stained with blood and soot, stood alone to view the wreckage.

Catherine came slowly across the lawn from the stable, where she and her spouse were currently lodging, her sympathetic gaze touching upon the weary slump of his shoulders. He needed sleep, but as always he neglected his own well-being.

That, she thought with new determination, would stop, for as his wife she was not about to stand idly by and watch as he ruined his health.

Coming to stand beside him, she put an arm about his lean middle, pressing against his uninjured side. "Come with me now," she said, gazing up into his face. "You need to rest, and there is nothing to be done about this today. Tomorrow is time enough to plan the rebuilding of Rosemunde."

Jase turned his gaze from the ruins and looked at Catherine. "I am not planning to rebuild," he said. "It was never really mine. I no more belonged to this place than I did in the Seneca towns, or Quebec . . . or anywhere, since Castle Ford."

There was no plea for sympathy in the simple statement. Catherine leaned her head against his shoulder, glad for his nearness. "You belong with me," she said.

A wicked grin spread slowly over Jase's mouth, a brilliant showing of teeth which caused his lady's heart to fall over itself in eagerness, prompted by his wordless promise. "Yes, I do belong with you," he said, "and I have been thinking about that."

"Oh?" she said. "Do you plan to tell me of those thoughts, or will you keep me guessing?"

"I was thinking of traveling south," he told her, "to New Orleans. I hear that a man of enterprise can make his fortune there. Unless, that is, you wish to go elsewhere."

Catherine squealed and hugged him tightly, forgetting about his injured shoulder. "You will love Rivercrest, I promise you!"

"I have no doubts, madam. As for this place, Tom has long been after me to sell it to him. He will give me a fair price for the land." Bending slightly, Jase kissed her parted lips, tasting smoke, and thought of the fragrant bed of hay awaiting them in the stable loft. The woman in his arms fitted him so perfectly, was so very pliant, so willing, that he almost forgot where they were, and would have slowly borne her to the ground had it not been for the clatter of hooves on the drive.

Reluctantly, Jase interrupted the passionate play and, lifting his head, glared at their visitor.

"Evening, Mr. St. Claire, Mrs. St. Claire. I am sorry indeed to hear of your misfortune."

"Reverend," Jase said, glancing from the mounted scarecrow to the figure just coming into view down the drive. He frowned, thinking the second rider looked familiar, then dismissed the notion, turning his attention once again to Hezekiah Rose.

"I was on my way to Nashville, but thought I'd stop by here first, since there is someone who is most anxious to see you. I thought he should wait, but he was more unceasing in his badgering than all the plagues of Egypt—"

Catherine failed to hear the rest of Hezekiah's statement. She was staring at the mule and rider just coming up the drive. "Mose?" she said, her hand fluttering to her throat.

And then she was running to greet him, crying her relief as she clasped his hand.

"Oh, Mose! Thank God you are here! I feared you had been killed!"

"Yes'm, I guess I nearly was." Mose dismounted from the saddle. "It took me nigh on a week to 'scape from those rascals who stole me, and I've been through some scary times since. I was walkin' to Natchez, not knowin' where you was, and come on Mr. Alonzo dressed in some Indian clothes. He'd hurt some poor man and was standin' over him, laughing. That's how I knew it was him. I tried to hide in the bushes, but he heard the noise and chased me. I managed to get away and shimmied my way into a hollow log to hide, but not before I cut my leg. Mr. Alonzo did some bad things, Miss Catherine. But I guess you know that now."

She nodded. "Are you sure you're all right, Mose?"

"Yes'm. Mr. Hezekiah come upon me and took real good care of me while I was ailing."

Mose glanced at Jase, who was striding across the lawn toward them. "You really married an' all, like the reverend says, Miss Catherine?" His voice betrayed his surprise.

"Yes, Mose, I'm truly married. His name is Jason St. Claire, and he is a good man . . . so unlike Alonzo."

"I'm sure glad to hear that. Mr. Alonzo—well, I jes' never imagined." Mose shook his head.

"No one could have known," Catherine agreed.

Jase took his place by Catherine's side, inclining his dark head in greeting. "For a man with an injured leg, you're exceedingly spry. How did you disappear so quickly that night in the hollow?"

Mose looked chagrined. "If I'd 'ave known you was family to Miss Catherine, I wouldn't have run off. I thought it might be one of Mr. Alonzo's men chasin' me, so I figured I better not let you catch me. There's always hidey-holes in the wood, Mr. Jase. I'd found one just before dark that evening, and was lookin' for some food to tide me over when you come along. I hid till morning." He lay a hand upon his leg. "By then my leg was fevered and started to fester. When Mr. Hezekiah found me, I was nigh out of my head with fever."

"It's over now," Catherine said, "and best forgotten. What matters now is the future."

Mose nodded and glanced at Hezekiah, who sat waiting a few yards away, before bringing his gaze back to Catherine. "Yes'm, and I've been givin' that a whole lot of thought. I figured I might use them manumission papers you gave me before we come north and stay a spell with Mr. Hezekiah. Ma won't mind, seein' as how I'll be doin' the Lord's work—" He saw Catherine's expression change to one of disappointment and hurried to add, "Unless you was still wantin' to catch that Black Lion? Then I guess I could stay."

Catherine would be sad to see Mose go, but his question made her smile. "I've more important things to do," she said, smiling up at Jase. "Besides, I've heard it said he went to Canada after the Indian Wars ... or maybe back to guard the gates of Hell for his dark compatriot."

Meeting her husband's gaze, Catherine softly questioned, "And what do you think, M'sieur Husband? What has become of the infamous renegade the Black Lion?"

Jase gave a derisive snort. "All this talk of Hell and Canada is a crock of bloody sh—"

Catherine swiftly covered his mouth with her hand. When she lowered it again, he finished more politely. "I prefer to think the man's come to his senses and found in life the pleasures that are most important, as I myself have done. Home and hearth, a loving wife, and children. Aye, perhaps he's planning to raise a house full of sons to carry on his name ... if not his bloody legacy."

It was a wonderful thought, and it caused Catherine's eyes to grow misty as, with a final wave, she watched Mose ride away.

Moments later, the lovers entered the stable. The barn was dark and smelled of horses, but Catherine didn't care. She would have slept on the cold ground to stay by Jase's side.

Sadist thrust his head over his stall to flick his ears at Catherine as she passed. It seemed that even he approved of their newfound happiness.

Upon their fragrant bed of hay they came together, trading heated kisses, boldly treading paths of pleasure which still were new and unexplored.

And then in passion's aftermath they lay with limbs entwined, drifting together into sleep, and toward a future that beckoned brightly.

Avon Romances—
the best in exceptional authors and unforgettable novels!

THE LION'S DAUGHTER   Loretta Chase
76647-7/$4.50 US/$5.50 Can

CAPTAIN OF MY HEART   Danelle Harmon
76676-0/$4.50 US/$5.50 Can

BELOVED INTRUDER   Joan Van Nuys
76476-8/$4.50 US/$5.50 Can

SURRENDER TO THE FURY   Cara Miles
76452-0/$4.50 US/$5.50 Can

SCARLET KISSES   Patricia Camden
76825-9/$4.50 US/$5.50 Can

WILDSTAR   Nicole Jordan
76622-1/$4.50 US/$5.50 Can

HEART OF THE WILD   Donna Stephens
77014-8/$4.50 US/$5.50 Can

TRAITOR'S KISS   Joy Tucker
76446-6/$4.50 US/$5.50 Can

SILVER AND SAPPHIRES   Shelly Thacker
77034-2/$4.50 US/$5.50 Can

SCOUNDREL'S DESIRE   Joann DeLazzari
76421-0/$4.50 US/$5.50 Can

If you enjoyed this book, take advantage of this special offer.
Subscribe now and get a

FREE
Historical Romance

No Obligation (a $4.50 value)

Each month the editors of True Value select the four *very best* novels from America's leading publishers of romantic fiction. Preview them in your home *Free* for 10 days. With the first four books you receive, we'll send you a FREE book as our introductory gift. No Obligation!

For any reason you decide not to keep them, just return them and owe nothing. If you like them as much as we think you will, you'll pay just $4.00 each and save at *least* $.50 each off the cover price. (Your savings are *guaranteed* to be at least $2.00 each month.) There is NO postage and handling – or other hidden charges. There are no minimum number of books to buy and you may cancel at any time.

Send in the Coupon Below

To get your FREE historical romance fill out the coupon below and mail it today. As soon as we receive it we'll send you your FREE Book along with your first month's selections.